James C. Öhlschläger

Ahn's New Practical and Easy Method of Learning the German Language

with a pronunciation, numerous corrections, additions and a remodelling of the whole of the exercises and reading lessons in the practical part

James C. Öhlschläger

Ahn's New Practical and Easy Method of Learning the German Language
with a pronunciation, numerous corrections, additions and a remodelling of the whole of the exercises and reading lessons in the practical part

ISBN/EAN: 9783337387389

Printed in Europe, USA, Canada, Australia, Japan

Cover: Foto ©Andreas Hilbeck / pixelio.de

More available books at **www.hansebooks.com**

AHN'S

NEW PRACTICAL AND EASY METHOD

OF

LEARNING

THE GERMAN LANGUAGE

WITH A PRONUNCIATION,

Numerous corrections, additions and a remodelling of the whole

OF THE

EXERCISES AND READING LESSONS

IN THE

PRACTICAL PART

BY

J. C. OEHLSCHLAGER.

First Course: The Practical Part.

NEW YORK:

PUBLISHED BY E. STEIGER,

late JOSEPH WIECK, Agt.,

17 NORTH WILLIAM STREET.

1865.

PREFACE.

The great revolution, which, since the last twenty years, has taken place in the system of teaching modern languages, has produced a number of works which differ entirely from those formerly in use. Among these, Ahn's method has enjoyed perhaps the greatest share of favor in Europe, and also in America the republication of Ahn's Grammar has been well received.

However, although every teacher, who has used this work, admits its practical usefulness, there are not a few, who complain of the insufficiency of the exercises on certain subjects, as also of the reading lessons. To remedy this defect, I have undertaken to republish this work.

Considerable alterations have been made in the grammatical part, but the first or practical part has been entirely remodelled, the length of the lessons has been increased, and a much larger vocabulary introduced, whilst new—and I believe, more appropriate reading lessons have been selected.

Professor Oehlschlager's system of pronunciation, published in his dictionaries and other elementary works on languages, has now stood a test of upwards of twelve years, during which period, nothing has been published that surpasses his system of indicating the sounds of one language by the signs and characters of another in accuracy and facility of application. Tens of thousands of these works have been sold here and in Europe and the demand is still unabated.

The pupil, who cannot procure a teacher of the German language, may with confidence follow the accurate instruction, as well as the interlineal pronunciation, laid down in the work, and he may rest assured that his German will be understood wherever he goes—nay, will be superior to that which many students obtain from incompetent or careless teachers.

In the first or practical part a number of references to the second or grammatical part has been introduced, which will enable the student to obtain a more general view of any particular subject treated in the first part.

Another new feature of this publication is the introduction of German writing, as well as in the exercises as in the reader. Many persons who read a german author with ease, are obliged to employ somebody to read their letters to them, because they are unacquainted with German writing. The introduction of whole pieces, printed in written characters, will certainly obviate this difficulty. This addition has been made at considerable cost, but I am certain, that the advantages resulting from it, will amply repay the outlay.

Everything that could be done, to make this a complete text-book for the acquirement of the German language has been done, and I am confident that a discriminating public will not long withhold their approbation.

THE PUBLISHER..

ON THE PRONUNCIATION.

I. *The Alphabet.*

A,	a,	â,	N,	n,	en,
B,	b,	bey,	O,	o,	o,
C,	c,	tsey,	P,	p,	pey,
D,	d,	dey,	Q,	q,	koo,
E,	e,	ey,	R,	r,	err,
F,	f,	ef,	S,	ſ, s,	ess,
G,	g,	ghey,	T,	t,	tey,
H,	h,	hâ,	U,	u,	oo,
I,	i,	e,	V,	v,	fou,
J,	j,	yot,	W,	w,	vey,
K,	k,	kâ,	X,	x,	icks,
L,	l,	el,	Y,	y,	ip′-se-lon,
M,	m,	em,	Z,	z,	tset.

Ae, Ä, ä, ai, Oe, Ö, ö, —* Ue, Ü, ü, —*

II. *Pronunciation of the Letters.*

I. THE SIMPLE VOWELS.

A, a, when long sounds like *a* in *father*, *car*; when short, like *a* in *cart* or in *castle*, as pronounced in England. This letter when long is represented by â or a' and when short by â.

Baden,† bâ-den;‡	Bad, bâ'd;	Schaf, shâ'f;
Katze, kât′-sai;	matt, mât;	an, ân.

E, e, when long and close like *ey* in obey; when long and open like *ai* in *hair*; when short like e in *hen*, *ell*, *error*. This letter when long and close is represented by ey, when long and open by ai and when short by ai.

Lehre, ley′-rai;	mehr, meyrr;	Meer, mairr;
Ende, en′-dai;	des, dess;	Stelle, stel′-lai.

* The sounds of ö and ü do not exist in the English language, the manner of forming them, will be found P. 78.

† The sounds of the words in the first lines of the examples are long, in the second lines, they are short.

‡ See explanation of the signs used in the pronunciation P. 83.

I, i, when long, like e in me or ee in meet, when short like i in ill, in, if. This letter when long is represented by e or ee, when short by e.

Igel, ee'-ghel; ihn, een; ihr, eerr;
in, in; winden, vin'-den; irren, irr'-en.

O, o, when long like *o* in *pope*, *so*, *no*, when short, it must not resemble the English *aw* sound, and in pronouncing i, the aperture between the lips must be much smaller than in pronouncing the English word *odd*. The long sound is indicated by o or o', the short sound by o.

So, zo; Boden, bo-den; Loth, lo't;
ob, op; Donner, don'-ner; toll, tol.

U, u, when long like *oo* in *fool*, when short like *oo* in *foot* or *u* in *put*, *pulpit*, never like *u* in *tub*. The long sound is indicated by oo or oo', the short sound by ŏŏ.

Ufer, oo'-fer; Tugend, too'-ghent; Uhr, oo'rr;
und, ŏŏnt; Ulme, ŏŏl'-mai; hurtig, hŏŏrr-tich.

Ae, ä, when long like ai in pair, when short like the German e or like e in hen, ell, error. The long sound of this letter is indicated by ai and the short by e.

Aehre, ai'-rai; Schäfer, shai'-fer; schälen, shai'-len;
Aeltern, el'-tern; Kälber, kel'-ber; färben, ferr'-ben.

Oe, ö, the sound of this letter is not to be found in the English language, it resembles somewhat the u in fur. To form it, the pulpil should first pronounce a very long o this will indicate the position of the organs and then, without altering this position, try to pronounce the German e (*ey* in *obey*). This will produce the long sound. To produce the short sound place the organs in the same position and try to pronounce, *ep*, *et*, *ef*, *eck*, *el*, *em*, *en*, *err*, *ess*. The long sound of this letter is indicated by ö or ö', the short by ö.

Oel, ö'l; Höhle, hö'-lai; Gehör, gai'-hö'rr;
Hölle, höl'-lai; gewönne, gai'-vön'-nai; Mörder, mörr'-der.

Ue, ü, has no correspondent sound in English. Sound a very long *oo* as in the word *ooze*, and without changing this position, try and pronounce the long *e* in *meet*, and you will produce the long sound of this letter, which is the same as the French u. To obtain the short sound, pronounce the syllables, ip, it, if, ick, il, im, in, irr, iss, preserving all the time, the above position. The long sound is indicated by ü or ü', the short by ü.

Ueben, ü'-ben; Güte, gü'-tai; Thür, tü'rr;
Küsse, küs'-sai; Kümmel, küm'-mel; Bürste, bürr'-stai.

Y, y, does not differ from the German i, which is now generally used in its place.

II. THE DIPHTHONGS.

Au, is pronounced like *ou* in *house* or *ow* in *how;* we indicate its sound by ou.

Auf, ouf; Haus, houss; Bauer, bou'-er.

Aeu, äu, and eu, like oi in oil, in some parts of Germany a slight difference is made in these sounds, the äu being pronounced a little broader, in others none is made.

Eule, oi'-lai; Häuser, hoi'-zer; Steuer, stoi'-er.

Ai, like a very long i or like the a in father joined to ee in meet.

Kaiser, ki'-zer; Aichen, i'-chen; Saite, zi'-tai.

Ei, like i, in like, not quite so long as the foregoing.

Eile, i'-lai; Seite, zi'-tai; Seil, zile.

Ui, ui, like *oo'ee* or *we* indicated by oo'ee.

III. THE PROLONGED VOWELS.

There are three ways in German by which a vowel is made long. The first is by doubling the vowel, as: Aal, Seele, Boot, this only occurs with a, e and o, they are pronounced as a, e and o, when long; that is â'l, zey'lai, bo't.

The cecond is by placing an h before or after the vowel, which letter in this situation has no sound; this occurs with all the vowels except with y.

Thal, tâ't; kahl, kâ'l; Mehl, mail; ihn, een; Hohn, hone; Uhr, oo'rr; Thür, tü'rr; Gehör, gai-hö'rr.

The third is by placing e after i; as: dienen, dee'-nen; lieben, lee'-ben; Sieb, zeep.

IV. THE CONSONANTS.

The letters F, f, K, k, L, l, M, m, N, n, P, p and X, x, are pronounced the same as in English.

B, b, at the beginning of a syllable B is pronounced the same as in English, at the end like p.

Beil, bile; Lob, lope; Bleib, blipe.

C, c, before ä, e, i and ö like German z or *ts*. It only occurs in foreign words, many of which are also spelled with Z.

Cisterne, tse-sterr'-nai; Circus, tsirr'-kööss.

Before any other letter, after a vowel when no e follows, and at the end of a syllable, it sounds like *k*, which, in most cases, may be used in its place.

Cabale, kâ-bâ'-lai; Clavier, klâ-veer'; Tact, tâckt.

D, d, at the beginning of a syllable like *d* in English, at the end like t.

Dein, dine; Rad, râ't; Ruder, roo'-der.

G, g, at the beginning of a syllable like *g* in *gale*, *get*, *gills*, (of a fish), *god*, *gull*, *growl*, also after an n.

Garten, gârr-ten;	Geld, gelt;	gib, geep;
Gott, got;	gut, goo't;	Graben, grâ'-ben;
Ding,* ding;*	sang, zâng;	Gattung, gât'-töông.

* The majority of Germans pronounce the g after the n like k, however the pronunciation like g is preferable.

After a vowel it has the sound of the German ch, which see under compound consonants, but it generally leaves the preceding vowel long.

Lag, lâ'ch; sagte, zâ'ch'-tai; Betrug, bai-troo'ch'.

H, h, like English *h* in *house*, when at the beginning of a syllable, when after a vowel, after a t or at the end of a syllable, it has no sound but only lengthens the sound of the vowel. Between two vowels the aspiration is very slight.

Heulen, hoi-len; Hammer, hâm'-mer;
Stehen, stey'-(h)en; sahen, zâ'-(h)en.

J, j, like *y* in *yes, ye, you.*

Ja, yâ; jeder, yey'der, Jude, yoo'-dai.,

Q, q, is only used before u and sounds as in the English words, quail, quaff, quill.

Quarz, quârts; Quelle, quel'-lai; quer, quairr.

R, r, almost like rr in English, it should be pronounced distinctly without being made guttural. In English the sounds of the vowels before this letter, when single, change; in fact all the vowels except the a, have the sound of u in *fur;* thus *her* sounds as if written *hur*, *fir* as if written *fur*, *world* as if written *wurld* and myrrh as if written *mur*. In German these vowels sound the same as they would before d that is as *e* in *error*, *i* in *irritate*, almost as o in *horror*.

Reiten, ri'-ten; Herz, herrts; Irrthum, irr'-toom;
ordnen, orrd'-nen; Urne, öörr'-nai; arm, ârm.

S, ſ, s, at the beginning of a syllable like z, at the end like ss.

Seil, zile; sausen, sou'-zen, das, dâss.

V, v, this letter has the same sound as f in all German words, in foreign words it is mostly pronounced like v.

Viel, feel; Verkehr, fer-keyrr'; voll, foll;
Visite, ve-ze'-tai; Visir, ve-zeer'; Vase, vâ'-zai.

W, w, like English *v*, the teeth should not be pressed quite so hard on the lower lip.

Wein, vine; werden, verr'-den; wohl, vo'l.

Z, z, like ts.

Zelt, tselt; Zauber, tsou'ber; Scherz, sherrts.

V. THE COMPOUND CONSONANTS.

The compound consonants are named as the simple ones. ch is called tsey hâ, ck, tsey kâ, &c.

Ch, ch, there is no corresponding sound in the English language; it is the Scotch *ch* in the word *loch*, lake, and the Spanish *j* in the word *Mejico* (Mexico). The sound lies between *g* hard and *k*. In pronouncing the syllable ig, the breath is drawn in, in pronouncing ick, it is forcibly and suddenly expelled, but in pronouncing ich, it is expelled softly and gradually, the breath passing between the palate and the tongue. The vowel a, e, i and o are always short before the ch, u is sometimes long and sometimes short; to indicate this sound we have used the German character ch.

In French words the ch has the sound of English sh. In words from other languages it has sometimes the sound of k.

Bach, bâch; Loch, loch; Gesicht, gai-zicht';
Buch, boc'ch; Gesuch, gai-zoo'ch'; durch, dŏŏrrch;
Chaise, shai'-zai; Chicane, she-kâ'-nai; Charpie, shârr-pee';
Chor, kore; Christ, krist; Chur, koo'rr;
China, chee'-nâ; Chemie, chai-mee'.

Chs, chs, like *x* or *cks*. When the s is the possessive case of a word terminating in ch, the ch retains its guttural sound.

Lachs, lâks; Ochse, ock'sai; Achse, âck'-sai.

Ck, ck, like *ck*.

Sch, sch, like *sh*.

Scheu, shoi; schauen, shou'-en; rasch, râsh.

St, st, and Sp, sp, as st and sp in English. In the South of Germany these are generally pronounced as if written sht and shp. The student who speaks English, will do better to adopt the former pronunciation.

ss, ss, has the sound of ss in English; it only occurs in the middle of words, when one of the letters is pronounced with each syllable, making the vowel in the first syllable short.

Masse, mâss'-sai; Messe, mess'-sai; lassen, lâss'-sen.

ß has the sound of ss in English; it stands at the end of syllables and in the middle of words; when in the middle of words it communicates no sound to the first of the two syllables, between which it occurs, when at the end, it makes the syllable short.

Maßen, mâ'-ssen; Straße, strâ'-ssai; daß, dâss.

ff, ff, the same as f.

ph, ph, the same as f.

Philosoph, fe-lo-zo'f'; Phantom, fâṇ-to'm'.

pf, pf, pronounce both letters rapidly one after the other without any hiatus. By pronouncing the words *up for* rapidly and frequently the sound will soon be acquired.

Pferd, p'faird; Pfeil, p'file; Pfennig, p'fen'-nich.

tz, like ts the same as z.

Platz, plâts, sitzen, et'-sen; Hetzen, het'-sen.

SYLLABIC ACCENT.

The accent is on the root of the word.

Heil′-ung, sen′-den, Säng′-er, gu′-ten.

Exceptions: 1. Many words introduced from foreign languages, as. Ba-ron′, Ad-vo-cat′, Mu-sik′.

2. German words with foreign terminations, as: Mo-rast′, Blu-mist′, Gla-sur′.

3. The words: le-ben′-dig, Ant′-wort, Ant′-litz, and their derivatives.

4. Words ending in ei, as: Kin-de-rei′, Bet-te-lei′.

5. Compound verbs which have separable prefixes, have the primary accent on the prefix, as: zu″-schrei′-ben, bei″-fü′-gen.

In compound words, the accented syllable of the qualifying word has generally the primary and that of the qualified word, the secondary accent, the former we indicate by ″ and the latter by ′. In the word Blumengarten, flowergarden, Blumen is the qualifying word, therefore Blu has the primary accent and gar, the accented syllable of the qualified word, the secondary accent, Blu″-men-gar′-ten.

DIVISION OF SYLLABLES IN SPEAKING.

1. When a single consonant occurs between two vowels, the consonant belongs to the second syllable, independent of the derivation of the word, as: gu′-te, not gut′-e, altho' the word is derived from gut. Lei′-den, schrei′-ben, Freu′-de.

2. When two consonants are in the middle of a word, they not being one of the compound consonants, mentioned P. 8, the first goes with the preceding, and the second with the following syllable, as: Er′-ben, Fel′-sen, freund′-lich, Gar′-be, Wes′-pe.

3. Ch, ck and sch, when these make the foregoing letter short, they communicate their sound to both syllables, when they stand between two vowels, as: lachen, pronounce läch′-chen; sprechen, sprech′-chen; waschen, vâsh′-shen; rücken, rück′-ken. When preceded by a vowel and followed by a consonant they, of course, belong to the first syllable, as:

wachsam, vâch′-sâm; rücklings, rück′-lingss.

4. ss, ß, see these letters under the pronunciation of double consonants.

5. In compound words, the component parts are pronounced separately, as: Kienapfel, keen″-ap′-fel; composed of Kien and apfel; Neunauge, noin″-ou′gai, of Neun and auge. Prefixes also retain their sound and do not combine with the following consonant or vowel, as: bestreiten, bai-stri′-ten; befreien, bai-fri′en; geblasen, gai-blâ′-zen; geirrt, gai-irrt′; beurkunden, bai-oor′-kōōn-den; erobern, err-o′-bern..

EXPLANATION

OF THE SIGNS USED IN THE PRONOUNCING PART.

When a vowel is immediately followed by one or more consonants, the vowel is short, âl, el, il, ol, ool are short.

When an apostrophe is placed after the vowel and a small space left between the consonant and the vowel, the latter is long, as: â'd, i'd, o'd, oo'd are long.

â represents the sound of the German a.

ai, the long open sound of e and ä, as in *air*, when this sound is unaccented, it must not be pronounced strongly or be drawn out long, but is something like the final a in the name Louisa.

ey, the long close sound of e as in *obey*.

oo', represents the sound of the German u or uh, it is the oo in *boot*, *ooze*.

oo, ŏŏ, represent the sound of the short u, it is the *oo* in *foot*, or the *u* in *put*.

ou, always sounds like ou in house.

', indicates the accented syllable, that is the syllable on which the stress of the voice is to fall.

", compound words have often two accents, a stronger one and a weaker one, the stronger one is called the primary and the weaker one, the secondary accent; the former is indicated by " and the latter by '.

ö, ü, ch, as these characters have no corresponding sounds in English, the student is referred for their explanation to the pronunciation of the letters.

Each syllable in the pronouncing part, is pronounced in the same manner as in English.

gh, represents the hard g, when according to English orthoepy it would be soft, and must always be pronounced as g in get.

THE WRITTEN ALPHABETH.

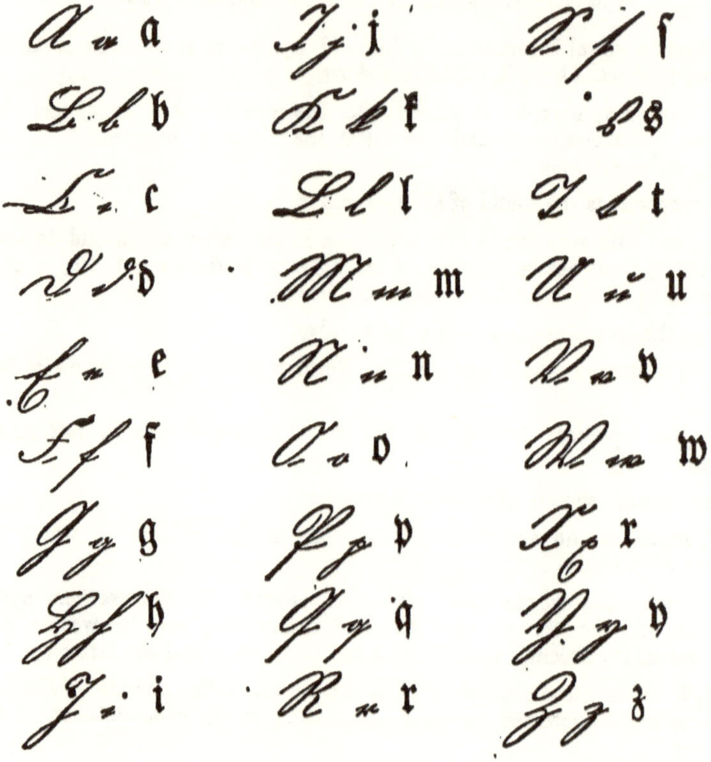

COMPOUND AND DOUBLE CONSONANTS.

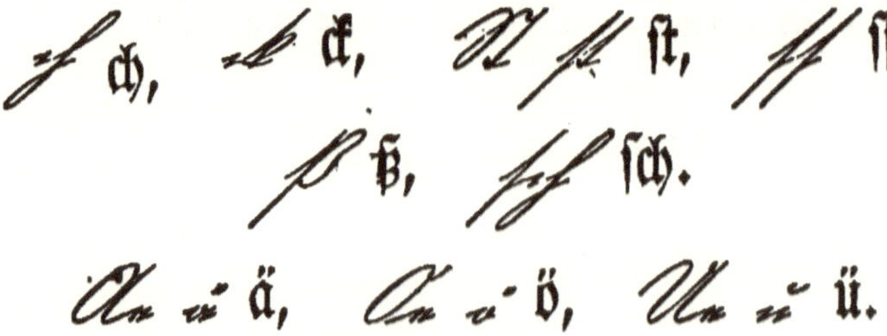

DIRECTIONS.

All sentences, as well as all substantives, and all words used as substantives, must begin with a capital letter.

The second person of the personal pronouns are written with a capital, also the words Sie and Er, when used instead of Du and Ihr.

Adjectives derived from proper substantives are not written with capitals, except those derived from the names of towns.

The long ſ is used at the beginning, the short s at the end of a syllable; the ſſ when the sharp sound of the s is divided between two syllables, the ß when the sharp s sound goes with the last syllable only. The latter is also used at the end of words or syllables (see p. 9).

(See the exercises p. 12.)

1.

Haben Sie? Ich habe, wir haben, hat er? Brod, Salz, Geld, Gold, viel, kein, ja. Haben Sie viel Brod?

2.

Hat er Brod? Er hat Brod. Hat er viel Salz? Er hat viel Salz.

3.

Hat sie? Wer, was, nicht, der Mann. Fleisch, Gras, Heu, Wasser, Glas, Feuer, Licht, wenig, nur, und, auch.

4.

Haben sie viel Fleisch? Sie haben kein Fleisch, sie haben nur Brod.

Der Affe, der Bäcker, der Schneider, der Knabe, der Soldat, das Mehl, das Kupfer, das Schmalz.

5.

Gekauft, gehabt, gesucht, gefunden, aber, oder, noch, das Pulver.

6.

Habe ich Schmalz gekauft? Sie haben viel Schmalz, aber kein Brod gekauft.

Der Zimmermann, der Schuhmacher, der Müller, der Offizier, das Leder, das Blei; geholt, gebracht.

7.

Geschickt, gegessen, getrunken, Bier, Gemüse, Eis, genug, mehr, als, welches, einiges, keins, etwas. Haben Sie Fleisch gegessen? Wir haben welches gegessen.

8.

Der Hund, der Maler, Vater, Sohn, Kaufmann, das Getreide, gepflanzt, empfangen, verloren, der Bauer.

9.

Hatten Sie? Ich hatte, so viel wie, nichts.

10.

Hatten Sie Getreide? Ich hatte welches. Wir hatten keins. Der Koch; Bauer; Russe, Engländer, das Roß; gekocht; gebraten; weggeschickt; verbrannt.

11.

Wo, hier, da, schon, noch nicht, zu Mittag gegessen, zu Abend, zu Hause, wann, heute, gestern, zu viel. Wo haben

Sie zu Mittag gegessen?

12.

Wo hatten Sie Geld verloren? Ich hatte hier welches verloren. Hatten Sie nicht da welches verloren?

13.

Sind Sie? Ich bin, er ist, schön, arm, reich, krank, wohl, groß, klein, durstig, hungrig, sehr.

14.

Bin ich schön? Sie sind nicht schön. Ist der Knabe so schön wie der Mann? Er ist so schön.

Naß, trocken, jung, müde, lustig, traurig, häßlich, blind, taub.

15.

Waren Sie? Ich war, warm, kalt, rein, schmutzig, hart, weich, schläfrig, lahm. Waren Sie naß oder trocken? Ich war naß, aber der Mann war trocken.

16.

Waren Sie krank? Ich war krank. War der Koch kalt? Zähe, scharf, stumpf, sauer, süß, weiß, eben, uneben, neu.

17

Sind Sie gewesen? irgendwo, nirgends, in Amerika, Deutschland, Frankreich, Rußland, oft, zuweilen, jemals, niemals, um ein Uhr, zwei, drei, vier, fünf, auf dem Lande, auf der Straße, vor einem Jahre.

18.

Der Koch ist sehr krank gewesen Ist er jetzt wohl? Spanien, Preußen, Holland, müde, auf dem Markte, in dem Hause, Garten, lange, wie, ein Jahr, zwei Jahre

19.

Dann, nicht mehr, verkauft. Ich war schon da gewesen.

20.

Wann war er zu Hause gewesen?

Er war um drei Uhr zu Hause gewesen.

21.

Das Kaufmanns, das Brod des Knaben. Hat der Soldat das Pulver des Offiziers. Er hat es nicht, aber er hat es gehabt.

22.

Haben Sie das Fleisch des Soldaten? Ich habe es nicht. Wer hat das Leder des Schuhmachers? Der Knabe des Zimmermanns hat es.

23.

Werden, er wird, gut, schlecht, auch, wieder, dunkel. Wer wird reich? Der Großvater wird reich.

24.

Werde ich alt? Sie werden alt und reich. Grün, theuer, roth, dick, dünn, hell, hart, weich.

25.

Kaufen, suchen, finden, holen, bringen, schicken, essen, pflanzen, verlieren;

kochen, wegschicken. Werden Sie kaufen? Morgen, übermorgen, heiß, des Mittags, um Mitternacht.

26.

Werde ich Feuer und Licht haben? Sie werden Feuer und Licht haben. Nähen, mähen, schneiden, geschnitten, anzünden, angezündet, backen, gebacken.

27.

Dieser, ein, einen, Ihr, Ihren, mein, meinen, sein, seinen, dieses Fleisch, ihnen.

28.

Hat der Sohn des Malers den Neffen des Bauern gesehen? Er hat ihn gesehen. Rufen, gerufen, fassen, gefaßt, schlagen, geschlagen, jener, jenen, jenes.

29.

Gehabt haben, gewesen sein, geworden sein, gekauft haben, unser, unsern, unseres, Ihres, der Schlächter.

30.

Werde ich mein Blei verkauft haben? Sie werden es dann verkauft haben. Wird der Knabe des Schneiders das Geld seines Vaters empfangen haben?

31.

Der gute Schneider, das gute Fleisch; mich. Haben Sie den guten Mann geliebt.

32.

Wird der gute Franzose mich rufen? Er wird Sie rufen. Werden Sie den kleinen Schlächter suchen? Der Schwager, der Enkel, der Bruder, der Oheim, der Vetter, alt, fleißig, träge.

33.

Ein guter Vater, mürbe, das

Rindfleisch, Kalbfleisch, Hammelfleisch. Der geliebte Knabe, das gebackene Brod; geschickt; der Freund; der Feind; das Wasser; Haus; Ei; Glas.

34.

Ihr armer Oheim ist ein sehr alter Mann. Mein alter lahmer Großvater hat keinen guten Freund. Das Band, Buch, Faß, Auge.

35.

Der Wein, Thee, Zucker, Käse, etwas, allerlei.

36.

Ist guter Kaffee da? Es ist welcher da. Alter Käse ist gut.

37.

Dem, diesem, keinem, schenken, geschenkt, geben, gegeben, senden, gesandt, leihen, geliehen, bezahlen, bezahlt, zeigen, gezeigt, der Rock, der Schuh, des Hutes, wem.

38.

Haben Sie dem Zimmermann viel Geld geliehen? Ich habe dem Zimmermann kein Geld, aber ich habe dem Maurer welches geliehen.

Schreiben, geschrieben, reisen, gereist, lassen, gelassen, wiedergeben, wiedergegeben.

39.

Mir, Ihnen, ihm, ihr, uns, ihnen, jemand, niemand, weder—noch. Haben Sie dem Franzosen seinen Hut geschickt? Ich habe ihm seinen Hut geschickt.

40.

Wollen Sie mir Geld schicken? Ich werde Ihnen Geld schicken.

41.

Hat der Soldat dem Hunde das Brod gegeben? Er hat es ihm gegeben.

42.

Hat der Kaufmann dem Zimmermann das Tuch verkauft? Er hat es ihm verkauft.

43.

Dem guten Freunde, einem schlechten Soldaten, diesem alten Deutschen. Um wie viel Uhr? Um halb eins. Der Brief, Rock, das Kleid, der Löffel, golden, silbern, eisern.

PART I.

1.

Haben Sie? hâ'ben zee,	have you?
Ich habe, ich hâ'bai,	I have
wir haben, veer hâ'ben,	we have
haben wir? hâ'-ben veer,	have we
hat er? hâ't airr,	has he
er hat, airr hâ't,	he has.

Brod, bro't, bread; Salz, zâlts, salt; Geld, ghelt, money; Gold, golt, gold; viel, feel, much; kein, kine, no; ja, yâ, yes.

Haben Sie Brod? Ich habe Brod. Haben Sie kein Brod? Ich habe kein Brod. Hat er viel Geld? Er hat viel Geld. Haben Sie viel Brod? Ja, ich habe viel Brod.

2.

Have you *any** bread? I have *some* bread. Has he *any* bread? He has no bread. Has he much salt? He has much salt. He has no salt. Have we *any* bread? We have no bread. We have *some* bread. Have I *any* gold? Yes, you have gold. Has he no money? He has much money.

Let the student form similar sentences, in writing or in speaking, with the following words:

Oel, ö'l, oil; Papier, pâ-peer', paper; Holz, holts, wood; Tuch, too'ch; Silber, zil'-ber.

3.

Hat sie? hâ't zee,	has she
sie hat, zee hâ't,	she has
sie haben, zee hâ'-ben,	they have
haben sie, hâ'ben zee,	have they
wer? vairr,	who?
was, vâss,	what
nicht, nicht,	not
der Mann, dairr mân,	the man
der, dairr, m. art. nom.	the.

Fleisch, fli'sh, meat, flesh; Gras, grâss, grass; Heu, hoi, hay; Wasser, vâs'-ser, water; Gas, gâ's; Feuer, foi'er, fire; Licht, licht, light; wenig,

* Words in italics are not to be translated.

wenig, vey'-nich, little (quantity); nur, noo'rr, only, but; und, öönt, and; auch, ouch, also.

Haben Sie viel Fleisch? Wir haben viel Fleisch. Hat sie viel Wasser? Sie hat viel Wasser. Hat sie wenig Licht? Sie hat viel Licht. Haben sie wenig Heu? Sie (they) haben wenig Heu. Wer hat kein Geld? Der Mann hat kein Geld. Wer hat kein Gras? Wir haben kein Gras.

4.

Have they much meat? They have no meat, they have only bread. Have they only salt? They have not only salt, they have also money and meat. What has she? She has fire and water. Who has gas? The man has gas. Have I *any* light? You have no light and no fire. Who has little meat? She has only little meat. Has he not much bread? He has no bread and no meat, he has but little salt. Have we bread and salt? We have only bread, we have no salt. What have you? I have much gold and little grass. What has the man? He has meat and salt.

Form similar sentences with the following words:

Der Ochse, ock'-sai, the ox; der Bäcker, beck'-ker, the baker; der Schneider, shni'-der, the tailor; der Knabe, k'nâ'-bai, the boy; der Soldat, zol-dât'; Mehl, mail, flour; Kupfer, kööp'-fer, copper; Schmalz, shmâlts, lard.

Eisen iron

5.

Gekauft, gai-kouft', bought; gehabt, gai-hâpt', had; gesucht, gai-zoo'cht', looked for; gefunden, gai-föön'den, found.

The past participle stands at the end of the sentence. German construction, have you bread bought?

Aber, â'-ber,	but
oder, o'-der,	or
noch, noch,	still, yet
noch kein, noch kine,	no . . . as yet
Pulver, pööl'-fer,	powder.

Haben Sie Kupfer gekauft? Hat der Ochse Gras gehabt? Er hat Gras gehabt. Hat der Schneider Tuch gekauft? Er hat Tuch gekauft. Hat der Soldat Pulver gehabt? Er hat kein Pulver gehabt. Haben sie Pulver gefunden? Sie haben Pulver gefunden. Hat der Knabe Gold gesucht? Er hat Gold gesucht. Er hat kein Gold, aber Kupfer gefunden. Haben Sie Brod oder Schmalz gekauft? Wir haben Brod und Salz, aber wir haben noch kein Schmalz gekauft.

6.

Have I bought *any* lard? You have bought much lard but no bread. Have they had no money? They have not had much money? Has the ox had *any* hay? He has had no hay but much grass and little water. What has the taylor had? He has had cloth. What has the soldier had? He has had iron. What has the boy found? He has found much money.

Has he found no powder? He has found* no powder but much iron. What has the boy looked for? He has looked for water. Has he found *any* water? He has found only little water but much gas and much fire. Have you gold or silver? I have gold and silver, the soldier has gold but no silver, and the boy has silver but no gold. Has the baker had flour or bread? He has had flour and bread but no money. Who has bought iron? The tailor has bought iron. Who has looked for paper? We have looked for paper.

Form similar sentences with the following words:

Der Zimmermann, tsim''-mer-mân', the carpenter; der Schuhmacher, shoo''-mâch'-cher, the shoemaker; der Müller, mül'-ler, the miller; der Offizier, of-fe-tseer', the officer; Leder, lai'-der, leather; Blei, bli, lead; geholt, gai-ho'lt', fetched, gone for, brought; gebracht, gai-brâcht', brought.

7.

Geschickt, gai-shickt',	sent
gegessen, gai-ges'-sen,	eaten
getrunken, gai-trŏŏnk-en,	drunk
Bier, beer,	beer
Gemüse, s. gai-mü'-zai,	vegetables
Eis, ice,	ice
genug, gai-noo'ch',	enough (stands after the noun)
mehr,..als, meyr âlss,	more,..than.

The nouns which have been used so far, with the exception of the personal nouns and the word ox, are all neuter. The words some and any, when standing before a noun, without the accent of the phrase being on them, are not translated, but when they stand alone in answer to a question, must be translated by welches or einiges, in which case welches is unlimited and einiges more limited. In the more elevated style the words welches, welche, are not much used, but dessen, deren put in their place.

Haben Sie Brod,	Have you any bread
Ich habe welches,	I have some (any quantity, small or large)
Ich habe einiges,	I have *some* (not much)
keins, ki'nss,	not any, none (not before a noun)
etwas, et'-vass,	some, a little.

Haben Sie Brod? Ich habe welches. Haben Sie Geld gehabt? Ich habe einiges gehabt. Haben Sie Fleisch gegessen? Wir haben welches gegessen. Haben sie Bier getrunken? Sie haben keins getrunken. Wer hat Gemüse geschickt? Der Soldat hat welches geschickt. Hat der Offizier genug Geld geholt? Er hat genug geholt. Was hat der Soldat gebracht? Er hat Pulver und Blei gebracht. Haben Sie mehr Mehl als Brod gekauft? Hat der Schneider mehr Holz als der Zimmermann? Er hat mehr. Haben Sie viel Silber? Ich habe nicht viel, aber genug.

8.

Have you brought any beer? We have not brought any. Have you drunk some water? I have drunk no water, but some beer. Who has

* At the end of the sentence.

eaten more meat, the tailor or the officer? The officer has eaten more than the tailor, but the tailor has drunk more water than the officer. Has she had any leather? She has had some, but not enough. Has the carpenter bought much wood? He has bought none. Who has bought cloth enough? The tailor has bought more than enough but the shoemaker has bought none, he has bought leather. Have you had ice enough? We have had more than enough. What has the tailor eaten? He has eaten meat, bread and vegetables. What has the shoemaker drunk? He has drunk nothing but (only) water. What has the miller bought? He has bought flour. Have they drunk any water? They have drunk some. They have drunk none. Have they seen no fire? They have seen none. Has she much lard? She has not much, but some. Has she more lard than salt? She has some lard, but no salt.

Form similar sentences with the following words:

Der Hund, hōōnt, the dog; der Maler, mâ'-ler, the painter; der Vater, fâ'-ter, the father; der Sohn, zone, the son; der Kaufmann, kouf'-mân, the merchant; das Getreide, n., gai-tri'-dai, grain, corn; gepflanzt, gai-pflântst', planted; empfangen, emp-fâng'-en, received; verloren, ver-lo'-ren, lost; der Bauer, bou'-er, the farmer, peasant.

9.

Hatten Sie,	hât'-ten zee,	had you
ich hatte,	ich hât'-tai,	I had
wir hatten,	veer hât'-ten,	we had
er hatte,	er hât'-tai,	he had
sie hatte,	zee hât'-tai,	she had
sie hatten,	zee hât'-ten,	they had
so viel wie,	zo feel vee,	as much as
ich hatte gehabt,		I had had
nichts,	nichts,	nothing.

Hatten Sie Korn? Ich hatte keins. Wer hatte welches? Der Vater hatte welches. Hatte der Sohn keins? Hatten Sie so viel wie ich? Ich hatte mehr als Sie? Hatte sie genug? Sie hatte mehr als genug. Wer hatte mehr als genug? Der Hund hatte mehr als genug. Was hatte er? Er hatte Fleisch und Wasser. Was hatte der Kaufmann gekauft? Er hatte nichts gekauft. Was haben sie empfangen? Sie haben nichts empfangen. Hatten Sie Leder empfangen? Ich hatte keins empfangen. Was hatte der Hund gegessen? Er hatte Fleisch gegessen.

10.

Had you any grain? I had some. We had none. What had you? I had money. Had he any gold? He had some but she had none. Had she no salt? She had more salt than bread. Who had grain? The father and the son had (3d Pers. plur.) some. Had the farmer any grain? He had more grain than flour but not much leather. What had the ox? He had much hay and some water. What had the tailor received? He had received cloth. What had the carpenter bought? He had bought more wood than leather. Had he received more ice than water? He had received much ice but only little water. Had they planted grain? They had planted some but not much. What had the ox eaten? He had eaten much hay and the dog had eaten much meat. Had you had flour and bread enough. We had had enough, but we had not had beer enough. Had the soldier powder and lead enough? He had powder enough, but not lead enough. Who had had more money, the father or the son? The father had had more than the son. Had we gone for no beer? You had gone for beer. Had you brought some? We had brought none. Had you bought nothing? I had bought nothing. What had the father seen? He had seen much fire.

Form similar sentences with the following words:

Der Koch, koch, cook; der Brauer, brou′-er, the brewer; der Neffe, nef′-fai, the nephew; der Engländer, eng′-len-der, the Englishman; Stroh, n., stro, straw; gekocht, gai-kocht′, boiled, cooked; gebraten, gai-brâ′-ten, roasted, fried; weggeschickt, vech″-gai-shickt′, sent away, verbrannt, fer-brânt′, burned, destroyed by fire.

11.

Wo, vo,	where
hier, here,	here
da, dâ,	there
schon, sho'n,	already
noch nicht, noch nicht,	not yet
zu Mittag gegessen, tsoo mit′-tâch-gai-ghes′-sen,	dined
zu Abend gegessen, tsoo â′-bent,	supped
zu Hause, tsoo hou′-zai,	at home
wann, vân,	when
heute, hoi′-tai,	to day
gestern, ghess′-tern,	yesterday
zu viel, tsoo feel,	too much
nicht so viel wie, nicht zo feel vee,	not so much as
nein, nine,	no.

Wo haben Sie zu Mittag gegessen? Wir haben zu Hause zu Mittag gegessen. Hatten Sie zu Abend gegessen? Ich hatte zu Abend gegessen, aber der Soldat und der Schneider hatten noch nicht zu Abend gegessen. Was hatten sie gegessen? Wir hatten Fleisch und Brod und Gemüse gegessen. Hatten Sie schon zu Abend gegessen? Ich hatte schon zu Abend gegessen, aber der Zimmermann hatte noch nicht zu Mittag gegessen. Wo haben Sie Geld verloren? Ich habe hier welches verloren. Wo hat der Schneider Tuch verbrannt? Er hat es hier verbrannt. Wann hat er es verbrannt? Er hat es heute verbrannt. Hat er zu viel gegessen? Er hat nicht genug gegessen. Hatte er zu viel getrunken? Er hatte zu viel Bier getrunken. Hat der Koch Fleisch gebraten? Er hat kein Fleisch gebraten, er hat welches gekocht. Hat der Knabe schon zu Abend gegessen? Ja, er hat schon zu Abend gegessen. Was hat er gegessen? Er hat noch nicht zu Abend, aber er hat schon zu Mittag gegessen. Hat er zu Hause zu Abend gegessen? Nein er hat hier zu Abend gegessen.

12.

Where had you lost *some* money? I had lost some here. Had you not lost some (keins) there? I had lost some there. Have you already supped? No, I have not yet dined. Has the tailor already supped? No, the tailor has not yet supped, but the shoemaker and the carpenter have already supped. Had the cook burnt much meat? He had burned none. When had he burned meat? He had burned some yesterday. Has he lost much money yesterday? He has lost some yesterday and some to-day. (Constr. He has yesterday and to-day some lost)? Had they already burned much grain? They had not yet burned any (noch keins). Had they boiled too many (viel) vegetables? They had not boiled too many vegetables, but they had roasted too much meat. Had they already planted as much corn as we? They had not yet planted so much as we, but they had already planted more vegetables than we. Had the boy not yet supped. He had already dined and supped. Where had he supped? He had supped at home. Has the miller already brought some flour? He has not yet brought any. Has he brought more than the baker? The baker has brought more than the miller.

13.

Sind Sie, zint zee,	are you?
ich bin, ich bin,	I am
er iſt, ſie iſt, air ist, zee ist,	he is, she is
der Mann iſt, ist,	the man is
wir ſind, veer zint,	we are
ſie ſind, zee zint,	they are.

Schön, shö'n, beautiful; arm, ârm, poor; reich, ri'ch, rich; krank, kränk, ill; wohl, vo'l, well; groß, gro'ss, large, big, great, tall; klein, kline, small, little (refers to size only); durſtig, döör'-stich, thirsty; hungrig, hööng'-rich, hungry; ſehr, zeyr, very.

Sind ſie hier? Sie ſind hier. Sind Sie hier? Ich bin hier. Wir ſind hier. Iſt er da? Er iſt da. Er iſt nicht da. Iſt der Soldat, oder der Offizier hier? Der Offizier iſt hier, aber der Soldat iſt nicht hier. Wo iſt der Soldat? Er iſt zu Hauſe. Iſt der Knabe ſchön? Er iſt ſehr ſchön. Iſt der Schneider ſo hungrig wie der Schuhmacher? Er iſt ſo hungrig wie der Schuhmacher, aber er iſt nicht ſo durſtig. Wer iſt durſtig? Der Bäcker iſt durſtig. Sind ſie wohl? Sie ſind wohl. Iſt der Knabe klein? Nein, er iſt groß und ſchön. Iſt der Koch ſo groß wie der Brauer?

14.

Am I beautiful? You are not beautiful. Is the boy as beautiful as the man? He is as beautiful as the man. Are you rich? I am not rich, I am very poor, but the farmer is rich and has much grain. Has he much money? He has much gold and much silver, he is as rich as the officer. Are they sick or well? He is sick, but she is very well. Where is she, she is at home. Am I not as rich as you? You are as rich as I. Who is thirsty and hungry? The shoemaker is hungry and the miller is thirsty. Are you thirsty already (already thirsty)? I am not yet thirsty. Who is tall, the soldier or the cook? The soldier is tall, but the cook is very small. Where is the father? He is here. Is he already here? He is here already.* Where is the son? He is at home. Has he already supped? He has not yet supped. Where is the baker to-day? He is at home to-day. Who is handsome? The farmer is very handsome. Is the baker sick to-day (to-day sick)? He is not sick to-day. Is he too tall? He is not too tall. Is she too handsome? She is not too handsome. Have you sent away *any* flour. I have sent none, but the miller has sent away some.

Form some more similar sentences with the following words:

Naß, nâss, wet; trocken, trock'-en, dry; jung, yŏŏng, young; müde, mü'-dai, tired; lustig, lŏŏs'-tich, merry; traurig, trou'-rich, sad; häßlich, hess'-lich; blind, blint, blind; taub, toup, deaf.

15.

Waren Sie? vâ'-ren zee,	were you?
ich war, ich vâ'rr,	I was;
er war, air vâ'rr,	he was;
sie war, zee vâ'rr,	she was;
wir waren, veerr vâ'-ren,	we were;
sie waren, zee vâ'ren,	they were.

(See § 54, 5.)

Warm, vârrm, warm; kalt, kâlt, cold; rein, rine, clean; schmutzig, shmŏŏt'-sig; hart, hârrt, hard; weich, vi'ch, soft; schläfrig, shlaif'-rich, sleepy; lahm, lâm', lame.

The characteristic letter of the neuter gender is s; es, it; das, the, is the neuter article; as it has been stated before, all the words introduced so far, except the personal nouns, are neuter and therefore take the article das before them, both in the nominative and in the accusative case. Es, is both, nom. and acc.

Das (dâss) Brod,	the bread;
das Fleisch,	the meat, &c.

Waren Sie naß oder trocken? Ich war naß, aber der Mann war trocken. Waren sie schläfrig? Sie waren nicht schläfrig, sie waren hungrig und durstig. Wer war warm? Der Soldat war warm. Wer war kalt? Der Bäcker war sehr kalt. Waren sie jung oder alt? Sie waren nicht jung, sie waren alt. Wo waren Sie? Wir waren hier. Waren sie schon da? Ich war noch nicht da. Wann waren wir zu Hause? Wir waren gestern zu Hause. Haben Sie das Gold und das Silber? Ich habe das Gold aber nicht das Silber. Haben Sie das Fleisch gehabt? Ich habe es gehabt. Hatten Sie das Eisen? Ich hatte es nicht, der Soldat hatte es. Wer hatte das Pulver und das Blei? Der Offizier hatte es. Wo war das Licht? Es war hier.

16.

Were you ill? I was very ill. Was the cook cold? He was not very cold. Was the meat hard? It was too hard. Was the soldier as blind as the tailor? The soldier was blind, the tailor was not blind. Who was

* The adverb of time precedes the adverb of place.

lame? The shoemaker was lame and had no meat. What had he? He had only bread and water. What is he? He is a carpenter. What is the son? He is an officer. Were you at home? We were not at home yet. When were you at home? We were at home yesterday. Were they already here? They were not yet here. Is the iron hard? It is hard. Is the bread soft or hard? It is hard to-day (to-day hard), yesterday it was (was it) soft. Was the boy not dirty? He was very wet and dirty. Where were they yesterday? They were at home. Are they blind and hungry and have they no money? They are blind and have no money. Who was sick? The cook and the carpenter were sick, but the officer was well.

Form similar sentences with these words:

Zähe, tsai'-hai, tough, tenacious; scharf, shârrf, sharp; stumpf, stöömpf, blunt; sauer, zourr, sour; süß, zü'ss, sweet; weiß, vi'ss, white; eben, ai'-ben, even; uneben, ööon''-ai'-ben, uneven; nun, noo'n, now.

17.

Sind Sie gewesen? gai-vai'zen,	have you been?
ich bin gewesen,	I have been;
er, sie, es ist gewesen,	he, she, it has been;
wir sind gewesen,	we have been;
sie sind gewesen,	they have been;
irgendwo, irr''-ghent-vo',	some where, any where;
nirgends, nirr'-ghents,	no where;
in Amerika, in â-mey'-re-kâ,	in America;
in Deutschland, doitsh'-lânt,	in Germany;
in Frankreich, frânk-ri'ch,	in France;
in Rußland, rööss'-lând,	in Russia.

Oft, oft, often; zuweilen, tsoo-vi'-len, sometimes; jemals, yey'-mâ'lss, ever; nie, nee; niemals, nee'-mâ'lss, never; um ein Uhr, ööm ine oo'rr, at one o'clock; um zwei Uhr, ööm tswi oo'rr, at two o'clock; drei, dri, three; vier, feerr, four; fünf, fünf, five; auf dem Lande, ouf dem lân'-dai, in the country; auf der Straße, ouf dair strâ'-ssai, in the street; vor einem Jahre, fo'r i'-nem yâ'-rai, a year ago.

Sind Sie da gewesen? Ich bin da gewesen. Ist er oft da gewesen? Er ist nicht oft da gewesen. Wann ist sie da gewesen? Sie ist um ein Uhr da gewesen. Ist er schon hier gewesen? Er ist noch nicht hier gewesen. Sind wir krank gewesen? Sie sind sehr krank gewesen. Wer ist lustig gewesen? Der Zimmermann ist lustig gewesen. Sind Sie irgendwo gewesen? Ja, ich bin auf dem Lande gewesen. Ist sie oft in Rußland gewesen? Sie ist niemals da gewesen. Ist der Mann auf der Straße gewesen? Er ist da gewesen.

18.

Have you been sick? I have not been sick. Who has been sick? The cook has been very sick. Is he well now? He is not yet well. Where has he been? He has been in the country. Have you ever been in Russia? I have never been there. Has she ever been in France? She has never been in France and in Germany. Has the miller been in

America? He has never been there. When was the baker in Russia? He was there last year. When has he had the wood? He has had it to-day. Has he not had it yesterday and to-day? He has had it yesterday and to-day. Where has the soldier been? He has been in America. When was he there? He was there last year. Has the bread been soft? No, it has been hard. Has he been as hungry as you? He has been as hungry as I. Has she been in the country? She has never been in the country. Have you been in the country? I have not been there. When have you been in the street? I have been there to-day. Has he not been blind? He has been blind and lame. Is he blind and lame now? He is not blind but lame. Who has been hungry and thirsty? The boy has been hungry and thirsty. Is he still hungry? He is now not hungry, but he is still very thirsty. Has he no water? He has some. Is the water here? It is not here, it is there. Have they lost the money? They have not lost it, they have it here. What have they lost? They have lost nothing. What have they had? They have had bread, meat, vegetables, beer and water.

Form similar sentences with the following words:

Spanien, spå′-ne-en, Spain; Preußen, proi′-ssen, Prussia; Holland, hol′-lånt, Holland; müde, mü′-dai, tired; auf dem Markte, ouf dem mårk′-tai, in the market; in dem Hause, in dem hou′-zai, in the house; in dem Garten, in dem gårr′-ten, in the garden; lange, lång′-ai, long, a long time; wie, vee, how; ein Jahr, ine yå′rr, one year; zwei Jahre, tswi yå′ray, two years.

19.

Waren Sie gewesen? vå′-ren zee gai-wai′-sen,	had you been?
Ich war gewesen, ich vå′rr gai-vai′-sen,	I had been;
er, sie, es war gewesen,	he, she, it had been;
wir waren gewesen,	we had been;
sie waren gewesen,	they had been;
der Engländer war gewesen,	the Englishman had been;
dann, dån,	then, at that time;
nicht mehr, nicht mair,	not any more, no longer;
verkauft, fer-kouft′,	sold.

Waren Sie schon da gewesen? Ich war schon da gewesen; er war noch nicht da gewesen. War sie schon in Frankreich gewesen? Sie war schon oft da gewesen. War der Kaufmann noch nicht in Holland gewesen? Er war schon in Holland und in England gewesen. War das Tuch schön gewesen? Es war sehr schön gewesen. Ist der Mann reich gewesen? Er ist sehr reich gewesen. War er arm gewesen? War das Stroh naß gewesen? Es war naß gewesen, dann war es trocken. War der Vater krank gewesen? Er war krank gewesen, aber gestern war er wohl. War das Brod gut gewesen? Es war gut gewesen, aber gestern war es sauer. War der Knabe blind gewesen? Er war lange blind gewesen, aber vor einem Jahre war er nicht mehr blind.

20.

Was he at home at one o'clock (see Exerc. 14)? He was not at home. When had he been at home? He had been at home at three o'clock

Had you been sick? I had been long sick. Was the German at home? He was not at home at two o'clock, but he had been at home at one o'clock. Were the tailor and the merchant in France? They were not in France last year, but they had been there. Had they been in Spain? They had never been in Spain. Where had they been? They had been no where. Was the officer here at four o'clock? He was not here at four o'clock, but he had been here at three o'clock. Was the dog handsome? He was not handsome, but he had been handsome. Had the shoemaker any leather? He had none, he had had some, but he had sold it. Was the boy thirsty? He was not thirsty, but he had been very thirsty, he had much water. Had the miller vegetables enough? He had not enough, he had had a great deal of (viel) vegetables (s.), but he had sent them (it) away. Had the brewer beer enough? He had enough, he had fetched (gone for) some. Had she not yet been in France? She had already been there. Had she been there long? She had not been there as long as you and I. I had been there as long as the merchant. Had the Englishman been lame? He had been lame *for* two years. How long had the nephew been lame? He had been lame *for* three years. Who had been in the garden? The brewer had been there. Who had been in the market? The father and the son had (3d pers. pl.) been in the market.

Form sentences with any words that have been introduced before.

21.

des Kaufmanns,	dess kouf'-mâns,	of the merchant;
des Knaben,	dess k'nâ'-ben,	of the boy, the boy's.

(Genitive case see § 9.)

All mascul. nouns terminating in e take n in the genitive singular, most the others take s or es.

des Malers, dess mâ'-lers,	of the painter or the painter's;
des Bauern, (exc.) dess bou'-ern,	of the peasant;
des Mannes, dess mân'-ness,	of the man;
des Ochsen, dess ock'-sen,	of the ox;
des Bäckers, dess beck'-kers,	of the baker;
des Soldaten, dess zol-dâ'-ten,	of the soldier;
das Brod des Knaben,	the bread of the boy, or the boy's bread.

Haben Sie das Brod des Knaben? Ich habe es. Hat der Soldat das Pulver des Offiziers? Er hat es nicht, aber er hat es gehabt. Haben Sie das Mehl des Müllers gehabt? Wir haben es gehabt. Haben sie das Salz des Koches (Kochs) gehabt? Sie haben es gehabt. Wer hat das Fleisch des Schneiders gegessen? Der Sohn des Offiziers hat es gegessen. Wer hat das Bier des Brauers getrunken? Der Neffe des Engländers hat es getrunken. Wo sind Sie gewesen? Ich bin in dem Garten des Schneiders gewesen. Sind sie in dem Garten des Kaufmanns oder in dem Garten des Zimmermanns gewesen? Ich bin in dem Garten des Kaufmanns gewesen. Wo waren Sie so lange? Ich war in dem Hause des Neffen und in dem Hause des Sohnes. Ist das Eisen des Soldaten hart? Es war hart, nun ist es weich. Ist das Fleisch des Bauern kalt oder warm? Um ein Uhr war es warm, nun ist es kalt. War das Leder des Schuhmachers gut? Es war gut gewesen, aber es war nicht mehr gut.

22.

Have you the meat of the soldier? I have it not. Who has the leather of the shoemaker? The boy of the carpenter has it. Who has had the wood of the carpenter? The nephew of the officer had had it, but he has it no more. Who has it now? The son of the brewer has it. Where were you at one o'clock? I was in the house of the Englishman. Was the wood of the carpenter smooth? It was smooth and hard. How long has the Englishman's nephew been (trans. the nephew of the Englishman) in the country? Were you yesterday in the house of the father or in the house of the son? I was in the house and in the garden of the son. Who has had the hay of the ox? The Englishman's boy has had it. When has he had it? He has had it yesterday. Who has planted the grain of the farmer? The father of the baker, the miller has planted it. Has he planted it to-day? He has planted it to-day. Where has he planted it? He has planted it in the garden of the cook. Has the soldier's nephew lost the officer's bread? Is she in the garden of the farmer? She is not in the garden of the farmer, she is in the garden of the baker. Has he seen the fire of the soldier? He has seen the fire of the officer. Have you sometimes drunk the brewer's beer? I have often drunk it. Have you seen the gold of the boy in the house of the merchant? I have not seen the gold of the boy in the house of the merchant, but I have seen the silver of the cook in the house of the baker.

Form similar sentences with the following words:

Der Tischler (s), tish′-ler, the cabinetmaker; der Franzose (n) från-tso′-zai, the Frenchman; der Deutsche (n), doit′-shai, the German; der Spanier (s), spå′-ne-er, the Spaniard; der Großvater (s), gro′ss″-få′-ter, the grandfather; der Maurer, mou′-rer, the mason; der Gärtner, gherrt′-ner, the gardner; in dem Zimmer, tsim′-mer, in the room.

23.

Werden, to get, to become, to be, will, shall, see § 54. 7.

Werden Sie? verr′-den zee,	do you get, become?
ich werde, ich verr′-dai,	I get;
er, sie, es wird, air virrt,	he, she, it gets;
wird er? virrt air,	does he get;
werden wir, verr′-den veer,	do we get;
werden sie,	do they get.

No auxiliary verb is used to form the negative and interrogative sentences, for the latter it is only necessary to place the verb before the nominative.

Wird der Mann (gets the man), is the man getting?

Gut, goo′t, good; schlecht, shlecht, bad; auch, ouch, also; wieder, ve′-der, again; dunkel, döönk′-el, dark.

Werden Sie krank? Ich werde krank. Wir werden nicht krank. Wird er wieder krank? Er wird wieder krank. Wer wird reich? Der Großvater wird reich. Wer wird arm? Der Soldat wird arm. Wann wird er müde? Er wird nun müde. Wird der Mann alt und blind? Er wird alt und blind. Wird das Wasser kalt? Es wird kalt. Wird es dunkel? Es wird sehr dunkel. Wird es kalt? Es wird sehr kalt. Wird der Schuhmacher so reich wie der Maurer? Er wird eben so reich. Wird der Knabe schlecht? Er wird sehr schlecht. Wird das Fleisch zähe? Es wird sehr zähe. Wird der Deutsche lustig? Er wird lustig. Wird der Knabe Kaufmann?

24.

Am I getting old? You are getting old and rich. Is the grandfather getting rich? He is getting rich. Who is getting poor? The officer and his nephew are getting poor. Is the German getting sad? He is not getting sad. Are the Spaniard and the Englishman getting wet? They are not getting wet, they are already very wet. What is the mason's son getting? He is becoming *a* merchant. What is the painter's nephew getting (learning to be)? He is getting *a* soldier. Is the son of the gardner not yet getting sleepy? He is getting sleepy. He is not getting sleepy, but thirsty and hungry. Is the paper getting white? It is getting very white. Is the boy getting handsome or ugly? He is getting good and handsome. Is the flour getting dry? It is not getting dry. We are getting dry but tired. Are they getting wet in the street? They are getting wet in the garden and in the market. Is the nephew of the gardener getting tall? He is getting as tall as I. Are you getting as tall as the German? I am not getting as tall as he, but he is getting as tall as the soldier's son. Have you any grain? I have some. We have none. Have they had any flour? They have had none. Had the dog any meat? He had meat and bread. What had the ox had? He had had nothing. Where is the dog? The dog is in the street. Am I not sick and old? You are sick but not old, you are not as old as I. Where they at home at two o'clock? They were not home at two o'clock, but they had been home at one o'clock. Have we been in the market? We have not been in the market, but in the country.

Form similar sentences with the following words:

Grün, grü'n, green; theuer, toi'-er, dear; roth, rote, red; dick, dick, thick; dünn, dūn, thin; hell, hell, light; hart, hârrt, hard; weich, vi'ch, soft.

25.

Haben, inf., to have.

Ich werde haben, ich verr'-dai hâ'-ben,	I shall have;
*du wirst haben, du virrst hâ'-ben,	thou wilt have;
er, sie, es wird haben, air virrt hâ'-ben,	he, she, it will have;
wir werden haben, veer verr'-den "	we shall have;
*ihr werdet haben, eer verr'-det "	you will have;
sie werden haben, zee verr'-den "	they will have;
Sie werden haben, " " "	you will have.

* Not to be used at present.

The first future tense is formed by placing the infinitive mood of the verb after the present tense of the verb werden.

Sein, zine, to be; ich werde sein, I shall be;
werden, verr'-den, to become (to get); ich werde werden, I shall become;
kaufen, kou'-fen, to buy; ich werde kaufen, I shall buy;
suchen, zoo'-chen, to seek; ich werde suchen, I shall look for;
finden, fin'-den, to find; ich werde finden, I shall find;
holen, ho'-len, to fetch, go for; ich werde holen, I shall go for;
bringen, bring'-en, to bring; ich werde bringen, I shall bring;
schicken, shick'-en, to send; ich werde schicken, I shall send;
essen, es'-sen, to eat; trinken, trink'-en, to drink;
pflanzen, pflänt'-sen, to plant; empfangen, emp-fäng'-en, to receive, obtain;
verlieren, fer-lee'-ren, to lose; verkaufen, fer-kou'-fen, to sell;
kochen, koch'-chen, to cook, to boil; braten, brå'-ten, to roast;
wegschicken, vech''-shick'-en, to send away.
Morgen, morr'-ghen, to-morrow; übermorgen, ü''-ber-morr'-ghen, the day after to-morrow.
Sechs, secks, six; (see the remaining cardinal numbers, § 24.)
des Morgens, dess mor'-ghenss, in the morning;
des Abends, dess å'-bents, in the evening;
des Mittags, des mit'-tå'chs, at noon;
um Mitternacht, ōōm mit''-ter-nåcht', at midnight.

Werden Sie morgen Geld haben? Ich werde morgen welches haben. Wir werden keins haben. Werden Sie viel haben? Wir werden nur wenig haben. Werden Sie um ein Uhr da sein? Ich werde um zwei Uhr da sein. Wer wird das Heu kaufen? Der Kaufmann wird es kaufen. Wer wird Eis holen? Der Koch wird welches holen. Werden wir keins holen? Wird sie Geld finden? Sie wird keins finden, aber er wird welches finden. Werde ich übermorgen Mehl verkaufen? Sie werden übermorgen einiges verkaufen. Was wird der Spanier pflanzen? Er wird Gemüse pflanzen. Was werden der Deutsche und der Spanier trinken? Sie werden Bier trinken.

26.

Shall I have fire and light? You will have fire and light. Will he have too much lard? He will have more than I. Shall we be sick to morrow?. We shall be sick to morrow and the day after to morrow. Will they get sick to morrow? They will get sick to-day. What will you sell to-day. I shall sell the iron and the copper. What will he buy? He will buy the officer's hay. What will you go for? I shall go for the bread. What will you bring? We shall bring much grain and much straw. What will the merchant's boy buy? He will buy powder and lead. What will the cook cook? He will cook the meat and the vegetables. Will he boil it or roast it? He will boil the vegetables and roast the meat. What will the gardener plant to morrow? He will plant vegetables. When shall we dine? We shall dine at three o'clock. When shall we sup? We shall sup at seven o'clock. Where will the tailor dine? He will dine in the house. What will he eat? He will eat vegetables and bread. What will he drink? He will drink beer. When will they be in the garden? They will be there at five o'clock.

Will they be there to-day or to morrow? They will be there to morrow. What will the boy become? He will become *a* brewer. Will you become *a* merchant? I shall become *a* merchant. Will she become handsome? She will become very handsome.

Form similar sentences with the following words:

Nähen, nai′-hen, to sew; mähen, mai′-hen, to mow; schneiden, to cut, geschnitten, gai-shnit′-ten, cut, past part.; anzünden, ån-tsün′-den, to light; angezündet, ån″-gai-tsün′-det, lighted; backen, båck′-ken, to bake; gebacken, gai-båck′-ken, baked.

27.

Nom. Der Mann, dair mån, the man;
Acc. den Mann, dain mån, the man;
Nom. dieser Mann, dee′-zer mån, this man;
Acc. diesen Mann, dee′-zen mån, this man;
Nom. der Knabe, dair knå-bai, the boy;
Acc. den Knaben, dain knå-ben, the boy;
Nom. m., ein, ine; Acc. m., einen, ei′-nen, a, one;
Nom. m., Ihr, eer; Acc. m., Ihren, ee′-ren, your;
Nom. and Acc. n., Ihr, eer, your.
Nom. m., mein, mine; Acc. m., meinen, mi′-nen, my;
Nom. m., sein, zine; Acc. m., seinen, zi′-nen, his;
Nom. and Acc. n., dieses Fleisch, dee′-zes, this meat;
Nom. and Acc. n., mein Fleisch, my meat;
Nom. and Acc. n., sein Fleisch, his meat;
Acc. m., ihn, him, it; Acc. m., wen, vain, whom.

Masc. nouns, which take n or en in the genitive case, have the dative and accusative singular and the whole of the plural in n or en. (§ 9, 1.) Lieben, leeben, to love; geliebt, gai-leept′, loved, past part.

Haben Sie den Ochsen gesehen? Ich habe ihn gesehen. Haben Sie diesen Hund gesehen? Ich habe ihn gesehen. Hat er einen Hund? Er hat einen Hund. Hat mein Neffe seinen Vater gefunden? Er hat ihn nicht gefunden. Wer hat den Knaben geschickt? Der Offizier hat den Knaben geschickt. Wer hat meinen Sohn gesucht? Der Brauer hat Ihren Sohn gesucht. Wann hat er ihn gesucht? Er hat ihn heute gesucht. Wann wird der Zimmermann diesen Bauern wegschicken? Er wird ihn morgen um ein Uhr wegschicken. Wird der Sohn den Vater lieben? Er wird ihn lieben. Wird der Deutsche je den Franzosen lieben? Er wird ihn nie lieben.

28.

Has the son (Nom.) of the painter (Gen.) seen the nephew (Acc.) of the farmer (Gen.)? He has seen him. Has the grandfather loved his son? He has loved him. Has the German sometimes seen a Frenchman? He has sometimes seen a Frenchman. Where has he seen a Frenchman? He has seen one (einen) in France. Have you lost your son? I have lost him. Who has sent the soldier away? The officer has sent him away. When has the officer sent the soldier away? He has sent him away at eight o'clock in the evening. Have you seen my nephew? I have seen him. Where have you seen him? I have seen him in the garden.

Have you seen him to-day or yesterday? I have seen him yesterday and to-day. Has this boy lost his father? He has lost his father and his grandfather. Will you lose your cook? I shall lose him. Will the Spaniard love the Frenchman? He will not love him. Will they love my father? They will love him. Will they love him always? They will always love him. Have you already seen this dog? I have already seen him. Have you not yet seen this painter? I have not yet seen him. Has the cook boiled this meat? He has not boiled it, he has roasted it. Has the baker baked the bread? He has baked this bread. Whom have you seen? I have seen the nephew of my cabinetmaker in my garden. Whom have you loved? I have loved my farmer's son.

Form some more sentences with the following words:

Rufen, roo′-fen, to call; gerufen, gai-roo′-fen, called; hassen, hâs′-sen, to hate; gehaßt, gai-hâsst′, hated; schlagen, shlâ′-ghen, to beat, to strike; geschlagen, gai-shlâ′-ghen, beaten.

Nom. m., Jener, yey′-ner; Acc. m., Jenen, yey′-nen, that.
Nom. and Acc., n., Jenes, yey′-ness, that.
Jener Knabe, that boy; jenes Licht, that light.

29.

Gehabt haben, have had, comp. part. gewesen sein, have been; geworden sein, have become; gekauft haben, have bought, &c.

The second future is formed by placing the compound past participle after the present tense of the verb werden. (§ 55.)

Ich werde gehabt haben,	I shall have had;
Sie werden gehabt haben,	you will have had;
er, sie, es wird gehabt haben,	he, she, it will have had;
wir werden gehabt haben,	we shall have had;
sie werden gehabt haben,	they will have had;
Ich werde gewesen sein,	I shall have been;
Ich werde geworden sein,	I shall have become;
Ich werde gekauft haben,	I shall have bought.

Nom. m., unser, oon′-zer; Acc. m., unsern, oon′-zern, our;
Nom. and Acc. n., unser, our.
Nom. m., ihr, eer; Acc. m., ihren, her, their;
Nom. and Acc. n., ihr, her.

Gen. m. and n.,	unseres,*	of our;
	ihres,	of their;
	Ihres,	of your;
	meines,	of my;
	seines,	of his;
	ihres,	of her;
	eines,	of a, of one;

Das Haus meines Vaters, the house of my father;
Meines Vaters Haus, my father's house;
der Schlachter, shlâch′-ter, the butcher

Werden Sie Gold und Silber gehabt haben? Wir werden welches gehabt haben. Wird der Koch Fleisch und Gemüse gekocht haben? Er wird welches

* or unsers, unsres.

gekocht haben. Werden Sie das Schmalz weggeschickt haben? Ich werde es dann weggeschickt haben. Werden sie ihr (fem.) Eisen geholt haben? Sie werden es geholt haben. Werden sie sein Fleisch gebraten haben? Sie werden es gebraten haben. Wird sie ihr Fleisch gekocht haben? Sie wird es gekocht haben. Wird der Schlachter übermorgen sein Fleisch verkauft haben? Er wird es schon morgen verkauft haben. Werden Sie um fünf Uhr Ihr Licht angezündet haben? Wir werden um fünf Uhr unser Licht angezündet haben. Wann wird der Bäcker sein Brod gebacken haben? Er wird es um drei Uhr des Morgens gebacken haben. Wann wird der Bauer sein Korn gepflanzt haben? Er wird es übermorgen gepflanzt haben. Was wird er gefunden haben? Er wird nichts gefunden haben. Wann werden wir gegessen haben? Wir werden um fünf Uhr gegessen haben.

30.

Shall I have sold my lead? You will have sold it then. Will the boy of the tailor have received the money of his father? He will have received it. When will he have received it? He will have received it to morrow at nine o'clock. When will the butcher have sold his meat? He will have sold it at eight o'clock in the morning. When will the nephew of the officer have eaten his bread? He will have eaten it at one o'clock. When will the son of my farmer have received his and her money? When will she have received his and her nephew? She will have received them at ten o'clock. Is your father at home? My father is not at home. Was her father at home at eleven o'clock? He was at home at eleven o'clock. Has the butcher of your cabinetmaker been in the market? He has not been there to-day. When has he been there? He has been there yesterday. Have you called the son of her painter? I have called him. Has the dog of the farmer been hungry. He has not been hungry, he had plenty meat. Have they lighted their fire? They have lighted their *fire* and our fire. Have they beaten the ox of his or of her father? They have beaten the ox of his father. Will you see the dog of my nephew? I shall see his dog. Have you bought the flour of a miller (a miller's)? I have bought it.

31.

Adjectives. § 20.

Masc.

Der gute Schneider,	the good tailor;
des guten Schneiders,	of the good tailor;
den guten Schneider,	the good tailor.

Neuter.

Das gute Fleisch,	the good meat;
des guten Fleisches,	of the good meat;
das gute Fleisch,	the good meat.

When the definite articles or demonstrative pronouns precede the adjective, the masc. and neut. nominative terminates in e; the neuter acc. is like the nom., and the other cases m. and n. are in en.

Sie, acc., zee, you, them; mich, acc. mich, me.

Haben Sie den guten Mann geliebt? Ich habe ihn geliebt? Hat der kleine Schneider Sie gesehen? Er hat mich gesehen. Haben Sie den kleinen Schneider gesehen? Ich habe ihn gesehen. Wer hat den kranken Deutschen gesucht? Sein Vater hat ihn gesucht. Wer hat den kleinen Franzosen gefunden? Der reiche Bauer hat ihn gefunden. Wo hat der reiche Bauer den kleinen Franzosen gefunden? Er hat ihn in dem Garten gefunden. Wer hat den traurigen Sohn des kleinen Tischlers empfangen? Der Neffe des reichen Kaufmanns hat ihn empfangen. Wann hat er ihn empfangen? Er hat ihn vorgestern empfangen. Wird der Bäcker meines Neffen dieses trockne Brod verkaufen? Er wird es verkaufen. Hat der hungrige Soldat das harte Fleisch des alten Schlachters gegessen? Nein, er hat das gute Fleisch des reichen Knaben gegessen. Der Knabe ist reich und schön. (§ 20.)

32.

Will the good Frenchman call me? He will call you. Shall I call the ugly Spaniard? You will call him. Will they look for the little butcher? They will look for him. Where will they look for the little butcher? They will look for him in the market. Where has the little boy seen the baker of the Englishman? He has seen him in the street. The shoemaker is lame (§ 20.) The lame shoemaker is very hungry. The young son of the lame shoemaker is sleepy and cold. The blind nephew of the rich Spaniard was in Germany. The deaf father of the ugly farmer is not as rich as the sick grandfather of the poor brewer. Will they love or hate the father of the big boy? They will always hate him. Had you seen the thirsty boy of the brewer any where. We had seen him no where? What had she seen? She had seen this good silver. Had she found this or that hard iron? She had found this *hard iron.* Had she found this or that? She has found that but not this. Has the dirty cook boiled the good vegetables (s.)? He has boiled them (it). Has the clean cook roasted the good meat? Will the big ox eat the clean hay and straw? He will not eat the dirty straw, but the clean hay. Is the grass green? Has he eaten the tough meat? He has not eaten the tough meat, but he has eaten all the dry bread. Has the big boy of the hungry baker baked the white flour? He has baked it yesterday.

Form similar sentences with the following words:

Der Schwager, shwä'-gher, the brother in law; der Enkel, en'-kel, the grand-son; der Bruder, broo'-der, the brother; der Oheim, o'-hime, the uncle; der Vetter, fet'-ter, cousin; alt, ält, old; fleißig, fli'-ssich, industrious; träge, trai'-gai, idle.

33.

Adjectives preceded by the indefinite article ein, a or an, or by the possessive pronouns, mein, dein, sein, &c., and the word kein have the nom. masc. in er and the other cases in en, the nom. and acc. neut. in es, and the other cases in en. (§ 20, 2.)

Ein guter Vater, ine goo'-ter fä'-ter, a good father;
eines guten Vaters, i'-ness goo'-ten fä'-ters, of a good father;
einen guten Vater, i'-nen goo'-ten fä'-ter, a good father.

Ein guter Deutscher,* a good German;
eines guten Deutschen, of a good German;
einen guten Deutschen, a good German.

Mürbe, mürr'-bai, tender; das Rindfleisch, rint'-fli'sh, the beef; das Kalbfleisch, kälp'-fli'sh, the veal; das Hammelfleisch, håm''-mel-fli'sh', the mutton.

Past participles when used as adjectives, are subject to the same rules as the latter:

Der geliebte Knabe, dair gai-leep'-tai knå'-bai, the beloved boy;
ein geliebter Knabe, ine gai-leep'-ter knå'-bai, a beloved boy;
das gebackne Brod, dass gai-båck'-nai bro't, the baked bread;
ein gebacknes Brod, ine gai-båck'-nes bro't, a baked loaf.

Geschickt, gai-shickt', skilful; der Freund, froint, the friend; der Feind, fi'nt, the enemy; das Messer, mes'-ser, the knife; das Haus, house, the house; das Ei, i, the egg; das Glas, glå'ss, the glass.

Mein lustiger Bruder ist ein guter Schuhmacher. Er ist ein kleiner Knabe. Ein alter Deutscher hatte einen häßlichen Hund. Unser alter Bauer hat einen großen Ochsen. Haben Sie keinen reichen Vetter? Ich habe einen, aber er ist in Rußland. Wird Ihr Oheim alt und häßlich? (§ 20.) Er wird es nicht, er ist es schon. Ist Ihr kleiner Vetter immer fleißig? Mein kleiner Vetter ist zuweilen fleißig und zuweilen träge. Ist er des Morgens oder des Abends träge? Werden Sie nicht einen guten Gärtner haben? Wir werden in Rußland einen geschickten und fleißigen Gärtner finden. Essen sie kein gutes Gemüse? Sie essen es nicht. Kochen Sie kein zähes Ochsenfleisch? Wir kochen kein zähes Rindfleisch. Wir braten unser gutes Hammelfleisch. Ein Mann ist ein Vater wenn er einen Sohn hat. Der lahme Oheim hat einen geliebten Sohn. Dieser alte Deutsche hatte immer ein gutes Feuer. Er war der Sohn eines reichen Bauern.

34.

Your poor uncle (Nom.) is a very old man (Nom.). My old lame grandfather has not a (no) good friend. Our little boy will have a handsome dog. Have you not seen a tall soldier and a young officer. We have seen a little soldier and an old blind officer. Were you going for (Imp.) a skillful tailor? I was going for one (einen). An old blind Frenchman had lost his ugly dog in the market, a little boy had found him. Have you a good and industrious tailor? I have a very good *one*. Had your handsome cousin a big ox? Has your little grandson his good meat? He has his good beef and vegetables, but he has no good water. Have they their dirty straw? They have their clean straw. Will they have our good hay? They will have your good hay. Will they have had a sharp knife? They will have had a sharp knife and a clean glass. Will a nephew of this rich man buy a large house in the market? He will buy a large house in this (dieser) street. Have they eaten a soft egg? They have eaten a boiled egg. Have they eaten no fried egg? They have also eaten a fried egg and drunk a glass of water. A friend of my father has bought a very dear glass in the market. An old soldier has been in the street and has lost a handsome knife of my uncle's.

* Adjectives and participles used as nouns, are declined like adjectives.

Form similar sentences with the following words:

Das Band, bânt, the ribbon; das Buch, boo'ch, the book; das Faß, fâss, the cask; das Auge, ou'-gai, the eye.

35.

When no qualifying word precedes the adjective, or when the qualifying word is indeclinable, the adjective is declined like the definite article, except in the gen. m. and n., where the es is changed into en for the sake of euphony. This is particularly the case when the noun has es in the gen.

Der Wein, vine, the wine;	der Käse, key'-zai, the cheese.
der Thee, tey, the tea,	der Kaffee, kâf-fey' or câf'-fay', the coffee.
der Zucker, tsöock'-ker, sugar.	

Guter Wein,	goo'-ter vine,	good wine;
gutes (en) Weines,	goo'-tes (ten) vi'-ness,	of good wine;*
guten Wein,	goo'-ten vine,	good wine;
Gutes Fleisch,	goo'-tes fli'sh,	good meat;
gutes (en) Fleisches,	goo'-tes (ten) fli'-shess,	of good meat;*
gutes Fleisch,	goo'-tes fli'sh,	good meat;

etwas, et-vâss, some; allerlei, al'-ler-lei'', all sorts of;

etwas guter Kaffee,	some good coffee;
viel schöner Thee,	much fine tea;
wenig gutes Fleisch,	little good meat.

Es ist, ess ist, there is; welcher, nom. m., vel'-cher, some;
welchen, acc. m., vel'-chen, some, any.

Es ist viel guter Wein hier. Guter Wein ist theuer. Es ist wenig gutes Salz in Richmond. Haben Sie gutes Salz? Wir haben viel gutes Salz. Es ist kein schlechter Käse da. Werden Sie guten Käse und gutes Brod verkaufen? Haben Sie schlechten Zucker verkauft? Ich habe welchen verkauft.

36.

Is there *any* good coffee? (nom.) There is some there. Old cheese is good. Old wine is not bad. Hard meat is not good. Have you received *any* wet salt? I have received *some* wet salt. Have you eaten roasted meat? I have eaten boiled meat. Have you had clean or dirty water? We have had clean water and good coffee. Have you sold warm tea? We have sold some. Had you then sold much tough meat? We had sold much, but not enough. Who had bought much good bread and much fine wine? What shall we receive? We shall receive clean straw and old copper. The carpenter and the cabinetmaker of the Englishman have some (etwas) good wood and much good iron. Is white paper dear? Do you eat good roast beef and well (gut) boiled vegetables (s.)? We eat well baked bread. We shall have *some* good, roasted veal. We drink cold beer. The brewer drinks only cold water. The good wine is dear. My fine wine is in the room. Fine wine is dear. We shall buy good lard. There is good lard in the market.

37.

Most verbs which have two nouns as objects, such as, geben, to give; schicken, to send; leihen, to lend; require one of those objects to be in the acc., and the

* Exercices on the genitive will be given later.

other, in the dative case; the former answers to the question whom or what, the latter to the question to whom or to what. The dative of the masc. and neuter articles pronouns and adjectives, when not preceded by a qualifying word, terminate in m or em.

Dem,	dem,	to the;	einem,	i'-nem,	to a;
diesem,	dee'-zem,	to this;	keinem,	ki'-nem,	to none;
jenem,	yey'-nem,	to that;	unserm,	öönzerm,	to our;
meinem,	mi'-nem,	to my;	Ihrem,	ee'-rem,	to your;
seinem,	zi'-nem,	to his;	ihrem,	ee'-rem,	to their.

Nouns, which in the genitive have s only, have the dat. like the nom.

Nom. Das Wasser, the water;
Gen. des Wassers, of the water;
Dat. dem Wasser, to the water.

Those which in the gen. have es, have in the dat. e.

Nom. Der Mann, the man;
Gen. des Mannes, of the man;
Dat. dem Manne, to the man.

Those which in the gen. have en, have the same in the dative.

Nom. Der Knabe, the boy;
Gen. des Knaben, of the boy;
Dat. dem Knaben, to the boy. (§ 9 to 13, and § 89, 6.)

Schenken, shenk'-en, geschenkt, gai-shenkt, to present;
geben, gai'-ben, gegeben, gai-gai'-ben, to give;
senden, zen'-den, gesandt, gai-zänt', to send;
leihen, li'-hen, geliehen, gai-lee'-hen, to lend;
bezahlen, bai-tsä'-len, bezahlt, bai-tsä'lt, to pay;
zeigen, tsi'-ghen, gezeigt, gai-tsich't, to show.
Der Rock (es) rock, the coat;
der Schuh (es), shoo, the shoe;
der Hut (es), hoo't, the hat; wem, vem, to whom.

Haben Sie dem Tischler das Holz verkauft? Ich habe es dem Tischler verkauft. Wer hat unserm Großvater einen Rock geschickt? Der kleine Schneider hat ihm einen geschickt. Wer wird dem Neffen des alten Soldaten einen neuen Hut schenken? Sein junger Offizier wird dem Neffen einen alten Hut schenken. Hat der kleine Schlachter dem Bruder des Bauern gutes Ochsenfleisch verkauft? Er hat dem Bruder des Bauern welches verkauft. Der Kaufmann hat dem Schuhmacher meines Großvaters Leder verkauft. Was haben Sie dem Soldaten gegeben? Ich habe ihm Pulver und Blei gegeben. Wir hatten dem Neffen des blinden Franzosen Geld und Mehl gegeben.

38.

Have you lent the carpenter much money? I have lent the carpenter no money, but I have lent the mason some. To whom have you presented (made a present of) an old coat? I have presented one to the American. What have you shown to the sleepy boy? I have shown gold and silver to the sleepy boy. The industrious German has presented a handsome book to the uncle of this Englishman. I have sent my brother in law, in France much grain. They have paid the painter *for* the leather (constr.

They have to the painter the leather). Have they paid the farmer *for* the vegetables (s.)? They have paid the farmer *for* the meat and *for* the vegetables? Has your brother paid the butcher *for* the veal and the mutton? He has paid the butcher *for* the tender veal but not for the tough mutton. Will they pay the Spaniard *for* the cask? They will pay the Spaniard *for* it. When shall we send the flour to the cook? We shall send it to the cook at twelve o'clock, at noon. Shall we send it to the cook in the morning or in the evening? You will send it to the cook in the morning. Who will lend SOME (etwas) money to my uncle? I shall lend some to your uncle. What will they send to his grandson? They will send silver and gold to his grandson.

Form some sentences with the following words:

schreiben, shri'-ben, geschrieben, gai-shree'-ben, to write;
reichen, ri'-chen, gereicht, gai-ri'cht', to hand;
lassen, lâs'-sen, gelassen, gai-lâs'-sen, to leave, to let have;
wiedergeben, vee"-der-gai'-ben, wiedergegeben, vee"-der-gai-gai'-ben, to restore, to return.

39.

The dative pronouns are as follows:

mir, meer, to me;
Ihnen, ee'-nen to you;
ihm, eem, to him, to it;
ihr, eer, to her;
uns, öönss, to us;
ihnen, ee'-nen, to them;
jemand, yey'-mânt, somebody;
niemand, nee'-mânt, nobody.
(Jemand und niemand, are declined like mein § 31 & 37.)
weder ... noch, 'vai'-der ... noch, neither ... nor.
Haben Sie weder Gold noch Silber? have you neither gold nor silver?

Haben Sie dem Franzosen seinen Hut geschickt? Ich habe ihm seinen Hut geschickt. Hat er Ihnen seinen Rock geschickt? Er hat mir seinen Hut geschickt. Hat der Amerikaner uns Salz gelassen? Er hat uns viel Salz gelassen. Hatte der taube Mann Ihnen seinen Hund gegeben? Er hatte mir seinen Hund geschenkt. Hatte jemand ihm einen Ochsen gezeigt? Niemand hatte ihm einen gezeigt. Hatte der Bruder des Maurers ihr Gold gegeben? Er hatte ihr Silber aber kein Gold gegeben. Haben Sie jemandem geschrieben? Ich habe niemandem geschrieben. Wollen Sie weder dem Freunde noch dem Feinde Pulver verkaufen? Ich will weder dem Feinde noch dem Freunde welches verkaufen.

40.

Will you send me *some* money? I shall send you *some* money. When will you send me *some* money? I shall send you *some* money the day after to morrow. Had you lent *some* paper to the merchant? I had lent him *some* paper. Has he returned you the paper? He has returned me the paper. Will he return you your money? He will return my money to me. Has the merchant returned to us his cloth? He has returned to us his cloth. Have you given them good corn and good flour? Have you presented somebody (dat.) *with* a new hat? I have presented my brother *with* a new hat. Has the farmer shown them his vegetables? He has shown them his vegetables. Will you show them his dog? I will show them his dog. Will you send me good beer? I will send you *some* good beer. How much will you send me? I will send you one cask. When will you send it? I will send it at ten o'clock. The German has sold me *some* good coffee. The Frenchman had sent me *some* dear lard.

Form similar sentences with the words of the foregoing exercises.

41.

When both, the acc. and the dat. are personal pronouns, the acc. precedes the dat.

Ihn mir, him (it) to me; es mir, it to me;
ihn ihm, him (it) to him; es ihm, it to him;
ihn Ihnen, him (it) to you; es Ihnen, it to you;
ihn uns, him (it) to us; es uns, it to us;
ihn ihnen, him (it) to them; es ihnen, it to them;
sie mir, her to me, sie mir, them to me.

The pronouns, jenes, dieses, welches, einiges, etwas, eins follow the dative:

Mir welches, some to me (me some);
Ihnen welchen, some to you (you some);
dem Manne welches, eins, some, one to the man.

When one of the cases is a noun, and the other a personal pronoun, the pronoun stands before the noun.

Ihn or es dem Manne, him or it to the man
ich gebe es dem Manne, I give it to the man;
ich gebe ihm das Fleisch, I give him the meat.

Hat der Soldat dem Hunde das Brot gegeben? Er hat es ihm gegeben. Hat er dem Knaben den Stock geschenkt? Er hat ihn ihm geschenkt. Haben die Bauern uns die Butter gebracht? Sie haben sie uns heute gebracht. Wird der Schneider Ihnen heute die Kleider bringen? Er wird sie mir morgen bringen. Wird der junge Kaufmann dem General gutes Papier verkaufen? Er wird ihm keins verkaufen. Hat der Koch ihm das Hammelfleisch gebraten oder gekocht? Er hat es ihm weder gebraten noch gekocht. Hat der Deutsche ihnen einen Ochsen verkauft? Er hat ihnen einen verkauft. Hat er ihn dem großen Holländer verkauft? Er hat ihn ihm verkauft.

42.

Has the merchant sold the cloth to the carpenter? He has sold it to him. To whom has the butcher sold the beef? He has sold it to a friend, in the market. Had he sold it at ten o'clock? He had sold it. Has the father of your friend sent you some fine cloth? He has sent me some. Has he also sent you some white paper? He has sent me none. Will he send us some? He will send you some to-day or to-morrow. Will you show me your big book? I will show it to you now. Who will send me the vegetables of the farmer? We shall send them to you to-day. Will the gardener not send some (s.) to the merchant? He will send him some. Will you present the nephew of the brewer *with* a hat? I shall present him *with* one. What will the Spaniards sell to their grandfather? They will sell him good coffee (m.). The merchant will sell it (m.) to him. Had you often sent me the paper? I had often sent it to you. Had you sent it to them? I had sent it to them. What had the Englishman brought us? He had brought us coffee. Has he brought it to us now? He has brought it to us at one o'clock. Have you written it to him? I have written it to him. Have you written it to them? I have written it to them.

43.

The dative of the adjective, when preceded by an article or a pronoun terminates in en, when not preceded by a declineable word, in em, the latter case scarcely ever occurs in conversation.

Dem guten Freunde,	to the good friend;
einem schlechten Soldaten,	to a bad soldier;
diesem alten Deutschen,	to this old German.

Um wie viel Uhr? ööm vee feel oo'r, at what o'clock?
Um halb eins, ööm hâlp i'nss, at half past twelve;

Um halb zwei, ööm hâlp tswi, at half past one; der Brief (es), breef, the letter; der Stock (es), stock, the stick, cane; das Kleid (es), klite, the dress; der Löffel, (s), löf'-fel, the spoon; golden, gol'-den, gold, golden; silbern, zil'-bern, silver, adj.; eisern, i'-zern, iron, adj.

Wer hat diesem alten Deutschen den goldenen Löffel geschenkt? Mein Vater hat ihn ihm geschenkt. Hat der Franzose dem großen Bauern das eiserne Messer gekauft? Er hat es ihm gekauft. Wann hat er es ihm gekauft? Er hat es ihm heute um halb eins auf dem Markte gekauft. Wo waren Sie um halb zwei? Ich war in meinem Zimmer. Der Kaufmann hat mir einen langen Brief geschrieben. Wann haben Sie ihn empfangen? Ich habe ihn heute empfangen. Ich habe dem guten Kaufmann einen langen Brief geschrieben. Werden Sie dem häßlichen Soldaten Ihr altes Messer leihen? Ich werde es ihm leihen. Hatte der Franzose uns einen silbernen Löffel geschickt? Er hatte uns einen geschickt.

44.

Will the rich brewer send his good beer to the thirsty tailor's boy? He will send it to him to morrow at half past three. Will you send the cask *of* wine to this young man? I shall send it to that young man. Will you send the golden spoon to this poor farmer? I shall send it to him. When will you send it to him? I shall send it to him at half past five o'clock. Have you presented to this good old man that gold ribbon? I have presented that *one* to him. Have you lent him this *one* or that one? I have lent him that *one*, but not this one. Who has sent good old cheese to the ugly old shoemaker? I have sent some to him. The little cook has given good veal to the old Frenchman. Has he paid him (dat.) *for* the veal? He has paid him *for* it. To whom have you given the blunt knife? I have given it to you or to him. Have you sent it to the handsome nephew of the industrious gardner? I have sent it to him. Have you sent neither to the lazy German nor to the merry Frenchman *any* good wine? I have sent some neither to the Frenchman nor to the German.

Form sentences by using the following words:

Papieren, pă-pee'-ren, paper, of paper; tuchen, too'-chen, cloth, of cloth; hölzern, hölt'-sern, wooden.

45.

Schön, shön, handsome, fine;	schöner, shö'-ner, handsomer, finer;
arm, ărrm, poor;	ärmer, err'-mer, poorer;
reich, ri'ch, rich;	reicher, ri'-cher, richer;
krank, krănk, sick;	kränker, krenk'-er, more sick;
uneben, öön"-ai'-ben, uneven;	unebner, öön"-aib'-ner, more uneven.

Zufrieden, tsoo"-free'-den, contented, satisfied; elend, ai'-lent, miserable; glücklich, glück'-lich happy, lucky fortunate; unglücklich, öön"-glück'-lich, unhappy.

In forming the comparative of adjectives, the radical vowels a, o and u, generally change in to ä, ö and ü. (§ 21.)

Adjectives terminating in er, el, en, drop the e before the consonant.

Edel, ai'-del, noble;	edler, aid'-ler, nobler;
eben, ai'-ben, even;	ebner, aib'-ner, more even.

Als, ălss, than; reicher als, ri'-cher ălss, richer than; so reich wie, zo ri'ch vee, as rich as; eben so ... wie, just as ... as; dieser, dee'-zer, this one, the latter; jener, yey'-ner, that one, the former.

Ist der Deutsche reicher als der Franzose? Dieser (the latter) ist reicher als jener (the former). Ist der Maler so fleißig wie der Tischler? Er ist fleißiger. Wer ist kleiner, der Spanier oder der Engländer? Der Engländer ist reicher als der Spanier, aber der Spanier ist schlechter als der Engländer. Ist das ebene Holz härter als das unebene? Das ebene ist härter. Ist Blei zäher als Eisen? Eisen ist zäher als Blei. Sind Sie nicht älter als Ihr guter Bruder? Ich bin nicht älter als er, aber mein Vetter ist älter als er. Sind wir nicht unglücklicher als unser Nachbar? Wir sind nicht unglücklicher als er, aber er ist reicher als wir. Ist dieses Bier so stark wie jenes? Es ist stärker, aber nicht so alt. Ist dieses Tuch dicker als jenes? Es ist dicker aber nicht so gut.

46.

Is the carpenter more thirsty than the cabinetmaker? The former (jener) is more thirsty than the latter (dieser). Is the flour dearer then the bread? Good bread is dearer than flour. Is the nephew taller than the uncle? The uncle is taller than the nephew. Is the ox as lame as the dog? The dog is lamer than the ox. Was the beef as tough as the mutton. The mutton was as tough as the beef. Were you more sick than we? We were more sick than you. Will not the gardener be more industrious than the little cook? He will be more industrious. Will the ice be harder than the iron? It will not be so hard. Will the beef be tougher than the veal? The veal will be tougher than the young beef. Are you more idle in the morning than in the evening? I am more idle in the morning than in the evening. Were they more sleepy at one o'clock than at two o'clock? They were more sleepy at half past two o'clock. Was the boy of the officer more sick than the boy of the brewer? The former was more sick. Has your good brother-in-law been more sleepy than your brother? Is this leather not thicker than that? This is thicker than that.

Form similar sentences with the following words:

Schwer, shwairr, heavy; leicht, li'cht, light; treu, troi, faithful, true; stark, stârrk, strong.

47.

Gut, goo't, good; besser, bes'-ser, better;
hoch,* ho'ch, high; höher, hö'-her, higher;
viel, feel, much; mehr, meyr, more;
das Schloß, shloss, the castle, the lock.

Ist dieser Zucker besser als jener? Er ist besser. Ist dieses Messer schärfer als das Messer des Schwagers? Das Messer des Schwagers ist schärfer. Ist das Schloß viel höher als das Haus? Es ist viel höher. Ist das Heu eben so naß wie das Gras? Das Gras ist nässer als das Heu. Ist dieses dünne Bier so stark wie jener gute Wein? Er ist stärker. Haben Sie mehr Geld empfangen als Ihr Bruder? Ich habe mehr Geld empfangen als er. Hat Ihr Schneider so viel Tuch gekauft wie der kleine Kaufmann? Er hat mehr Tuch gekauft. Haben Sie so viel Thee wie Kaffee getrunken? Ich habe eben so viel Kaffee wie Thee getrunken; mein kleiner Neffe hat mehr Kaffee getrunken, mein alter Großvater hat mehr Thee getrunken und mein Oheim hat weder Kaffee noch Thee getrunken, er hat nur Wasser getrunken.

48.

Is your house higher than my castle? Your castle is higher than my house. Is the straw of the peasant better than his hay? It is much better but not so good as the straw of the gardener. Had you had more money than your brother? I had more than my brother and my cousin, but not so much as my uncle. Are *there* more vegetables (s.) in the market than in the garden of the gardener? There are (es ist) more vegetables in the garden of the gardener. Have you less (reg.) water than wine? I have less water than wine. Have you drunk more coffee than tea? We have drunk more tea than coffee. Has your son eaten more bread than cheese? He has eaten as much good bread as soft cheese. Who is more hungry, the old officer or the young soldier? The young soldier is more hungry. Is the flour of the baker better than that of the miller? The flour of the miller is better than that of the baker. Have you paid more money to the shoemaker than to the tailor? I have paid more to the former.

* Before the noun hoh, ho, is used, das hohe Haus, the high house.

49.

Der reiche, ri'che, the rich; der reichere, ri'-chai-rai, the richer; der reichste, ri'ch'-stai, the richest;
der harte, hâr'-tai, the hard; der härtere, herr'-tai-rai, the harder; der härteste, herr'-tai-stai, the hardest.

The comparatives and superlatives of adjectives are declined in the same manner as the adjectives in the positive form.

Ein reicherer Mann, a richer man;
Mein kleinster Knabe, my smallest boy; (see § 23.)

viel, much; mehr, more; meist, mi'st; am meisten, âm mi-'sten, most;
nahe, near; näher, nai'-her, nearer; nächst, naichst, nearest;
hoch, high; höher, higher; höchst, hö'chst, highest;
der gute, goo'-tai, the good; der bessere, bes'-sai-rai, the better; der beste, bess'-tai, the best.

Der Degen (s), dai'-gen, the sword;
der Tisch (es), tish, the table;
der Stuhl (es), stoo'l, the chair;
der Teller (s), tel'-ler, the plate;
der Schinken (s), shin'-ken, the ham.

Nehmen, nai'-men, to take; genommen, gai-nom'-men, taken; sondern, zon'-dern, but (used after a negative); von allen, fon âl'-len, of all.

Haben Sie nicht den schärferen Degen des Offiziers genommen? Ich habe nicht den schärferen genommen. Hat der alte Mann den kleineren Knaben weggeschickt? Er hat nicht den kleineren, sondern den größeren weggeschickt. Haben Sie nicht einen kleineren Tisch gekauft? Ich habe einen kleineren gekauft. Hat der Bäcker besseres Brod geschickt? Er hat besseres geschickt. Wer hat besseren Zucker gekauft? Der reiche Schuhmacher hat welchen gekauft. Wird der Schneider einen höheren Tisch kaufen? Er wird einen viel höheren kaufen. Wird der Franzose das beste Gemüse essen? Er wird das beste Gemüse und das schönste Fleisch essen. Haben Sie Ihren besten Rock verloren? Wir haben unsern schlechtesten Rock aber unsern besten Hut verloren. Hat der Schneider sein bestes Tuch verkauft? Er hat sein bestes Tuch verkauft. Ist dieser Hut höher als jener? Dieser ist höher als jener, aber mein Hut ist der höchste von allen. Wer hat den reichsten Vater? Dieser kleine Knabe hat den reichsten Vater. Wer hat den fleißigsten Sohn? Der Brauer hat den fleißigsten Sohn. Ist Ihr jüngster Sohn der fleißigste Knabe? Er ist nicht der fleißigste, er ist der trägste. Wird der Koch das zäheste Ochsenfleisch kochen? Er wird das zäheste kochen. Hatte der Engländer viel Geld? Der Engländer hatte viel, der Deutsche hatte mehr, aber der Spanier hatte am meisten. Ist der höhere Baum der nächste? Der kleinere Baum ist der nächste.

50.

The big man is rich, the bigger man is richer and the biggest man is the richest. The dearest sugar was the best. Who has the larger shoe? The cabinetmaker has the larger. Who will see the hardest cheese? Your nephew will see the hardest. Who will write the longest letter to my grandfather? The good German will write to him the longest. Had you given your brother-in-law the dearest wine? I had given him the dearest wine. Who was the wettest, the mason or his son? The mason was the wettest. Have you given him the sharper knife? I have given him the sharpest. Have you sent him better wine then me? I have sent him as good wine as you but no better *wine.* Will the boy become a greater soldier than his father? He will become a better man. Has your nephew become a handsome man? He has become a handsome man. Has the baker sent us lighter bread? He has sent us heavier bread. Will you not buy *some* whiter flour? I shall buy *some* whiter. Have you presented the smallest book to this young boy? I have presented it to him. Will you not give us some (etwas) colder water? I have none colder, but I have colder beer. Will you roast (for) them (dat.) some good mutton? I have no good mutton but I shall boil them good beef and good vegetables. Will they show us their best ribbon? They will show you their best and their dearest ribbon. Had he given you his longest stick? He had given it to me. When had he given it to you? He had given it to me the day before yesterday at five o'clock. Had the boy become more hungry than the man? He had become more hungry and more sleepy. The old Spaniard is getting more ugly than the old German, but the young Englishman is getting the ugliest of all. Are the streets getting dryer? They are getting much dryer. The poor shoemaker is getting still blinder than he was.

51.

Die Frau, dee frou, the woman, (§ 12 & 13.), the wife; die Mutter, mööt'-ter, the mother; eine Frau, i'-nai frou, a woman; die Schwester, shwess'-ter, the sister; sie, zee, nom. & acc., she, her; ihr, eer, to her (her); meine, mi'-nai, my; Ihre, ee'-rai, your; ihre, ee'-rai, their; unsere, öön'-zai-rai; die Tochter, toch'-ter, the daughter; die Nichte, nich'-tai, the niece; die Königinn, kö'-neghin, the queen; die Französin, frânt'-sö-zin, the French woman; die Deutsche, doit'-shai, the German woman.

Feminine nouns remain unaltered in the singular.

Nom.	die gute, the good;	eine gute, a good;
Gen.	der guten, of the good;	einer guten, of a good;
Dat.	der guten, to the good;	einer guten, to a good.
Acc.	die gute, the good;	eine gute, a good.

Diese, dee'-zai, this; jene, yey'-nai, that (declined like die).

Ist die Frau gut? Die Frau ist gut. Ist die Königinn schön? Sie ist sehr schön. War die Deutsche arm? Sie war arm. Wird die Deutsche arm? Sie wird nicht arm, sie wird sehr reich. Ist meine Tochter so jung wie Ihre Nichte? Sie ist jünger. Ist seine Frau so gut wie meine Frau? Sie ist besser als Ihre Frau. Wird die Schwester schön? Sie wird schön. Ist die Französinn häßlich geworden? Sie ist häßlich geworden. Wird die Königinn alt werden? Sie wird alt werden. Haben Sie der Schwester den Brief gegeben? Ich habe ihr den Brief gegeben. Werden sie ihr einen Brief schreiben? Sie werden ihr einen schreiben. Haben Sie unsere Mutter gesehen? Ich habe sie gesehen. Wo haben Sie sie gesehen? Hat die kleine Deutsche keine Mutter? Sie hat eine Mutter aber keinen Vater. Wer hat meine gute Nichte weggeschickt? Niemand hat sie weggeschickt. Haben Sie der Tochter der armen Frau Geld gegeben? Ich habe ihr welches gegeben. Werden Sie die Tochter des Spaniers immer lieben? Ich werde sie immer lieben. Wird der Offizier die Nichte der Königinn lieben? Er wird sie immer lieben. Ist die Mutter der kleinen Französinn nicht zu Hause? Sie ist jetzt nicht zu Hause, aber sie wird um acht Uhr des Abends zu Hause sein.

52.

Was the woman sick? She was very sick. Has the daughter of the tailor been poor? She has been very poor. Will the niece of the German *woman* grow rich. She will grow rich and handsome. Has the daughter of the queen been in Holland? She has not been there. Who will receive my wife? The queen will receive her. When will she receive her? She will receive her to morrow. Where will she receive her? She will receive her in the room. Is the old woman sick? She was sick yesterday, she is well now. Was the ugly niece of the French woman here to-day? She was not here. Will the old mother of the good German woman send some money to the young niece of the poor soldier. She will send some to his niece. Has your wife been at home? She has not yet been home. What have you sent to the good queen? I have sent her much gold and much silver. Have you sent her too much? I have not sent her too much but too little. Will the French *woman* have lighted the fire and the candle? She will have lighted them. What will the merry French woman roast? She will roast *some* good beef. Has the niece of the queen given (to) the daughter of the German *woman some* lead? She has given her no lead, she has given her *some* gold. Where have you sent your youngest daughter? I have sent her to Prussia. Will the good queen hate the ugly old mother of the German *woman?* She will not hate her, she will love her. Whom will she hate? She will hate nobody.

Form similar sentences with the following words:

Die Waschfrau, vâsh′-frou, the washerwoman;
die Nähterinn, nai′-tai-rin, the seamstress;
die Magd, mâ′cht, the servant girl;
die Witwe, vit′-vai, the widow;
die Großmutter, gro′ss′′-mööt′-ter, the grand-mother;
die Enkelinn, enk′-ai-lin, the grand-child;
die Tante, tân′-tai, the aunt.

53.

Sie ihr,	zee eer,	her, (it) to her;
ihn ihr,	een eer,	him, (it) to her;
es ihr,	ess eer,	it to her;
Sie ihr,	zee eer,	you to her;
sie ihr,	zee eer,	them to her;
uns ihr,	öönss eer,	us to her;

ihr welchen, welche, welches, welche, some to her;
ihr keinen, keine, keins, keine, none to her.

When the adjective stands without any determinating particle it is conjugated as follow:

Nom. gute, goo' tai, good;
Gen. guter, goo'-ter, of good;
Dat. guter, goo'-ter, to good;
Acc. gute, goo'-tai, good.

Die Taube, tou'-bai, the pigeon; die Katze, cât'-sai, the cat; die Henne, hen'-nai, the hen; die Seife, zi'-fai, the soap; die Suppe, zōōp'-pai, the soup; die Kuh, koo, the cow; die Butter, bōōt'-ter, the butter; die Limonade, le-mo-nâ'-dai, the limonade; liebenswürdig, lee'-benss-vür'-dig, amiable; deutsch, doitsh, German; amerikanisch, â-mai-re-kâ'-nish, American; englisch, Eng'-lish; französisch, frân-tsō'-zish, French.

Most masculine names of persons and animals are made feminine by adding inn, (see § 18).

Der Sänger, seng'-er, the singer (male);
die Sängerinn, seng'-ai-rin, the singer (female);
der Löwe, lö'-vai, the lion;
die Löwinn, lö'-vin, the lioness;
der Engländer, eng'-len-der, the Englishman;
die Engländerinn, eng'-len-dai-rin, the English woman.

	Masc.	*Fem.*	*Neut.*
Nom.	Ihr guter,	ihre gute,	ihr gutes, her good;
Gen.	ihres guten,	ihrer guten,	ihres guten, of her good;
Dat.	ihrem guten,	ihrer guten,	ihrem guten, to her good;
Acc.	ihren guten,	ihre gute,	ihr gutes, her good;
		welche, some.	

Haben Sie der alten Waschfrau gute Seife gegeben? Ich habe ihr welche gegeben. Werden Sie der kleinen Magd die warme Butter bringen? Ich werde sie ihr bringen. Wird die schmutzige Magd uns gute Suppe kochen? Sie wird uns welche kochen. Haben Sie der schönen Sängerinn die weiße Taube geschickt? Ich habe sie ihr geschickt. Hatten Sie der lahmen Bäuerinn den grünen seidenen Schuh geschenkt? Ich hatte ihn ihr geschenkt. Werden Sie der liebenswürdigen Spanierinn dieses goldene Band leihen? Ich werde es ihr leihen. Wird die blinde Tante ihrer Tochter die weiche Butter schicken? Sie wird ihr nicht die weiche aber die harte schicken. Sie wird sie ihr nicht schicken. Hatten Sie dieser liebenswürdigen Frau eine schwarze Katze geschickt? Sie hatten ihr keine geschickt. Hatte die Köchinn uns und ihr keine Suppe gekocht? Sie hatte weder uns noch ihr welche gekocht. Werden wir heute eine gebratene Taube essen? Sie werden keine essen. Was werden wir essen? Wir werden ihr gutes Ochsenfleisch und ihren weichen Käse essen. Ist ihre alte Waschfrau stark und häßlich? Sie ist stark aber nicht häßlich. Was haben Sie ihrer liebenswürdigen Gärtnerinn gegeben? Ich habe ihr Suppe und Brod gegeben.

54.

Are you not my dear aunt? Yes my dear, I am your old aunt and shall always love you. Is your niece not getting very handsome and very amiable? She is getting very handsome but not very amiable. Was not the American *woman* very amiable? She was as amiable as handsome. What have you sent to your old grandmother? I have sent her a paper bonnet. Has the mother not called her youngest daughter? She has not called her youngest, but her oldest daughter. Will the merchant love his wife? He will love her, for she is not only handsome but also good and amiable. Has the poor widow lost her black cat? She has lost it (her) yesterday. Is this white soap better than the red *soap?* The white is better than the red. What has your deaf old servant bought in the market to-day? She has bought a tough old hen and a hard pigeon, *some* bad vegetables and some hard cheese. What has the rich baker's *wife* sold to your mother? She has sold her some stale (alt) bread. Was your sister in America? She was not in America but her daughter, my niece was there. Has your seamstress bought the good butter? She has bought it (f.)? Has she paid *for* it? She has paid for it. Have you a French or German gardener-woman? I have a French one, but I have a German gardener. Had your good grandmother bought her old cheese, her tender veal, and her good butter? She had bought her old cheese, but neither her tender veal nor her good butter. Her tender veal she will buy to-day and her good butter to morrow.

55.

	Masc.	*Fem.*	*Neut.*
Nom.	Der meinige,*	die meinige,	das meinige, mine;
	der seinige,	die seinige,	das seinige, his, its;
	der ihrige,	die ihrige,	das ihrige, hers;
	der unsrige,	die unsrige,	das unsrige, ours;
	der Ihrige,	die Ihrige,	das Ihrige, yours;
	der ihrige,	die ihrige,	das ihrige, theirs;

mi′-ne-ghai, zi′-ne-ghai, ee′-re-ghai, un′-zre-ghai;
these are declined like, der, die, das gute (§ 20, 1.)

Derselbe, dair-zel′-bai; dieselbe, dee-zel′-bai; dasselbe, dâs-sel′-bai, the same, also are declined like der gute.

Gütig, gü′-tich, kind; höflich, hö′f′-lich, polite; die Dame, dâ′-mai, the lady; der Herr, herr, the master, gentleman; das Fräulein, froi′-line, the young lady;

mein Herr, mine herr, Sir;
Madame, mâ-dâmm′, Mam (Madam);
mein Fräulein, mine froi′-line, Miss;
Herr Miller, Mr. Miller;
Madame Miller, Mrs. Miller.

Welcher, vel′-cher, welche, vel′-chai, welches, vel′-ches, which.

This interrogative pronoun is declined like the definite articles der, die das.

Welcher Mann,	which man;
welche Frau,	which woman;
welches Kind,	which child.

Das Kind, kint, the child; ist dies? ist deess? is this?
das Mädchen, mait′-chen, the girl, lass.

Haben Sie gutes Brod. mein Herr? Ja Madame, ich habe welches. Haben Sie kein Geld mein Herr? Ja mein Fräulein, ich habe Papiergeld, aber kein Silbergeld. Ist Herr Miller zu Hause? Nein mein Herr, er ist jetzt nicht zu Hause. Wann wird er zu Hause sein? Er wird um halb zwölf

* Der meine, der seine, der ihre, der unsere, der Ihre and der ihre are used instead of these.

Uhr zu Hause sein. Waren Sie zu Hause, mein Herr? Ich war nicht zu Hause. Ist dies (instead of dieser) Ihr Hut? Es ist der meinige. Ist dies Ihr Papier? Es ist das meinige. Hatten Sie dem Mädchen ihr Geld gegeben? Ich hatte ihr das ihrige gegeben. Werden Sie mir meine Suppe kochen? Ich werde Ihnen die Ihrige kochen. Ist dies Ihr Licht? Es ist nicht das meinige, es ist das seinige. Werden Sie Ihre Schwester oder die seinige hier empfangen? Ich werde weder die meinige noch die seinige hier empfangen. Haben Sie meinem Vater oder ihrem Vater die Kuh geschenkt? Ich habe sie dem ihrigen geschenkt. Ist dies das Haus ihres Vaters oder das Haus seines Vaters? Es ist das Haus des ihrigen. Haben Sie noch dasselbe Mädchen? Wir haben noch dasselbe. Werden sie noch dieselbe Köchinn haben? Ich werde noch dieselbe haben. Haben Sie diesen Mann bezahlt? Ich habe denselben bezahlt (instead of ihn). Haben Sie demselben das Geld gegeben? Ich hatte es ihm schon gegeben. Werden Sie heute nicht ein Glas Wein trinken, mein Fräulein? Nein mein Herr, ich werde ein Glas Wasser trinken. Welcher Mann ist glücklich? Der reiche Mann ist glücklich. Welche Frau hat ein Glas Limonade getrunken? Die kleine Französinn hat eins getrunken. Welches Mädchen war hier? Das hübsche Mädchen meiner Tante war hier. Welchem Knaben haben Sie es gegeben? Ich habe es dem Knaben meines Bauern gegeben. Welcher Witwe haben Sie das silberne Band geschenkt? Ich habe es der schönen Witwe geschenkt.

56.

Miss, have you been in the market? Yes Sir, I have been there. Have you bought any thing there? Yes, I have bought *some* good veal, good cheese and good butter. Is the meat dear now? It is very dear. Is this your black tea? It is mine (masc.). Has the tall German his strong beer? He has his. Has she had her good soup? She has had hers. Have you your soft leather? I have mine. Had he my long letter? He had not yours, he had mine. Had the cook roasted your hen or mine? He had not roasted yours but mine. Had the queen given the ribbon to your *daughter* or to my daughter? He had given it to mine. Is this the shoe of your servant or of mine? It is the shoe of mine. Madam, have you already been in the garden to-day? No Sir, I have not yet been there. Is this the same money? It is the same. Had the washer-woman sent the soap to the lady? She had sent it to the same. Have you ever seen this man? I have often seen the same. Will the son of the merchant lend *some* money to the officer? He will lent some to the same (const. to the same some). Which German *woman* is sick? The big German *woman* was sick, but she is very well now. Which German had bought the best butter? The merry German had bought it. Which child will bring us some soup? The French child will bring us soup, meat and bread. Which Frenchman have you hated? I have hated the ugly old Frenchman. Which woman has the officer loved? He has loved the amiable little Spanish woman. To which carpenter have you sold the wood? I have sold it to the English carpenter. To which seamstress have you paid the money? I have paid it to the deaf seamstress.

57.

On the Plural of Nouns, &c.

Almost all masc. and neut. mono-syllabic nouns form their plural by taking e in the nom,. gen. and acc., and en in the dat.* Generally the vowels a, o, u, au change into ä, ö, ü and äu.

Sing. Der Freund (es), froint, the friend; Pl. die Freunde, froin'-dai, the friends.

Nom.	Die Freunde,	the friends;
Gen.	der Freunde,	of the friends;
Dat.	den Freunden,	to the friends;
Acc.	die Freunde,	the friends.

Die Jahre, yâ'-rai, the years; das Band, bânt, the band; die Bande, bân'-dai, the bonds; die Söhne, zö'-nai, the sons; die Röcke, rök'-kai, the coats; die Briefe, bree'-fai, the letters; die Stöcke, stök'-kai, the sticks; die Tische, tish'-shai, the tables; die Köche, köch'-chai, the cooks; die Stühle, stü'-lai, the chairs; die Könige, kö'-ne-gai, the kings; der General, gai-nai-râ'l, the general; die Generäle, gai-nai-rai'-lai, the generals; die Offiziere, of-fe-tsee'-rai, the officers; der Knopf, k'nopf, the button; die Knöpfe, knöp'-fai.*

Articles, adjective pronouns, and adjectives not preceded by a determinative word terminate as follows: Nom. e; Gen. er; Dat. en; Acc. e.

N. diese,	these,	meine,	my;	welche,	which, some;
G. dieser,	of these,	meiner,	of my;	welcher,	of which;
D. diesen,	to these,	meinen,	to my;	welchen,	to which;
A. diese,	these,	meine,	my;	welche,	which.

N.	Keine,	no, none;	gute,	good;
G.	keiner,	of no;	guter,	of good;
D.	keinen,	to no;	guten,	to good;
A.	keine,	no;	gute,	good;

ihn, sie, es ihnen,	him, her, it to them;
sie ihnen,	them to them;
ihnen welchen, welche, welches,	some (sing.) to them;
ihnen welche,	some (plur.) to them.

Sind Ihre Freunde reich? Meine Freunde sind nicht so reich wie ich. Waren unsere Freunde glücklich? Sie waren nicht glücklich. Sind die Köche auf dem Markte gewesen? Sie sind da gewesen. Wann sind sie auf dem Markte gewesen? Sie sind gestern da gewesen. Haben Sie meine Papiere gehabt? Ich habe sie gehabt. Haben Sie diese Röcke verkauft? Ich habe nicht diese aber jene verkauft. Welche Offiziere haben Sie gesehen? Ich habe keine Offiziere gesehen. Werden Sie mir lange Briefe schicken? Ich werde Ihnen keine schicken. Werden die Offiziere Generäle geworden sein? Sie werden Generäle geworden sein. Hatten Sie die Tische schon fortgeschickt? Waren unsere Oheime zu Hause? Sie wären nicht zu Hause. Hat Ihnen der Mann schöne silberne Knöpfe geschenkt? Er hat mir keine silberne aber goldene Knöpfe geschenkt. Was haben die Könige ihren Generälen gegeben? Sie haben ihnen Geld gegeben. Hatten Sie keine grüne Tische und Stühle? Wir hatten grüne und rothe Tische gehabt. Sind die Söhne des Kaufmanns

* The dative pl. of all nouns, adject. and interrogative pronouns, adjectives and articles, is in en (n).

auf dem Markte? Die Söhne des Schneiders sind in der Stube. Haben Sie den Söhnen des Schuhmachers große Schuhe geschickt? Werden die Oheime der Könige den Generälen lange Briefe schreiben? Sie werden ihnen welche schreiben.

58.

Have you many friends? We have many. Who has had our buttons? The officer has had them. Have the generals as many chairs as tables? They have as many chairs as tables. Will these kings have good generals? They will have *some* good *ones*. Will the officers have sold their chairs? They will have sold them. Will they have paid them (dat.), *for* them (acc.)? They will have paid them for them. Where are your sticks? They are in the room. Had you received your letters? I had received them at five o'clock. Are the sons of the cooks as industrious as the sons of the officers? They are more industrious. Have you bought some handsome chairs? I have bought very handsome chairs. Have your sons sent gold and silver buttons to the generals? They have sent them some. Have they lost those buttons? They have not lost these but those. Have the sons of the brewer showed wooden tables to the generals of the kings? They have shown them *some* wooden *ones*. Have they seen French or German officers? They have seen German *ones*. Shall we given these sticks to our good friends? We shall give them to them. Have you lent money to these officers? I have lent some to these cooks. Have you roasted some beef *for* the (dat.) uncles of the officers? I have roasted some *for* them (dat.). Have the cooks boiled good soup *for* the kings (dat.)? They have boiled some *for* them.

59.

Masc. and neuter nouns terminating in the nom. sing. in el, en, er and the diminutives in lein and chen have the nom. plur. like the nom. sing. and the dative in n, when the word does not terminate in n. The vowels a, o, u and au in the radical syllable of the neuter nouns of these terminations do not change, except in das Kloster, pl. die Klöster.

N.	Die Brüder,	the brothers;
G.	der Brüder,	of the brothers;
D.	den Brüdern,	to the brothers;
A.	die Brüder,	the brothers.

N.	Die Degen	the swords;	die Mädchen,	the girls;
G.	der Degen,	of the swords;	der Mädchen,	of the girls;
D.	den Degen,	to the swords;	den Mädchen,	to the girls;
A.	die Degen,	the swords;	die Mädchen,	the girls.

Der Spiegel, spee'-ghel, the looking glass; der Garten, gār'-ten, the garden; die Gärten, gerr'-ten, the gardens; der Holländer, hol'-len-der, the Dutchman; die Holländer, hol-len'-der, the Dutch (people); der Irländer, irr'-len-der, the Irishman; der Europäer, oi-ro-pai'-er, the European; der Buchdrucker, boo'ch''-droock'-er, the printer; das Zimmer, tsim'-mer, the room; der Schlüssel, shlüss'-sel, the key; der Aermel, err'-mel, the sleeve; der Finger, fing'-er, the finger; der Nagel, nā'-ghel, the nail.

Schuldig, shööl'-dich, guilty; unschuldig, öön''-shööl'-dich, innocent, not guilty; tugendhaft, too''-ghent-häft, virtuous.

When the adjective is preceded by a determinative word, such as an article or a pronoun, it takes en in all the cases of the plural. (§ 20, 1,)

N.	Die armen Freunde, Spanier,	the poor friends, Spaniards;
G.	der armen Freunde, Spanier,	of the poor friends, Spaniards;
D.	den armen Freunden, Spaniern,	to the poor friends, Spaniards;
A.	die armen Freunde, Spanier,	the poor friends, Spaniards.

Denn, den, for; bald, bält, soon.

Sind die Brüder glücklich oder unglücklich? Sie sind sehr unglücklich, denn sie sind krank und haben kein Geld. Haben die Maurer den guten Offizieren die scharfen Degen der Generäle gegeben? Sie haben sie ihnen gegeben. Was haben die Irländer den Amerikanern gegeben? Sie haben ihnen die Schlüssel der Zimmer gegeben. Wessen Vettern haben die Engländer Gold und Silber geschickt? Sie haben den Vettern der Maurer welches geschickt. Haben Sie den Buchdruckern das Papier verkauft? Ich habe es ihnen nicht verkauft, denn ich hatte keins, aber die Schwäger der Schuhmacher haben es ihnen theuer verkauft. Werden wir die Amerikaner heute Abend sehen? Sie werden sie heute und morgen sehen. Sind sie zuweilen hier gewesen? Haben die durstigen Schneider nichts zu trinken? Werden die unschuldigen Mädchen nicht weggeschickt werden? Sie werden heute weggeschickt werden. Die geschickten Tischler haben den alten Holländern die hölzernen Tische der französischen Sänger geschickt. Diese tugendhaften Brüder haben ihren kranken Oheimen sechs silberne Teller geschenkt. Haben die kleinen Amerikaner ihre drei Mädchen in Deutschland gelassen? Die Gärtner werden den Schneidern die Röcke nicht mehr bezahlen, denn sie sind sehr arm.

60.

Are the knives of these shoemakers sharp or blunt? They are very sharp. Will they not become blunt? They will become blunt soon. Are the fathers of these French officers good cabinetmakers? They are not cabinetmakers but they are industrious and virtuous masons. Have the polite printers their clean paper? They have it. Will the generals of these kings beat the Americans? They will never beat the Americans but they will beat the Irish and the English. Will the industrious Dutch send sharp swords to the brothers of the millers? We shall buy these six silver spoons *for* our girls (dat). Will these grandchildren of the English generals have their handsome swords? They will have them. Have you eaten the boiled hams of the Irishmen? I have not eaten the hams of the Irish but I have eaten the meat of the sleepy Dutchmen. Have the young girls not sewed the sleeves of your coat? They have sewed them this morning. Have the same boiled for the bakers their coffee? They have boiled it for them. Will these amiable girls love the brothers of their fathers? They will love them. Have the young cousins of these idle Spaniards sewed the long sleeves of the red coats *for* their kind grandfather (dat.)? They have sewed them for them.

61.

Masc. nouns, which in the genitive singular have en (n), and which designate living beings, have all the cases of their plural in en (§ 9.).

Der Knabe, des Knaben, die Knaben, the boys;
der Herr, des Herrn, die Herren, the masters.

Nom.	Die Knaben,	the boys;
Gen.	der Knaben,	of the boys;
Dat.	den Knaben,	to the boys;
Acc.	die Knaben,	the boys.

Der meinige, mine; der seinige, his; der ihrige, hers, &c., are in the plural declined like die guten.

Die Soldaten, zol-dâ'-ten; the soldiers; die Bauern, bou'-ern, the peasants; der Fürst (en), fürrst, the prince; der Mensch (en), mensh, the man (the human being); der Affe (n), âf'-fai, the ape; der Graf, grâ'f, the count; der Hirt, hirrt, the shepherd; der Preuße, proi'-ssai, the Prussian; der Däne, dai'-nai, the Dane; der Schwede, shwey'-dai, the Swede; der Türke, tür'-kai, the Turk; der Advokat, ât-vo-kâ't', the lawyer.

Es sind, they are, there are.

Tapfer, tap'-fer, brave; feige, fi'-ghai, cowardly; ehrlich, eyr'-lich, honest; angenehm, ân''-gai-naim'; ungeschickt, öön''-gai-shickt', unskillful, clumsy; todt, to't, dead.

Machen, mâ'-chen, to make; gemacht, gai-mâcht', made; besiegen, bai-zee'-ghen, to conquer; besiegt, bai-zeecht', conquered; verrathen, inf. and p. part. to betray, betrayed.

Warum, vâ'-rööm, wherefore; weil, vile, because. Weil, like most relative pronouns, adverbs and many conjunctions, sends the principal verb, or the auxiliary verb, when there is one, to the end of the sentence.

Weil ich krank bin, because I am sick;
weil ich kein Geld habe, because I have no money;
weil wir die Feinde geschlagen haben, because we have beaten the enemy;
weil die Frau krank geworden ist, because the woman has become sick.

Die Freiheit, fri'-hite, liberty.

Haben die tapfern Schweden diese schlechten Soldaten der Prinzen besiegt? Sie haben sie mehr als einmal besiegt. Was haben die Bauern den ehrlichen Knaben der fleißigen Hirten gegeben? Sie haben ihnen diesen schönen Ochsen gegeben. Wer hat den guten Deutschen diese kleinen Ochsen geschickt? Die Türken haben sie ihnen geschickt. Werden die Bauern dieser Fürsten reich werden? Die Fürsten werden reich werden, aber nicht die Bauern. Werden diese kleinen Franzosen gute Soldaten werden? Sie werden gute und tapfere Soldaten werden. Sind Sie Dänen? Wir sind Schweden. Sind die Ochsen dieser Bauern besser als die Ochsen der alten Hirten? Sie sind nicht besser. Werden die feigen Dänen diese tapfern Franzosen verrathen? Warum haben die Fürsten der Deutschen ihren Bauern keine Freiheit gegeben? Sie haben ihnen keine gegeben weil sie zu träge sind. Warum haben die Knaben nichts gegessen? Sie haben nichts gegessen weil sie krank sind. Warum haben diese Menschen kein Geld erhalten? Sie haben keins erhalten, weil sie träge und ungeschickt gewesen sind. Warum haben Sie diesen Knaben Brod gegeben? Ich habe ihnen welches gegeben weil sie gut und fleißig gewesen sind. Warum haben die Deutschen keinen Kaffee getrunken? Weil wir ihnen keinen gegeben haben. Warum werden die Hirten ihre alten Ochsen nicht verkaufen? Sie werden sie nicht verkaufen, weil die Bauern kein Geld haben sie zu kaufen.

62.

Will the peasants of these princes betray their masters? They will betray them. Have the monkeys of these boys eaten all the bread? They have eaten it. Which soldiers have conquered the Danes? The American soldiers have conquered them. Where have they conquered them? They have conquered them in Germany. Have the small boys of the poor shepherds found the oxen? They have found them. Where have they found them? They have found them in the market. Will the Germans beat these brave Frenchmen? They will beat them. Have the boys of the honest Swedes found money in the street? They have found no money but they have found *some* bread and *some* water in the market. Do these Germans write as much as these Frenchmen? Those write more than these. Had the American lawyers written as much as the German lawyers? The former (those) had written more than the latter. Which soldiers had conquered the enemies? The brave Danish soldiers had conquered them. Where had they conquered them. They had conquered them in Prussia and in Holland. Why have you bought no paper? I have bought no paper because I had received no money. Why had the industrious farmers not paid *for* their wine? They had not paid *for* it (masc. acc.), because they had no money. Why have you not returned the candle to the poor people? I have not returned it to them because I had lost it. Why have you boiled no beef to-day? We have boiled none (keins) because we had no water. Why are these soldiers so sad? They are sad because the French have conquered them. Soldiers! shall we not conquer these English peasants? We shall conquer them. Are all men good and virtuous? All men are not good and virtuous; many are bad. Are the boys of this lady very unskillful? They are not unskillful, but they are idle. What are these men (people)? They are shepherds. Have you given the hay to the oxen of the farmer? I have given it to them. At what o'clock have you given it them? I have given it to them at half past six o'clock. Is this* your hat? It is mine. It is not his, it is ours or hers. Is this your cat? It is mine. Are these your boys? They (it) are mine. Are these monkeys yours? They are not mine. They are either his or hers.

63.

Some neuter nouns have in the nom., gen. and acc. pl. er and in the dat. ern, (§ 15).

Nom.	Die Bücher,	the books;
Gen.	der Bücher,	of the books;
Dat.	den Büchern,	to the books;
Acc.	die Bücher,	the books.

* When the noun, which the word this or these represents, is in the same part of the sentence, dies is used instead of dieser, dieses and diese.

These change the vowels a, o and u into ä, ö and ü.

Die Bänder, ben′-der, the ribbons; die Fässer, fes′-ser, the casks; die Gelder, gel′-der, moneys; die Kräuter, kroi′-ter, herbs; die Tücher, tü′-cher, the handkerchiefs, cloths; die Gräser, grai′-zer, the grasses; die Lichter, lich′-ter, (Lichte), the lights, the candles; die Kleider, kli′-der, the dresses, clothes; die Häuser, hoi′-zer, the houses; die Schlösser, shlös′-ser, the castles, locks; die Kinder, kin′-der, the children.

The Relative Pronoun.

	Masc.	*Fem.*	*Neut.*	*Pl.*	
Nom.	welcher,	welche,	welches,	welche,	who, which, that;
Nom.	der,	die,	das,	die,	who, which;
Gen.	dessen,*	deren,	dessen,	deren,	whose, of which.

The Dat. and Acc. of der, die, das are like the Dat. and Acc. of the article. (§ 39).

All relative pronouns send the principal or the auxiliary verb to the end of the sentence.

Das Buch welches (das) ich habe,	The book which I have;
die Bänder welche (die) ich gesehen habe,	the ribbons which I have seen.

Der Fleischer (s), fli′-sher; der Schlachter (s), shlach′-ter, the butcher.

Hat der Buchdrucker die Bücher welche Sie haben? Er hat die Bücher welche ich habe. Hat der Prinz die Schlösser welche sein Vater hatte? Er hat nicht die Schlösser welche sein Vater hatte, er hat schönere und größere. Der Kaufmann hat die Gelder erhalten, die ich ihm geschickt habe. Welcher Koch hat die Fässer gekauft, welche ich verkauft habe? Der höfliche Koch hat sie gekauft. Hat ihre Tochter die Gelder verloren, welche ich ihr geliehen habe? Der Gärtner hat dieselben Kräuter und Gräser gepflanzt, die der Bauer gepflanzt hat. Werden wir den Knaben finden, dessen Vater krank ist? Wir werden ihn hier finden. Sie werden die Kinder sehen, deren Brüder sehr unglücklich sind. Wann wird der Schneider die Kleider bringen, welche er gemacht hat? Haben Sie den Mann, dem Sie Ihre Bücher geschenkt haben, gesehen? Haben Sie die Waschfrau, deren Tochter so schön ist, gesehen? Warum haben Sie mir das Geld, welches ich Ihnen geliehen habe, nicht wieder gegeben? Ich habe es Ihnen nicht wiedergegeben, weil ich es nicht mehr habe. Wann werden die armen Kinder, die ihre Mutter und ihren Vater verloren haben, wieder glücklich werden? Die schönen Bänder, die Sie mir geschenkt haben, werde ich (§ 89, 2.) Ihnen nicht wiedergeben. Haben diese Herren schon die Hüte gesehen, die ich meiner Schwester gekauft habe? Haben Sie denselben Kaufleuten geschrieben, denen ich geschrieben habe? Hat die Köchinn das Ochsenfleisch gekocht, welches wir ihr geschickt haben? Sie hat nicht das Ochsenfleisch, welches Sie ihr geschickt haben, sondern das Kalbfleisch, welches der alte Schlachter ihr gestern verkauft hat, gekocht.

64.

Where are the ribbons which you have bought? They are in my room. Which are the houses which the Germans have sold? They (es)

* The gen. sing. has also, deß, der, deß.

are these. Are these the lights which the servant woman has brought? They are not the lights which the servant woman has brought. Will these officers hate the boy, whose father is dead? They will not hate him, they will love him. Why have you hated the friends of your father? I have hated them because they have betrayed me. Will you love the woman whose daughter has betrayed you? I shall not love her, I shall hate her. Have you found the old cook (*masc.*). to whom you had given the dry salt? I have not found the old cook, to whom I had given the dry salt but the young handsome cook (*fem.*), who had given me *some* fine roast mutton, *some* white bread and good butter. Have you already been in the houses of the Germans? I have already been in the houses of the Germans whose grandfather was an American. Have you not received the lady to whom I had sent my cook (*fem.*)? I have not received her but I shall receive her to morrow. What will the Prussians plant? They will plant grasses and herbs. Will they plant the same grasses and herbs which the Turcs have planted? They will plant the same. Will you receive at (in dat.) your house the same Germans whom I receive in mine. I shall receive the same. Why did you not go for (have you not fetched) the brave gentlemen to whom I had given the handsome swords? I have gone for them. Where are they? They are in the garden. In mine (*dat.*) or in yours? Neither in mine nor in yours, but in the garden of the old French gentleman, to whom the father of the German prince has presented a handsome castle and two fine houses. Have the Danes lost all the officers (to) whom the king had presented (*with*) handsome swords? Where have you been? We have been in the houses of the Swedes whose uncle and whose father are now in America.

65.

Feminine nouns form their nom. pl. in e or en, the former take n in the dat., the latter, in en, have all four cases alike; with the former a, o, u and au change to ä, ö, ü and äu. (§ 12.)

Nom.	Die Mägde,	the servants;	Die Frauen,	the women;
Gen.	der Mägde,	of the servants;	der Frauen,	of the women;
Dat.	den Mägden,	to the servants,	den Frauen,	to the women;
Acc.	die Mägde,	the servants;	die Frauen,	the women.

Mutter and Tochter are irregular and have in the plural, die Mütter and die Töchter.

Die Braut, brout, the bride, the affianced; die Bräute, broi'-tai; die Haut, hout, the skin, the hide; die Häute, hoi'-tai; die Frucht, frŏŏcht, the fruit; die Früchte, früch'-tai; die Gans, gânss, the goose; die Gänse, ghen'-zai; die Kuh, koo, the cow; Kühe, kü'-hai.

All the feminine nouns which have been introduced before, and which are not mentioned above, form their plur. in en; as: die Nichten, die Königinnen, u. s. w.

Ich liebe,	lee'-bai,	I love;
er liebt,	leept,	he loves;
wir lieben,	leeben,	we love;
sie lieben,	lee'-ben,	they love;
Sie lieben,	lee'-ben,	you love.

In the same manner are conjugated all the verbs that occur in the following Exercise:

Selbst, zelpst, self, selves. **Ich... selbst**, I...myself; **wir... selbst**, we...ourselves. **Wohnen**, vo'-nen, to live, to dwell, to reside. **Loben**, lo'-ben, to praise; **hören**, hö'-ren, to hear; **das Geräusch (es)**, gai-roish', the noise; **das Bellen (s)**, bel'-len, the barking; **die Stimme**, stim'-mai, the voice; **Die Feder (pl. n)**, the pen; **die Blume**, bloo'-mai, the flower; **die Birne**, birr-'nai; **kaufen von (bei)**, to buy from (**von** and **bei** govern the dative).

Suchen Sie die Gänse Ihrer Schwester? Ich suche nicht die Gänse meiner Schwester. Wo wohnen Sie? Ich wohne auf dem Markte. Wo wohnt Ihr Sohn? Er wohnt auch auf dem Markte. Wo wohnen Ihre Nichten? Sie wohnen in dem Hause des schwedischen Offiziers der das Feuer angezündet hat. Wer wohnt in diesem Hause? In diesem Hause wohnt der Gärtner, dessen Sohn schon drei Jahre in Amerika ist. Loben die Generäle die tapfern Soldaten, die den Feind in Frankreich geschlagen haben? Sie loben nicht allein die Soldaten, sondern auch die Offiziere. Loben die Damen die Mägde, welche gut kochen? Sie loben sie. Haben die Herren die Gärtner gelobt, welche schöne Blumen pflanzen? Sie haben sie noch nicht gelobt, aber sie werden sie loben, wenn sie hören wie viele schöne Blumen sie gepflanzt haben. Hören (to obey) die Töchter ihren Müttern? Sie hören ihnen nicht immer. Loben die Königinnen ihre Generäle und Offiziere? Lieben die Mütter ihre Kinder? Kochen Sie Ihre Suppe selbst? Ich koche sie nicht selbst, meine Köchinn kocht sie, aber ich mache meinen Kaffee selbst. Kauft Ihre Schwester selbst ihr Gemüse auf dem Markte? Sie kauft es nicht selbst, die Köchinn holt es. Holen Sie Brod? Ich hole Brod und Butter. Bei wem kaufen Sie Ihr Brod? Ich kaufe es bei dem Bäcker, aber meine Blumen und meine Früchte kaufe ich bei dem deutschen Gärtner. Die Deutschen kaufen ihre Ochsen von den Dänen und ihr Eisen von den Schweden.

66.

Does your brother love his mother? He loves his father and his mother but he does not love me, his brother. Does the cook (*fem.*) boil the fruit? She boils it (fem.) Which fruit does she boil? She boils the pears and the apples. How many pears and how many apples does she boil? She boils twenty pears and fifteen apples. What do the English women boil? They boil soups. Do they roast their pigeons? They roast them. Which pigeons do they roast? They roast those, which they bought from the sisters of the washerwoman. Which cows have you paid *for*? I have paid *for* the cows which my father has sent me. Do you pay *for* the geese, which you buy? I pay *for* the geese which I buy from the farmerwoman, but not for the geese which I receive from the widow of the count, she presents *me with them* (them to me). Do the affianced of the Germans love them? They love them. Do we not hear the barking of the hungry dogs in our garden? We hear it in the garden and in the room. Do the sleepy ladies hear what we say? They do not hear it. Do these kind mothers love their amiable daughters as much (sehr) as *the latter* (these) love them? They love them as much. What do these merchants buy? They buy the skins, which the American has sent to his son. Do the washerwomen sell soap? They do not sell soap but they buy some. From whom do they buy their soap? They buy it from the old merchant who lives in the market. Does he not live in the house of your nephew? He does not live in the house of my nephew but in the house of my brother, which is also in the market. Why do you not boil these hens? We do not boil them because we have no water; we roast them. Where do these ladies live? This young lady lives in the house, which is in the market, and the old *one* lives in my small house in the country. Do your aunts make their soups themselves? They always make them themselves. Who praises my little cats? The two old widows, who live in my grandfather's house, praise them amd love them. Why does this old woman not show her daughters? She does not show them because they are so very ugly. Why do these nieces of the sick countess always praise their old servant (f.)? They praise her, because she is industrious and virtuous. Do you not hear the voice of your wife? I hear her voice, but I do not find her. From whom have you bought these flowers? I have bought them from the English gardener, who lives in the old house of my shoemaker. What do you hear? We hear a noise. Where, in the house or in the garden? Neither in the house, nor in the garden.

67.

Derjenige (der), welcher (der), the one (he) who; (see § 35 & 41)

Ich liebte,	leep'-tai,	I loved;
er liebte,	leep'-tai,	he loved;
wir liebten,	leep'-ten,	we loved;
sie liebten,	leep'-ten,	they loved;
Sie liebten,	leep'-ten,	you loved.

Lachen, lāch'-chen, to laugh; weinen, wi'-nen, to weep; sagen, zā'-gen, to say; reisen, ri'-zen, to travel, erzählen, err-tsai'-len, to relate; geliebt, gai-leept', loved; gelacht, gāi-lācht', laughed; geweint, gai-vi'nt', wept; gereis't, gai-riz't', travelled.

Verbs, the root of which terminates in d or t, retain the e after the root in the 2d and 3d person sing. of the present tense, in all the persons of the imperf., and in the past part.; as: reden, to speak; er redet, rai'-det, he speaks; ich redete, rai'-dai-tai, I spoke; geredet, gai-rai'-det, spoken.

In the same manner are conjugated:

Tödten, tö'-ten, to kill; schlachten, schlāch'-ten, to kill (cattle); kleiden, kli'-den, to clothe, to dress; leiten, li'-ten, to conduct, lead.

Die Sprache, sprā'-chai, the language, the speech; wovon, vo-fon', of what, where of; fett, fet, fat; damals, dā'-māls, at that time.

Suchten Sie mich? Ich suchte Sie. Wer suchte meinen Vater? Ihre Mutter suchte ihn. Hassen Sie den Soldaten, welchen Ihr Bruder haßt? Ich hasse nicht denjenigen, welchen mein Bruder haßt. Lieben Sie die Dame, die ich liebe? Ich liebe nicht diejenige die (welche) Sie lieben, ich liebe eine andere. Liebte die Mutter den Sohn, welchen der Vater liebte? Sie liebte nicht den (denjenigen), welchen der Vater liebte. Lobten Sie die Frauen welche ich lobte? Ich lobte nicht diejenigen welche Sie lobten, ich lobte meine Frau. Lachte die kleine Waschfrau als unsere alte Köchinn lachte? Sie lachte nicht, sie weinte. Warum weinte dieses kleine Mädchen? Sie weinte weil sie kein Brod hatte. Was sagen Sie mein Herr? Ich sage nichts. Wovon redeten die Spanier? Sie redeten von der Freiheit. Was schlachteten die Fleischer? Sie schlachteten einen großen Ochsen. Hat der Fleischer einen fetten Ochsen geschlachtet? Er hat keinen fetten Ochsen, aber zwei fette Kühe geschlachtet. Reisen Sie viel? Ich reise nicht viel. Reis'ten Ihre Brüder damals in Frankreich? Sie reis'ten nicht in Frankreich, sondern in Amerika. Haßt uns der Mann, der in diesem Hause wohnt? Derjenige der in diesem Hause wohnt haßt uns nicht, aber derjenige, der auf dem Markte wohnt, haßt uns. Bezahlte der Fleischer dem Kaufmanne, der Ihnen bezahlte? Der Fleischer bezahlte nicht demjenigen, der (welcher) uns bezahlte, er bezahlte demjenigen, der ihm Fleisch verkaufte. Liebten ihre Schwestern die Töchter der Frau, die in diesem Hause wohnte? Sie liebten nicht die Töchter derjenigen, die in diesem Hause wohnte.

68.

Did you love the officer whom I loved? I did not love the one, whom you loved. Did the butcher who lives in this house pay you? The one, who lives in this house did not pay me. Did the merchant, who had two handsome nieces, live in this house? The one, who had two handsome nieces did not live here, but in the market. Did the farmer, whose brother was so poor, sell his oxen? The one, whose brother was so poor, sold them. Did the baker, to whom you had sold the flour pay you (dat.)? The one, to whom I had sold the flour, did not pay me. Did the tailor, whom we praised, sew your coat? The one, whom we praised did not sew it. Do you hear the voice of the gardener, who is in the garden? I do not hear the voice of the one who is in the garden, I hear the voice of the one who is in the room. Did the soldier kill the general of the prince, whose mother is in America? He did not kill the general of the one, whose mother is in America. Did your nephews buy the sword of the officer to whom you had presented it? They bought the sword of the one to whom we had presented it. Did the shoemaker make the shoe of the man whom we sent away. He made the shoe of the one, whom we sent away. Did you sell your horse to the Englishman, who lives in the market? I sold it to the one who lives in the country. Did you give the money to the boy, whose grandfather is sick? I gave it to the one, whose grandfather is blind. Did you buy your beef from the butcher, to whom the farmer-woman has sold her cow? I bought it from the one, to whom she has sold her. Did you *present the Turk with* (present to the Turk), whom our soldiers had conquered a silver spoon? I presented one to the one whom our brave soldiers had conquered. Do you bring the tea which is so good? I bring that (the one) which is so good. Did the ladies praise the officer, whose sword they had looked for? They praised the one, whose sword they had looked for. Did the French soldiers hate the general, to whom we had sent money? They hated the one to whom we had sent some. Did you look for the one (m.), for whom we were looking? We looked for the one for whom you were looking.

69.

Das Wort, vorrt, the word; **die Wörter**, vörr'-ter, the words; **die Worte**, vörr'-tai, the words (connected in a sentence); **die Geschichte**, gai-shich'-tai, the story, the history.

Schickte Ihnen die Dame, welche so reich ist das Geld? Diejenige welche so reich ist schickte es mir. Erzählten Sie die Geschichte der Königinn, die jetzt in Frankreich ist? Ich erzählte die Geschichte derjenigen, welche jetzt in Frankreich ist. Hassen Sie nicht die Tochter der Deutschen, welche den König getödtet hat? Ich hasse die Tochter derjenigen welche ihn verrathen hat. Schickten Sie Ihre Butter der Witwe, welche hungrig war? Ich schickte sie derjenigen welche höflich war.

70

Did you relate to them the story, which you had heard from me? I related to them the one which I had heard from your brother. Is the singer (f.), whose father is sick, as handsome as people say (man sagt)? The one whose father is sick, is not so handsome as people say but her sister is handsomer. Is the son of the woman, whose husband is in Paris, a cabinetmaker or a carpenter? The son of the one, whose husband is in Paris, is neither a cabinetmaker nor a carpenter, he is a watchmaker, but the son of the one, whose husband is dead, is a carpenter. To which servant (f.) have you lent your bonnet? I have lent it to the one, whose eyes are blue. Which lady did you show him in the garden? I showed him the one, whose gardener had sent me these red paper flowers. Which washerwoman sent my clothes (dresses)? The one to whom you had paid the money, sent them. Was the sister of the queen, to whom you showed the castle, guilty or not guilty? The sister of the one to whom I showed, the castle was innocent. To which gardenerwoman did you tell the story? I told it to the one, to whom you had said the word. Which butter did you buy? I bought that in which *there* was so much salt. Which seamstress sews the dresses of the princess? The one whom you have seen in my house. The voice of which woman is best? The voice of that one is best, whom we heard yesterday. To which woman have you written? I have written to the one whom you hate. Which goose has the farmer woman given away? She has given away the one which you have presented her with. Did you praise the beer which you had drunk? I did not praise that which I had drunk to-day, but that which I had drunk yesterday. Which meat did the cook (*m.*) boil? He boiled that which the cook (f.) had bought. In which castle did the princess reside? In that which her father had presented her *with*. Of which silver did you speak? We spoke of that which you have received to-day. In which house did your grandmother live at that time? She lived in that which my grand-oncle had bought *for* her (dat.).

71.

Arbeiten, ârr'-bi-ten, to work; bewundern, bai-wöön'-dern, to admire; lehren, ley'-ren; to teach; lernen, lerr'-nen; to learn; füttern, füt'-tern, to feed; pflücken, pflük'-ken, to pluck; die Rose, ro'-zai, the rose; das Veilchen, file'-chen, the violet; die Lilie, le'-le-al, the lily; blau, blou, blue; grau, grou gray; hellblau, hell'-blou, light blue. — Das Kalb, kâlp, the calf; die Kälber, kel'-ber, the calves; die Armee, ârr-mai', the army; reif, rife, ripe.

Welche Männer arbeiten fleißig?* Diejenigen arbeiten fleißig, die kein Geld haben. Die Soldaten welcher Armeen bewundern Sie? Ich bewundere die Soldaten der Armeen, die die Feinde besiegen. Welche Sprachen reden Sie? Ich rede die, welche mein Vater redet. Welchen Offizieren schickten die Generäle Geld? Sie schickten denen welches, die Alles verloren hatten. Welchen Bauern haben Sie Mehl verkauft? Ich habe denen welches verkauft, die mir Geld gebracht haben. Die Kälber welcher Kühe werden die Fleischer schlachten? Sie werden die Kälber derjenigen schlachten, die keine Milch geben. Welchen deutschen Bauern werden Sie Blumen schenken? Ich werde denjenigen welche schenken, die noch keine empfangen haben.

72.

Which girls are happy? Those who are still young, are happy. What languages do you learn? I learn the language of those who love me. To which gentlemen do you teach languages? We teach some to those who travel much. Which pears do you pluck? We pluck those which are ripe. Do you admire the ladies whose eyes are gray? I admire those whose eyes are blue. Do you send violets to the ladies whose gardener is sick? I send some to those whose gardener is dead. Which flowers are in the garden? Those which the gardener woman has planted there. To which German women do these English *women* write letters? They write some to those, from whom they have received some. To which Frenchman did you relate your history? I related it to those who had not yet heard it. To which girls did you say a word? I said a word to those, whose brothers were soldiers. Which lilies did your sisters admire? They admired those which nobody admired. Did you pluck white or red roses in the beautiful garden of the German princess? We plucked roses and the handsomest violets that I have ever seen. How many calves have your cows? My two cows have three calves. How much milk will your cows give? They will give 32 quarts (Quartier). Do these tailors work industriously? They sometimes work industriously and sometimes *they are* (are they) very idle. Do you feed your cows? No, I feed those of my neighbor (f.). Do you feed them with grass? I feed them with hay.

73.

Können Sie, kön'-nen, can you, may you;
ich kann, kân, I can, I may;
er kann, kân, he can, he may;

* The adjective in German is used as an adverb without its form being altered.

wir können,	kön'-nen,	we can, we may;
sie können,	kön'-nen,	they can, they may.

This verb können not only expresses capacity but also permission.

Sie können gehen,	ghey'-hen,	you may go;
er kann kommen,	kom'-men	he may come.
Wollen Sie,	vol'-len,	will you, are you willing;
ich will,	vill,	I will;
er will,	vill,	he will;
wir wollen,	vol'-len,	we will;
sie wollen,	vol'-len,	they will.

Gehen, to go; kommen, to come; nach, nâch, after, to (when speaking of a house, &c. It governs the dative); zu, tsoo, (Dat.), to; zu mir, to my house; nach der Stadt gehen, to go to (the) town; nach der Kirche gehen, to go to (the) church.

Die Stadt, stâtt, the town; die Schule, shoo'-lai, the school; die Kirche, kirr'-chai, the church; die Börse, bö'r'-zai, the exchange; das Dorf, dorrf, the village; wo...hin, wohin, vo-hin', whither, where to? dahin, dâ'-hin, thither, there (to); denn, den, for; nach Hause gehen, to go home; zu Hause sein, to be at home; sogleich, zo-gli'ch', immediately; ich danke Ihnen, dân'-kai, I thank you.

Können Sie schreiben? Nein, ich kann nicht schreiben. Kann der Vetter des Arztes lesen? Er kann lesen. Kann die Tochter der alten Bäuerinn nach der Stadt gehen? Sie kann morgen oder heute dahin gehen. Kann der Knabe die Kühe und die Ochsen füttern? Er kann sie nicht füttern, denn er hat weder Heu noch Gras. Können diese Mädchen mir kein Geld geben? Sie können Ihnen keins geben, denn sie haben keins. Wollen die Holländer mit mir gehen? Sie können nicht mit Ihnen gehen. Kann ich jetzt nach Hause gehen? Sie können jetzt gehen. Können die französischen Soldaten die Deutschen besiegen? Sie können sie nicht besiegen. Können Sie morgen zu mir kommen? Ich kann morgen nicht zu Ihnen kommen. Warum können Sie nicht zu mir kommen? Ich kann nicht zu Ihnen kommen, weil ich nach der Kirche gehen werde. Wollen Sie dieses Haus kaufen? Ich will es kaufen. Will Ihr Bruder mir das Pferd schenken, welches er von dem deutschen Offizier gekauft hat? Er will Ihnen nicht dasjenige, welches er von dem deutschen Offizier, aber dasjenige, welches er von dem französischen Soldaten gekauft hat, schenken. Wollen die Damen nach der Stadt gehen? Sie wollen nicht nach der Stadt, sie wollen nach dem Dorfe gehen. Will die Magd heute das Hammelfleisch oder das Ochsenfleisch kochen? Sie will weder das Hammelfleisch noch das Ochsenfleisch kochen, sie will Brod backen. Um wie viel Uhr wollen Sie nach Hause gehen? Ich will um zehn Uhr nach Hause gehen. Können Sie mir einen silbernen Löffel machen? Ich kann Ihnen einen machen. Werden Sie nach mir kommen? Ich werde nach Ihnen kommen. Werden Sie heute nach der Börse gehen? Ich werde sogleich dahin gehen. Wo gehen Sie hin? Ich gehe nach dem Hause meines Bruders. Ich gehe zu meiner Schwester. Was wollen Sie essen? Ich will etwas Fleisch und Brod essen.

74.

Can you speak German? I can speak it. Can you speak it well? I can speak it as well as my father, who is a german. Can your sister sew a dress? She can sew one. Can their cousins (*f.*) roast meat? They can roast and boil meat. Can (may) we go to the country? You may go there, your older brother will go with you. Can you buy this handsome gold watch? I cannot buy it, for I have not money enough, but that rich baker who has many handsome houses, will buy it from you and present it to his daughter who is an amiable and handsome young lady. When can you come to town? I can come thither to morrow. At what o'clock can you go to the exchange? I can go thither at three o'clock. Can you give me back my handsome gold ring? I cannot give it back to you, I have lost it in the street, but I will buy you (dat.) another. Can these young ladies not drink? They cannot drink any thing now, they have just drunk a glass of water. Can we pay them what they have lent us? We cannot pay it to them. Will you buy me a hat to-day? I cannot buy you one (keinen) to-day, I have but very little money. Can these young ladies read this French book? They can read it very well. Will the cooks light the fire? They will light the fire immediately. When will the servant light the candles? She will light them when it is getting dark. Will (*fut.*) the Danes conquer the Swedes? They cannot conquer them, the Danes have too many soldiers. Will you show me your coffee and your tea? I have no coffee, but I will show you my tea and my sugar. Where will these farmer go to? They will go to the village. When can you come to *my house* (me, dat.)? We can come to you to morrow at six o'clock. Will you come to *my father's house* (my father) to-day? I will come to him to morrow. Will the daughters of these farmers come with us? They will not go with you, they will go with their cousins. Can you write a French letter *for* me (dat.) immediately? I cannot write you one now. May I give you some bread and butter? No Sir, I thank you, I have some. May I go with my grandfather? You cannot go with him, your coat is not good enough.

75.

Müssen, müs'-sen, to be obliged.

Müssen Sie? must you?	Ich muß, mŏŏss, I must;
er muß, he must;	wir müssen, we must;
sie müssen, they must.	

Sollen, zoll'-en, to be to, shall.

Ich soll,	zoll,	I shall,	I am to;
er soll,	zoll,	he shall,	he is to;
wir sollen,	zol'-len,	we shall,	we are to;
sie sollen,		they shall,	they are to;
Sie sollen,		you shall,	you are to.

Ausgehen, ouss'-gai-hen, to go out; bleiben bei, bli'-ben, to remain with (at the house of); wann? vân, when?

Auf das Land, auf die Straße, auf den Markt gehen.	To go into the country, into the street, to the market.
Auf dem Lande, auf der Straße, auf dem Markte sein.	To be in the country, in the street, in the market.

Auf, on, upon (§ 73, 4.) fahren, fā'-ren, to drive; ri'-ten, to ride.

Der Bediente, bai-deen'-tai, the servant, m.; bis, biss, until; um...zu, (ŏŏm), in order to; um einen Brief zu schreiben, in order to write a letter; vorig, fo'-rich, former, last; (die) vorige Woche, last week; (den) vorigen Monat, last month; das vorige (voriges) Jahr, last year; die Woche, voch'-chai, the week; der Monat, mo'-na't, month; das Stück, stück, the piece; das Stück Brod, the piece of bread.

Müssen Sie Brod backen? Ich muß welches backen, wenn ich welches essen will. Muß der Bediente auf den Markt gehen? Er muß alle Tage auf den Markt gehen. Muß die Bäuerinn auf dem Markte bleiben? Sie muß bis fünf Uhr da bleiben. Müssen wir auf das Land fahren? Wir müssen heute noch dahin fahren. Müssen die Kaufleute nach der Kirche gehen? Sie müssen mit ihren Frauen und ihren Kindern dahin gehen. Müssen diese armen Bauern ihre Häuser und ihre Felder für so wenig Geld verkaufen? Sie müssen sie für sehr wenig Geld verkaufen. Muß der König den Feind besiegen? Er muß ihn besiegen wenn er es kann. Warum müssen Sie auf das Land reiten? Ich muß dahin reiten, um Getreide und Heu zu kaufen. Was müssen die Soldaten haben um die Feinde zu besiegen? Sie müssen Pulver und Blei haben. Was muß der Schneider haben um einen Rock zu machen? Er muß Tuch haben. Ist Ihr Schwager auf dem Lande oder in der Stadt? Er ist jetzt in der Stadt, vorige Woche war er auf dem Lande. Wann wird Ihre Schwägerinn auf das Land gehen? Sie ist jetzt auf dem Lande, nächsten Monat wird sie in die (nach der) Stadt kommen. Soll ich auf der Straße bleiben? Nein, Sie können in das Haus gehen. Soll ich in das Haus Ihres Freundes oder in das Ihrer Mutter gehen? Sie können in das meiner Mutter gehen. Soll der alte Bediente Licht bringen? Er soll sogleich welches bringen. Wo soll er es hinbringen? Er soll es in das Zimmer bringen. Wo ist das Licht jetzt? Es ist in dem kleinen Zimmer meiner Tante. Müssen die Bedienten diesen Morgen auf den Markt gehen um Brod, Fleisch und Gemüse zu kaufen? Sie müssen dahin gehen um Kaffee, Zucker und Thee zu kaufen. Wie lange können die deutschen Bedienten hier bleiben? Sie können, wenn sie wollen, bis acht Uhr hier bleiben, aber sie müssen bis halb sieben Uhr hier bleiben, um meinen Oheim und meine Tante zu empfangen, die um sieben oder um halb sieben Uhr nach Hause kommen werden.

76.

Must these farmers go into the country to-day or to morrow? They must go there (thither) to-day. Why must they go there to-day? They must go there to-day to sow grain. Must this cook (*f.*) boil or roast the beef? She must boil the big piece and roast the small piece. Must we go to the village at midnight? You must not go there at midnight, but in the morning. Must these children not make a (no) noise? They must make no noise for I am obliged to write and I cannot write when they make *a* noise. Must these poor children cry, because these bad servants will not give them any bread? They shall not cry, for these servants shall give them not only bread, but also (sondern auch) meat and vegetables. Am I to go to (in, acc.) church or into the kitchen? You shall go to church and the ugly cook (f.) shall go into the kitchen. Am I to write a French or a German letter to the cousin of your friend? You must write him a French letter, he can not read German. Is he a Frenchman? No Sir, he is a Spaniard who has long lived in Paris, where he has learned the French language. At what o'clock am I to come home? You must come home at five o'clock; you can remain in the country until four o'clock and then ride into (the) town. Shall the small boys now read or write? They shall now read and then write. Shall the strong farmers cut this ripe grain? They shall not cut it, but they shall mow it next week. Who is to light the fire when our servant is in the country? You may light it yourself. Are these soldiers to eat nothing but dry bread and drink nothing but water? How can they conquer our enemies, who have good meat and good wine, if they have nothing but dry bread and bad water? Can not this honest old man remain in his house? He shall not remain in it, he must sell it to pay me the money which I I have lent him. Are the servant-girls or the cooks to go to the market, in order to buy mutton and vegetables? The cook's are to go to the market to buy mutton and vegetables, and the servant-girls are to go for coffee and sugar. Where are they to buy the coffee and sugar? They are to buy the sugar from Mr. Paul who lives in (the) New Street and the coffee from Mr. Fetts, who lives in the house of the Englishman. Are we to have no more money (no money more)? You are to have no more, why have you lost that which I have given you. We have not lost that which you have given us, we have made it a present to an unfortunate woman, who had lost her clothes and her money in the great fire. It is very agreeable to me, that I am to go into the conntry with my grandfather. It would not be so agreeable to me to (remain in the town)* with my sad old aunt, who is always crying, because her cat is lame and her old dog is blind. Must the children of the neighbours write letters to their grandmother? They must write some to her. When can you come to town? I can come to town to morrow. Where are the daughters of the singer (f.)? They are in the street. Must they go into the street? They must go thither. When were you in (the) church? I was there last month.

77.

Dürfen, dürr'-fen, to be allowed, may.

Ich darf,	dârrf,	I may;
er darf,	dârrf,	he may;
wir dürfen,	dürr'-fen,	we may;
sie dürfen,	dürr'-fen,	they may;
Sie dürfen,	dürr'-fen,	you may.

Bitten...zu, bit'-ten, to request...to; gebeten, gai-bai'-ten, requested; haben Sie Lust...zu, lööst, have you a mind to? zu, tsoo, to, (Dat.).

Bei mir, at my house; zu mir, to my house; bei meinem Nachbar, at my neighbor's; bei meiner Schwester, at my sister's; zu meiner Schwester, to my sister's; bei wem? at whose house? zu wem, to whose house; nächst, naichst, next; nächste Woche, naich'-ste, next week.

Auf dem Felde sein, fel'-dai, to be in the field; auf das (aufs) Feld gehen, to go into the field (see § 74.). Wenigstens, vai'-nich-stens, at least; alle Tage, al'-lai

* At the end of the sentence.

tâ'-gai, every day; alle Morgen, al'-lai morr'-ghen, every morning. Jeder, jede, jedes, yai'-der, yai'-dai, yai'-des, each, every.

Lassen, lâs'-sen, to let, to cause to; gelassen, gai-las'-sen, let.

Ich lasse,	lâs'-sai,	I let;
er läßt,	lest,	he lets;
wir lassen,	lâs'-sen,	we let;
sie lassen,	lâs'-sen,	they let;
Sie lassen,	lâs'-sen,	you let.

Holen lassen, to send for; ich lasse holen, I send for; ich habe holen lassen,* I have sent for; rufen lassen, to have called, to send for; mit Vergnügen, mit fer-gnü'-ghen, with pleasure; der Tag, tâ'ch, the day.

Darf ich Sie bitten, mir diese Rosen und diese Veilchen zu geben? Ich gebe sie Ihnen mit Vergnügen. Darf dieser Offizier diesen Soldaten schlagen? Er darf ihn nicht schlagen. Dürfen wir ausgehen? Sie können ausgehen. Warum darf dieses kleine Mädchen kein Fleisch essen? Sie darf keins essen, weil es sie krank macht. Haben Sie Lust ein Feuer anzuzünden? Ich habe Lust eins anzuzünden, denn es ist kalt. Hat der reiche Bauer Lust sein gutes Bier zu verkaufen? Er hat Lust es zu verkaufen. Darf ich Sie bitten zu mir zu kommen und eine Woche bei mir zu bleiben? Ich werde mit Vergnügen zu Ihnen kommen und so lange bei Ihnen bleiben wie Sie wollen. Sind Sie schon bei meiner hübschen Nachbarinn gewesen? Ich bin noch nicht da gewesen, aber mein Bruder ist schon bei ihr gewesen und wird morgen wieder zu ihr gehen. Wo ist der Bauer? Er ist auf dem Felde. Wo soll der Sohn des Bauern hinfahren? Er soll auf das Feld fahren. Warum läßt der Zimmermann den Schneider holen? Er läßt ihn holen weil er ihm einen neuen Tuchrock machen soll. Lassen diese Gärtnerinnen ihre Töchter ausgehen wann sie wollen? Sie lassen sie nicht ausgehen wann sie wollen. Lassen Sie Bier und Wein von dem Kaufmann holen? Ich lasse Wein aber kein Bier von ihm holen. Wollen Sie mir einige Blumen geben? Wie oft dürfen diese Kinder auf das Land gehen? Sie dürfen alle Tage auf das Land gehen, aber jene Kinder dürfen nur alle Woche einmal hingehen. Dürfen Sie jeden Morgen in die Kirche gehen? Ich darf jeden Morgen dahin gehen.

78.

May we request you to send us the money which we have lent you last year? I shall send it to you next week with pleasure, but this week, I have none. Is this little boy allowed to go to his aunt? He is allowed to go there, when he is *a* good *boy*. Are these soldiers allowed to go out when they *please* (wollen)? They are not allowed to go out when they please, they are allowed to go out in the morning. At whose house are you allowed to stay? I am allowed to stay at my uncle's or at my cousin's. To whose house are the nephews of the Englishman allowed to go? They are allowed to stay at the house of the countess and of the princess. When are you allowed to come to my house? I am allowed to come to your house next week and to stay a month with (bei) you. May every soldier cook his meat? Every soldier may cook his. Is every officer allowed to beat the soldier? He is not allowed to beat him. Are we al-

* The inf. is used here instead of the past part. (§ 82, 5.)

lowed to sell our gold spoons and our silver plates? You are not allowed to sell them. Will you let your children go to (in the) school? I will let them go to school. How often do they go to school? They go to school every day. Do they not go to shool every morning and every evening? They go there every morning. Has every child a silver spoon? Every child that goes to this school must bring a silver spoon and a silver plate. Do you let your son go out, when he has a mind? I do not let him always go out, when he has a mind, but I let him go out, when he has been industrious. Why will you have this man called? I will have him called in order to buy his copper and his iron. I will have him called in order to relate something to him. Will the enemies let the soldiers go? They will not let them go, but they will let the officers go. May I have some meat brought to me by (von) the butcher? You may have some brought to you by the cook, but not by the butcher, for the cook will bring you boiled or roasted meat, but the butcher will bring you uncooked meat.

79.

Ich bin gegangen,	gai-gång'-en,	I have gone,* (I am gone);
Sind Sie gegangen,	gai-gång'-en,	have you gone;
Sind Sie gekommen,	gai-kom'-men,	have you come;
Ich war gegangen,	I had gone;	
Ich war gekommen,	I had come;	
Ich bin gefallen,	gai-fål'-len,	I have fallen;
er ist geflogen,	gai-flo'-ghen,	he has flown.
Ich bin gefahren,	gai-få'-ren,	I have driven;
Ich bin geritten,	gai-rit'-ten,	I have ridden;
Ich bin gesegelt,	gai-zai'-gelt,	I have sailed;
Ich bin geblieben,	gai-blee'-ben,	I have remained.

Das Schiff, shif, the vessel, ship; das Boot, bo't, the boat; die Insel, in'-zel, the island; der erste, eyr'stai, the first; der zweite, tsvi'-tai, the second; der dritte, drit'tai, the third; der vierte, feer'-tai, the fourth; (see § 25.)

Am ersten des Monats, the first of the month; am zweiten Januar, yå-noo-å'r', the second of January; Februar, fai-broo-å'r', February; März, merrts, March; April, å-pril', April; Mai, mi, May; Juni, you'-nee, June.

Das Dach, dåch, the roof; als, åls, when; (sends the verb to the end § 90, 6.)

Wo ist Ihr Bedienter hingegangen? Er ist in die Stadt gegangen. Wo ist der Hund geblieben? Er ist auf dem Felde geblieben. Wo sind Ihre hübschen Nichten hingereis't? Sie sind nach Frankreich gereis't. War der Spanier aufs Land gegangen? Er war nicht auf das Land gegangen. Ist der Bediente des Engländers gekommen? Er ist schon vorigen Monat gekommen. Der Tag der Freiheit war gekommen. Die goldene Feder meines Lehrers ist vom Tische gefallen. Wer ist von dem Dache des Schlosses gefallen? Der Zimmermann ist herunter (down) gefallen. Sind Sie auf das Land geritten? Nein Madame, ich bin nicht dahin geritten, ich bin dahin gefahren und mein Bruder ist dahin gegangen. War der Kaufmann schon nach Amerika gesegelt als Sie in seinem Hause waren? Er war schon dahin gesegelt. Mit

* Most intransitive verbs are conjugated with the auxiliary verb sein (see § 55).

welchem Schiffe war er dahin gesegelt? Er war mit dem Schiffe „Johann" dahin gesegelt. Haben Sie Ihren Bruder nicht gesehen? Ja mein Herr, er ist so eben mit seinem kleinen Boote nach jener schönen grünen Insel gesegelt. Wann ist der General nach England gesegelt? Er ist am sechsten vorigen Monats dahin gesegelt. Wann ist er zu Ihnen gekommen? Er kam am zehnten dieses Monats zu mir. Wie lange ist er bei Ihnen geblieben? Er ist bis zum Neunzehnten bei mir geblieben. Wann ist die Tochter des Bauern auf's Land gefahren? Die Tochter des Bauern ist nicht aufs Land gefahren, sie ist in der Stadt geblieben; aber die des deutschen Kochs ist mit ihrem Vater am 5. Juni auf's Land gefahren. Wann wird sie wiederkommen? Sie wird am zwanzigsten August wiederkommen. Der kleine Tischler ist nach Philadelphia gegangen um Holz zu kaufen.

80.

Where is your mother? She is gone to church. Was your grand-father at home, when you were at his house (bei ihm)? He was not at home, he had gone to France. How had he gone there? He had driven there. Had the servant of the Frenchman come when you saw him? He had come. Where had he come from? He had come from the market. Why had he gone there? He had gone there to buy mutton and veal. Is your cook at home? No, he is gone to your house, to bring you some roses and lilies which we have plucked in our garden. Who has fallen (fell)? The pretty little child of the seamstress has fallen from the table. Where has the pigeon of the old brewer flown to? She has flown upon the roof of the church. Have you remained with your grand-father? I have remained with him until the (bis zum) fifteenth of March, then I went (am I gone) to Germany, where I remained (have remained) five weeks. How many years *were you* (have you been) in Germany? I *was* (have been) there five years and six months. How many years was the aunt of the deaf Dutchman in America? She was there two years. Why *did you drive* (have you driven) to (the) town? We have driven there to buy cloth and leather. What did you want to do with it (damit)? We wanted to make coats of the cloth, and boots and shoes of the leather. *Did you ride* (have you ridden) into the country? I have ridden into the country this morning. Where is the French count gone to? He is *gone* (has traveled) to Paris, to buy a handsome castle. *Did you remain* (have you remained) in the boat? I have remained in it and sailed to the green island which you can see from here. Had the German princess *gone* (travelled) to Germany, when (als) you received her letter? She had gone there. When had she gone there? She had gone there on the tenth of March. May I (ich mir) take the liberty to ask you where your sister is? The younger or the elder? The elder. She is gone to the market, to buy sugar and coffee. The younger is gone to (in) the kitchen to cook a soup for her grand-mother, who is very sick. Can you buy me (dat.) some knives? I can buy you some, if you will give me *some* money. Here is some, is that enough? It is not enough, I must have five dollars (Thaler).

81.

In the following verbs the prefixes are separat e and stand after the verbs, generally at the end of the sentence. The ge, which forms the past participle, is placed between the prefix and the simple verb, also the preposition zu, where it occurs before the verb, goes between the prefix and the verb (see § 70.).

Ankommen, ân′′-kom′-men, to arrive. * Ich komme....an, I arrive; angekommen, ân′-gai-kom-men, arrived. Abreisen, âp′-ri′-zen, to depart, to leave; ich reise ab, I depart; ich bin abgereis't, I have departed. Weggehen, vech′′-gey′-hen, to go away (see Exc. 80). Aufgehen, ouf′′-gey′-hen, to rise; untergehen, to set, to go down; absegeln, to depart, to sail off; anfangen, ân′′-fâng′-en, to begin (auxil. haben); ich fange an, I begin; ich habe angefangen, I have begun; anfangen zu, to begin to; aufstehen, ouf′′-stey′-hen, to rise; die Sonne, zon′-nai, the sun; der Mond, mo'nt, the moon; der Stern, sterrn, the star; der Arzt, ârrtst′, the physician. Der Thaler, tâ′-ler, the dollar; schuldig sein, shööl′-dich zine, to be indebted, to owe (with the dat. and acc.); zumachen, tsoo′-mâch-chen, to shut; aufmachen, to open (a door, a window); die Thür, tü'rr, the door; das Fenster, fen′-ster, the window; der Kasten, kâss′-ten, the box; der Koffer, kof′-fer, the trunk; ohne, o′-nai, without; allein, âl-line′, alone; die Minute, me-noo′-tai, the minute; offen, of′-fen, open.

Wann werden die lustigen Maurer in London ankommen? Sie werden am 10. Juni da ankommen. Ist der arme Müller noch nicht angekommen? Er ist schon um fünf Uhr diesen Morgen angekommen. Haben die alten Frauen Lust heute noch abzureisen? Sie haben keine Lust heute noch abzureisen, aber sie wollen morgen um sechs Uhr abreisen. Wann ist der Bediente des Offiziers hier angekommen? Er ist schon vorige Woche mit den Pferden seines Herrn hier angekommen. Waren die deutschen Grafen schon abgereis't als Sie in London ankamen? Sie waren noch nicht abgereis't. Würden Sie ohne mich abreisen? Ich würde nicht ohne Sie abreisen können. Wann sind die liebenswürdigen Freundinnen Ihrer Schwestern weggegangen? Sie sind um halb acht Uhr weggegangen. Sind sie allein weggegangen? Sie sind nicht allein, sondern mit meinem Neffen weggegangen, der sie nach Hause gebracht hat. War die Sonne schon aufgegangen als Sie von Hamburg absegelten?* Sie war noch nicht aufgegangen. Um welche Uhr geht die Sonne jetzt auf? Sie geht um sechs Uhr auf. Wann geht der Mond unter? Er geht um acht Uhr Morgens unter. Um wie viel Uhr sind die Bauern auf dem Markte angekommen? Sie sind um halb fünf Uhr mit ihren Pferden und Ochsen da angekommen. Haben Sie den Arzt holen lassen? Ich habe ihn schon gestern holen lassen. Fangen ihre Schwestern schon an französisch zu sprechen? Sie fangen an es zu lesen, aber nicht zu sprechen. Warum ist der Soldat so früh aufgestanden? Er ist so früh aufgestanden um dem Offizier seinen Kaffee zu machen. Segelt das englische Schiff ohne seinen Koch von hier ab? Es segelt ohne ihn ab. Haben die kleinen deutschen Mädchen angefangen französisch zu lernen? Sie haben noch nicht angefangen es zu lernen, aber sie werden nächsten Monat anfangen.

82.

Can your friends still arrive to-day? They can still arrive to-day. Have the enemies arrived in the town? They have already arrived in

* When a conjunction, adverb or relative pronoun sends the verb to the end, it must be joined again to the prefix.

the town. When does the new servant arrive? He arrives to-day. Has the doctor already departed? Not yet, but he will depart in a week (dat.). At what o'clock have you departed? We have departed at half past eleven. Had the soldiers departed when you arrived in Paris? They had not yet departed. Does the washer-woman go away in the morning? She goes away in the evening at eight o'clock. Where does she go to? She goes home. Is your mother gone away? My mother and my sister are gone away. Why are they gone away? They are gone away because they were thirsty and there was no water here. At what o'clock may the cooks (f.) go away? They may go away at seven o'clock. Why do the butchers go away? They go away in order to kill an ox and two calves. What will they do with them (damit)? They will take (bringen) them to the market, in order to sell them. When do these vessels sail? They sail on the third of next month (gen.). Can you tell me when the sun rises on the twenty-first of June? I can tell (it) you, it is the longest day in the year, it rises at 4 o'clock thirty-one minutes. When does it set on the day? It sets at 7 o'clock thirty-one minutes. Is the moon already risen? She (*m.*) is not yet risen. When will she rise? She will rise at half past nine. When the stars had risen we departed (departed we). Do these farmers begin to sow their grain? They begin to sow it. Do you begin to teach your children German? I begin to teach (it) them. Does this little girl begin to learn German? She begins to learn it. Can these French ladies begin to learn *to* cook (cook to learn)? Had the moon risen, when you sailed? She had risen. Will you begin to write? I cannot begin to write, I have no pens, will you give me some? With pleasure, here are some. Now I have pens and shall begin to write immediately. Can your servants rise as early as mine? They can rise earlier. At what o'clock have they risen this morning? They have risen at five minutes past (nach) six. Do the children of these ladies rise early? They do not rise early, they rise late. Why do they rise so late? They rise so late, because they are too idle to rise. Does this physician owe you *any* money? He owes me some. How much does he owe you? He owes me fifty dollars (*sing.*). To whom do you owe this money? I owe it to the one, who has lent it to me. Why do you not pay it to the one, to whom you owe it? Because he will not take it. Do the servants of the Spanish woman open the doors and the windows every morning? They open them every morning and leave them open two hours. When do they shut them? They shut them, when they go to the market. Why do you shut the door? I shut it because it is cold in this room, have you no fire? I have a very good fire, but you are always cold, you remain too much in the (*contract*) warm room. Is the door open? Yes Sir, it is open. Who has opened it? The baker's boy has opened it and has left it open, when he came for (holen) the flour.

83.

Abschreiben, ap''-shri'-ben, to copy; abgeschrieben, ap''-gai-shree'-ben, p. p. copied; wegnehmen, to take away; wiederkommen, ve''-der-kom'-men, to come

again; wiedergekommen, ve′-der-gai-kom′-men, come back, p. p.; zurückkehren, tsoo-rück″-kai′-ren, to return; auffliegen, to fly up; aussuchen, to select; heute Abend, this evening; heute Morgen, this morning; gestern Abend, yesterday (last) evening; gestern Nachmittag, näch″-mit′-tach, yesterday afternoon; morgen früh, to-morrow, morning.

Haben Sie Zeit...zu? have you time to? keine (nicht) Zeit...zu, no time to. Loben Sie (imperat.), praise (you); schreiben Sie...ab, copy; seien Sie, be.* Thun, too'n, to do; gethan, gai′tâ′n′, done.

Instead of *it* and *they*, when these pronouns follow prepositions, and refer to things, we use in German the word there, da; with it, with them, damit, of it, of them, davon, when the preposition commences with a vowel, da is changed to dar; as, darauf, upon it; darin, in it, there in. — In the same manner, wo is used for the relative and interrogative pronouns; as, with what (which), womit; for what (which), wofür; in what (which), worin; the r being inserted for the sake of euphony.

Die Dinte, din′-tai, the ink; gefälligst, gai-fel′-lichst, if you please; also, âl′-zo, therefore; ander, ân′-der, other; der, die, das andere, the other; die andern, the others.

Wollen Sie gefälligst diesen Brief abschreiben? Ich kann ihn nicht abschreiben, ich habe kein Papier, keine Federn und keine Dinte, also womit soll ich ihn abschreiben? Hier ist Papier; Federn und Dinte finden Sie in jenem kleinen hölzernen Kasten, der auf dem großen Tische in Ihrem Zimmer steht. Ich danke Ihnen, jetzt werde ich ihn sogleich abschreiben. Diese Feder ist nicht gut, ich will mir eine andere aussuchen. Haben Sie sich schon Tuch zu einem Rocke ausgesucht? Ich habe mir noch keins ausgesucht, aber ich werde mir sogleich welches aussuchen. Wann kommen diese Bäuerinnen wieder? Sie kommen am siebenten nächsten Monats wieder. Wann werden diese häßlichen alten Frauen nach ihrem schmutzigen Dorfe zurückkehren? Sie werden heute Abend dahin zurückkehren. Wo war Ihr Großvater, als Sie von Amerika zurückkehrten? Er war in Hamburg. Haben Sie Zeit, heute auf das Land zu fahren? Ich habe heute keine Zeit dahin zu fahren, aber morgen Nachmittag werde ich mit Vergnügen mit Ihnen fahren. Geben Sie mir gefälligst einen silbernen Löffel, ich kann nicht mit einem hölzernen essen. Sein Sie so gut und geben Sie mir ein Stück Brod und Butter. Holen Sie mir gefälligst ein Stück Fleisch von dem Markte. Reisen Sie gefälligst gleich ab und kehren Sie nicht mehr hierher zurück. Womit soll ich die Suppe essen? Mit dem Löffel. Worin soll die Köchinn das Fleisch kochen? Sie soll es in Wasser kochen. Essen Sie Ihr Fleisch mit einem Messer? Ich esse es damit. Kleiden diese Bauern sich in Tuch? Sie kleiden sich darin. Ist dies das Haus, wofür Ihre Schwägerin tausend Thaler gegeben hat? Es ist es. Dies ist nicht die Feder womit ich geschrieben habe, es ist eine andere.

84.

Who has copied these letters? My cousins have copied them, are they not well copied? They are not as well copied as those which that little boy has copied, who has only commenced to learn *to* write. Will you please (gefälligst) *to* take away these plates, spoons and knives? I will

* The imperatives of all other verbs, when Sie is used, are like their infinitives.

take them away immediately. Have the little dogs of the old Frenchman who lives in (the) Broad Street come back? They have not come back. When do you return to Germany? I shall return (thither) on the twentieth of July, if I and my wife and my children are well, but if we are not well (so), we shall remain here until the fifteenth of August. When does your father return to (nach) (the) town? He returns to morrow morning. Has the brother of the gardener already returned into the country. He has not yet returned thither. When will these ladies go out? They will go out to morrow morning. Why can they not go out this afternoon? They cannot go out, because they have no time. Copy these lttecrs immediately. Bring me a calf and an ox. Please take these books with *you*, and give them to the brother of the butcher who lives in the next village. Of what shall I make these tables? You must make them of wood. How much money shall I (am I to) give you for these violets? You are to give me five cents for them. . The table for which I have paid you twenty dollars is very handsome. What have you written this letter with? I have written it with the fine ink of which you have given me some. Do not do that? Why not? Because it is not right (recht) to do it. Open this door, why do you not open it when I tell you (it)? Shut the window, it is too cold in this room. Please to come this evening to my house and bring your wife, and your daughters with *you*, we shall have much pleasure. What shall we do? We shall eat and drink and be merry. The house in which you live is larger, than the one in which you lived last year, but it is not so large as that in which your uncle lives, he lives in the largest house of the town. Will you have this beer? No, I will have the other. Will you send me this ink? No, I will send you the other, which is in that wooden box. Will you give this bread to these children? No, I will give it to the others. Is the tailor to make the coat of these soldiers or those of the others. He is to make those of the others.

85.

Dissonant Verbs of the first Class. 1 and 2. (see § 54.)

1.

Schieben, shee'-ben, to push; ich schob, sho'p, I pushed; geschoben, gai-sho'-ben, pushed;
aufschieben, ouf-shee'-ben, to put off; verschieben, ferr-shee'-ben, (insep.) to put out of place;
fliegen, flee'-ghen, to fly; flog, flo'ch; geflogen, gai-flo'-ghen;
verlieren, fer-lee'-ren, to lose; verlor, fer-lo'r'; verloren, fer-lo'-ren;
ziehen, tsee'-hen, to draw; zog, tso'ch; gezogen, gai-tso'-ghen; ausziehen, to undress, to strip; anziehen, to dress, to put on; vorziehen, to prefer, (dat. and acc.)
wiegen, vee'-ghen, to weigh; wog, vo'ch; gewogen, gai-vo'-ghen.

2.

Schießen auf (acc.), shee'-ssen, to fire at, to shoot at; schoß, shoss; geschossen, gai-shos'-sen;
erschießen (insep.), err-shee'-ssen, to shoot (shoot dead); erschoß, err-shoss'; erschossen, err-shos'-sen;

gießen, gee'-ssen, to pour; goß, goss; gegossen, gai-gos'-sen; ausgießen, to pour out; vergießen, ferr-ghee'-ssen, to shed;
riechen, ree'-chen, to smell; roch, roch; gerochen, gai-roch'-chen;
saufen, zou'-fen, to drink (of animals), to be a drunkard; soff, zof; gesoffen, gai-zof'-fen; versaufen (insep.), ferr'-zou''-fen, to spend in drink;
verbieten...zu, ferr-bee'-ten, to forbid to (dat.); verbot, ferr-bo't; verboten, ferr-bo''-ten.

Der Karren, kârr-ren, the wheelborrow, cart; die Strafe, strâ-fai, the punishment, fine; das Bierglas, beer'-gla's, the tumbler; man, mânn, one, people, we, they (3d pers. sing.); alles was, all that; gern, gherrn, willingly; gern lesen, to like to read; gern essen, to like to eat; gern sehen, to like to see.

The adverb gern is treated in the same manner as a separable prefix, and occupies the same place in the sentence.

Der Vogel, fo'-ghel, the bird; der Wagen, vâ'-ghen, the carriage, wagon; die Weste, ves'-tai, waistcoat, vest; der Strumpf, ströömpf, stocking; das Pfund, pfööni, the pound; die Unze, öön'-tzai, the ounce; das Blut, bloo't, blood; die Thräne, trai'-nai, the tear; das Gesetz, gai-sets', the law; die Arbeit, ârr'-bite, work, labor, task; das Volk, fol'k, the people, nation.

Schieben Sie gefälligst Ihren Stuhl an das Fenster. Wer schob den Tisch an das Fenster? Wer hat den Karren geschoben? Der kleine Knabe hat ihn in den Garten geschoben. Hat man seine Strafe aufgeschoben? Man hat sie bis nächsten Monat aufgeschoben. Warum schoben Ihre Töchter ihre Arbeit auf? Sie schoben sie auf weil sie zu träge waren, sie zu thun. Wer hat diese Bücher verschoben? Heinrich hat sie so eben verschoben. Verschieben Sie mir meine Sachen nicht. Wo ist die Taube? Sie ist weggeflogen. Wo ist sie hingeflogen? Sie ist auf das Dach des Nachbars geflogen. Wohin wird sie von dort fliegen? Sie wird auf den Baum, der in dem Garten ist, fliegen. Wie viele Pferde zogen den Wagen? Vier Pferde zogen ihn. Zogen oder schoben die Kinder den Karren? Zuweilen zogen und zuweilen schoben sie ihn. Welches Volk verlor seine Freiheit? Dasjenige welches die Franzosen besiegten. Welchen Rock zog der Graf an? Werden Sie Ihren blauen oder Ihren grünen Rock anziehen. Zog er nicht seine Weste und seinen Rock aus? Wenn ich nach Hause komme ziehe ich meinen Rock aus und ziehe einen alten an. Zog sie ein blaues oder ein weißes Kleid vor? Gestern zog sie ein blaues vor. Zog er es nicht vor in Paris zu wohnen? Wir haben es immer vorgezogen auf dem Lande zu wohnen. Haben die Schlächter dieses Fleisch gewogen? Sie haben es gewogen. Wie viel wog es? Es wog zwanzig Pfund. Wie viel wiegen Sie? Wer schoß auf den Vogel? Der Offizier schoß darauf. Wer hat diesen tapfern Soldaten erschossen? Goß der Brauer das Bier in das Faß? Er goß es hinein. Warum vergoß diese liebenswürdige Dame so viele Thränen? Weil man ihren Mann, den Offizier erschossen hatte. Können Sie nicht riechen was man hier kocht? Ich kann es nicht riechen. Riechen die Rosen und Veilchen, die man in jenem Garten gepflanzt hatte, nicht sehr schön? Von einem Thiere, sagt man, es säuft, von einem Menschen, er trinkt. Auch sagt man von einem Menschen, der zu viel Wein oder Bier trinkt, er säuft. Was ist aus dem Enkel dieses alten Tischlers geworden? Er verlor viel Geld, versoff noch mehr und ging (went) dann nach Amerika. Wer hat Ihnen verboten auf den Markt zu gehen? Mein Oheim hat mir verboten dahin zu gehen. Verboten Sie Ihrem Sohne in die Armee zu gehen? Ich verbot es ihm. Warum hat man seine Strafe aufgeschoben? Man schob sie auf, weil er krank war. Zog oder schob der Bauer den Karren? Zuweilen zog er denselben, zuweilen schob er ihn. Was sagt man Neues? Man sagt nichts Neues.

86.

Who pushed the wheelbarrow? The gardener pushed it. Where did he push it? In the garden? Where did he push it to? Into the garden. You have pushed all the tables out of place. Has not the punishment of this soldiers been put off until (bis zu) the first of (the) next month? It has been put off until the last of (the) next month. Did the birds fly on the roofs? They flew on the trees and not on the roofs of the houses. What will the bird do when you fire at it? It will fly away. My dear Sir, can you lent me some money, for I have lost all mine? Do you prefer roast meat to boiled meat? I prefer that to this. Do the ladies (es) prefer going to the country? They prefer going there (thither). Did you prefer the roses to the violets? No, we preferred violets to roses. Do not the farmers prefer good vegetables to bad meat? What will one do with the soldier who has beaten his officer? He will be shot (one will shoot him). When will they shoot him? They will shoot him the fifth of next month. What have they done to the officer who has betrayed his country? They have shot him in the garden of the Dutchman. Throw (pour) out the water which is in the big cask. Pour the water into the tumbler. This lady shed many tears when she heard that they (one) had killed her brother and her husband. Who has shed the blood of this innocent man? The French soldiers have shed it. The king will kill all those who shed innocent blood. Forbid your daughter to go out. Why do these washer-women forbid the servants of your aunt to speak to (mit) our seamstress, who is a very good and industrious young woman? They do not forbid them to speak to her, but she will not speak to them, because she is too tired. Does this man drink (to excess)? He drinks always. He spends all his money in drink. What has the tailor done with the money we paid him for the coat? He has spent it in drink. Has he forbidden you to make a noise. He forbade us to make a noise, when he wanted to write his letters, afterwards, (nachher) he told us, we might make as much noise as we wanted *to make.*

87.

DISSONANT VERBS OF THE SECOND CLASS. (See § 52.

Pfeifen, pfi'-fen, to whistle; pfiff, pfif, whistled; gepfiffen, gai-pfif'-fen, whistled;

greifen (nach), gri'-fen, to seize, to grasp at; griff, grif; gegriffen, gai-grif'-fen; angreifen, an''-gri'-fen, to attack; ergreifen, err-gri'-fen, to lay hold of, to seize;

reißen, ri'-ssen, to pull; riß, riss; gerissen, gai-ris'-sen; zerreißen, tser-ri'-ssen, to tear; abreißen, åp''-ri'-ssen, to tear off;

schreiben, an (acc.) shri'-ben, to write to; schrieb, shreep; geschrieben, gai-shree'-ben;
leihen, li'-hen, to lend; lieh, lee; geliehen, gai-lee'-hen;
schreien, shri'-en, to scream, cry; schrie, shree; geschrien, gai-shree'-en;
schneiden, shni'-den, to cut; schnitt, shnit; geschnitten, gai-shnit'-ten; zerschneiden, tzer-shni''-den, to cut to pieces, to cut up.

Anstatt zu schreiben, ân-stât', insteat of writing; gern mögen, to like; ich mag gern, ma'ch, I like; gern, willingly; lieber, more willingly, rather; am liebsten, most willingly; während, during, whilst (sends the verb to the end, when it is a conjunction); so, zo, thus, in this manner; spielen, spee'-len, to play; Branntwein, brânt'-vine', brandy; laut, lout, aloud; der Schüler, shü'-ler, the pupil; der Lehrer, lay'-rer, the teacher; die Aufgabe, ouf''-gâ'-bai, the exercise; die Gelegenheit, gai-lai'-ghen-hite; der Matrose, mâ-tro'-zai, the sailor.

Wer hat gepfiffen? Der Soldat hat gepfiffen. Pfiff der Matrose als die Vögel sangen? Er pfiff lustig. Wann griffen die Feinde das Dorf an? Sie griffen es um halb fünf Uhr des Morgens an. Wie viele Male haben die Feinde schon angegriffen? Sie haben schon dreimal angegriffen und wir haben sie jedes Mal geschlagen. Gute Kinder zerreißen nicht ihre Bücher. Wer hat dieses Papier zerrissen? Der ungeschickte Knabe Ihres Nachbars hat es zerrissen. Was that der Kaufmann mit den Briefen, die er erhalten hatte? Er zerriß sie anstatt sie zu lesen. Warum zerreißt das kleine Mädchen ihre Bücher? Sie zerreißt sie, weil sie nicht gerne lernt. Mag sie lieber nähen als lernen? Sie mag weder nähen noch lernen, sie mag nur spielen. Mögen diese Kinder lieber Kaffee als Thee? Sie mögen lieber Kaffee. Trinken diese Matrosen lieber Bier als Wein? Sie trinken lieber Wein als Bier, aber sie trinken am liebsten Branntwein. Schreiben die jungen Prinzessinnen lieber als daß sie lesen? Sie lesen lieber als daß sie schreiben. Wer hat diese Blumen abgerissen? Niemand hat sie abgerissen, aber die Kuh hat sie abgefressen. Was that der Knabe während Sie Ihre Briefe schrieben? Er schrieb Briefe ab. Soll ich einen Brief an Herrn Simms in London schreiben? Ja, Sie können heute an ihn schreiben und ihm sagen, daß das Volk die Soldaten angegriffen hat. Wer lieh Ihrem Vetter immer Geld als er in Paris war? Ein reicher Bäcker lieh ihm welches. Haben Sie ihm das Geld, welches er Ihnen geliehen hat, zurück bezahlt? Ich habe es ihm schon voriges Jahr zurückbezahlt. Was thaten die Kinder, während die Witwe des tapfern Offiziers weinte? Sie schrieen so laut sie konnten. Was thaten die Matrosen als sie besoffen waren? Sie schrieen und machten viel Geräusch. Schreiben Ihre Schüler lieber als daß sie spielen? Sie mögen lieber spielen als schreiben.

188.

Why do you whistle so loud? I cannot work here. I shall not whistle *any* more, give me the book, if you please, and I shall copy the letters which you have written. I must request you not to whistle, I do not like to hear it. The birds whistled very loud and flew away. Whistle Sir, and I will come to you. The bird has whistled until he was tired. The child grasps at (every thing) (allem). They seized the soldier and sent him to the army. Why did the painter's son seize a stick? He seized one in order to beat the dog. Where was the dog? He was in the room of the painter. Have you already found an opportunity to write to (an, acc.) your friend in London? I have not yet found an opportunity to write to him, but I shall seize the first opportunity of doing so (it to do) which I can find. I seize this opportunity to tell you that the tea which you have sent me is not so good as that, which you sent me last month. If the enemy attack us, we are (so are we) lost. The enemy attacked us three times (an, dat.) in one day, and every time we fled. When the soldier said this to the sailor, the latter seized a sword and attacked him, but the former (that one) fled into the garden, and shut the door. Does your sister learn her exercise? No Miss, instead of learning her exercise, she tears her books and cuts up her paper with your knife. What has the tailor done? He has cut up my new coat. Did he cut it up when you were in the room? No, he cut it up when we were in the garden. Did you ride every day (acc.) into the country when you were living in (the) town? Where were you riding to yesterday? I was riding to my uncle, who lives in B. and who has there a very handsome house and large garden, in which *there* are apples and pears. To whom did you lend your money when you were in Hamburg? I lent it to those friends, who had often lent me some when I was poor and had nothing. Do not scream so, why do you scream so? That sailor has attacked me with a big stick. Why did he scream? He screamed because he had lost all his money. Why did the child scream? It screamed because its mother had gone out. What is the servant doing? He is boiling the soup instead of roasting the meat. Was the farmer working in the field? Instead of working in the field, he rode to (the) town. Do you like riding better than driving? I like riding better than driving when it is not too warm. Do you prefer reading (lesen Sie lieber) German or French books? I prefer reading German books. Do you prefer living in the country or in the town? Do you prefer beef or mutton? I like beef very well, but I prefer veal. What do you like (to eat) best? I like a good piece *of* beef and a good piece *of* bread best. Had the pupil made his exercise? He had made it, but it was so badly written, that he was obliged (mußte) to copy it.

89.

Dissonant Verbs of the Third Class. (§ 50, p. 34.)

Those which have e in the infinitive, have o in the past particle, and those which have i in the infinitive, have u in the past part. (See obs. p. 35.)

1.

Finden, fin′-den, to find; fand, fânt, gefunden, gai-fōōn′-den; erfinden, err-fin′-den, to invent, to find out; wiederfinden, to find again; binden, bin′-den, to bind; singen, zing′-en, to sing; anbinden, ân″-bin′-den, to tie to, (mit) to attach; trinken, trink′-en, to drink; austrinken, ouss-trink′-en, to finish (drinking).

2.

Sprechen, sprech′chen, to speak; sprach, sprâ′ch; gesprochen, gai-sproch′-chen; versprechen, fer-sprech′-chen, to promise; aussprechen, ous″-sprech′-chen, to pronounce.—Nehmeu, nai′-men, to take; nahm, nâ′m; genommen, gai-nom′-men; Imp. nimm, nim. Annehmen, ân″-nai′-men, to accept, to suppose;

die Maschine, mâ-shee′-nai, the machine; die Dampfmaschine, dâmpf″-mâ-shee′-nai, the steam-engine; die Uhr, oo′r, the watch, clock; die Taschenuhr, tâsh′-shen-oo′r, the watch. Was für ein, vâs fü′rr ine, what kind of a; füllen, (reg.) fül′-len, to fill.

Was haben Sie gefunden? Ich habe nichts gefunden. Fanden die Damen eine Börse als sie in der Stadt waren? Sie fanden eine goldene. Wer hat die Taschenuhren erfunden? Hele hat sie erfunden. Was für eine Maschine hat dieser Mann erfunden? Er hat eine Dampfmaschine erfunden. Er erfand sie während er in Deutschland war. Ich hatte mein Buch verloren aber ich habe es wiedergefunden. Fanden die Bäuerinnen die Gänse die sie suchten? Sie fanden sie in ihrem Dorfe. Wo bindet der kleine Preuße sein Pferd an? Er bindet es an den großen Baum, der vor unserm Hause steht. Waren die Bücher gebunden? Sie waren gebunden, der Buchbinder hatte sie schon vorige Woche gebunden. Was tranken die Matrosen als sie in Ihrem Hause waren? Sie tranken Branntwein. Warum trinken Sie Ihre Gläser nicht aus, meine Herren? Wir danken Ihnen, wir haben schon zu viel getrunken. Meine Herren, trinken Sie gefälligst Ihre Gläser aus und füllen Sie sie wieder. Was für Wein ist dies? Es ist Rheinwein. Was für Briefe sind dies? Dies sind die Briefe, die von England gekommen sind. Was für ein Haus haben Sie in dieser Straße gekauft? Was für einen Tisch hat der Tischler Ihnen gemacht? Was für eine Uhr hat er Ihnen geschenkt? Er hat mir eine schöne goldene Uhr geschenkt. Sprach der Preuße deutsch oder französisch zu Ihnen? Er sprach englisch zu mir. Haben Sie schon mit dem russischen Kaufmanne, der hier gestern angekommen ist, gesprochen? Versprechen Sie mir, nicht auszugehen. Was für Geld versprach Ihnen die Tante? Sie versprach uns Goldgeld. Dieser Mann hat das Pulver nicht erfunden.*

90.

What kind of water did you find in England. We found very good water. Did I find a gold watch when I was in England? Who invented (the) looking glasses? When did Hele of Nurnberg invent the watc es? He invented them in the year 1510. Has your brother invented this wooden machine? He has not invented it, but my uncle has invented it. Have these carpenters found the wood again, which they had lost? They have found it again in the village in which our baker's mother lives. Where did your sister find her gold watch again? She found it again in the school. Are the books of which our teacher was speaking, bound or unbound? They are all well bound. Can you tie up this calf? Yes, I can tie it to this iron ring which is here below (unter, dat.) the window. Who has invented the powder? Schwarz, a German (nom.) has invented it. Where did the soldiers tie up their horses? They tied them up in the marked. When you were in the Russian army, did you find that the Germans drank as much as the Russians? I found that the Germans drank more beer and more wine, and the Russians more brandy. When these old soldiers had finished their glasses we filled them again *for* them.

* Equivalent to the English proverb, this man will never set the Thames on fire.

(dat.) Will you fill this barrel with beer, when you shall have poured out the water which is in it now? Did the Englishman speak German to you? No, he always speaks English to me, he cannot *speak* much German. What where you speaking off (von)? We were speaking of the watch which your sister had found in the church. He pronounces French very well, but not so well as his eldest sisters, who pronounces it as well as a French woman. What did the officer promise you when you showed him, where the village was? He promised me five dollars, but he has not yet given them to me. Please take a glass *of* wine, Sir. I thank you Sir, I have taken one just now. The poor women accepted the money which was offered to them. Has your grandfather accepted the castle, which the King of Prussia offered to him? Will you take three dollars for this cloth? No, I cannot take less than four.

91.

Fourth Class of dissonant Verbs. (§ 50, p. 35.)

Fahren, fâ'-ren, to drive in a carriage; fuhr, foo'rr; gefahren, gai-fâ'-ren, driven; ausfahren, ouss''-fâ'-ren, to take a drive; erfahren, err-fâ'-ren, to learn, to hear, to experience; geben, gai'-ben, to give; gab, gâ'p; gegeben, gai-gai'-ben; vergeben, ferr-gai'-ben, to forgive (dat.); ausgeben, ouss''-gai'-ben, to spend, give out; ich aß, â'ss, I ate; lesen, lai'-zen, to read; las, lâ'ss; gelesen, gai-lai'-zen; er lies't leest, he reads; vorlesen, fore''-lai'-zen, to read aloud to (dat.); bitten, bit'-ten, to pray, to request; bat, bâ't; gebeten, gai-bai'-ten; bitten um, to ask for; sehen, zey'-hen, to see; sah, zâ, gesehen, gai-zai'-hen, seen; aussehen, ous''-zai'-hen, to look; ich briet, breet, roasted; schlafen, shlâ'-fen, to sleep; schlief, shleef; geschlafen, gai-shlâ'-fen; ich fing an, fing ân, I commenced; ich ließ, leess, I let, left, allowed, got, had; er läßt, lest, he lets (see obs. p. 36.).

Die Gabel, gâ'-bel, the fork; die Lektion, leck'-tse-o'n', the lesson; nöthig haben, nö'-tich, to require; der Stein, stine, the stone; die Tasse, tâs'-sai; the cup; die Zeitung, tsi'-tööng, newspaper; täglich, taich'-lich, daily; monatlich, mo'-nâ't-lich, monthly; erst, eyrrst, only, not untill.

Wo fuhren Sie hin als ich Sie sah? Wir fuhren nach B.... um dort zu Mittag zu essen. Fahren Sie gern? Ich fahre gern aber meine Schwester reitet lieber. Sind Sie heute Morgen ausgefahren? Wir sind nicht heute, aber gestern Morgen ausgefahren. Hat der General schon erfahren daß der Feind geschlagen ist? Er hat es so eben erfahren. Darf ich Sie bitten, mir ein Stück Brod und eine Tasse Thee zu geben? Mit Vergnügen mein Herr. Hat seine Mutter ihm nicht vergeben? Sie hat ihm nicht vergeben und wird ihm nie vergeben. Was gab der Bediente diesen Herren? Er gab jedem ein Messer, eine Gabel und einen Löffel. Wie viel Geld geben Sie täglich aus? Ich gebe täglich einen Thaler aus, aber mein Vetter, der eine Frau und fünf Kinder hat, giebt täglich sechs Thaler aus. Wann aßen Sie zu Mittag, als Sie in London waren? Ich aß immer um drei Uhr, aber meine Brüder aßen erst um fünf Uhr zu Mittag. Was haben diese Knaben heute gegessen? Sie haben alles gegessen was wir gegessen haben. Lasen Sie als wir ankamen? Wir lasen nicht, aber wir schrieben. Hatten Ihre Nichten das Buch, welches ich ihnen geschickt habe, schon gelesen? Sie hatten es schon zweimal gelesen.

Meine Tochter lies't mir jeden Abend vor. Wollen Sie mir gefälligst etwas vorlesen? Darf ich Sie bitten mir etwas vorzulesen? Die Kinder baten den Vater um ein Stück Brod und er gab ihnen einen Stein. Wie sah der Offizier aus? Er sah gesund aus. Wie wird die Armee aussehen, wenn sie aus dem Felde kommt? Schliefen die Mägde als Sie in die Küche traten? Sie schliefen alle. Wie lange habe ich geschlafen? Sie haben keine Stunde geschlafen. Haben Sie Zeit auf das Land zu gehen? Wir haben Zeit aber keine Lust dahin zu gehen. Lassen Sie uns nach Hause gehen. Lassen Sie das Feuer nicht ausgehen. Haben die englischen Damen ihr Ochsenfleisch kochen oder braten lassen? Ließen sie ihre Kinder in die Schule gehen?

92.

Do you like (mögen) driving *in a carriage* better, than riding *on horseback?* I like neither riding nor driving, I like walking. Where were you driving to yesterday? I was driving to my friend, the merchant, who has a handsome country-house in the village *of* S. Have (sind) you driven out to-day to P...? I have driven with my intended to P.... This old man has experienced much. The officers of the army have just learned that they must all depart to-morrow. Yesterday I learned that my brother had died (gestorben sei). Have you learned nothing new in the market? What did the farmer give the lame soldier? He gave him a cent. Has your father forgiven you? He has forgiven me. Will you not forgive those who hate you? Forgive me, I shall not do it again. What did you spend, when you were travelling in France? I spent 3 dollars a day. Did you read much, when you were in Germany? I read the whole day and half the (the half) night. Will you read this good book? I cannot read it, please read it to me. I was reading to my old uncle, when you and your little cousin came into the room, and brought your dog with *you*. I request you to lent me that book. I cannot lend it to you to-day, I have promised it to my aunt. The poor soldiers begged the rich merchants to give them some bread, but they did not give them any. May I ask you for a little soup? May I ask you to let me sleep (me sleep to let)? You have slept enough, it is time to rise and to learn your lesson, How does the general look? He looks like his brother, the doctor. I asked him for a glass of limonade and he brought me a glass of brandy. What is the neighbour's servant doing? He is reading. What is he reading? He is reading the history of France. What were you reading when I was eating my dinner? I was reading the newspaper. What are you in want of? I am in want of money (require). Who is in want of boots and shoes? The children of these poor peasants are in want of them. Are you not in want of a cup *of* tea or *of* coffee? I am much (sehr) in want of a cup of coffee, for I am very cold. How does your grand-father look? He looks old, and is almost (beinahe) lame. Do you let your son go out every day? I let him go out when he is good and industrious. What did you send for? I send for beer and wine. Whom did you send for (rufen lassen)? I send for Doctor P...

93.

Kennen, ken'-nen, to know, to be acquainted with; ich kannte, kân'-tai, I knew; gekannt, known.

Senden, sen'-den, to send; sandte, sân'-tai, gesandt. (see § 53.)

IRREGULAR VERBS. (see § 54.)

Wissen, vis'-sen, to know; wußte, vöös'-tai; gewußt, gai-vööst'; ich weiß, vi'ss, I know; ich wußte, vööss-tai, I knew.

Kennen implies a knowledge derived from having seen a person or thing. Ich kenne den Mann, das Haus, das Pferd, weil ich ihn, es gesehen habe; wissen implies a knowledge obtained by having heard of an event, or by having studied a thing; the latter is often followed by the conjunction daß. Ich weiß daß er todt ist. Ich weiß meine Lection.

Ich mußte, möös'-tai, I was obliged; ich durfte, döörf'-tai; ich konnte, kon'-tai, I could; ich mochte, moch'-tai, I liked, might; ich wollte, vol'-tai, I wanted to, would; ich sollte, zol'-tai, I was to, I should; ich brachte, brâch'-tai, I brought; ich that, tâ't, I did; ich ging, ging, I went; stehen, stey'-hen, to stand; stand, stânt; gestanden, gai-stân'-den, stood (aux. haben); denken (an, acc.), denk'-en, to think of; dachte, dâch'-tai; gedacht, gai-dâcht'.

Beinahe, bi-nâ'-hai; fast, fâst, almost, nearly; einem begegnen (reg.), bai-gaich'-nen, to meet a person; (dat., aux. sein), ich bin ihm, ihr, ihnen begegnet,* I have met him (her, them); kosten, kos'-ten, to cost, to taste; da, dâ, as, since; die Kartoffel, kârr-tof'-fel, the potatoe; der Mitmensch, mit'-mensh, the fellow creature; durch, döörch, through (acc.); aus, ouss, out (dat.); das Haar, hâ'rr, the hair.

Kennen Sie diesen Franzosen? Ich kenne ihn. Kannten Sie ihn schon als Sie in Frankreich waren? Wissen Sie wie alt der König von England ist? Ich weiß es nicht, aber ich kann es von meinem Lehrer erfahren. Wußten diese Damen daß der Präsident angekommen ist? Sie wußten es nicht. Wissen Ihre Schüler und Schülerinnen ihre Lectionen? Einige wissen sie und andere wissen sie nicht. Als er fand, daß er sein Geld verloren hatte, mußte er nach Amerika gehen. Da die Köchinn kein Ochsenfleisch hatte, mußte sie Kalbfleisch kochen. Was mußte die Köchinn des Kaufmanns thun? Sie mußte Kalbfleisch braten, Kartoffeln kochen und Brod backen. Durften die Bedienten ausgehen, wenn sie wollten? Mochten Sie gern reiten als sie jung waren? Ich mochte lieber reiten als fahren. Ich wollte eben ausgehen, als meine Freunde hereintraten. Sie sollten dieses nicht thun, es ist unrecht. Wir sollten unsere Mitmenschen lieben und nicht hassen. Was brachten Sie mit, als Sie von Californien kamen? Ich brachte viel Gold mit. Was that Ihr Sohn, als Sie nach Hause kamen? Er sah aus dem Fenster. Warum gingen diese Mädchen nicht aus? Sie gingen nicht aus, weil man es ihnen verboten hatte. Woran denkt dieser Herr? Er denkt an seine Braut und dieses Mädchen denkt an ihren Bruder. Wir haben oft an Sie gedacht, während Sie in Deutschland waren. Ich kann fast so gut schreiben wie er, aber er kann besser lesen. Er hat beinahe so viel Geld wie sein Bruder, der Buchbinder. Ich bin meinem Oheim in der Heinrichsstraße begegnet. Wir begegnen diesen Damen alle Tage in der Straße. Wo gingen Sie gestern hin als ich ihnen auf dem Markte begegnete.

* We also say, er ist mir begegnet, he has met me.

94.

Did you know this German teacher when you where in Germany? I knew him very well, I have known (pres. tense) him *these* (already) three years, he is a very industrious man. Did you know (have you known) my grand-father? I did know him, he was a tall (groß) man, and had white hair and blue eyes, I often met (perf. t.) him at the exchange and in the church. Does your tailor know how much this cloth costs? He does not know it. Do you know when your father will return from France? I know it, but I dare not tell you, as no one must (dürfen) know it. What kind of goods did you send to France? We sent there coffee and tea. Have you sent any powder to London? The king will send this count to Russia to ask for the hand (die Hand) of the princess. Did you like to go to the country, when you lived in Canada? I liked it much. Why did you not bring your daughter with you? I did not like to do it. Could these men not come earlier? They were obliged to stay at home. I wanted to go out, but I could not, I had no boots. What was I to do? I had no money, no friends, nothing to eat and no clothes. These kind ladies brought these poor soldiers daily something to eat and to drink. What were you doing in the country? I was buying oxen and calves in order to kill them. What did your brother do in this house? He was learning German. Where were your sisters going, when I met them yesterday? They were going to church. When we saw you yesterday, you were standing in the door of the exchange. Have you not met the queen? I have met her in the door of the church. Many sailors were standing on the roofs of the houses, when the king rode *on horseback* through the streets. Should we hate our fellow men, because they do not think (so) as we *do*. Can you not eat any potatoes? I cannot eat them, they make me sick, if they did not make me sick, (so) I should eat them three times a day (des Tags). Did the man, whom you were looking for, come out of this house, or out of that? He came neither out of this nor out of that, he came out of the garden of the English merchant.

95.

When the principal verb of a conditional sentence is in the 1st conditional or in the imperfect of the subj., the verb expressing the condition after wenn, is in the imperfect or pluperfect of the subj. When the principal verb is in the 2d conditional or in the pluperfect of the subj., the dependent verb is in the pluperfect of the subj. (For the formation of these tenses see § 44 and 65.)

When the dependent verb precedes the principal verb, the nominative of the latter is placed after the verb and the word so may be placed before it.

Ich (wäre zufrieden) würde zufrieden sein wenn ich genug hätte.	I should be satisfied if I had enough.
Sie (wären) würden nicht so lustig sein, wenn Sie so viel wie ich gelitten hätten.	You would not be so merry, if you had suffered as much as I.
Ich (wäre zufrieden gewesen) würde zufrieden gewesen sein, wenn ich genug gehabt hätte.	I should have been satisfied, if I had had enough.
Wenn ich genug hätte, (so) würde ich zufrieden sein (wäre ich zufrieden).	If I had enough, I should be satisfied.

Ich würde, I should; wir würden, we should;
er würde, he would; Sie würden, you would;
sie würden, they would.
würde, vürr'-dai; würden, vürr'-den.

Vor Gram, grâ'm, with grief; vor Freude, froi'-dai, with joy; das Wetter vet'-ter, the weather; die Nase, nâ'-zai, the nose.

Ich würde Geld genug haben, wenn ich es nicht ausgegeben hätte. Mein Vater würde zufrieden sein, wenn er seine Kinder glücklich sähe. Diese Kühe würden fett werden, wenn sie Heu genug hätten. Diese junge Witwe würde den Tischler lieben, wenn er nicht so häßlich wäre. Wenn mein Sohn französisch spräche, so würde er nach Frankreich gehen. Ich stürbe vor Gram, wenn ich meine Kinder verlöre. Sie würde nicht so liebenswürdig sein, wenn sie nicht eine so liebenswürdige Mutter gehabt hätte. Was würden diese Grafen gethan haben, wenn man sie geschlagen hätte? Sie würden diejenigen, die sie geschlagen hätten, getödtet haben. Wenn diese Franzosen Brod gehabt hätten, so würden sie keine Kartoffeln gegessen haben.

96.

The cook would roast his meat, if he had any wood. I should rise immediately, if I were not sick. My father would go (travel) to Germany, if he spoke German. I could (imp. subj.) make a watch, if I had time. These ladies could remain here, if they wanted. I should die with grief, if my mother did not love me. If we had a carriage and horses, we should take a drive every day into the country. These young ladies would not know so much, if they had not been in so good a school (a so good). I should have remained in my room, if the weather had not been so fine. The bride would have gone with us, if she had had her bonnet. If you had put (thun) more sugar into the tea, it would have been too sweet. Had the pupils learned their lessons, their teachers would not have punished them? What army would have conquered the enemy, if ours had not done it. Would the sailors drink the wine which is on board of their ship, if they were thirsty and had no water? Would you not have sent for the physician if your daughter had become (geworden wäre) sick? I should have sent for him. The countess would have died with joy, if she had known that the count was (subj.) safe. The mother would have wept with joy, if she had found her daughter innocent. The soldiers would have set fire to the house, if they had known that the officers of the enemy (feindlich, adj.) were in it. If I had meat and vegetables, I should cook a soup for these wretched women, but I have nothing but a little weak tea and a piece *of* hard bread, which I give them willingly. If I were not so tired, I should go out and buy a piece of ham. Would not the whole army and the whole country have admired our general, if he had beaten the enemy, that was much stronger? This dog would have died if the neighbor's little girl had not given him some thing to eat. This washer-woman would not have brought back the clothes, if you had not sent for them to-day. The eyes of your pupil (*f.*) would not be so red, if she had not cried so much. This old shoemaker would not have so red a nose, if he had not drunk so much brandy. The little bird would still be alive (live), if these boys had not thrown a stone at it and had killed it. I should come to *see* you some times, if I knew at what o'clock I should find (subj. imp.) you at home.

97.

To accustom the pupil to use the person pron. Sie, you, sing. and plur. and to avoid confusion, we have not before introduced the second person singular du and the plural ihr; in the following exercise "thou" will be translated by du, and "you" by ihr. (See the formation of these persons § 47.)

INDICATIVE.

Present.

Du hast, doo ha'st, thou hast;	ihr habt, hâ'pt, you have;
du bist, bist, thou art;	ihr seid, zite, you are;
du wirst, virrst, thou wilt;	ihr werdet, you will;
du liebst, leepst, thou lovest;	ihr liebt, you love.

Imperfect.

Du hattest, hât'-test, thou hadst;	ihr hattet, hât'-tet, you had;
du warst, vâ'rst, thou wast;	ihr waret, vâ'-ret, you were;
du wurdest, vöör'-dest, thou becamest;	ihr wurdet, vöör'-det, you became;
du liebtest, leep'-test, thou lovedst;	ihr liebtet, leep'-tet, you loved.

Imper. habe, hâ'-bai; sei, zi; werde, verr'-dai; liebe, lee'-bai;
habet, hâ'-bet; seid, zite, werdet, verr'-det; liebet, lee'-bet.

SUBJUNCTIVE.

Imperfect.

Du hättest, het'-test, thou hadst;	ihr hättet, het'-tet, you had;
du seiest, zi'-est, thou beest;	ihr seiet, zi'-et, you be;
du würdest, vürr'-dest, thou becamest;*	ihr würdet, vürr'-det, you became;
du liebtest, leep'-test, thou lovedst;	ihr liebetet, lee'-bai-tet, you loved.

Dein,† dine, thy; euer,† oir, your; der deinige,‡ di'-ne-gai, thine; der eurige,‡ oi'-re-gai, yours? dich, dich, thee; dir, deer, to thee; euch, oich, you, to you.

Meine Tochter, du hast heute deine Lection nicht gelernt, morgen mußt du sie besser lernen. Meine Kinder, wenn ihr heute eure Aufgaben gut macht, so sollt ihr diesen Nachmittag mit mir und eurer Mutter aufs Land fahren. Ihr seid noch nicht fleißig genug, ihr müßt fleißiger sein. Du wirst morgen mit deiner Schwester und deinem Oheime nach England reisen. Mein Sohn, du magst lieber spielen als arbeiten. Geliebte Freunde und Nachbarn, ihr seid hungrig und durstig, esset und trinket. O Gott, zu dir bete ich, dich bitte ich um mein tägliches Brod. Wenn ihr todt wäret würdet ihr nichts mehr nöthig haben. Wenn du eine Gelegenheit findest an deinen Bruder zu schreiben, so thue es. Kinder, ihr würdet eure Aufgaben besser gemacht haben, wenn ihr nicht immer an das Spielen gedacht hättet. Warum schreibt ihr eure Aufgaben nicht heute Abend, morgen werdet ihr keine Zeit haben, und dann werden euer Lehrer und euer Vater mit euch unzufrieden sein. Wer hat dir dieses schöne Buch geschenkt? Meine gute Tante hat es mir geschenkt. Seid ihr taub, ich habe euch schon mehrere Male gerufen. Du kleines Thier, komm doch ein wenig her zu mir.

* wouldst, shouldst, &c. † declined like mein, see § 37. ‡ declined like der gute.

98.

Thou art a good boy, give me thy (the) hand. How old art thou? How many brothers and sisters hast thou? What is thy father? *Doest* thou go to school? Who teaches thee (acc.) *to* read? Who gives thee (dat.) something to eat? Does thou love thy teacher, thy father and thy mother? Does not thy teacher praise thee? Wilt thou not be a great man? If thou art industrious, thou will become a great and good man, every lady will love thee. Children, if you are good (artig), I will tell you this evening a very pretty story of a lion and a soldier. You ought to love your fellow men. You have lost a fine opportunity to do something good. Who has shown thee this handsome bird? The farmer's son has shown it to me. Who has made you the blue vest which you wear? My tailor has made it *for* me. Who has forbidden thee to go out? Thy father has forbidden thee to depart and has ordered my sister (dat.) to remain. Thou wouldst die, if thou atest of this meat. Thou wouldst have lost thy money, if thou hadst gone to America. You would have cried, if you had seen the wretched old people without clothes, without any thing to eat.

99.

The Passive Voice. (see § 63.)

The passive voice is formed by adding to the verb werden, in all its tenses, the past participle of the verb to be conjugated. After the passive voice the preposition von is used for by, sometimes durch.

Artig, ärr'-tich, well-behaved, good; unartig, bad, (of a child), impolite; bestrafen, bai'-strâ-fen, to punish; strenge, streng'-ai, severely; belohnen, bai-lo'-nen, to reward.

Wird der gute Knabe belohnt? Er wird von seinen Lehrern belohnt. Von wem wird das Feuer angemacht? Es wird von dem Bedienten angemacht. Sind Sie für das was Sie gethan haben, bezahlt worden? Ich bin dafür bezahlt worden. Wurden Sie nicht geliebt, während ihr Bruder gehaßt wurde? Wurden diese Mädchen nicht immer gut empfangen, wenn sie zu ihrem Vetter kamen? Wurde das Fleisch gebraten oder gekocht? Es wurde weder gebraten noch gekocht. Wird dieser träge Mensch aus der Stadt geschickt werden? Würden diese Kinder belohnt werden, wenn sie ihre Arbeit nicht gethan hätten? Würden die Mägde bestraft worden sein, wenn sie die Tassen nicht zerbrochen hätten? Diese Maschine ist von einem Franzosen erfunden worden. War der Arzt schon geholt worden als der Vater ankam? Waren die Kühe noch nicht gefüttert worden, als die Sonne unterging? Das Gras war noch nicht gemähet worden, als das Wetter schon sehr kalt wurde. Was sagte dieser Mensch als er getödtet wurde? Er sagte daß er unschuldig wäre. Die Soldaten sagten, daß sie schuldig wären, als sie bestraft wurden. Von wem sind diese Briefe erhalten worden? Sie sind von meinem Sohne durch einen Bauern erhalten worden. Von wem bist du zu Hause gebracht worden? Diese armen kleinen Kinder werden von diesem Kaufmanne gekleidet. Diese schönen großen Bäume sind von meinem Großvater im Jahre ein tausend sieben hundert und sechs und sechszig, gepflanzt worden. Er ist zum Könige gemacht worden.

100.

By whom are these children brought (holen) from school? By the servant. Are you loved by your fellow men? I do nothing (in order) to be hated by them. It is not enough, that you do nothing to be hated by them, you ought to do something to be loved by them. Is the little boy (being) rewarded when he does his work well? He is rewarded. By whom is he rewarded? By his teachers. By whom were these houses (being) sold? They were sold by the old uncle of our mason. Were you not betrayed, when you were in Paris? I was betrayed by the court. How many soldiers were killed on (an, dat.) that day? More then three thousand men (Mann, sing.) were killed. This watch has been made by me, John Peters. These pupils have been severely punished, because they had not made their exercises and had not learned their lessons. The good children have been rewarded and the bad children have been punished by their father and their mother. Have these potatoes been eaten by you or by the little Dutchman? I do not know by whom these clothes have been torn. This door will be opened by you every morning and be shut every evening. His punishment will be put off till the seventeenth of this month. Thou wilt be called immediately by the master. If they had need of the servant, he would be called. I should be admired, if I were as handsome as this young lady. If they lived in the country they would be admired. If they had been betrayed, they would have been killed by the Germans and Englishmen. Could not these Frenchmen be sent out of the town? They would be sent to France, for they have betrayed the country.

101.

The Reflective Verb. (see § 64 and 65.)

Sich beklagen über, sich bai-klâ'-ghen ü'-ber (acc.), to complain of; sich schlagen,* mit, to fight with; sich freuen über, froi'-en, to rejoice at; sich ärgern über, err'-ghern, to fret about; sich täuschen, in (dat.), toi'-shen, to deceive one's self in, to be deceived; sich verwundern über (acc.), to be astonished at; sich ankleiden, ân''-kli'-den, to dress one's self; sich entkleiden, ent-kli'-den, to undress; sich befinden, bai-fin'-den, to be (in health), to find one's self; sich wehthun, vey'-toon (with the dative); sich schmeicheln, (dat.) to flatter one's self; sich vergeben, fer-gai'-ben, (dat.) to forgive one's self.

Das Betragen, bai-trâ'-ghen, the conduct; die Rückkehr, rück'-kair, the return; der Geizhals, gites'-hâls, the miser; Ihre Frau Gemahlinn, gal-mâ'-lin, your good lady; Ihr Fräulein Schwester, your sister; der Verlust, ferr-lööst', the loss; das Vaterland, fâ'-ter-lând, the native land.

Ich binde mich an diesen Baum. Er beklagte sich über seine Frau. Du schlugst dich mit dem Buchdrucker. Die Tante freute sich über das Kleid, welches Sie ihr geschenkt haben. Wir freuten uns Sie wohl zu sehen. Wir haben uns über sein Betragen genug geärgert. Ihr hattet euch schon oft genug in dieser Frau getäuscht, um von ihr nicht wieder verrathen zu werden. Ich werde mich sogleich ankleiden und ausgehen. Wenn sie erst um zwölf Uhr

* Sich schlagen without the preposition mit is a reciprocal verb. (see § 64.)

kommen, werde ich mich schon entkleidet haben. Ich würde mich entkleiden, wenn ich nicht noch ausgehen müßte. Wenn wir dem Kinde das Messer gelassen hätten, würde es sich weh gethan haben. Wenn du mit dem Messer spielst, wirst du dir weh thun. Wie befinden Sie sich? Ich befinde mich wohl. Wie befindet sich Ihr Herr Vater? Er befindet sich nicht wohl. Ich hoffe daß er sich bald besser befinden wird. Wie befanden sich Ihre Fräulein Schwestern, als Sie bei ihnen auf dem Lande waren? Wenn das Wetter besser wäre, würde ich mich bald besser befinden. Wie haben Sie sich befunden seit ich Sie nicht gesehen habe? Ich habe mich stets wohl befunden.

102.

What do you complain of? I complain of your conduct and of that of your cousin. Do these people complain? They do complain. What do they complain of? They complain of the bad bread and of the bad water which they (one) give them. With whom were you fighthing when I arrived? I was fighting with the French officer, whom you know. With whom have you fought? I have fought with nobody. Will the queen not rejoice at the return of the king and the prince? She will certainly rejoice at it. Had not this miser fretted at the loss of his money? He had fretted at it. I should have wondered (been astonished), if I had found him in her house. I should be astonished, if he were not sick to-day. It would have been better if you had dressed (yourself) immediately. If you had not been here at twelve o'clock, I should have undressed myself and should have gone to bed. How do you do Mr. P.? I thank you, I am (find myself) very well and how is your good lady? She is pretty well. Have you heard from your son lately? I have heard from him (vor) two weeks *ago*. How was he?. He was then quite well, but he had been sick. Would these ladies not be better, if they were in the country? I think that they would be better, if they were in the country. In my native land I shall find myself better. My child, hast thou hurt thyself? Yes, (my) father I have hurt myself with this knife. Will this child not hurt itself, if we leave him this fork? It might (subj.) hurt itself, we will take it away *from* him (dat.). I flattered myself that I spoke (subj. imp.) French as well as you, but I see now that I have deceived myself. Do not flatter yourself that he will give you back the money, which you have lent him. I shall never forgive myself *for having* (to have) struck him. We should not have forgiven ourselves if we had told him *of* it.

103.

The Impersonal Verb. (see § 66 and 67.)

Es regnet, raich'-net, it rains; es schneit, shnite, it snows; donnern, don'-nern, to thunder; es giebt, there is, are; es stürmt, stürrmt, it blows hard; es wehet, vai'-het, it blows; es blitzt, blitst, it lightens; es hagelt, hâ'-ghelt, it hails; es freut mich...zu, I am glad of; es thut mir leid, lite, I am sorry; es gelingt mir, gai-lingt', I succeed; gelingen, to succeed; gelang, gai-lâng'; gelungen, gal-lööng'-en (aux. sein); es ist mir gelungen, I have succeeded; es wird mir gelingen, I shall succeed; glauben, glou'-ben, to believe (reg.); hoffen, hof'-fen, to hope; aufhören...zu, ouf′′-hö′-ren, to cease, to stop; das Unglück, ōōn′-gluck, the misfortune, bad fortune; das Glück, the good luck, happiness; die Ausdauer, ouss′-dou-er, the perseverance; heftig, hef′-tich, violent, -ly; nicht mehr, no longer; entdecken, ent-deck′-en, to discover.

Es fängt an zu donnern und zu blitzen. Regnet es? Es regnet ein wenig. Schneite es als Sie zu Hause kamen? Es schneite nicht, aber es hagelte. Hat es diesen Monat nicht viel geregnet? Es hat nicht so viel geregnet wie im vorigen. Glauben Sie nicht, daß es im nächsten Monate viel schneien wird? Wenn es nicht so kalt wäre, würde es regnen. Es freut mich Sie zu sehen. Freut es Ihren Großvater, alle seine Enkel bei sich zu haben? Es freut ihn sehr. Hat es den König nicht sehr gefreut die Königinn wieder zu sehen? Es hat ihn sehr gefreut. Hätte es Sie nicht gefreut, wenn Ihre Freundinn glücklich geworden wäre? Es thut mir leid daß Sie krank sind. That es diesen armen Bauern nicht leid, daß unsere Kühe gestorben waren? Es würde mir sehr leid thun, wenn er durch meine Schuld sein Geld verlöre. Ich hoffe daß es heute nicht regnen wird. Ich hoffte daß es aufhören würde zu schneien. Ich glaube daß es den Damen leid thun würde, sich über die Diener beklagt zu haben. Es muß mir gelingen meine Aufgabe zu machen. Ist es diesem Manne je gelungen sein verlornes Kind wieder zu finden? Es ist ihm gelungen. Wird es uns nie gelingen unser Geld wieder zu erhalten? Es würde Ihnen gewiß gelingen deutsch zu lernen, wenn Sie mehr Zeit hätten.

104.

Is it still raining? It is raining no longer. Did it thunder when you were in the country? It thundered and lightened very violently. Did it not blow very hard when you were in (auf) the vessel? It blew harder than I had ever seen (inf., see § 82, 5.) it blow. Has it hailed this morning? It has not hailed but rained. Will it blow hard to night? I believe that it will blow and rain hard this night. The sailors hoped that it would not rain to-day. It does not always blow when it snows. How long has it been snowing (pres. t., § 85.) already? It has been snowing already more than two hours. Do you think that it will snow the whole day? I think so (es). It would rain, if it were not so cold. Are you not glad that your father has returned? I am very glad that he has returned. Where you not glad to hear that your friends were well? I was very glad to hear that they were well (found themselves well). I should be glad to hear of you and of your friends. We should have been glad if you had come with your mother. I am sorry that you are not well. Was the servant sorry to have torn the handkerchief? He was sorry for having torn it. I hoped that the teacher would be sorry to have innocently punished this industrious pupil. I shall be very glad to hear of your good fortune. I have been sorry to hear of your bad luck. They would have been very sorry to hear of your misfortune. Do you succeed in learning (to learn) German? I believe that I succeed in it. Did your teacher succeed in teaching these pupils French? He succeeded in it. Have you succeeded in finding that happiness, which you were searching *for*? I have not succeeded in finding it. Do you believe that the enemy will succeed in beating our army? Have the farmers succeeded in mowing their hay? They have succeeded in it. Columbus would not have succeeded in discovering America, if he had not had so much perseverance. This poor woman hoped to succeed (that she would succeed) in recovering her lost child. They could (es wollte) not succeed in finding what (das was) they were looking for.

105.

Prepositions which govern the Accusative. (see § 73, 3.)

Durch, döörch, through, by; für, fü'r, for; gegen, gai'-ghen, against, towards; wider, vee'-der, against; ohne o'nai, without; um, ööm, around, about, at for; um....herum, ööm....her-ööm', around about.—Herumlaufen, her-ööm''-lou'-fen, to run about; herumgehen, to walk about, around; das ganze Jahr durch, the whole year (through); einen Tag um den andern, every other day; um keinen Preis, for no money, price; bitten um, to ask for, to request; marschiren, marshee'-ren, to march; ziehen, to move, to march; sorgen für, zorr'-ghen, to care for; halten für, hål'-ten, to take for, to hold; stellen, stel'-len, to put, to place; sich stellen, to place one's self; setzen, zet'-sen, to put, to place; sich setzen, to seat one's self, to sit down; der Kreis, kri'ss, the circle; um baares Geld, (ba'-ress), for cash; der Krieg, kreech, the war.

Durch wen haben Sie diesen Brief empfangen? Ich habe ihn durch den Herrn N. empfangen. Diese Leute sind durch ihn glücklich geworden. Der Gärtner ging mit seinem Sohne durch den Wald. Die Katze lief durch die Stube. Durch dich hoffte ich meine verlorne Tochter wieder zu finden. Für wen haben Sie diese silbernen Leuchter gekauft? Ich habe sie für meine Schwester gekauft. Diese Briefe sind für Sie. Du bist ein undankbarer Mensch, ich werde nichts mehr für dich thun. Dieser General sorgt immer für seine Soldaten. Für mich ist alles verloren. Wieviel Mehl bekommen Sie für einen Thaler? Wer nicht für mich ist, ist gegen mich. Die Grafen waren gegen den König. Ist der alte Herr nicht immer gut gegen alle seine Bedienten gewesen? Morgen ziehen wir wider (gegen) den Feind. Wir kamen gegen fünf Uhr an. Können diese Leute nicht ohne mich in die Stadt gehen? Ohne Sie kann ich nicht leben. Meine Herren, wollen Sie sich gefälligst um diesen Tisch setzen. Wir müssen entweder durch den Wald oder um denselben herum fahren. Er kam um dieselbe Zeit. Er kommt hier einen Tag um den andern. Er that es ums Geld. Der alte Tischler hat meinen Sohn um ein Stück Brod gebeten. Bittet Gott um euer tägliches Brod. Er kam um eine halbe Stunde zu spät.

106.

By whom will your friends send me my trunk? They will send it to you by one of their servants. Did you go (perf.) through my field or through that of my neighbor? I went through that of your neighbor. I hoped to obtain my money through you. Will the soldiers march through the town or not? They will not march through it. What will you give me for my black horse? I will give you (one) hundred dollars for it, if you will sell it. This coat is too small for me, but it is large enough for you. For whom do you work so industriously? I work for my wife and my children and that (is what) every one should do. For a dollar one can buy much. My brother is gone (ziehen) for me to (in) the war. Has your father not paid your boots for you? For what (wofür) do you take me? I take you for a good man. Will you always be so amiable towards your bride as you are now? These farmers are very hard to the poor. Has he not fought against the king and the queen, who had always been so kind towards him? When did he depart (perf.)? He departed towards the seventh hour. We drove against the wind. They marched against the Germans. What can you do without me? I can live without you and without your money. Without this kind lady I should have (subj. imp.) lost my life. We will place ourselves around this tree. Do you not see the circle around the moon, it will rain to-morrow. I do not like to have him about me. These boys asked their father for a dollar and he gave them a cent. He has sold his house for ready money. What do these poor laborers work for? They work for their daily bread.

107.

PREPOSITIONS GOVERNING THE DATIVE. (see § 73, 2.)

Mit, mit, with; nächst, neychst, next to; nebst, naipst, together with; sammt, zămt, together with; bei, bi, with, at the house of; seit, zite, since; von, fon, of, from; nach, nâch, after, to; gemäß, gai-maiss', according to; aus, ouss, out of; außer, ou'-sser, besides; binnen, bin'-nen, within; zu, tsoo, to; zuwider, tsoo-vee'-der; entgegen, ent-gai'-ghen, opposed to; gegenüber, ghey'-ghen-ü''-ber, opposite to.

In speaking of the different parts of the body the definite article is used where in English the possessive pronoun is applied.

Er schüttelte den Kopf (mit dem Kopfe).	He shook his head (with his head).
Wir sehen mit den Augen.	We see with our eyes.

After the verb weh thun, to hurt; schmerzen, to pain, &c., we use the dat. or acc. case and the definite article, instead of the possessive pronoun.

D e r Fuß schmerzt m i c h.	*My* foot pains *me*.
Der Kopf thut ihr weh.	Her head aches.

Der Befehl, bai-fail', the order, command; was fehlt Ihnen? failt, what ails you, what is the matter with you? das Theater, tai-â'-ter, the theatre; zuwider sein (dat.) to dislike; er ist mir zuwider, I dislike him.

Womit schneiden Sie Ihr Fleisch? Ich schneide es mit dem Messer. Ich esse mit der Gabel und mit dem Messer. Haben Sie nicht mit meinem Vater gesprochen? Wollen Sie nicht zu mir kommen? Ich werde mit Vergnügen zu Ihnen kommen. Der Minister fuhr in einem Wagen mit vier Pferden. Sehen Sie den Mann da nicht mit dem schwarzen Rocke? Ich sehe nicht den mit dem schwarzen, aber den mit dem blauen Rocke. Er schlug mich mit der Hand. Nächst dem Hause war ein kleiner Garten. Hier finden Sie Papier nebst Federn und Dinte. Ich werde sammt meiner Frau und meinen Kindern in die Stadt ziehen. Das Schiff ist sammt den Leuten untergegangen. Wo ist Ihr Herr Vater? Er ist bei uns. Sind Sie heute schon bei dem Nachbar gewesen? Wo saß Ihr Fräulein Schwester? Sie saß bei meiner Mutter. Wo ward die größte Schlacht geschlagen? Bei Leipzig. Jacob war bei seinem Vater als sein Bruder eintrat. Wann haben Sie meinen Bruder gesehen? Ich habe ihn seit vorgestern nicht gesehen. Seit wann ist die Mutter dieser Mädchen todt? Sie ist seit einem Jahre todt. Ihr Schwager ist seit drei Wochen nicht bei uns gewesen. Wo kommen diese Truppen her? Sie kommen von der nächsten kleinen Stadt. Diese Bauern kommen vom Felde. Von wem erhalten Sie ihre Bücher? Es schneite vom zwölften November bis zum fünfzehnten December. Gehen Sie heute mit der Schwester des Generals nach der Kirche? Wer kam nach mir? Der Bruder des Generals kam nach Ihnen. Nach der Arbeit können die Bedienten ausgehen. Nach der Zeitung vom ersten dieses Monats ist das Schiff am 3ten (des) vorigen Monats angekommen. Ihrem Befehle gemäß, werden diese Leute morgen aus der Stadt ziehen. Außer mir und meinem Bruder war niemand in dem Zimmer. Wo gehen Sie hin? Ich gehe zu meinem Oheim. Er ist immer zu Hause. Was fehlt ihrer Schwester? Der Kopf thut ihr weh. Meinen Vetter schmerzt das Auge.

108.

With what have you cut yourself? I have cut myself with the knife of my teacher. Will you go with me to (nach) the town? I will go with you this morning. The father, together with his children, sailed for America. When were your aunts and your cousins at your house? They were there yesterday. With us people (man) never play. Do people eat the pigeons boiled or roasted with you (in your country)? They eat them roasted. Since when have the French troops been here (pres. i.)? They have been here since the 23d of last month. From which merchant do you receive your coffee? I receive it from the one from whom your brother receives his. What kind of a boy has brought you the papers? It was a boy of ten years *old*. Have you sent for (nach) the physician? I have sent for him, but he has not yet come. For (nach) whom does he inquire? He inquires for Mr. Moor who lives No. 15. When will your farmer drive to town? He will drive there to-morrow morning. Where are you riding to? I am riding to my country house. Was he not punished for what (das, was) he had done? He was punished according to (the) law. Where do these pretty little children come from? They come from (aus) (the) school. When do these ladies come out (of) the theatre. They come at 11 o'clock out of the theatre. Do you know any body in London, besides Mr. Peters? I know nobody besides him. When will your brother return? He will return within six days. Do you not dislike these cowardly men? I dislike them much. I dislike (the) beer so *much*, that I cannot even taste it. Who lives opposite you (§ 73, 2.)? An old physician lives opposite me. Who stood opposite your daughter? A young and handsome officer stood opposite to her. Will you not drive out to meet (entgegen fahren) your friend? I would drive out to meet him, if I had a better carriage and better horses. How is your father to-day? He is not well Sir. What ails him? His eyes hurt him. I have walked so much that my feet ache me. Does your head ache still? It aches still a little, but not so much.

109.

Prepositions governing the Genitive. (§ 73, 1.)

Unweit, ōōn'-vite, near, not far from; während, vai'-rent, during; diesseit, deess'-site, on this side of; jenseit, yen'-zite, on that side of; oberhalb, o'-ber-hålp, above; unterhalb, ōōn'-ter-hålp, below; kraft, krȧft, by virtue of; wegen, vai'-ghen, on account of (§ 73, 1.); meinethalben, mi''-net-hȧl'-ben, on my account, for my sake; ungeachtet, ōōn''-gai-ȧch'-tet, notwithstanding; statt, anstatt, stȧtt, ȧn-stȧtt', instead of; längs, lengss, along; trotz, trots, inspite of; zufolge, tsoo-fol'-gai, in consequence of (these last three prep. govern the gen. and dat., see § 73, 1, p. 54).

Der Sommer, zom'-mer, the summer; der Winter, vin'-ter, the winter; der Frühling, frü'-ling, the spring; der Herbst, herrpst, the autumn; die Brücke, brück'-kai, the bridge; der Weg, vaich, the road; die Nacht, nȧcht, the night; der Tag, tȧ'ch, the day; die Mauer, mou'-er, the wall, rampart; der Dieb, deep, the thief; führen, fü'-ren, to lead; die See, zey, the sea; der See, the lake.

Haben Sie ihn sterben sehen? Have you seen him die? (§ 82, 5.)
Wir haben nicht ausgehen dürfen, We were not allowed to go out.
Erstaunt, er-stount', astonished; ruhen, roo'-hen, to rest, repose.

Der Engländer wohnt unweit des Schlosses. Was machen diese Kinder während des Tages? Sie lernen und spielen. Wir waren noch diesseit des Flusses, als der Feind uns angriff. Jenseit dieser hohen Berge gibt es andere schöne Länder. Dieser unglückliche Schneider wohnt jetzt oberhalb der Marktstraße. Fort Mifflin liegt unterhalb Philadelphia, am Delaware Flusse. Der Feind liegt außerhalb dieser Mauern. Er hat sich ihrethalben (f.) getödtet. Unserthalben wollten Ihre Freunde nicht ausgehen. Wegen dieses Geräusches werde ich nicht ausgehen. Meinetwegen können diese Kinder nach Hause gehen. Anstatt des Sohnes wurde der Vater ergriffen. Der alte Herr kam statt des jungen Herrn. Statt des Brodes gab er ihnen einen Stein. Wir fuhren längs der Mauer hin, während sein Vetter längs des Flusses hinritt. Kraft eines Befehles seines Generals ist er strenge bestraft worden. Wegen seiner Krankheit hat er mich nicht besuchen können. Während des Winters habe ich nicht zu meinen Cousinen gehen können. Kraft des Gesetzes hätte er den Dieb bestrafen sollen. Während des ganzen Sommers habe ich keine Früchte essen dürfen.

110.

Where did you meet (perf. t.) your aunt's friend? I met (perf. t.) her near my father's house. Where did your servants meet the scholars of your teachers? They met them not far from the school. Not far from this town is a bridge, which leads over the (über acc.) river. During the winter the rich people (Leute) of this town reside in town and, during the summer they reside in the country or near the sea. Not far from this lake there are high mountains. Did you cross (fahren über, acc.) the lake below or above the bridge? We crossed below the bridge, but the enemy crossed above the same. Does the castle of the king stand on this side or on that side of the river.* It stands on that side. In virtue

* When "on this side" or "on that side" is not followed by a noun or pronoun, which it governs, the adverbs diesseits and jenseits must be used.

of your orders we have sent all the officers and soldiers to that side of the river. For your sake and for the sake of your amiable sister, I shall do what you demand of me. For our part you may depart as (so) soon *as* you wish. Notwithstanding the orders of the general, the soldiers had left the town during the night, and at five o'clock in the morning were already beyond the forest, near the Hudson river, above the bridge which leads over (über, acc.) this river. He was astonished to see, the soldiers come instead of the farmers. Instead of me, my brother came into the room and gave her the letter of her grand-mother. During the night we drove along the river (hin), and during the day we rested not far from a thick forest. Which father will give his son a stone instead of a loaf? By virtue of the order of the king he loses his life during this night. In consequence of the order of the general he will be shot to (this) night. Have you been able to live in the country during the autumn? I have not been able to live there during the autumn, but during the spring and (the) summer. During the autumn and (the) winter I have been obliged to live in town, on account of my father, who was very ill. During the whole afternoon I have neither seen him go out, nor seen him come home. Would you not have assisted me *to* write (in writing) during the evening, if you had not had too much to do? This bird sings very beautifully in the spring, have you never heard him sing? Has the teacher heard the children read in spite of the noise which some of them were making?

111.

Prepositions which sometimes govern the Dative and sometimes the Accusative. (§ 73, 4, and 74.)

An, ân, on, at, to; auf, ouf, on, upon, up; in, in, in (with the dat.), into (with the acc.); über, ü'-ber, over, above; unter, ŏŏn'-ter, under, beneath; vor, fore, before; hinter, hin'-ter, behind; neben, nai'-ben; zwischen, tswish'-shen, between, among.

Der Ball, bâll, the bal; auf dem Balle sein, to be at the ball; auf den Ball gehen, to go to the ball; das Thor, tore, gate; schreiben an, to write to; stehen, stey'-hen, to stand; der Kessel, kess'-sel, the kettle; steigen, sti'-ghen, to mount, to ascend; hangen (neut. irr.), hâng'-en, to hang; hängen, heng'-en (act. r.), to hang; vor einem Jahre (dat.), a year ago; die Wolke, vol'-kai, the cloud; der Richter, rich'-ter, the judge; das Gefängniß, gai-feng'-niss, the prison; ertrinken, er-trink'-en, to be drowning (drowned), (with sein); ungefähr, ŏŏn-gai-fair', about, nearly; kaum, koum, scarcely.

Wer steht an der Thür? Der Sohn des Arbeiters steht an der Thür und seine Schwester steht an dem Fenster. Gehen Sie an die Thür und sehen Sie zu wer kommt. Stellen Sie den Kessel an das Feuer. Waren Sie heute auf dem Markte? Ich war heute nicht da, aber ich werde morgen auf den Markt gehen. Vor einer Stunde stieg der Zimmermann auf das Dach, jetzt sitzt er auf dem Dache und arbeitet. Wohnen die jungen englischen Damen jetzt in der Stadt? Nein sie wohnen noch auf dem Lande, aber sie werden bald in die Stadt ziehen. Wann ziehen diese reichen Kaufleute auf das Land? Sie ziehen im Monate Mai auf das Land und kommen im Monate November wieder in d i e Stadt. Wie oft gehen diese Mädchen in d i e Kirche? Sie gehen öfter in d i e Kirche als Ihre Cousinen. Sein Name steht über der Thür. Der Vogel fliegt über der Wolke (higher than the cloud). Wohnt der Schneider noch über d e m Lehrer? Er wohnt nicht über i h m aber nächste Woche zieht er über d i e kleine Französinn. Wo sahen Sie das Pferd des Russen. Ich sah es auf der Brücke, über dem Eise. Gingen Sie über d a s Eis? Nein, ich ging über d i e Brücke. Wo liegt das Papier? Es liegt unter m e i n e m Buche. Haben Sie das alte Messer unter d e n Tisch geworfen? Er steht unter d e n Soldaten. Er geht unter d i e Soldaten (turns soldier). Kaum hatte der General diese Worte gesagt als der König unter d i e Offiziere trat. Der Soldat steht vor d e m Hause. Stellen Sie sich vor das Zimmer. Warum steht diese Dame immer vor d e m Spiegel? Sie stellt sich nur vor d e n Spiegel wenn sie sich entkleiden will. Der Schuhmacher kam vor d e m Schneider an. Der Dieb muß sich vor d e n Richter stellen. Wo ist der Hund? Er liegt hinter d e r Thür. Stellen Sie sich hinter d i e Thür, wenn er herein kommt. Der Soldat geht hinter dem Offiziere. Ihre fleißige Cousine saß neben m e i n e r alten Schwester, da setzte sich meine lahme Nichte neben I h r e Cousine. Wo lag Ihre goldne Uhr? Sie lag zwischen d e m Buche und d e r Börse. Legen Sie die Uhr zwischen das Buch und die Börse.

112.

Where lies Philadelphia? On the river Delaware (Delaware river). Please put the book upon the table and come upon the roof, to see the birds fly *about* over the house. Put the kettle by (an) the fire, Caroline. Where is the kettle now? It stands by the (contraction) fire? When we came to the river, we found that the enemy was already beyond it (the same); we therefere remained at the river to feed our horses. How long was this thief in (the) prison? He was there (in) three years. Why was he sent to (into the) prison? He was sent there because he had stolen. Why do these women not go into the house when it rains? They do not go into this house, because they have something to do in (auf) the street. When I was walking over the bridge, the child fell into the river and would have been drowned, if a young man had not jumped into the water and had saved it (subj.). Where did the officers sword hang? It hung over his bed. Where (whither) did you hang my watch? I hung it over the door. I wrote your name over the window. Where is the kettle? It is under the table in the kitchen. Put it under the chair. Before the castle is a beautiful garden, and behind it (the same) a thick forest. The thief was brought before this good judge, who sent him to (into the) prison, because he had stolen a gold watch and twelve silver spoons *from* a (dat.) French count. He gave the soldier the order to place himself behind the door. Please to sit down (seat yourself) a long side of this lady. I thank you Sir, I do not like to sit. Along side of him stood a tall handsome man of about thirty years *of age*. Where do you live? I live between (the) third and fourth street. The plate stands between the box and the trunk. The servant walked between the two officers. Sit down between me and my brother. Put the table between the two chairs.

113.

Her, hair, this way; hin, hin, that way. (see § 76.)

Die Treppe (*f. s.*), trep′-pai, the stairs; bald, bâlt, soon; so bald, as soon as; treten, trai′-ten, to step; ziemlich, tseem′-lich, pretty, rather, adv.; vorgestern, fore″-ghess′-tern, the day before yesterday; die Gesellschaft, gai-zel′-shâft, the company, society; oben, o′-ben, above, up stairs; unten, ŏŏnten, below, down stairs.

Kommen Sie gefälligst herein. Gehen Sie hinaus. Wann werden Sie aufs Land gehen? Ich werde morgen dahin gehen. Wo kommen Sie her? Ich komme vom Hause. Wo gehen Sie hin? Ich gehe auf den Ball, nach der Stadt, zu meinem Oheime. Gehen diese Kinder diese Treppe hinauf? Sie gehen sie nicht hinauf, sie fallen sie hinunter. Kommen Sie herauf zu uns. Gehen Sie hinunter zu meinem Sohne und sagen Sie ihm, er möchte zu mir herauf kommen. Bringen Sie mir gefälligst meinen Ring herüber. Ich würde gleich hinüber kommen wenn ich nicht so viel zu thun hätte, aber sobald ich fertig bin, werde ich hinüber kommen.

114.

Will you please to step in, Gentlemen? I thank you Sir, we shall step in with pleasure. Will these ladies please to come up *stairs?* They will come up immediately. As soon as it begins to rain we shall go in. As soon as it ceases to snow, we shall go out (hinaus). Do not fall down the stairs, it is pretty dark here. When did you go up the mountain? We went up *the day* before yesterday. Will you tell your sister to come over to us. I shall tell her to come over to you, and I know she will come with pleasure, for she likes to be (is willingly) in your company and in the company of your amiable sister. Come out (2d p. pl.) children and see how it snows. Let us go into the garden, there are fine flowers there, we can pick them. If you will not come up, I shall come down *and* (to) fetch you. I must ride over to our neighbor, the farmer, and buy some of his good potatoes. Come over to our house this evening, we shall have *some* company. Where are you? I am here up-stairs, come up. I cannot come up, I am too tired. Come down, I am below. If you want to see something beautiful, (so) you must come here (hither) and look that way.

115.

The Subjunctive Mood. (§ 47, 50 & 80, 2, and Exerc. 95.)

After verbs which express, thinking, feeling, wishing and stating, the subjunctive mood is used when doubt or uncertainty is implied. After verbs which express stating or asking, the dependent phrase is generally in the present or future tense, no matter whether the principal verb is in the present or in a past tense. The following verbs are some of those which may take the subjunctive mood after them: meinen, to mean, to believe; glauben, to believe; vermuthen, to suppose; zweifeln, to doubt; scheinen, to appear; hoffen, to hope; fürchten, to fear;

wollen, to want, to wish; bitten, to request; befehlen, to command; verlangen, to demand; rathen, to advise; sagen, to say; erzählen, to relate; melden, mel'-den, to announce; fragen, to ask.

Der Offizier meldete dem General, daß der Gefangene angekommen sei.	**The officer informed the general, that the prisoner had arrived.**
Er sagte daß das Wasser schlecht sei.	**He said that the water was bad.**
Er fürchtet daß er krank sei.	**He fears that he is sick.**

The conjunction daß is frequently omitted:

Er sagte er sei krank.	**He said he was sick.**

In this case the verb is not placed at the end.

The subjunctive mood is also used to express a wish, in form of an interjection; in the present tense when the fulfilment of the wish is possible or probable, in the past tense, when the wish expresses the contrary of what exists.

Gott gebe uns bald den Frieden.	**May God soon grant us peace.**
Lange lebe die Königinn.	**Long live (life to) the queen.**
Möchte er doch genesen!	**Oh, that he might recover!**
O, daß mein Sohn noch hier wäre!	**Oh, that my son was still here!**

Was...auch, whatever; wer...auch, whoever; wenn...auch, although; wie... auch, however. Der Krieg, kreech, the war; die Post, poss't, the mail; erwähnen, er-vai'-nen, to mention; das Vermögen, fer-mö'-ghen, the fortune, property; zur See, tsoo'r zey, at sea; genesen, gai-nai'-zen, to recover.

Der König fragte den General ob seine Soldaten Pulver und Blei hätten? Der General antwortete, wenn meine Soldaten Pulver und Blei hätten, so würde der Feind jetzt schon geschlagen sein. Sagte der Knabe nicht daß seine Mutter während der Nacht gestorben sei? Zweifeln Sie, daß ich Ihnen bezahlen werde? Glauben Sie daß Ihr Vaterland Sie nicht belohnen werde? O, daß wir Geld hätten um dieses schöne Haus zu kaufen! O, daß man diesen unglücklichen Krieg nie angefangen hätte! Wie glücklich würde dieser Mann sein, wenn er seine Kinder nicht verloren hätte.

116.

He asked me if I had money. I told him that I had none. Did you not tell us that you were (pres.) sick and could not leave the house. The physician told me that I must (pres.) remain in (the) bed. He mentioned that the mail had arrived (perf.). Do you believe that it is good to live always in the country? I suppose that the little daughter of our neighbor will be here before seven o'clock. I doubt it (daran), that he will ever be well again (gesund werden). Did it not appear to you that the house of the merchant was (pres.) too small for you? I hope that your son will have arrived when you arrive at home (zu Hause). I feared that he was sick and could not come. Did you not fear that he had lost his property? I demanded that he should go home (pres.) immediately, and bring (holen) his father here. It is not good for man to be alone (that man be alone). He informed us that his father and mother had died (perf.) at six. The farmer said he came (pres.) from his youngest son, the lawyer, who, as the physician thought, was (pres.) very sick. I feared his arm would pain him (fut.). May he return (subj. pres.) safely (glücklich)! May God reward you for what (that which) you have done for me!

Whatever it may be (subj. of ſein), tell it me. Whatever he may have done, he will not be punished. Whoever he may be, (ſo...doch) he must still obey. However small she may be, (ſo...doch) she can work well. Let him depart early, so (auf) that he may not arrive too late. If we had had time, we should have stopped a week longer in London. I gave him the money that he might buy something to eat *for* himself.

117.

Adjectives are used adverbally without undergoing any change (§ 77).

The superlative of comparison is generally formed by placing the preposition an, with the definite article contracted, before it:

Schön, beautifully; ſchöner, more beautifully; am ſchönſten, most beautifully;
Gut, well; beſſer, better; am beſten, best.

When the superlative expresses the highest degree without forming a comparison, the preposition auf with the def. art. contracted, is placed before the adverb, aufs ſchönſte, in the most beautiful manner; or it stands without any preposition; as: höchſt, in the highest degree; eiligſt, with the utmost haste; gehorſamſt, most obediently, or it takes the termination ens; as: ſchönſtens, in the most beautiful manner; beſtens, in the best manner; nächſtens, very soon.

When adjectives are undeclinable, that is, when they stand after the verb, and express the highest degree without a comparison, their superlatives should have am before them.

Wenn die Noth am größten*, iſt die Hülf am nächſten.	When night is darkest, dawn is nearest.

Fließen, flee'-ssen, to flow; fließend, fluently; ſich betragen, bai-trâ'-ghen, to conduct one's self; tanzen, tânt'-sen, to dance; vertreiben, fer-tri'-ben, to drive away; grü'-ssen, to salute, greet; grüßen Sie ihren Vater, give my respects to your father; gefallen, gai-fâl'-len, to please; bedürfen, bai-dür'-fen, to require; dreifach, dri'-fâch, threefold; feſt, fest, firm, -ly, soundly; gar nicht, gâ'r nicht, not at all; geſund, healthy, safely, soundly; das Zahnweh, tsâ'hn'-vai, tooth-ache; das Zahnweh haben, to have the tooth-ache; einſchlafen, ine''-shlâ-fen, to fall asleep; der Matroſe, mâ'-tro-zai, the sailor; langſam, lâng'-zâ'm, slow, -ly.

Warum geht dieſes Mädchen ſo langſam? Es geht ſo langſam weil es krank iſt. Konnte es nicht ſchneller gehen, wenn es wollte? Ich glaube es kaum. Tanzt Caroline ſo gut wie ihre Schweſter? Sie tanzt beſſer als ſie, aber ſie tanzt nicht ſo gut als die kleine Emma, die am beſten von allen Mädchen in dem Dorfe tanzt. Wollen Sie gefälligſt hereintreten? Ich danke Ihnen, ich habe keine Zeit. Der Knabe kam eiligſt gelaufen (§ 81.) und ſagte daß der Feind ſchon vor dem Thore ſei. Der König war höchſt erſtaunt als er hörte, daß es dem jungen General P.... gelungen ſei, den dreifach ſtärkern Feind aus dem Lande zu vertreiben. Ich verbleibe gehorſamſt. Er grüßte mich freundlichſt. Grüßen Sie ihn höflichſt und ſagen Sie ihm er möchte mich nächſtens beſuchen. Haben Sie gut geſchlafen, mein Fräulein? Nein, ich habe gar nicht gut geſchlafen, ich hatte ein ſehr heftiges Zahnweh, und als dieſes aufhörte, machten die Leute des Hauſes ein ſolches Geräuſch, daß ich nicht einſchlafen konnte.

* Literally, when the distress is greatest, help is nearest.

118.

Can you write as rapidly as your brother? I can write more rapidly than he. Who of all these boys can write most rapidly? Henry can write most rapidly. Who works most industriously? The sons and the daughters of the old Englishman work most industriously. Who speaks most politely, the Frenchman, the Englishman or the German? The Frenchman speaks most politely. Who saluted us so politely? My cousin, Miss Smith saluted us so politely. Do these Dutchmen speak French as fluently as these Germans? They speak it more fluently, but the Russians speak it most fluently. When is man (der Mensch) happiest? He is happiest when he requires least. When do you sleep most quietly, before or after midnight? I sleep more quietly towards (the) morning. In which month is it warmest here? It is warmest here in the month of July, and it is coldest in the month of January. When can this woman write best? She can write best in the evening, but her sister, the baker's wife can write best in the morning. They said: we remain most obediently and went away. Give my best respects (grüßen) to your uncle, and tell him that I shall very soon call upon him (besuchen). Which bird flies swiftest? The eagle flies swiftest. The room looked in the highest degree dirty. The sailors came running most hastily in order to go on bord (an Bord). Which horse runs fastest, yours, his, or mine? Mine runs faster than yours, but his runs the fastest of all the horses in (the) town. Which of these young ladies do you like best (pleases you best)? The one who is sitting near your aunt I like best. When it freezes most violently, there is only very little or no wind? He was most highly astonished, when I told him that all his friends had safely (glücklich) arrived in London. Does not this child sleep very quietly? I have never seen a child sleep so quietly. Do you speak German more fluently than English? I speak the one as fluently as the other. How did these boys conduct themselves, when they were in the country? They conducted themselves very badly. What have they (has one) done to them? One has punished them most severely. When does this teacher punish his pupils most severely? He punishes them most severely, when they laugh at him (über, acc.). What *do* you *like to* eat best? I like beef best. What does the French ladies like to drink best? They like good light wine best.

119.

CONJUNCTIONS. (§ 78.)

Wenn, ven, when, if; als, âlss, when, as, than. Als is used of some past event or occurrence, the time of which is determined; wenn is used, where in English whenever may be substituted for when.

Als ich in Frankreich war, fühlte ich mich sehr glücklich.	When I was in France, I felt very happy.
Als ich in Paris ankam, fand ich meinen Bruder schon dort.	When I arrived in Paris, I found my brother already there.
Wenn ich in Paris bin, wohne ich bei meinem Freunde L....	When (whenever) I am in Paris, I live with my friend L....
Wenn ich ausgehe, begegne ich immer diese Frau.	When I go out, I always meet this woman.

Da, dā, as, since; Weil, vile, because;
Denn, den, for; Je...desto, yey, dess'-to, the.. the.

Je...je, the...the.

Je länger je lieber.	The longer the better.
Je mehr er hat, desto mehr will er haben.	The more he has, the more he wants to have.
Um so schöner...je	So much the more beautiful as.
So...als (wie).	as...as, so...as.
Sie ist so schön als liebenswürdig.	She is as handsome as amiable.
Sie ist so schön wie ihre Schwester.	She is as beautiful as her sister.
Schöner als,	More beautiful than.

Der (die) Verwandte, fer-vân'-tai, the relative; der Sturm, stöörm, storm; die Meile, mi'-lai, mile; das Recht, recht, the right, justice, law; Recht haben, to be right; Unrecht haben, öönrecht', to be wrong; der Bürger, bürr'-gher, the citizen; der Fluß, flööss, the river; schlimm, shlim, sore, bad; das Bein, bine, leg; dunkel, döönk'-el, dark; verlassen, fer-lâs'-sen, to leave, abandon; trauen, trou'-en, to trust; dumm, dööm, stupid; gewöhnlich, gai-vö'n'-lich, usual, -ly.

Wissen Sie wo der General Peters wohnt, wenn er in New-York ist? Er wohnt im Astor Hotel. Wo wohnte Ihre Frau Mutter, als sie in New-York war? Sie wohnte bei einer Verwandten. Wenn die Sonne roth untergeht, bekommen wir gewöhnlich Sturm. Als die Sonne unterging, waren wir schon zwanzig Meilen von unserer Vaterstadt entfernt. Warum gehen die Brüder Ihrer Freunde nicht ins Theater? Sie gehen nicht hinein, weil sie kein Geld haben. Da ich kein Geld habe, kann ich nicht ins Theater gehen. Ich will nicht ausgehen, denn ich habe keine Schuhe. Warum regnet es nicht? Es regnet nicht, weil es zu kalt ist, aber es wird bald schneien. Von diesem Manne kann man mit Recht sagen, je älter, je dümmer. Je mehr Geld der Mensch hat, desto mehr will er haben. Je freundlicher er gegen mich ist, desto weniger traue ich ihm. Je fleißiger Sie sind, um so mehr werden Sie verdienen. Sie werden um so mehr lernen, je fleißiger Sie studiren. Je öfter Sie französisch sprechen, um so fließender werden Sie sprechen. Glauben Sie daß dieses Wetter so gesund als angenehm ist? Sagten Sie nicht daß dieser Mann so ehrlich als arm sei? Ich sagte daß dieser Mann so ehrlich wie jener sei, und daß die Nichte des erstern viel geschickter sei als die des letztern. Hat der kleine Buchdrucker Recht oder Unrecht? Er hat Unrecht. Sie haben nicht das Recht in meinen Garten zu gehen und die Blumen zu pflücken.

120.

When I have money I go to the theatre. When these geese see water, (so) they want to drink. What do you do, when you are sick? I send for a physician. When it rains the street gets dirty. When (whenever) the Romans conquered a nation, (so) they made them (to) citizens. When the Romans conquered the Germans, (so) they found that they were quite savage (wild). When I was in London, the king was not (§ 89, 2.) there. When the moon rose, we saw that we were near the town. Where did you find yourself, when the sun rose. We found ourselves on the ice, not far from a bridge, which leads over the river. Being (as he is) sick, he must not go out. Being poor she cannot keep a servant. As it was raining I would not go out. Why can the baker bake no bread B ecause he has no flour. Why do you not put your coat on? Because it is at the tailor's. Why do you not come up? Because I have a sore leg. Why does this child not open its (his) eyes? Because it has sore eyes. This cow cannot be hungry, for I have fed her. Can this child be thirsty? It cannot be thirsty, for I have just given it something to drink. You cannot have seen Mr. Town to-day, for he has been dead these (schon) six weeks. Come, the sooner the better. Remain with us, the longer the better. Give these people something to eat, the sooner the better. The older she gets, the more stupid she gets. This wine tastes, the older the better. The longer *we are* here, the later *we shall be* there. The richer these people grow, the more money they will want. The sooner (eher) you leave Paris, the better it will be for you. The more wood this cabinet-maker can buy, the more chairs and tables will he make. The more oxen this butcher kills, the more meat he will have to sell. The more you study, the sooner you will succeed in learning (Inf. with zu) German. The older the young lady gets the more beautiful and the more amiable she grows. The more these people drink, the more thirsty they become. What do you think of these two young ladies? I think that they are as good as amiable. Are they not as beautiful as amiable? Is the weather as fine in the month *of* October as in the month *of* May? It is finer in the month *of* October, than in the month *of* May. Are these flowers as dear as those? They are dearer than those. Is your room as light as mine? It is neither as light as yours, nor as light as that of your brother, but it is lighter than that of my daughter, whose room is the darkest in the whole (ganz) house.

121.

Some verbs, besides the acc., govern the gen. case.

Sich erinnern, er-in'-nern, to remember; *sich rühmen, rü'-men, to boast; des Dienstes entlassen, to discharge; sich annehmen, to take pity upon, to take charge of; sich bemächtigen, bai-mech'-tig-en, to possess one's self of; sich bedienen, bai-de'-nen, to make use of, to help one's self; sich schämen, shai'-men, to be ashamed; versichern, fer-zich'-chern, to assure, to make sure of; bedürfen, bai-dür'-fen, to require, be in want of; gedenken, to think of; des Todes sterben, to'-des, to die the death; eines Amts warten, âmts, to attend to an office; Hungers sterben, hööng'-ers, to die of hunger; meiner, of me; deiner, of thee; seiner, of him; unser, of us; euer, of you; ihrer, of her, of them, of you; dessen, m. and n., of him, it; deren, f. and pl., of her, of them; die Krankheit, krânk'-hite, sickness, disease; an einer Krankheit sterben, to die of a disease; die Blattern, blâttern, the small pox; die Masern, mâ'-zern, the measles; die Schwindsucht, shwint'-zööcht, the consumption; die That, tâ't, deed; die Stärke, ster'-kai, strength; die Ehre, ey'-rai, honor; die Hülfe, hül'-fai, help, assistance; fremd, fremt, strange, foreign; der (die) Fremde, frem'-dai, the stranger; anzünden, ân'-tsün-den, to set fire to.

Erinnern Sie sich noch der Zeit, da wir zusammen in die Schule gingen? Ich erinnere mich deren noch. Weß* rühmte sich dieser Soldat? Er rühmte sich seiner Stärke. Ich habe heute meinen Bedienten seines Dienstes entlassen. Werden diese reichen Kaufleute sich nicht dieser armen verlassenen Waisen annehmen? Sie werden sich ihrer annehmen. Wissen Sie, ob der Feind sich

* Anstatt wessen, of what.

schon der Stadt Mexico bemächtigt hat? Werden Sie sich meiner Kleider bedienen können? Hat er Sie nicht seiner Hochachtung versichert? Er hat mich seiner Freundschaft versichert. Schämt Euch dieser Thränen nicht, sie machen euch Ehre. Ihr Bruder ist arm, aber deswegen sollten Sie sich seiner nicht schämen. Wenn ihr meiner Hülfe bedürft, so ruft mich nur, ich werde sogleich da sein. Sie haben meinen Bruder in Amerika gesehen, gedenkt er unser noch im fremden Lande? Welches Todes ist er gestorben? Er ist ertrunken. Jeder sollte seines Amtes warten. Er ist an den Blattern gestorben.

122.

Do you still remember the beautiful days we spent (verleben) in Germany? I remember them very well. Do not boast of your beauty, it soon fades (vergehen). The king has discharged many of his officers. If you will not take pity upon my poor children after my death, what will become of them? The French took possession of all the money that was in the town, and then set fire to it. Why will you not make use of the money, which I offer (anbieten) you (dat.), I know that you are in want of it. This man is ashamed of his native land. Are you not ashamed of this deed? I am not ashamed of it, I boast of it, as of a good deed. I am ashamed of them, they look like beggars. Sir, allow me to assure you of my friendship and of my esteem. Let us make sure of (take) these thieves, or they will rob (berauben) somebody. Do you require me? I do not want you, but I want your sister, please, tell her to come to me. Do you still think of the many opportunities, (which) you had to learn something. We still remember the many days (which) we were together in prison. How (is) did she die (died)? She died of (the) small pox. What (woran) did these pretty children die of? They died of the measles. What death, do you think that you will die? I know that I shall die of consumption, my father, my uncle, my mother and my aunt, all died of this disease. It must be dreadful (schrecklich) to die of hunger.

123.

The present participle of the German verb is seldom used in prose, the compound participle (having loved) never. When the former occurs, it should be paraphrased by the pres. or imperf. tense and such a conjunction as best expresses the idea: "Finding that he (can) could not open the door, he (calls) called the servant," may be paraphrased by: when (als) he found; whenever (wenn) he (finds) found; whilst (indem) he found; as, since, (da) he (finds) found; because (weil) he finds (found).

The compound participle must be paraphrased by the perfect or pluperfect tense and a conjunction; as, having found the door open, may be paraphrased, when (als) he (has) had found, whenever (wenn) he (has) had found, after (nachdem) he had found; as, since (da) he (has) had found; because (weil) he (has) had found.

Der Fehler, fai'-ler, fault, error, mistake; der Regenschirm, rai''-ghen-shirrm, the umbrella; der Kunde, kōōn'-dai, customer; der Reiter, ri'-ter, rider; das Geschöpf, gai-shōpf', creature; die Bank, bånk, bench, bank; der Jünger, yüng'-er, disciple; die Waare, vå'-rai, merchandize, goods; auslöschen, ouss-lösh'-shen, to extinguish; stehlen, stai'-len, to steal; schöpfen, shöp'-fen, to inhale, draw (water); begraben, bai-grå'-ben, to bury; Jahre lang, for years; betrunken, bai-trōōnk'-en, drunk, intoxicated.

Da der Arzt hörte, daß ich krank war, kam er zu mir. Wenn der Mann ins Wasser springt, folgt ihm der Hund. Als der General sah daß er einen Fehler gemacht hatte, gab er andere Befehle. Indem er hinausging, machte er die Thür zu. Weil ich heute ausgehen muß, kann ich Ihnen nicht meinen Regenschirm leihen. Weil er kein Geld hat, kann er nicht ins Theater gehen. Weil er betrunken ist, weiß er nicht was er sagt. Wenn er nüchtern ist, ist er ein sehr vernünftiger Mann. Da er seinen Bruder nicht zu Hause fand, ging er wieder aus. Da ich dieses Stück schon gesehen habe, werde ich heute Abend nicht ins Theater gehen. Als mein Vater gestorben war, nahm mein Oheim mich und meine Schwester in sein Haus. Da die Kinder das Licht ausgelöscht hatten, zündete ich es wieder an. Als die Sonne aufgegangen war, befanden wir uns unweit einer Stadt. Nachdem der Bäcker das Brod gebacken hatte, schickte er es zu seinen Kunden. Nachdem der Kaufmann seine Briefe geschrieben hatte, trug er sie auf die Post. Nachdem das Schiff angekommen war, fuhr der Capitain ans Land. Als wir drei Jahre gereis't hatten, kehrten wir in unser Vaterland zurück. Als die Wilden von Amerika zuerst einen Reiter zu Pferde sahen, glaubten sie, daß der Mensch und das Thier nur ein Geschöpf sei.

124.

Charles seeing his sisters weep, feared that they had met with some misfortune (a misfortune had met them). The calf being stolen, they shut the door. The ladies seeing that there were no chairs, sat down on the benches. Ascending the mountain, he inhaled the fresh air. Being obliged to leave my trunk here, I shall send for it to-morrow. Not requiring any money this evening, I shall leave my purse with you. He being my brother, I shall not strike him. These customers having no money, I cannot sell them any goods. These children having no books, I could not teach them. These clothes being wet, I cannot put them on. My father being sick, he cannot go to church to-day. The ship having arrived (angekommen war), we went to see it. The soldiers having died, we buried them in the field. After having sent the servant, he went himself. Having slept enough, they got up and went to (the) work. Having flattered themselves for years, that they knew (können) French, they find now that they understand nothing of it. Having put his stockings on, he put on his shoes. Having seen the sun rise, we returned to the village. Having said these words, he died. After having written these letters, you most copy them, and after having copied them, you must take them to the post office. It having struck twelve, we shall go home. Having cried long enough, he stopped. Having broken the bread, he gave it his disciples. Having distinguished the light, we went to bed and fell asleep. Having risen, these children washed and dressed themselves.

PART II.

THE GERMAN READER.

1. Das kluge Kind.
dâss kloo′-gai kint.

Ein Bischof sagte einst zu einem sehr klugen Kinde: Mein
ine bish′-shof zâ′ch′-tai i′nst tsoo i′-nem zair kloo′-ghen kin′-dai mine
Kind, ich will dir einen Apfel geben, wenn du mir sagst, wo Gott ist.
kint ich vil deer i′-nen âp′-fel gai′-ben ven doo meer zâ′chst vo got ist
Das Kind antwortete: Und ich will Ihnen zwei geben, wenn Sie mir
dâss kint ânt″-vorr′-tai-tai öönt ich vil ee′nen tswi gai′-ben ven zee meer
sagen, wo er nicht ist.
zâ′-ghen vo air nicht ist.

2. Der Platz beim Feuer.
dair plâts bi′m foir.

Ein Reisender kam an einem sehr kalten Abend in einem Wirths-
ine ri′-zen-der kâ′m ân i′-nem zeyr kâl′-ten â′-bent in i′-nem virrts″-
hause an. Alle Plätze um das Feuer waren besetzt und keiner der
hou′-zai ân âl′-lai plet′-sai ööm dâss foir v′â-ren bai-zetst′ öönt ki′-ner dair
Gäste machte Miene, ihm seinen Platz überlassen zu wollen. Der
ghes′-tai mâch′-tai mee′-nai eem zi′-nen plâts ü′-ber-lâs″-sen tsoo vol′-len dair
Reisende rief also den Stallknecht und befahl demselben, seinem Pferde
ri′-zen-dai reef âl′-zo dain stâl′-k′necht öönt bai-fâl′ dem-zel′-ben zi′-nem pfairr′-dai
sechs Dutzend Austern zu geben. Austern? sagte der Stallknecht, aber
zecks dööt′-sent ou′-stern tsoo gai′-ben ou′-stern zâ′ch-tai dair stâl′-k′necht â′-ber
ein Pferd ißt doch keine Austern. Thu, was ich dir sage, erwiederte
ine pfairt ist doch ki′-nai ou′-stern too vâss ich deer zâ′-gai er-vee″-der′tai
der Reisende, du wirst schon sehen. Der Stallknecht ging in den
dair ri′-zen′-dai doo virrst sho′n zey′-hen dair stâl′-k′necht ging in dain
Stall um dem Pferde die Austern zu geben, und alle Gäste verlie-
stâl ööm dem pfair′-dai dee ou′-stern tsoo gai′-ben öönt âl′-lai guess′-tai fer-lee′-
ßen jetzt ihre Plätze um ein Pferd Austern essen zu sehen. Inzwi-
ssen jetst ee′-rai plet′-sai ööm ine pfairt ou′-stern es′-sen tsoo zey′-hen in-tswish′-
schen nahm der Reisende den besten Platz beim Feuer ein. Bald nachher
shen nâ′m dair ri-zen′-dai den bes′-ten plâts bime foir ine bâlt nach-hair′

kam der Stallknecht wieder herein und sagte, das Pferd wolle keine
kâ'm dair stâl'-k'necht ve'-der her-ine' öönt zâ'ch'-tai dâss pfairt vol'-lai ki'-nai
Austern fressen. Schon recht, sagte der Reisende, so bringe mir die
ou'-stern fres'-sen sho'n recht zâ'ch'-tai dair ri'-zen-dai zo bring'-ai meer dee
Austern und gieb dem Pferde eine Metze Hafer.
ou'-stern öönt gheep dem pfair'-dai i'-nai met'-sai hâ'-fer.

3. Der Esel und das Salz.
dair ai'-zel öönt dâss zâlts.

Ein Esel trug eine Last Salz. Indem er damit durch einen Fluß
ine ai'-zel troo'ch i'-nai lâst zâlts in-dem' air dâ'-mit döörch i'-nen flööss
watete, glitt er auf den glatten Kieselsteinen aus und fiel sammt sei-
vâ'-tai-tai glit air ouf dain glât'-ten kee''-zel-sti'-nen ous öönt feel zâmt zi'-
nen Säcken ins Wasser. Nachdem er wieder aufgestanden war und
nen zeck'-ken inss vâs'-ser nâch-dem' air vee'-der ouf''gai-stân'-den wâr öönt
das Wasser aus den Säcken allmählig abtropfte, spürte er, daß seine
dâss vâs'-ser ouss den zeck'-ken âl-mai'-lich âp''tropff'tai spü'rr'-tai air dâss zi'-nai
Last immer leichter wurde, denn das Salz war in den Säcken ge-
lâst im'-mer li'ch'-ter vöör'-dai den dâss zâlts vâ'rr in dain zeck'-ken gai-
schmolzen und mit dem Wasser abgeflossen. „Dies," sagte er, „werde ich
shmolt'-sen öönt mit dem vâs'-ser âp''-gai-flos'-sen dees zâ'ch'-tai air verr'-dai ich
mir merken, und wenn ich künftig durchs Wasser gehe mich immer mit
meer merr'-ken öönt ven ich künf'-tich döörchss vâs'-ser gey'-hai mich im'-mer mit
meiner Last niederlegen, dann werde ich nur halb so schwer zu tra-
mi'-ner lâst nee''-der-lai'-ghen dân verr'-dai ich noo'r hâlp zo shwair tsoo trâ'-
gen haben."
ghen hâ'-ben.

Das nächste Mal wurde er mit Schwämmen beladen und sollte da-
dâss naich'-stai mâ'l vöör'-dai air mit shwem'-men bai-lâ'-den öönt zol'-tai dâ-
mit durch den Fluß gehen. Wie er beschlossen, legte er sich nieder,
mit' döörch dain flööss gey'-hen vee air bai-shlos'-sen laich'-tai air zich nee'-der
aber die Schwämme sogen so viel Wasser ein, daß er unter der Last
â'-ber dee shwem'-mai zo'-ghen zo fiel vâs'-ser ine dâss air öönter dair lâst
zusammenbrach und beinahe ertrunken wäre.
tsoo-sâm''-men-brâch' öönt bi-nâ'-hai er-trööṅk'-en vai'rai.

4. Der kluge Staar.
dair klöö'-gai stâ'r.

Ein durstiger Staar wollte aus einer Wasserflasche trinken und
ine döör'-stig-er stâ'r vol'-tai ouss i'-ner vâs''ser-flâsh'-shai trink'en öönt
konnte das Wasser in derselben mit seinem kurzen Schnabel nicht erreichen.
kon'-tai dâss vâs'-ser in dair-zel'ben mit zi'-nem kÖört'-sen shnâ'-bel nicht er-ri'-chen
Er hackte ins dicke Glas, und vermochte nicht es zu zerbrechen.
air hâck'tai inss dick'-kai glâ'ss öönt fer-moch'-tai nicht ess tsoo tser-brech'-chen
Er versuchte die Flasche umzuwerfen; aber dazu war er zu
air fer-zoo'ch'-tai die flâsh'-shai ööm''-tsoo-verr'-fen 'âber dâ'-tsoo vâ'r air tsoo

schwach; endlich kam er auf den Einfall, kleine Steine in die Flasche
shwâch ent'-lich kâ'm air ouf dain ine'-fâl kli'-nai sti'-nai in de flâsh'-shai

zu werfen und bald stieg das Wasser in der Flasche so hoch, daß er
tsoo verr'-fen öönt bâlt steech dâss vâs'-ser in dair flâsh'-shai zo ho'ch dâss air

es mit seinem Schnabel erreichen und seinen Durst löschen konnte.
ess mit zi'-nem shnâ'-bel er-ri'-chen öönt zi'-nen döörst lösh'-shen kon'-tai.

5. Der Elephant.

dair ey-lai-fânt'.

Ein Elephant ward eines Tages, wie gewöhnlich zur Tränke ge-
ine ey-lai-fânt vârrt i'-ness tâ'-ghes vee gai-vö'n'-lich tsoo'r trenk'-ai gai-

führt. Auf diesem Wege kam er bei der Werkstätte eines Schneiders
fü'rt ouf deezem vai'-ghai kâ'm air bi dair verrk'-stât i'-nes shni'-ders

vorbei; dieser saß an seinem offnen Fenster und arbeitete. Neben ihm
fore-bi' dee'-ser zâ'ss ân zi'-nem of'-nen fen'-ster öönt âr'-bi-tai-tai nai'-ben eem

lagen einige Aepfel. Als der Elephant die Aepfel sah, streckte er sei-
lâ'-ghen i'-ni-ghai ep-fel âlss dair ey-lai-fânt' dee ep'-fel zâ streck'-tai air zi'-

nen Rüssel aus und holte sich die Aepfel, einen nach dem andern, her-
nen rüs'-sel ouss öönt ho'l'-tai zich dee ep'-fel i'-nen nâch dem ân'-dern herr-

aus. Als der Elephant seinen Rüssel zum dritten Male in das Fen-
ouss' âlss dair ey-lai-fânt' zi'-nen rüs-sel tsööm drit'-ten mâ'l in dâss fen'-

ster steckte, stach ihn der Schneider mit seiner Nadel. Der Elephant
ster steck'-tai stâ'ch een dair shni'-der mit zi'-ner nâ'-del. dair ey-lai-fânt'

zog seinen Rüssel zurück und ging zur Tränke. Nachdem er sich satt
tso'ch zi'-nen rüs'-sel tsoo-rück' öönt ging tsoo'r trenk'-ai nâch-dem air zich zât

getrunken, rührte er das Wasser mit dem Fuße um und füllte dann
gai-tröönk'-en rü'r'-tai air dâss vâs'ser mit dem foo'-ssai ööm öönt fül'-tai dân

seinen Rüssel damit. Als er nun wieder zu dem Schneider kam,
zi'-nen rüs'-sel dâ-mit' âlss air noo'n ve'-der tsoo dem shni'-der kâ'm

steckte er den Rüssel zum Fenster hinein und blies dem armen Schnei-
steck'-tai air den rüs'-sel tsööm fen'-ster hin-ine' öönt bleess dem âr'-men shni'-

der das Wasser ins Gesicht und über den ganzen Körper.
der dâss vâs'-ser inss gai-zicht' öönt ü'-ber dain gânt'-sen kör'-per.

6. Ossian.

os'-se-â'n.

Ossian, Fingal's Sohn, der blinde Sänger von Morven, saß einst,
os'-se-â'n fing'-â'ls zone dair blin'-dai zeng'-er fon morr'-ven zâ'ss i'nst

als der Tag sich neigte, am Eingange seiner felsigten Halle. Malvina,
âlss dair tâ'ch zich ni'ch'-tai âm ine-gâng'-al zi'-ner fel'-zich-ten hâl'-lai mâl-ve'-na

Toskars blühende Tochter, stand neben dem schweigenden Greise.
toss'-kârrs blü'-hen-dai toch'-ter stânt nai'-ben dem shwi'-ghen-den gri'-zai.

Da fragte er, hat die Sonne schon ihren Lauf vollendet, und ist
dâ frâ'ch'-tai air hât dee zon'-nai sho'n ee'-ren louf fol-len'-det öönt ist

das Abendroth am westlichen Himmel?
dâss â''-bent-rote' âm vest'-lich-chen him'-mel

Sie sinket in diesem Augenblick hernieder, antwortete Mal-
zee zink'-et in dee'-zem ou''-ghen-blick' her-nee'-der ânt''-vorr'-tai-tai mâl-
vina und seufzte.
ve'-nâ öönt zoifts'-tai.

Warum seufzest du, Malvina? fragte der blinde Greis.
vâ'-rööm zoif'-tsest doo mâl-ve'-nâ frâ'ch' tai dair blin'-dai grice.

Ach, mein Vater, antwortete die Jungfrau, daß du kein Morgen-
âch mine fâ'-ter ânt''-vorr'-tai-tai dee yööng'-frou dâss doo kine mor'-ghen
und kein Abendroth siehest.
öönt kine â''-bent-rote' zee'-hest.

Und ach! — setzte der Greis mit lächelnder Lippe hinzu — auch
öönt âch zets'-tai dair grice, mit lech-cheln'-der lip'-pai hint-soo' ouch
nicht Malvina's, meiner Tochter freundliches Antlitz. — Aber hör' ich
nicht mâl-ve'-nâ'ss mi'-ner toch'-ter froint'-lich-ches ânt'-lits â'-ber hö'rr ich
nicht, Malvina, den Laut deiner süßen Stimme zu dem Klange meiner
nicht mâl-ve'-nâ dain lout di'-ner zü'-ssen stim'-mai tsoo dem klâng'-ai mi'-ner
Harfe, und das Schweben der Geister um ihre Saiten?
hârr'-fai öönt dâss shwe'-ben dair ghi'-ster ööm ee'-re zi'-ten.

Wie vermagst du denn die Laute der unsichtbaren Geister zu ver-
vee fer-mâ'chst' doo den dee lou'-tai dair öön''-zicht-bâren ghi'-ster tsoo fer-
nehmen, mein Vater? fragte Malvina.
nai'-men mine fâ'-ter frâ'ch'-tai mâl-ve'-nâ.

Nur ihm, Malvina, sprach der Greis, dem die äußere Welt erstarb
noo'r eem mâl-ve'-nâ sprâch dair grice dem dee oi'-ssai-re velt er-stârrp'
und unterging, ertönet das leise Säuseln höherer Welten. Siehe,
öönt öön'-ter-ging err-tö'-net dâss li'-zai zoi'-zeln hö'-hai-rer vel'-ten zee'.hai
Malvina, sein Auge ist schon geschlossen, ehe der Tod kommt, und die
mâl-ve'-nâ zine ou'-gai ist sho'n gai-shlos'-sen ey'-hai dair to't komt öönt dee
Erde ruhet vor ihm in Nacht und Dunkel verhüllt. So wie der ver-
err'-dai roo'-het fore eem in nâcht öönt döönk'-el fer-hült' zo vee dair fer-
dunkelten Erde nur der Sterne Glanz erscheint, so schweben von
döönk'-el-ten err'-dai noo'r dair sterr'-nai glânts er-shi'-net zo shwai'-ben fon
oben auf ihn tönende Strahlen hernieder, und berühren die Saiten seiner
o'-ben ouf een tö'-nen-dai strâ'-len her-nee'-der öönt be-rü'-ren dee zi'-ten zi'-ner-
Harfe und seines sehenden Geistes . . . Reiche mir die Harfe Malvina.
hârr'-fai öönt zi'-nes zey'-hen-den ghi'-stes . . . ri'-chai meer dee hâr'-fai mâl-ve'nâ.

So redete Ossian, Malvina reichte ihm schweigend die Harfe und
zo rai'-dai-tai os'-se-â'n mâl-ve'-nâ ri'ch'-tai eem shwi'-ghent dee hârr'-fai öönt
nun stürmte der blinde Greis in ihre Saiten.
nöö'n stürm'-tai dair blin'-dai grice in ee'-rai zi'-ten.

7. Die Nachtigall im Käfig.
dee nâch'-te-gâl im kai'-fich.

Ein Landmann kam eines Tages in die prächtige Wohnung eines
ine lânt'-mân kâ'm i'-nes tâ'-ghes in dee prech'-te-gai vo'-nööng i'-nes

reichen und vornehmen Mannes. Da vernahm er den hellen Gesang
ri'-chen öönt fore'-nai-men mân'-ness dâ fer-nâ'm' air den hel'-len gaizâng
eines Vogels in einem vergoldeten Käfig. Er trat hinzu, und siehe,
i'-ness fo'-ghels in i'-nem fer-gol'-dai-ten kai'-fich air trâ't hin'-tsoo öönt zee'-hai
es war eine Nachtigall. Mit wehmüthigem Herzen stand er auf seinem
ess vâ'rr i'-nai nâch'-te-gâl mit vey"-mü'-ti-ghem herrt'-sen stânt air ouf zi'-nen
Stab gelehnt und hörete.
stâ'p gai-laint' öönt hö'rai-tai.

Da traten die Diener des vornehmen Mannes zu ihm und sprachen:
dâ trâ'-ten dee dee'-ner dess fore'-nai-men mân'-nes tsoo eem öönt sprâ'-chen
Was befremdet dich, daß du also sinnend da stehest?
vâss bai-frem'-det dich dâss doo âl'-zo zin'-nent dâ stey'-hest.

Der Landmann antwortete: Es befremdet und wundert mich, wie
dair lânt'-mân ânt"-vor'-tai-tai ess bai-frem'-det öönt vöön'-dert mich ve
ihr und euer Herr den traurigen Klagegesang des gefangenen
eer öönt oirr herr dain trou'-re-ghen klâ"-gai-gai-zâng' dess gai-fâng'-ai-nen
Vogels ertragen mögt, in eurer schimmernden Wohnung.
fo'-ghels er-trâ'-ghen mö'cht in oi'-rer shim'-mern-den vo'-nööng

Du Thor, versetzte einer der Diener, dünkt dir denn auch der Nach-
du to'r fer-zets'-tai i'-ner dair dee'-ner dünkt deer den ouch dair nâch'-
tigallen Gesang traurig in deinen Feldern und Gebüschen?
te-gâl-len gai-zâng' trou'-rich in di'-nen fel'-dern öönt gai-büsh'-shen

Mit nichten, antwortete der Landmann, sondern er erfüllet mein
mit nich'-ten ânt"-vorr'-tai-tai dair lânt'-mân zon'-dern air er-fül'-let mine
Herz mit stiller Freude und Bewunderung.
herrts mit stil'-ler froi'-dai öönt bai-vöön'-dai-rööng

Singen denn jene in andern Tönen und Weisen als diese, fragte
sing'-en denn yey'nai in ân'-dern tö'-nen öönt vi'-zen âlss dee'-zai frâ'ch'-tai
der Diener mit spöttischem Lächeln.
dair dee'-ner mit spöt'-tish-shem lech'-cheln

Freilich, sagte der Landmann, unsere Nachtigallen verkünden
fri'-lich zâ'ch'-tai dair lânt'-mân öön'-zai-rai nâch"-te-gâl'-len ferr-kün'-den
zwischen grünen und blühenden Zweigen das Lob der verjüngten
tswish'-shen grü'-nen öönt blü'-hen-den tswi'-ghen dâss lope dair fer-yüng'-ten
Schöpfung, sie singen unter dem blauen offenen Himmel das Lied der
shöp'-fööng zee zing'-en öön'-ter dem blou'-en of'-fai-nen him'-mel dâs leet dair
Freiheit und über ihren brütenden Weibchen den Hochgesang der
fri'-hite öönt ü'-ber ee'-ren brü'-ten-den vipe'-chen den ho'ch"-gai-zâng' dair
Liebe.
lee'-bai

Bei diesen Worten erhoben die Knechte ein lautes Gelächter und
bi dee'-zen vorr'-ten er-ho'-ben dee k'nech'-tai ine lou'-tess gai-lech'-ter öönt
schalten den Bauern einen Thoren. Der Landmann aber schwieg und
shâl'-ten den bou'-ern i'-nen to'-ren dair lânt'-mân â'-ber shweech öönt
kehrte zurück in seine ländliche Wohnung und zu seinem Acker.
keyrr'-tai tsoo-rück' in zi'-nai lent'-lich-chai vo'-nööng öönt tsoo zi'-nem âck'-ker.

8. Das Kind und die Biene.
dâss kint öönt dee bee′-nai.

In eine Blume war ein Bienchen einst gekrochen.
in i′-nai bloo′-mai vâr ine been′-chen i′nst gai-kroch′-chen
Die Blume pflückte sich ein Kind zu einem Strauß,
dee bloo′-mai pflück′-tai zich ine kint tsoo i′-nem strouss
Und trieb dabei den kleinen Gast heraus.
öönt treep dâ′-bi dain kli′-nen gâst herr-ous′
„So herrisch?" rief das Bienchen zürnend aus,
zo her′-rish reef dâss been′-chen tsür′-nent ouss
„Vermuthlich wardst du nie gestochen?
fer-moot′-lich vârrtst doo nee gai-stoch′-chen
„Du sahst doch wohl daß ich auf diese Blume flog,
doo zâ′st doch vo′l dâss ich ouf dee′-zai bloomai flo′ch
„Und ruhig meinen Honig sog?
öönt roo′-hich mi′-nen ho′-nich zo′ch
„Denkst du vielleicht ich sei zu klein,
denkst doo feel′-li′cht ich zi tsoo kline
„Dich kleiner Mensch zu strafen? nein!
dich kli′-ner mensh tsoo strâ′fen nine
„So klein ich bin, so soll dich's reu'n."
zo kline ich bin zo zoll · dich'ss roin
So sprach sie, und den Augenblick
zo sprâ′ch zee öönt dain ou″-ghen-blick′
Wars auch geschehen. Doch ach der Stachel blieb zurück,
vâ′rss ouch gai-sheyn′ doch âch dair stâch′-chel bleep tsoo-rück′
Drum starb sie und erfuhr zu spät, daß, wer gern Rache
dröóm stârp zee öönt er-foor′ tsoo spait dâss vair gerrn râ′-chai
An andern übt, sich selber elend mache.
ân ân′-dern ü′pt zich zel′-ber ai′-lent mâch′-chai

9. Der Rabe.
dair râ′-bai.

Ein Rabe schleppte tausend Dinge,
ine râ′-bai shlep′-tai tou′-zent ding′-ai
Geld, Glaskorallen, Perlen, Ringe,
gelt glâss″-ko-râl′-len perr′-len ring′-ai
In einen Winkel, wo er schlief.
in i′-nen vink′-el vo air shleef
Der Haushahn sahe dies und rief:
dair 'houss′-hâ'n zâ′hai dees öönt reef
Was thust du denn mit diesen Sachen,
vâss toost doo den mit dee′-zen zâ′-chen
„Die dich doch niemals glücklich machen?"
dee dich doch nee′-mâls glück′-lich mâch′-chen
„Ich weiß es selbst nicht," sprach der Rabe,
ich vice ess zelpst nicht sprâch dair râ′-bai
„Ich nehm' es nur damit ichs habe."
ich naim ess noo′r dâ-mit′ ichss hâ′-bai.

10. Der Philosoph.

Im ersten halben Jahr und schon
Ganz voll Philosophie,
Kam Fritz, der hoffnungsvolle Sohn,
Von der Akademie.

Kaum kommt er in der Eltern Haus,
Kramt der gelehrte Mann
Bei Tisch der Weisheit Schätze aus,
Und zeiget, was er kann.

Gelt, spricht er, werthester Herr Papa,
Sie sagen, es sind zwei
Gebraten junge Hühnchen da;
Ich aber, es sind drei.

Nicht wahr? es sind zwei Braten hier,
Und eins steckt ja in zwei:
Ergo, so zeigt die Logik mir,
Sind auch der Braten drei.

Recht so, versetzt der Herr Papa,
Gott segne dein Bemüh'n;
Ich nehme den, den die Mama,
Nimm du den dritten hin.

11. Das Kanarienvögelchen.

Ein kleines Mädchen, Namens Karoline, hatte ein allerliebstes Kanarienvögelchen. Das Thierchen sang vom frühen Morgen bis an den Abend, und war sehr schön, goldgelb mit schwarzem Häubchen. Karoline aber gab ihm zu essen Samen und kühlendes Kraut, auch zuweilen ein Stückchen Zucker, und täglich frisches Wasser.

Aber plötzlich begann das Vögelchen zu trauern, und eines Morgens, als Karoline ihm Wasser bringen wollte, lag es todt in dem Käfig.

Da erhob die Kleine ein lautes Wehklagen um das geliebte Thier, und weinte sehr. Die Mutter des Mägdleins aber ging hin, und kaufte ein anderes, das noch schöner war an Farbe, und eben so lieblich sang wie jenes, und that es in den Käfig.

Allein das Mägdlein weinte noch lauter, als es das neue Vögelchen sah.

Da wunderte sich die Mutter sehr und sprach: Mein liebes Kind, warum weinest du noch, und bist so sehr betrübt? Deine Thränen werden das verstorbene Vögelchen nicht in das Leben rufen, und hier hast du ja ein anderes, das nicht schlechter ist, denn jenes!

Da sprach das Kind: Ach, liebe Mutter, ich habe Unrecht gegen das Thierchen gehandelt, und nicht alles an ihm gethan, was ich sollte und konnte.

Liebe Lina, antwortete die Mutter, du hast sein ja sorgfältig gepflegt!

Ach nein — erwiederte das Kind — ich habe noch kurz vor seinem Tode ein Stückchen Zucker, das du mir für dasselbe gabst, ihm nicht gebracht, sondern selbst gegessen. So sprach das Mädchen mit betrübtem Herzen.

Die Mutter aber lächelte nicht über die Klagen des Mädchens — denn sie erkannte wohl und verehrte die heilige Stimme der Natur in dem Herzen des Kindes. —

Ach! sagte sie, wie mag dem undankbaren Kinde zu Muthe sein am Grabe der Aeltern!

Krummacher.

12. Der Hund mit dem Fleische.

Mit einem Stückchen Fleisch, das er dem
Koch genommen,
Springt Spitz, Verfolgern zu entkommen,
In einen Fluß. Er schwimmt und
sieht hinein,
Sieht sich und auch das Fleisch. Ihm dünkt dieser Schein

Ein andrer Hund mit Fleisch zu sein.
Sogleich nimmt ihn die Lust, auch dies zu haben, ein.
Besiegt von der Gewalt des Neides,
Schnappt er nach jenem; weg war beides!
Ein Geiziger ist nimmer satt,
Und so verliert er oft auch das noch, was er hat.

Nach Aesop.

13. Rabbi Möir und seine Gattinn.

Rabbi Möir, der große Lehrer, saß am Sabbath in der Lehrschule und unterwies das Volk. Unterdessen starben seine beiden Söhne, beide schön von Wuchs und wohl unterrichtet im Gesetze. Seine Hausfrau nahm sie und trug sie auf den Söller, legte sie auf ihr Bett und breitete ein weißes Gewand über ihre Leichname. Abends kam Rabbi Möir zu Hause. „Wo sind meine Söhne," fragte er, „daß ich ihnen den Segen gebe?" „Sie sind in die Lehrschule gegangen," war ihre Antwort. „Ich habe mich umgesehen," erwiederte er, „und bin ihrer nicht gewahr geworden." Sie reichte ihm einen Becher, er lobte den Herrn, trank und fragte abermals: „Wo sind meine Söhne, daß sie auch trinken vom Weine des Segens?" „Sie werden nicht weit sein," sprach sie und setzte ihm vor zu essen. Als er nach der Mahlzeit gedankt hatte, sprach sie: „Rabbi, erlaube mir eine Frage!" „Sage an, meine Liebe!" antwortete er. — „Vor wenig Tagen," sprach sie, „gab mir Jemand Kleinodien in Verwahrung, und jetzt fordert er sie zurück. Soll ich sie ihm wiedergeben?" „Dies sollte meine Frau nicht erst fragen," sagte Rabbi Möir; „wolltest du Anstand nehmen, einem Jeden das Seine wiederzugeben?" „O nein!" versetzte sie; „aber auch wiedergeben wollt ich ohne dein Vorwissen nicht." Bald darauf führte sie ihn auf den Söller, trat hin und nahm das Gewand von den Leichnamen. „Ach, meine Söhne," jammerte der Vater — „meine Söhne!" Sie wandte sich hinweg und weinte. Endlich ergriff sie ihn bei der Hand und sprach: „Rabbi, hast du mich nicht gelehrt, man müsse sich nicht weigern, wiederzugeben, was uns zur Verwahrung anvertraut ward? Siehe, der Herr hat's gegeben, der Herr hat's genommen, der Name des Herrn sei gelobet!" — „Der Name des Herrn sei gelobet!" — stimmte Rabbi Möir mit ein.

Talmud.

14. Nuschirwan und der Greis.

Nuschirwan, Schach von Persien, fand auf einer Jagdpartie einen Greis, der einen Nußbaum pflanzte. „Alter," redete er ihn an, „denkst du, daß dieser Baum dir noch Früchte geben soll?" — „Früchte soll er geben," antwortete der Alte, „das denk' ich, wenn nicht mir, doch meinen Enkeln. Andere pflanzten und ich genoß: nun will ich pflanzen, damit Andere genießen mögen."— „Sih," rief Nuschirwan. Nun ist zu wissen, daß, so oft Nuschirwan das Wörtchen Sih ausrief, der Schatzmeister viertausend Dirhem auszahlen mußte. Sih war eine Anweisung von viertausend Dirhem, die auf der Stelle bezahlt wurden, und der Pflanzer erhielt dieselben zur Belohnung seiner treffenden Antwort. „Herr!" fuhr er fort, „es ist wahrlich keine geringe Seltenheit um den Baum, der so schnell Früchte trägt, als mir dieser getragen." — „Sih!" rief Nuschirwan, und andere viertausend Dirhem folgten der ersten. — „Nur deine Huld, o großer König," sprach der Alte, „vermag ein Wunder, wie dieses hervorzubringen, daß derselbe Baum in kurzer Zeit, zweimal Früchte giebt." Diese Antwort entlockte dem König ein drittes verwunderungsvolles Sih! und dem Beutel des Schatzmeisters viertausend andere blanke Dirhem. Schwerlich ward eine treffende Antwort je besser belohnt.

v. Hammer.

15. Der Kukuk.

Der Kukuk sprach mit einem Staar,
Der aus der Stadt entflohen war.
Was spricht man, fing er an zu schreien,
Was spricht man in der Stadt von unsern
Melodien?
Was spricht man von der Nachtigall?
„Die ganze Stadt lobt ihre Lieder."
Und von der Lerche?" rief er wieder.
„Die halbe Stadt lobt ihrer Stimme Schall."
Und von der Amsel? fuhr er fort.
„Auch diese lobt man hier und dort."

Ich muß dich doch noch etwas fragen:
Was, rief er, „spricht man denn von mir?"
„Das," sprach der Staar; „das weiß ich nicht zu sagen;
Denn keine Seele spricht von dir."
So will ich, fuhr er fort, mich an dem Undank rächen
Und ewig von mir selber sprechen.

Gellert.

16. Das Kind und die Wölfe.

Auf dem Riesengebirge lebte eine arme Frau; diese hatte ein kleines Kind, und hütete für andere Leute eine Viehheerde. Ein Mal saß sie mit ihrem Kinde im Walde, und gab dem Kinde Brei aus dem Napfe; die Kühe aber weideten auf der Wiese. Von der Weide gingen die Kühe in den Wald. Die Frau lief zu den Kühen hin und wollte dieselben forttreiben. Unterdessen kam eine große Wölfinn aus dem Dickicht des Waldes, ging auf das Kind los, packte es an seinem Röckchen und trug es in das Innere des Waldes. Die Mutter kam von den Kühen zurück, fand aber ihr Kind nicht mehr; auch fehlte der Eßlöffel. Die Mutter lief zu ihrem Dorfe zurück und jammerte gar sehr um ihr Kind. — Unterdessen kam ein Bote durch den Wald gegangen und verirrte sich. Aus einem Gebüsche vernahm er die Worte: „Geh, oder ich gebe dir Eins; geh, oder ich gebe dir Eins." Er geht in das Gebüsch, findet auf dem Boden ein kleines Kind und sechs junge Wölfe um dasselbe; die jungen Wölfe fuhren immer auf das Kind zu, schnappten nach seinen Händchen; das Kind aber schlug ihnen stets mit dem hölzernen Löffel auf die Nase, und sagte dabei die Worte: „Geh, oder ich gebe dir Eins." Der Bote verwunderte sich, lief geschwind hin, holte einen Prügel und schlug damit die sechs jungen Wölfe todt. Das Kind nahm er geschwind auf die Arme, und eilte aus allen Kräften aus dem Gebüsche. Am Ende des Waldes kamen ihm Bauern mit Heugabeln und Dreschflegeln entgegen und wollten den Wolf erlegen. Die Mutter war unter den Suchenden und empfing zu ihrer großen Freude aus den Händen des Boten ihr kleines Kind wieder. Das Kind ließ bis dahin den hölzernen Löffel nicht aus den Händen fahren.

17. Der große Hund.

Unten in der Wirthsstube einer kleinen Stadt saß ein Bärenführer und verzehrte sein Abendbrod. Der Bär stand draußen im Hofe angebunden. Oben im Zimmer spielten beim Mondschein drei kleine Kinder; das älteste war wohl sechs Jahre alt, das jüngste nicht mehr als zwei. Da kam etwas die Treppe heraufgetappt; wer mochte das sein? Die Thür sprang auf — es war der zottige Bär! Er hatte sich losgemacht und aus dem Hofe den Weg zur Treppe hinauf gefunden. Die Kinder waren über das große, zottige Thier erschrocken; sie krochen in einen Winkel, aber er fand sie alle drei; berührte sie mit der Schnauze, that ihnen aber nichts. Das ist der große Hund dachten sie, und dann streichelten sie ihn. Er legte sich auf den Fußboden, der kleine Knabe wälzte sich oben drauf und spielte Versteck mit seinem Köpfchen in dem dicken, schwarzen Pelz des Bären. Nun nahm der älteste Knabe seine Trommel; schlug darauf, daß es donnerte, und der Bär stand auf und fing an zu tanzen, das war allerliebst! Jeder Knabe nahm sein Gewehr, der Bär mußte auch eins haben; er hielt es ordentlich fest, und nun gingen sie: „Eins, zwei; eins zwei!“ Da kam wieder Jemand an die Thür, sie ging auf, es war die Mutter der Kinder. Ihr hättet sie sehen sollen, und ihren Schrecken und ihr kreideweißes Gesicht! Der kleinste der Knaben nickte vergnügt und rief ihr ganz laut zu: „Wir spielen nur Soldaten!“ Aber die erschrockene Mutter lief nach dem Bärenführer und dankte Gott, daß ihre Kinder noch am Leben waren. Der liebe Gott hatte sie beschützt. Hebel.

18. Die Maus und der Löwe.

Ein Löwe schlief in seiner Höhle, und um ihn her spielte eine lustige Mäuseschaar. Eine derselben kroch eben auf einen hervorstehenden Felsen, fiel herab und erweckte den Löwen, der sie mit seiner gewaltigen Tatze festhielt. „Ach," bat sie, „sei doch großmüthig gegen mich armes, unbedeutendes Geschöpf! Ich habe dich nicht beleidigen wollen; ich habe nur einen Fehltritt gethan, und bin von dem Felsen herabgefallen. Was kann dir mein Tod nützen? Schenke mir das Leben, und ich will dir zeitlebens dankbar sein." „Geh' hin sagte der Löwe großmüthig, und ließ das Mäuschen springen. Bei sich aber lachte er und sprach: „dankbar sein! Nun das möchte ich doch sehen, wie ein Mäuschen sich einem Löwen dankbar bezeigen könnte!"

Kurze Zeit darauf lief das nämliche Mäuschen durch den Wald und suchte sich Nüsse: da hörte es das klägliche Gebrülle eines Löwen. „Der ist in Gefahr!" sprach es bei sich und ging der Stelle zu, wo das Gebrülle herübertönte. Es fand den großmüthigen Löwen von einem starken Netze umschlungen, das der Jäger künstlich ausgespannt hatte, um damit große Waldthiere zu fangen. Die Stricke hatten sich so künstlich zusammengezogen, daß der Löwe weder seine Zähne, noch die Stärke seiner Tatzen gebrauchen konnte, um sie zu zerreißen.

„Warte nur, mein Freund," sagte das Mäuschen, „da kann ich dir wohl am besten helfen." Es lief hinzu, zernagte die Stricke, welche seine Vordertatzen gefesselt hatten, und als diese frei waren, zerriß er das übrige Netz, und ward so durch die Hülfe des Mäuschens wieder frei. Aesop.

19. Eine Erzählung des Barons von Münchhausen.

Als ich Sclave in der Türkei war, mußte ich des Sultans Bienen alle Morgen auf die Weide treiben. Eines Abends vermisse ich eine Biene, wurde aber sogleich gewahr, daß zwei Bären sie angefallen hatten und ihres Honigs wegen zerreißen wollten. Da ich nun nichts anderes waffenähnliches in Händen hatte, als die silberne Axt, welche das Kennzeichen der Gärtner und Landarbeiter des Sultans ist, so warf ich diese nach den beiden Räubern, bloß in der Absicht, sie damit wegzuscheuchen. Die arme Biene setzte ich auch wirklich dadurch in Freiheit; allein durch einen unglücklichen allzustarken Schwung meines Armes flog die Axt in die Höhe, und hörte nicht auf zu steigen, bis sie im Mond niederfiel. Wie sollte ich sie nun wiederkriegen? Mit welcher Leiter auf Erden sie herunterholen?

Da fiel mir ein, daß die türkischen Bohnen sehr geschwind und zu einer ganz erstaunlichen Höhe emporwüchsen. Augenblicklich pflanzte ich also eine solche Bohne, welche wirklich emporwuchs, und sich an eins von des Mondes Hörnern von selbst anrankte. Nun kletterte ich getrost nach dem Monde empor, wo ich auch glücklich anlangte. Es war ein ziemlich mühseliges Stückchen Arbeit, meine silberne Axt an einem Orte wieder zu finden, wo alle anderen Dinge gleichfalls wie Silber glänzen. Endlich aber fand ich sie doch auf einem Haufen Spreu und Häckerling.

Nun wollte ich wieder zurückkehren, aber ach! die Sonnenhitze hatte indessen meine Bohne aufgetrocknet, so daß daran schlechterdings nicht wieder hinabzusteigen war. Was war nun zu thun? — Ich flocht mir einen Strick aus dem

Häckerling, so lang ich ihn nur immer machen konnte. Diesen befestigte ich an eins von des Mondes Hörnern, und ließ mich daran herunter. Mit der rechten Hand hielt ich mich fest, und in der linken führte ich meine Axt. So wie ich nun eine Strecke hinuntergeglitten war, so hieb ich immer das überflüssige Stück über mir ab, und knüpfte dasselbe unten wieder an, wodurch ich denn ziemlich weit herunter gelangte. Dieses wiederholte Abhauen und Anknüpfen machte nun freilich den Strick eben so wenig besser als er mich völlig auf des Sultans Landgut brachte.

Ich mochte wohl noch ein paar Meilen weit droben in den Wolken sein, als mein Strick auf einmal zerriß, und ich mit solcher Heftigkeit herab zu Gottes Erdboden fiel, daß ich ganz betäubt davon wurde. Durch die Schwere meines von einer solchen Höhe herabfallenden Körpers fiel ich ein Loch, wenigstens neun Klafter tief, in die Erde hinein. Ich erholte mich zwar endlich wieder, wußte aber nun nicht, wie ich wieder herauskommen sollte. Allein was thut nicht die Noth! Ich grub mir mit meinen Nägeln, deren Wuchs damals vierzigjährig war, eine Art von Treppe, und förderte mich dadurch glücklich an den Tag.

20. Der Rabe Noahs.

Ängstlich blickte Noah umher aus seinem schwimmenden Kasten, und wartete, bis die Wasser der Sündfluth fielen. Kaum sahen der Berge Spitzen hervor, als er alles Gefieder um sich rief. „Wer," sprach er, „unter euch will Bote sein, ob unsere Rettung nahe ist?"

Da drängte sich vor allen der

Rabe hervor mit großem Geschrei; er witterte nach seiner Lieblingsspeise. Kaum war das Fenster geöffnet, so flog er hin, und kehrte nicht zurück. Der Undankbare vergaß des Retters und seines Geschäfts; er hing am Aase.

Aber die Rache blieb nicht aus. Noch war die Luft von giftigen Dämpfen voll, und schwere Dünste hingen über den Leichen; die benebelten ihm sein Gesicht, und schwärzten seine Federn.

Zur Strafe seiner Vergessenheit ward ihm auch sein Gedächtniß wie sein Auge düster;

selbst seine neugeborenen Jungen erkennt er nicht, und genießt er ihnen keine Vaterfreude. Erschrocken über ihre Häßlichkeit flieht er hinweg und verläßt sie. Der Undankbare zeugt ein Undankbar Geschlecht; entbehren muß er des schönsten Lohnes, des Dankes seiner Kinder.

Herder.

21. Die Taube Noahs.

Acht Tage hatte der Vater der neuen Welt auf die Wiederkunft des trägen Raben gewartet, als er auf's neue seine Scharen um sich rief, Kundschafter auszuwählen. Schüchtern flog die Taube auf seinen Arm und bot sich zur Sendung an.

„Tochter der Trauer," sprach Noah, „du wärest mir wohl eine Dienerin guter Botschaft; wie aber willst du deine Reise thun, und dein Geschäft vollenden? Wie, wenn dein Flügel ermattet, und dich der Sturm ergreift, und wirft dich in die trübe Welle des Todes? Auch scheuen deine Füße Schlamm, und deiner Zunge widert unreine Speise."

„Wer," sprach die Taube, „giebt den Müden Kraft, und Stärke genug den Unvermögenden? Laß mich, ich werde dir gewiß eine Dienerin guter Botschaft."

Sie entflog und schwebte hin und her, und nirgends fand sie, wo sie ruhen könnte; als schnell der Berg des Paradieses sich vor ihr erhob mit seinem grünenden Wipfel. Ueber ihn hatten nichts vermocht die Wasser der Sündfluth, und der Taube war die Zuflucht zu ihm unverboten. Freudig eilte sie und flog hinan, und ließ demüthig sich am Fuße des Berges nieder. Ein schöner Oelbaum blühete da: sie brach ein Blatt des Baumes, eilte gestärkt zurück und legte den Zweig auf des schlummernden Noah Brust.

Er erwachte, und roch dann den Geruch des Paradieses.

Da erquickte sich sein Herz; das grüne Friedensblatt erquickte die Seinigen, bis ihm sein Retter selbst erschien, bekräftigend der Taube gute Botschaft.

Seitdem denn ward die Taube Dienerin der Liebe und des Friedens. Wie Silber glänzen ihre Flügel, sagt das Lied; ein Schimmer noch vom Glanze des Paradieses, das sie auf ihrer Wanderschaft erquickte.

Herder.

22. Der Wolf und der Mensch.

Der Fuchs erzählte einmal dem Wolfe von der Stärke des Menschen. Kein Thier, sagte er, könnte ihm widerstehen, und sie müßten List gebrauchen, um sich vor ihm zu retten. Da antwortete der Wolf: wenn ich nur einmal einen zu sehen bekäme, ich wollte doch wohl auf ihn losgehen! „Dazu kann Rath werden,“ sagte der Fuchs, „komm nur morgen früh zu mir, so will ich dir einen zeigen.“ Der Wolf stellte sich frühzeitig ein, und der Fuchs ging mit ihm an den Weg, wo der Jäger alle Tage herkam. Zuerst kam ein alter, abgedankter Soldat. „Ist das ein Mensch?“ fragte der Wolf. „Nein,“ antwortete der Fuchs, „das ist einer gewesen.“ Darnach kam ein kleiner Knabe, der zur Schule wollte. „Ist das ein Mensch?“ — „Nein, das will erst einer werden.“ Endlich kam der Jäger, die Doppelflinte auf dem Rücken und den Hirschfänger an der Seite. Da sprach der Fuchs zum Wolfe: „Siehst du, dort kommt ein Mensch, auf den mußt du losgehen, ich aber will mich fort in meine Höhle machen.

Der Wolf ging nun auf den Menschen los. Der Jäger, als er ihn erblickte, sprach: Es ist Schade, daß ich keine Kugel geladen habe, legte an und schoß dem Wolfe das Schrot in's Gesicht. Der Wolf verzog das Gesicht gewaltig, doch ließ er sich nicht schrecken und ging vorwärts. Da gab ihm der Jäger die zweite Ladung. Der Wolf verbiß den Schmerz und rückte dem Jäger doch zu Leibe. Da zog dieser seinen Hirschfänger, und gab ihm links und rechts tüchtige Hiebe, daß er über und über blutend und heulend zu dem Fuchse zurücklief.

„Nun, Bruder Wolf,“ sprach der Fuchs, „wie bist du mit dem Menschen fertig geworden? „Ach,“ antwortete der Wolf, so hab' ich mir die Stärke des Menschen nicht vorgestellt. Erst nahm er einen Stock von der Schulter und blies hinein; da flog mir etwas in's Gesicht, das kitzelte mich ganz entsetzlich. Darnach blies er noch einmal in den Stock, da flog mir's um die Nase, wie Blitz und Hagelwetter; und wie ich ganz nahe war, da zog er eine blanke Rippe aus dem Leibe; damit hat er so auf mich losgeschlagen, daß ich beinahe todt liegen geblieben wäre.“ — „Siehst du,“ sprach der Fuchs, „was für ein Prahlhans du bist?“

23. Der Vater und die drei Söhne.

An Jahren alt, an Gütern reich,
Theilt' einst ein Vater sein Vermögen
Und den mit Müh' erworbnen Segen
Selbst unter die drei Söhne gleich.
„Ein Diamant ist's,“ sprach der Alte,
„Den ich für den von euch behalte,
Der mittelst einer edlen That
Darauf den größten Anspruch hat.“

Um diesen Anspruch zu erlangen,
Sieht man die Söhne sich zerstreun.
Drei Monden waren kaum vergangen,
Da stellten sie sich wieder ein.

Drauf sprach der älteste der Brüder:
„Hört, es vertraut' ein fremder Mann
Sein Gut ohn' einen Schein mir an;
Dem gab ich es getreulich wieder.
Sagt, war die That nicht lobenswerth?" —
„Du thatst, mein Sohn, was sich gehört,"
Ließ sich der Vater hier vernehmen,
„Wer anders thut, der muß sich schämen;
Denn ehrlich sein, heißt uns die Pflicht.
Die That ist gut, doch edel nicht."

Der zweite sprach: „Auf meiner Reise
Fiel einstmals unachtsamer Weise
Ein armes Kind in einen See.
Ich stürzt ihm nach, zog's in die Höh'
Und rettete dem Kind das Leben.
Ein Dorf kann davon Zeugniß geben." —
„Du thatest," sprach der Greis, „mein Kind,
Was wir als Menschen schuldig sind."

Der jüngste sprach: „Bei seinen Schafen
War einst mein Feind fest eingeschlafen
An eines tiefen Abgrunds Rand.
Sein Leben stand in meiner Hand:
Ich weckt' ihn und zog ihn zurücke."
„O!" rief der Greis mit holdem Blicke,
„Der Ring ist dein! Welch edler Muth,
Wenn man dem Feinde Gutes thut!"

Lichtwer.

24. Dornröschen.

(Märchen, von den Brüdern Grimm.)

Vor Zeiten war ein König und eine Königinn, die sprachen jeden Tag: „Ach wenn wir doch ein Kind hätten!" und kriegten immer keins. Endlich aber bekamen sie ein so schönes Mädcheu, daß der König vor Freude sich nicht zu lassen wußte und ein großes Fest anstellte. Er lud nicht blos seine Verwandten, Freunde und Bekannten, sondern auch die weisen Frauen dazu ein, damit sie dem Kind hold und gewogen würden. Es waren ihrer dreizehn in seinem Reich, weil er aber nur zwölf goldene Teller hatte, von welchen sie essen sollten, konnte er eine nicht einladen. Die geladen waren kamen, und nachdem das Fest gehalten war, beschenkten sie das Kind mit ihren Wundergaben; die eine mit Tugend, die andere mit Schönheit, die dritte mit Reichthum, und so mit allem, was Herrliches auf der Welt ist. Als elf ihre Wünsche eben gethan hatten, kam die dreizehnte herein, die nicht eingeladen war und sich dafür rächen wollte. Sie rief: „Die Königstochter soll sich in ihrem fünfzehnten Jahre an einer Spindel stechen und todt hinfallen." Da trat die zwölfte hervor, die noch einen Wunsch übrig hatte; zwar konnte sie den bösen Ausspruch nicht aufheben. aber sie konnte ihn doch mildern, und sprach: „Es soll aber kein Tod sein, sondern ein hundertjähriger tiefer Schlaf, in den die Königstochter fällt."

Der König hoffte sein liebes Kind noch vor dem Ausspruch zu bewahren, und ließ den Befehl ausgehen, daß alle Spindeln im ganzen Königreich sollten abgeschafft werden. An dem Mädchen aber wurden alle die Gaben der weisen Frauen erfüllt, denn es war so schön, sittsam, freundlich und verständig, daß es jedermann, der es ansah, lieb haben mußte. Es geschah, daß an dem Tage, wo es gerade fünfzehn Jahr alt ward, der König und die Königinn nicht zu Haus waren und das Fräulein ganz allein im Schloß zurückblieb. Da ging es aller Orten herum, besah Stuben und Kammern, wie es Lust hatte, und kam endlich auch an einen alten Thurm. Es stieg eine enge Treppe hinauf und gelangte zu einer kleinen Thüre. In dem Schloß steckte ein gelber Schlüssel, und als es umdrehte, sprang die Thüre auf und saß da in einem kleinen Stübchen eine alte Frau und spann emsig ihren Flachs. „Ei du altes Mütterchen," sprach die Königstochter, „was machst du da?" „Ich spinne," sagte die Alte und nickte mit dem Kopf. „Wie das Ding herumspringt!" sprach das Fräulein, und nahm die Spindel und wollte auch spinnen. Kaum hatte sie die Spindel angerührt, so ging die Verwünschung des Zauberweibes in Erfüllung und sie stach sich damit.

In dem Augenblicke aber, wo sie sich gestochen hatte, fiel sie auch nieder in einen tiefen Schlaf. Und der König und die Königinn, die eben zurückgekommen waren, fingen an, mit dem ganzen Hofstagt einzuschlafen. Da schliefen auch die Pferde im Stall ein, die Hunde im Hofe, die Tauben auf dem Dach, die Fliegen an der Wand, ja das Feuer, das auf dem Herde flackerte, ward still und schlief ein, und der Braten hörte auf zu brutzeln, und der Koch, der den Küchenjungen, weil er etwas versehen hatte, in den Haaren ziehen wollte, ließ ihn los und schlief, und alles, was lebendigen Athem hatte, ward still und schlief.

Um das Schloß aber begann eine Dornenhecke zu wachsen, die jedes Jahr höher ward und endlich das ganze Schloß so umzog und drüber hinauswuchs, daß gar nichts mehr, selbst nicht die Fahnen auf den Dächern, zu sehen war. Es ging aber die Sage in dem Land von dem schönen, schlafenden Dornröschen, denn so wurde die Königstochter genannt, also, daß von Zeit zu Zeit Königssöhne kamen und durch die Hecke in das Schloß dringen wollten. Es war ihnen aber nicht möglich, denn die Dornen hielten sich gleichsam wie an Händen zusammen und sie blieben darin hängen und starben jämmerlich. Nach langen, langen Jahren kam wieder ein Königssohn durch das Land; dem erzählte ein alter Mann von der Dornhecke: es solle ein Schloß dahinter stehen, in welchem ein wunderschönes Königsfräulein, Dornröschen genannt, schlafe mit dem ganzen Hofstaat. Er erzählte auch, daß er von seinem Großvater gehört, wie viele Königssöhne gekommen wären, um durch die Dornhecke zu dringen, aber darin hängen geblieben und eines traurigen Todes gestorben. Da sprach der Jüngling: „Das soll mich nicht abschrecken, ich will hindurch und das schöne Dornröschen sehen." Der Alte mochte ihm abrathen, wie er wollte, er hörte gar nicht darauf.

Nun waren aber gerade an dem Tage, wo der Königssohn kam, die hundert Jahre verflossen. Und als er sich der Dornhecke näherte, waren es lauter große, schöne Blumen, die thaten sich von selbst auseinander, daß er unbeschädigt dadurch ging; hinter ihm aber thaten sie sich wieder als eine Hecke zusammen.

Er kam ins Schloß; da lagen im Hof die Pferde und scheckigen Jagdhunde und schliefen, auf dem Dache saßen die Tauben und hatten das Köpfchen unter den Flügel gesteckt. Und als er ins Haus kam, schliefen die Fliegen an der Wand, der Koch in der Küche hielt noch die Hand, als wollte er den Jungen anpacken, und die Magd saß vor dem schwarzen Huhn, das sollte gerupft werden. Da ging er weiter und sah den ganzen Hofstaat da liegen und schlafen, und oben drüber den König und die Königinn. Da ging er noch weiter, und alles war so still, daß einer seinen Athem hören konnte, und endlich kam er zu dem Thurm und öffnete die Thüre zu der kleinen Stube, in welcher Dornröschen schlief. Da lag es und war so schön, daß er die Augen nicht abwenden konnte, und er bückte sich und gab ihm einen Kuß. Wie er ihm den Kuß gegeben, schlug Dornröschen die Augen auf, erwachte und sah ihn freundlich an. Da gingen sie zusammen herab, und der König erwachte und die Königinn und der ganze Hofstaat, und sahen einander mit großen Augen an. Und die Pferde im Hof stunden auf und rüttelten sich, die Jagdhunde sprangen und wedelten; die Tauben auf dem Dach zogen das Köpfchen unterm Flügel hervor, sahen umher und flogen ins Feld; die Fliegen an den Wänden krochen weiter; das Feuer in der Küche erhub sich, flackerte und kochte das Essen, und der Braten brutzelte fort; der Koch gab dem Jungen eine Ohrfeige, daß er schrie, und die Magd rupfte das Huhn fertig. Und da wurde die Hochzeit des Königssohns mit dem Dornröschen in aller Pracht gefeiert, und sie lebten vergnügt bis an ihr Ende.

25. Der blinde König.

Was steht der nord'schen Fechter Schaar
Hoch auf des Meeres Bord?
Was will in seinem grauen Haar
Der blinde König dort?
Er ruft, in bitterm Harme
Auf seinen Stab gelehnt,
Daß über'm Meeresarme
Das Eiland widertönt:

„Gib, Räuber aus dem Felsverlies
Die Tochter mir zurück!
Ihr Harfenspiel, ihr Lied so süß
War meines Alters Glück.
Vom Tanz auf grünem Strande
Hast du sie weggeraubt,
Dir ist es ewig Schande,
Mir beugt's das graue Haupt.“

Da tritt aus seiner Schlucht hervor
Der Räuber groß und wild,
Er schwingt sein Hünenschwert empor
Und schlägt an seinen Schild:
„Du hast ja viele Wächter,
Warum denn litten's die?

Dir dient so mancher Fechter
Und keiner kämpft um sie?"

Noch stehn die Fechter alle stumm;
Tritt keiner aus den Reihn?
Der blinde König kehrt sich um:
„Bin ich denn ganz allein?" —
Da faßt des Vaters Rechte
Sein junger Sohn, so warm:
„Vergönnt' mir's, daß ich fechte!
Wohl fühl' ich Kraft im Arm."

„O Sohn! der Feind ist riesenstark,
Ihm hielt noch Keiner Stand;
Und doch in dir ist edles Mark,
Ich fühl's am Druck der Hand.
Nimm hier die alte Klinge!
Sie ist der Skalden Preis.
Und fällst du, so verschlinge
Die Fluth mich armen Greis!

Und horch, es schäumet und es rauscht
Der Nachen über's Meer.
Der blinde König steht und lauscht,
Und alles schweigt umher;
Bis drüben sich erhoben
Der Schild' und Schwerter Schall
Und Kampfgeschrei und Toben
Und dumpfer Wiederhall.

Da ruft der Greis so freudig bang':
„Sagt an, was ihr erschaut!
Mein Schwert, ich kenn's am guten Klang,
Es gab so scharfen Laut." —
„Der Räuber ist gefallen,
Er hat den blut'gen Lohn,
Heil dir, du Held vor Allen,
Du starker Königssohn!"

Und wieder wird es still umher.
Der König steht und lauscht:
„Was hör' ich kommen über's Meer?
Es rudert und es rauscht." —
„Sie kommen angefahren,
Dein Sohn mit Schwert und Schild.
Mit sonnenhellen Haaren
Dein Töchterlein Gunild."

„Willkommen!" ruft vom hohen Stein
Der blinde Greis hinab.

„Nun wird mein Alter wonnig sein
Und ehrenvoll mein Grab.
Du legst mir, Sohn zur Seite
Das Schwert von gutem Klang,
Gunilde, du Befreite,
Singst mir den Grabgesang."

Uhland.

26. Ein Gleichniß.

Als der fromme Winfried, vom Geiste getrieben, ausziehen wollte aus seinem Vaterlande um seiner Verwandtschaft das Evangelium zu verkündigen unter den abgöttischen Deutschen, wehrten ihm seine Freunde und Verwandte und sprachen: Bleib in der Heimath, da magst du auch des Guten genug schaffen, wofern du nur dieses begehrest.

Winfried aber antwortete und sprach: Höret zuvor eine Geschichte, darnach urtheilt. Als vor etlichen Jahren des Krieges Wuth unseres Landes Grenzen verheert hatte, zog ein reicher Mann durch die verwüstete Gegend. Da traf er auf dem Gebirge ein Häuflein Kinder nackend und bloß, und sie nagten an den Wurzeln, die sie aus der Erde wühlten. Da jammerten ihn die Kinder und er fragte sie: Wo ist euer Haus und euer Vater und die Mutter? Die Kinder sagten: Unser Haus ist verbrannt, und wir haben keinen Vater und keine Mutter mehr, der Krieg hat sie getödtet.

Darauf nahm der reiche Mann die Kinder in seinen Wagen und führte sie in sein Haus und gab ihnen Alles, was sie bedurften, auch lehrte er sie arbeiten, und ließ sie unterrichten in allerlei Künsten und Weisheit.

Nach einiger Zeit kamen die Kinder zu ihm und sagten: Du bist groß und reich, aber noch größer, als dein Reichthum, ist deine Güte, womit du dich unserer erbarmt hast; ach! sage uns, mit welchem Namen wir dich nennen sollen?

Da neigte sich der barmherzige Mann zu den Kindern und sagte: nennet mich Vater, denn ich will euer Vater sein, und ihr sollt meine Kinder sein.

Als der fromme Winfried diese Geschichte erzählt hatte, lobeten alle die Güte des reichen Mannes. Da erhob er sich und sagte: Dort, wohin mein Herz verlanget, ist ein ganz verwais'tes Völkchen. Gold und Silber habe ich nicht, aber ich will ihnen Besseres geben. Ich will sie zum Vater führen.

Darum zog er hinaus gen Deutschland und that die Götzen hinweg und lehrte das Evangelium vom Glauben und von der Liebe. Und sie nannten ihn Bonifazius, d. h. Wohlthäter und sprachen: Er hat ein gutes Werk an uns gethan.

Krummacher.

27. Till.

Till Eulenspiegel zog einmal mit Andern über Land und

Thal; so oft, als sie zu einem Berge kamen, ging Till an seinem Wanderstab den Berg ganz sacht und ganz betrübt hinab; allein, wenn sie bergenwärts stiegen, war Eulenspiegel voll Vergnügen. Warum, fing Einer an, gehst du bergan so froh? bergunter so betrübt? Ich bin, sprach Till, nun so. Wenn ich den Berg hinunter gehe, so denk' ich Narr schon an die Höhe, die folgen wird, und da vergeht mir denn der Scherz. Allein, wenn ich bergenwärts gehe, so denk' ich an das Thal, das folgt, und fass' ein Herz.

Willst du dich in dem Glück nicht ausgelassen freu'n, im Unglück nicht unmäßig kränken, so lerne klug wie Eulenspiegel sein; im Unglück gern an's Glück, im Glück an's Unglück denken.

Gellert.

28. Der reiche Fürst.

Preisend mit viel schönen Reden
Ihrer Länder Werth und Zahl
Saßen viele deutsche Fürsten
Einst zu Worms im Kaisersaal.

Herrlich, sprach der Fürst von Sachsen,
Ist mein Land und seine Macht,
Silber hegen seine Berge
Wohl in manchem tiefen Schacht.

Seht mein Land in üpp'ger Fülle
Sprach der Kurfürst von dem Rhein,
Goldne Saaten in den Thälern.
Auf den Bergen edlen Wein.

Große Städte, reiche Klöster
Ludwig, Herr zu Bayern, sprach,
Schaffen, daß mein Land den euern
Wohl nicht steht an Schätzen nach.

Eberhard, der mit dem Barte,
Würtembergs geliebter Herr,
Sprach: mein Land hat kleine Städte,
Trägt nicht Berge silberschwer.

Doch ein Kleinod hält's verborgen
Daß in Wäldern noch so groß
Ich mein Haupt kann kühnlich legen
Jedem Unterthan in Schooß!

Und es rief der Herr von Sachsen,
Der von Bayern, der vom Rhein:
Graf im Bart, ihr seid der reichste
Euer Land trägt Edelstein!

Justinus Kerner.

29. Die Schatzgräber.

Hört, Kinder! sprach ein kranker Mann, der durch den Weinbau viel gewann: in unserem Berge liegt ein Schatz; grabt nur danach. — An welchem Platz? so fragten Alle, sagt den Ort! — Grabt! grabt! Er starb bei diesem Wort.

Kaum war der Greis zur Gruft gebracht, so ward gegraben Tag und Nacht; mit Hacke, Karst und Spaten ward der Weinberg um und um gescharrt. Da war kein Kloß, der ruhig blieb; man warf die Erde gar durch's Sieb; zog Harken in die Läng' und Quer nach jedem Steinchen hin und her. Allein, es ward kein Schatz verspürt, und jeder hielt sich angeführt.

Doch kaum erschien das nächste Jahr, so nahm man mit Erstaunen wahr, daß jeder Weinstock dreifach trug. Da wurden erst die Söhne klug, und gruben nun, Jahr ein, Jahr aus, des Schatzes immer mehr heraus. Bürger.

30. Der kluge Pudel.

Der Eigenthümer eines wohlabgerichteten Pudels ging einst mit einem Freunde durch einen Wald. Er ließ unterwegs den Hund mehrere seiner Kunststückchen machen und versicherte, daß derselbe etwas Verlorenes auf eine ganze Stunde Entfernung suche und wieder bringe. Als sein Freund dieses in Zweifel ziehen wollte, zog der Herr des Pudels seinen Geldbeutel heraus, warf ihn in einen nahen Busch und wanderte mit seinem Freunde weiter.

Als sie wohl eine Stunde zurückgelegt hatten, rief der Herr seinem Pudel zu: „Phylax! such' Verlornes!" und der Hund eilte, die Nase nahe am Boden haltend, mit der größten Schnelligkeit zurück.

Inzwischen kam ein Handwerksbursche denselben Weg. Ermüdet setzte er sich neben einem Haselstrauch, um auszuruhen, und als er sich vollends niederlegen wollte, erblickte er mit freudiger Ueberraschung in dem Gesträuche den Geldbeutel, welchen der Herr des Pudels dahin geworfen hatte. Er zählte das Geld, steckte es zu sich und war seelenvergnügt über den glücklichen Fund.

Es dauerte nicht lange, so kam der Pudel zurück. Er näherte sich dem Gebüsche und beroch dasselbe so wie den Handwerksburschen von allen Seiten. Dieser schmeichelte dem schönen Thiere, welches sich dieses willig gefallen ließ und sich endlich zu seinen Füßen niederlegte.

„Was das doch heute für ein glücklicher Tag ist," sagte der Wanderer zu sich selbst, „zuerst finde ich eine Börse mit 3 Thalern, und nun läuft mir noch ein so schöner Hund zu, den ich vielleicht gelegentlich theuer verkaufen kann;" denn daß er nach dem Eigenthümer dieser Sachen fragen wolle, fiel dem unredlichen Menschen nicht ein.

Er wanderte wohlgemuth weiter und blieb in dem nächsten Dorfe über Nacht. Sein heutiges Glück hatte ihn übermüthig gemacht und er ließ sich nach einer guten Mahlzeit auch einen guten Trunk schmecken, worauf man ihm endlich sein Schlafgemach anwies, das sich zu ebener Erde befand.

Dem heißen Tage war ein herrlicher Abend gefolgt. Der Handwerksbursche öffnete ein Fenster, entkleidete sich hierauf und legte sich zu Bette. Als der Pudel dies wahrnahm, faßte er schnell die Beinkleider, worin die Börse seines Herrn befindlich war und sprang mit denselben zum offenen Fenster hinaus. Alles Rufen des Handwerksburschen war vergeblich; er hatte das bloße Nachsehen für sich. Der Herr des Pudels aber war nicht wenig verwundert, als er spät in der Nacht seinen Hund mit einem Paar Hosen ankommen sah, in welchen man beim Durchsuchen den weggeworfenen Geldbeutel fand. H. R.

31. Wintermärchen.

Die Erde schläft! mit weißer Hülle hat sie der Winter zugedeckt; sie ist nicht todt, sie schläft nur stille, bis daß der Lenz sie wieder weckt.

Und wie das Kindlein ohne Sorgen sich an den Mutterbusen schmiegt, so ruhn an ihrer Brust geborgen die Blumenkinder eingewiegt.

Da träumen sie von milden Lüften, vom Sonnenschein, vom klaren Thau; und sehn, berauscht von süßen Düften, den grünen Wald, die bunte Au.

Sie lauschen, was die Vögel singen, und was die Welle sagt im Bach; sie kosen mit den Schmetterlingen, die Bienen summen: Guten Tag!

Die Blumen streben sich nach oben, die Pracht zu schauen fern und nah; da ist der schöne Traum zerstoben, und sieh, der Lenz ist wirklich da. Ebelmann.

32. Der Reisende.

Ein Wandrer bat den Gott der Götter
Den Zevs bei ungestümem Wetter
Um stille Luft und Sonnenschein.
Umsonst! Zevs läßt sich nicht bewegen
Der Himmel stürmt mit Wind und Regen;
Denn stürmisch sollt' es heute sein.
Der Wandrer setzt mit bittrer Klage,
Daß Zevs mit Fleiß die Menschen plage
Die saure Reise mühsam fort.
So oft ein neuer Sturmwind wüthet
Und schnell ihm still zu stehn, gebietet,
So oft ertönt ein Lästerwort.
Ein naher Wald soll ihn beschirmen.
Er eilt, dem Regen und den Stürmen
In diesem Holze zu entgehn;
Doch eh' der Wald ihn aufgenommen,
So sieht er einen Räuber kommen
Und bleibt vor Furcht im Regen stehn.
Der Räuber greift nach seinem Bogen,
Den schon die Nässe schlaff gezogen.
Er zielt und faßt den Pilger wohl;
Doch Wind und Regen sind zuwider,
Der Pfeil fällt matt vor dem darnieder,
Dem er das Herz durchbohren soll.
„O Thor," läßt Zevs sich zornig hören,
„Wird dich der nahe Pfeil nun lehren,
Ob ich dem Sturm zu Viel erlaubt?
Hätt' ich dir Sonnenschein gegeben,
So hätte dir der Pfeil das Leben,
Das dir der Sturm erhielt, geraubt."

Gellert.

33. Der Kaiser als Anwalt.

Ein alter Soldat, der lange unter dem Kaiser Augustus gedient, und namentlich in der entscheidenden Schlacht bei Actium für ihn gefochten hatte, war in einen Rechtshandel verwickelt, der kein Ende nehmen zu wollen schien. Als er vor Gericht erscheinen sollte, wandte er sich auf öffentlicher Straße an den Kaiser und bat ihn um Beistand. Augustus rief einen von seinem Gefolge und übertrug ihm die Sache des Beklagten. Der alte Soldat war aber damit nicht zufrieden und rief mit lauter Stimme: „O Kaiser, da du in der Schlacht bei Aktium in Gefahr schwebtest, habe ich keinen Stellvertreter ausgesucht, sondern in eigener Person für dich gekämpft!“ Zugleich entblößte er seine narbige Brust, um auf die Wunden hinzudeuten, die er für den Kaiser empfangen hatte. Dieser ward dadurch gerührt. Um nicht undankbar zu scheinen, ging er mit dem Beklagten vor Gericht und verteidigte ihn mit Wärme und Eifer und verhalf ihm dadurch zu seinem Rechte.

v. Schulze.

34. Des Sängers Fluch.

Es stand in alten Zeiten ein Schloß, so hoch und hehr,
Weit glänzt' es über die Lande bis an das blaue Meer,
Und rings von duft'gen Gärten ein blüthenreicher Kranz,
Drin sprangen frische Brunnen im Regenbogenglanz.

Dort saß ein stolzer König, an Land und Siegen reich,
Er saß auf seinem Throne so finster und so bleich;
Denn was er sinnt, ist Schrecken, und was er blickt, ist Wuth,
Und was er spricht, ist Geisel, und was er schreibt, ist Blut.

Einst zog nach diesem Schlosse ein edles Sängerpaar,
Der Ein' in goldnen Locken, der Andre grau von Haar;
Der Alte mit der Harfe, er saß auf schmuckem Roß,
Es schritt ihm frisch zur Seite der blühende Genoß.

Der Alte sprach zum Jungen: „Nun sei bereit, mein Sohn!
Denk' unsrer tiefsten Lieder, stimm' an den vollsten Ton,
Nimm alle Kraft zusammen, die Lust und auch den Schmerz!
Es gilt uns heut, zu rühren des Königs steinern Herz."

Schon stehn die beiden Sänger im hohen Säulensaal,
Und auf dem Throne sitzen der König und sein Gemal;
Der König, furchtbar prächtig, wie blut'ger Nordlichtschein,
Die Königinn, süß und milde, als blickte Vollmond drein.

Da schlug der Greis die Saiten, er schlug sie wundervoll,
Daß reicher, immer reicher der Klang zum Ohre schwoll.
Dann strömte himmlischhelle des Jünglings Stimme vor,
Des Alten Sang dazwischen, wie dumpfer Geisterchor.

Sie singen von Lenz und Liebe, von sel'ger goldner Zeit,
Von Freiheit, Männerwürde, von Treu und Heiligkeit.
Sie singen von allem Süßen, was Menschenbrust durchbebt,
Sie singen von allem Hohen, was Menschenherz erhebt.

Die Höflingsschar im Kreise verlernet jeden Spott,
Des Königs trotz'ge Krieger, sie beugen sich vor Gott.
Die Königinn, zerflossen in Wehmuth und in Lust,
Sie wirft den Sängern nieder die Rose von ihrer Brust,

„Ihr habt mein Volk verführet, verlockt ihr nun mein Weib?"
Der König schreit es wüthend, er bebt am ganzen Leib,
Er wirft sein Schwert, das blitzend des Jünglings Brust durchdringt,
Draus, statt der goldnen Lieder ein Blutstrahl hoch aufspringt.

Und wie vom Sturm zerstoben ist all der Hörer Schwarm,
Der Jüngling hat verröchelt in seines Meisters Arm,
Der schlägt um ihn den Mantel und setzt ihn auf das Roß,
Er bindt ihn aufrecht feste, verläßt mit ihm das Schloß.

Doch vor dem hohen Thore, da hält der Sängergreis,
Da faßt er seine Harfe, sie, aller Harfen Preis,

An einer Marmorsäule, da hat er sie zerschellt,
Dann ruft er, daß es schaurig durch Schloß und Garten gellt:

„Weh euch, ihr stolzen Hallen! nie töne süßer Klang
Durch eure Räume wieder, nie Saite noch Gesang,
Nein! Seufzer nur und Stöhnen und scheuer Sclavenschritt,
Bis euch zu Schutt und Moder der Rachegeist zertritt!

Weh euch, ihr duft'gen Gärten im holden Maienlicht!
Euch zeig' ich dieses Todten entstelltes Angesicht,
Daß ihr darob verdorret, daß jeder Quell versiegt,
Daß ihr in künft'gen Tagen, versteint, verödet liegt.

Weh dir, verruchter Mörder, du Fluch des Sängerthums!
Umsonst sei all dein Ringen nach Kränzen blut'gen Ruhms,
Dein Name sei vergessen, in ew'ge Nacht getaucht,
Sei, wie ein letztes Röcheln, in leere Luft verhaucht."

Der Alte hat's gerufen, der Himmel hat's gehört,
Die Mauern liegen nieder, die Hallen sind zerstört,
Noch eine hohe Säule zeigt von verschwundner Pracht,
Auch diese, schon geborsten, kann stürzen über Nacht.

Und rings, statt duft'ger Gärten, ein ödes Haideland.
Kein Baum versendet Schatten, kein Quell durchdringt den Sand,
Des Königs Namen meldet kein Lied, kein Heldenbuch;
Versunken und vergessen! das ist des Sängers Fluch.

Uhland.

35. Das Chamounithal.

Chamouni, den 4. November, Abends gegen Neun.

Nur daß ich mit diesem Blatt Ihnen um so viel näher rücken kann, nehme ich die Feder; sonst wäre es besser, meine Geister ruhen zu lassen. Wir ließen Salenche in einem schönen, offnen Thale hinter uns, der Himmel hatte sich während unserer Mittagrast mit weißen Schäfchen überzogen, von denen ich hier eine besondere Anmerkung machen muß. Wir haben sie so schön und noch schöner an einem heitern Tag von den Berner Eisbergen aufsteigen sehen. Auch hier schien es uns wieder so, als wenn die Sonne die leisesten Ausdünstungen von den höchsten Schneegebirgen gegen sich aufzöge, und diese ganz feinen Dünste von einer leichten Luft, wie eine Schaumwolle, durch die Atmosphäre gekämmt würden. Ich erinnere mich nie in den höchsten Sommertagen bei uns, wo dergleichen Lufterscheinungen auch vorkommen, etwas so Durchsichtiges, Lichtgewobenes gesehen zu haben. Schon sahen wir die Schneegebirge, von denen sie aufsteigen, vor uns, das Thal fing an zu stocken, die Arve schoß aus einer Felskluft hervor, wir mußten einen Berg hinan, und wanden uns, die Schneegebirge rechts vor uns, immer höher. Abwechselnde Berge, alte Fichtenwälder zeigten sich uns rechts, theils in der Tiefe, theils in gleicher Höhe mit uns. Links über uns waren die Berge kahl und spitzig. Wir fühlten, daß wir einem stärkern und mächtigern Satz von Bergen immer näher rückten. Wir kamen über ein breites trocknes Bett von Kieseln und Steinen, das die

Wasserfluthen die Länge des Berges hinab zerreißen und wieder füllen; von da in ein sehr angenehmes, rundgeschlossenes flaches Thal, worin das Dörfchen Servos liegt. Von da geht der Weg um einige sehr bunte Felsen, wieder gegen die Arve. Wenn man über sie weg ist, steigt man einen Berg hinan, die Massen werden hier immer größer, die Natur hat hier mit sachter Hand das Ungeheure zu bereiten angefangen. Es wurde dunkler, wir kamen dem Thale Chamouni näher und endlich darein. Nur die großen Massen waren uns sichtbar. Die Sterne gingen nach einander auf, und wir bemerkten über den Gipfeln der Berge, rechts vor uns, ein Licht das wir nicht erklären konnten. Hell, ohne Glanz wie die Milchstraße, doch dichter, fast wie die Plejaden, nur größer, unterhielt es lange unsere Aufmerksamkeit, bis es endlich, da wir unsern Standpunkt änderten, wie eine Pyramide, von einem innern geheimnißvollen Lichte durchzogen, das dem Schein eines Johanniswurmes am besten verglichen werden kann, über den Gipfeln aller Berge hervorragte, und uns gewiß machte, daß es der Gipfel des Montblanc war. Es war die Schönheit dieses Anblicks ganz außerordentlich; denn da er mit den Sternen, die um ihn herum stunden, zwar nicht in gleich raschem Licht, doch in einer breitern zusammenhängendern Masse leuchtete, so schien er den Augen zu einer höhern Sphäre zu gehören, und man hatte Mühe, in Gedanken seine Wurzeln wieder an die Erde zu befestigen.

von Göthe.

36. Aufmunterung zur Freude.

Wer wollte sich mit Grillen plagen, so lang uns Lenz und Jugend blühn? Wer wollt' in seinen Blüthentagen die Stirn in düstre Falten ziehn?

Die Freude winkt auf allen Wegen, die durch dies Pilgerleben gehn; sie bringt uns selbst den Kranz entgegen, wenn wir am Scheidewege stehn.

Noch rinnt und rauscht die Wiesenquelle, noch ist die Laube kühl und grün, noch scheint der liebe Mond so helle, wie er durch Adams Bäume schien.

Noch tönt der Busch von Nachtigallen dem Jüngling hohe Wonne zu; noch strömt, wenn ihre Lieder schallen, selbst in zerrißne Seelen Ruh.

O! wunderschön ist Gottes Erde und wert, darauf vergnügt zu sein; drum will ich, bis ich Asche werde, mich dieser schönen Erde freuen!

Hölty.

37. Bestrafte Anmaßung.

Immanuel Kant, der berühmte Königsberger Philosoph, aß eines Tages im Wirthshause an öffentlicher Tafel; ein junger Edelmann aus der Nachbarschaft, der überall sehr anmaßend aufzutreten pflegte, saß ihm gegenüber. Die Speisen wurden aufgetragen, unter diesen auch eine, die besonders den Appetit der Gäste reizte. Der junge Edelmann schien zu glauben, daß auf eine solche Delicatesse nur sein Gaumen einen Anspruch habe; denn er ergriff ohne Weiteres das Pfefferfaß und schüttete es über die Speise aus, indem er trocken hinzufügte: „Ich esse diese Speise gern mit Pfeffer!“ Alle übrigen Gäste waren über diese Anmaßung eben so betroffen, wie empört; Kant aber ergriff mit vollkommenster Ruhe seine Schnupftabacksdose, schüttete auch diese über die Speise aus und sagte ganz eben so trocken: „Und ich esse sie gern mit Schnupftaback!“ (Mündlich.)

38. Der junge Napoleon.

Napoleon gab schon in seiner Jugend oft sehr treffende Antworten. Als er zum ersten Male zum heiligen Abendmahle ging, zauderte der Erzbischof, ihm dasselbe zu reichen, weil sein Taufname: „Napoleon“ nicht im Kalender stehe. „Was? rief Buonaparte lebhaft, es giebt eine sehr große Menge von Heiligen, und das Jahr hat nur 365 Tage!“ Der Erzbischof staunte über diesen Ausruf und reichte ihm das Abendmahl.

39. Swift.

Der berühmte brittische Gelehrte Doctor Jonathan Swift war ein Mann von vielem Humor, und er hatte selbst in seinen reiferen Mannesjahren noch manchmal seine Freude, Jemandem einen kleinen Schalksstreich zu spielen. Einst, auf einer seiner Fußreisen, kam er des Abends in ein Städtchen, wo eben Jahrmarkt gehalten wurde. Er beschloß, dort zu übernachten, da er schon sehr müde war. Alle guten Herbergen waren schon überfüllt, und er mußte es sich in einem eben nicht sehr honetten Wirthshause gefallen lassen, mit einem vor ihm angekommenen Pächter zusammen zu schlafen; denn auch hier war Mangel an Gemächern, Betten und Bettzeug. Obgleich ihm nun die Bettgenossenschaft sehr ungelegen kam, so äußerte er doch nichts. Kaum hatten sich Beide zur Ruhe gelegt, als der Pächter, weil er nicht schlafen konnte, eine Unterhaltung anknüpfte, in welcher er seine auf dem Markte gemachten Geschäfte rühmte. — „Ich bin nicht so glücklich gewesen, sagte Swift; denn seit der Eröffnung der Assisen hab' ich erst sechs Burschen gehenkt.“ — „Wie? Gehenkt? rief der Pächter erschrocken. Was habt Ihr denn eigentlich für ein Geschäft?“ — „Es ist, meiner Treu'! ein gutes; ich bin der Scharfrichter der Grafschaft.“ —„Ist es möglich! Ihr, ein Scharfrichter?“ — „Ja! und ich denk' am nächsten Sonnabend zu Tyburn noch acht Kerls zu hängen und einen zu viertheilen.“ — Der Pächter, ohne weiter Etwas hören zu wollen, sprang auf, warf sich schnell in seine Oberkleider, nahm Hut und Stock und rannte die Treppe hinab zum Wirth, den er einen Spitzbuben schalt, daß er ihn mit dem Scharfrichter zusammengebettet habe. Der Gescholtene schüttelte den Kopf und glaubte, der Pächter sei übergeschnappt. Dieser warf ihm das Zechgeld vor die

Füße und stürmte zum Hause hinaus. Swift aber genoß die Früchte seines Schelmenstreichs und schlief ruhig bis an den hellen Tag.

40. Der Alpenjäger.

Willst du nicht das Lämmlein hüten?
Lämmlein ist so fromm und sanft,
Nährt sich von des Grases Blüthen,
Spielend an des Baches Ranft.
„Mutter, Mutter, laß mich gehen,
Jagen nach des Berges Höhen.“

Willst du nicht die Heerde locken
Mit des Hornes muntrem Klang?
Lieblich tönt der Schall der Glocken
In des Waldes Lustgesang.
„Mutter, Mutter, laß mich gehen,
Schweifen auf den wilden Höhen!“

Willst du nicht der Blümlein warten,
Die im Beete freundlich stehn?
Draußen ladet dich kein Garten;
Wild ist's auf den wilden Höh'n!
„Laß die Blümlein, laß sie blühen;
Mutter, Mutter, laß mich ziehen!“

Und der Knabe ging zu jagen,
Und es treibt und reißt ihn fort,
Rastlos fort mit blindem Wagen
An des Berges finstern Ort;
Vor ihm her mit Windesschnelle
Flieht die zitternde Gazelle.

Auf der Felsen nackte Rippen
Klettert sie mit leichtem Schwung,
Durch den Riß zerborstner Klippen
Trägt sie der gewagte Sprung.
Aber hinter ihr verwogen
Folgt er mit dem Todesbogen.

Jetzo auf den schroffen Zinken
Hängt sie, auf dem höchsten Grat,
Wo die Felsen jäh versinken,
Und verschwunden ist der Pfad.
Unter sich die steile Höhe,
Hinter sich des Feindes Nähe.

Mit des Jammers stummen Blicken
Fleht sie zu dem harten Mann,
Fleht umsonst, denn loszudrücken
Legt er schon den Bogen an.

Plötzlich aus der Felsenspalte,
Tritt der Geist, der Bergesalte.
Und mit seinen Götterhänden
Schützt er das gequälte Thier.
„Mußt du Tod und Jammer senden,
Ruft er bis herauf zu mir?
Raum für alle hat die Erde!
Was verfolgst du meine Heerde?“

Schiller.

41. Ritter Toggenburg.

„Ritter, treue Schwesterliebe
Widmet euch dies Herz.
Fodert keine andre Liebe!
Denn es macht mir Schmerz;
Ruhig mag ich euch erscheinen,
Ruhig gehen seh'n.
Eurer Augen stilles Weinen
Kann ich nicht versteh'n.

Und er hört's mit stummem Harme,
Reißt sich blutend los,
Preßt sie heftig in die Arme,
Schwingt sich auf sein Roß,
Schickt zu seinen Mannen allen
In dem Lande Schweiz!
Nach dem heil'gen Grab sie wallen,
Auf der Brust das Kreuz.

Große Thaten dort geschehen
Durch der Helden Arm!
Ihres Helmes Büsche wehen
In der Feinde Schwarm,
Und des Toggenburgers Name
Schreckt den Muselmann!
Doch das Herz von seinem Grame
Nicht genesen kann.

Und ein Jahr hat er's getragen,
Trägt's nicht länger mehr,
Ruhe kann er nicht erjagen,
Und verläßt das Heer,
Sieht ein Schiff an Joppes Strande,
Das die Segel bläht,
Schiffet heim zum theuern Lande,
Wo ihr Athem weht.

Und an ihres Schlosses Pforte
Klopft der Pilger an,
Ach! und mit dem Donnerworte
Wird sie aufgethan:

„Die ihr suchet trägt den Schleier
Ist des Himmels Braut.
Gestern war des Tages Feier,
Der sie Gott getraut!“

Da verlässet er auf immer
Seiner Väter Schloß,
Seine Waffen sieht er nimmer
Noch sein treues Roß.
Von der Toggenburg hernieder
Steigt er unbekannt,
Denn es deckt die edeln Glieder
Härenes Gewand.

Und er baut sich eine Hütte,
Jener Gegend nah,
Wo das Kloster aus der Mitte
Düst'rer Linden sah;
Harrend von des Morgens Lichte
Bis zu Abends Schein,
Stille Hoffnung im Gesichte,
Saß er da allein.

Blickte nach dem Kloster drüben,
Blickte Stunden lang
Nach dem Fenster seiner Lieben,
Bis das Fenster klang,
Bis die Liebliche sich zeigte,
Bis das theure Bild
Sich ins Thal herunterneigte
Ruhig, engelmild.

Und dann legt er froh sich nieder,
Schlief getröstet ein,
Still sich freuend, wenn es wieder
Morgen würde sein.
Und so saß er viele Tage,
Saß viel Jahre lang,
Harrend ohne Schmerz und Klage,
Bis das Fenster klang.

Bis die Liebliche sich zeigte
Bis das theure Bild
Sich ins Thal herunterneigte,
Ruhig, engelmild.
Und so saß er, eine Leiche,
Eines Morgens da;
Nach dem Fenster noch das bleiche
Stille Antlitz sah.

Schiller.

42. Alexander in Afrika.

Alexander der Große kam einst in eine entlegene goldreiche Gegend von Afrika; die Einwohner gingen ihm entgegen und brachten ihm Schalen dar voll goldener Aepfel und Früchte. — „Ißt man diese Früchte bei euch?" sprach Alexander; „ich bin nicht gekommen, eure Reichthümer zu sehen, sondern von euren Sitten zu lernen." — Da führten sie ihn auf den Markt, wo ihr König Gericht hielt.

Eben trat ein Bürger vor und sprach: „Ich habe, o König, von diesem Manne ein Grundstück gekauft, und als ich den Boden durchgrub, fand ich einen Schatz. Dieser ist nicht mein; denn ich habe nur das Grundstück gekauft, nicht den darin verborgenen Schatz, und gleichwohl will ihn der Verkäufer nicht wieder nehmen." — Und sein Gegner antwortete: „Ich bin ebenso gewissenhaft als mein Mitbürger. Ich habe ihm das Gut, sammt Allem, was darin verborgen war, verkauft und also auch den Schatz."

Der König wiederholte ihre Worte, damit sie sähen, ob er sie recht verstanden hätte; und nach einiger Ueberlegung sprach er: „Du hast einen Sohn, Freund?" — „Ja." — „Und du eine Tochter?" — „Ja." — Eure Kinder lieben sich?" — „O sehr!" — „Nun wohl! verheirathet eure Kinder, und gebet ihnen den gefundenen Schatz zur Heiratsgabe! das ist meine Entscheidung."

Alexander erstaunte, da er diesen Ausspruch hörte: „Habe ich unrecht gerichtet" sprach der König, „daß du also erstaunst?" „O nein," antwortete Alexander; „aber in unserm Lande würde man anders richten." — „Und wie denn?" fragte der afrikanische König. — „Die Wahrheit zu gestehen," antwortete Alexander, „wir würden beide Männer in Verwahrung gehalten und den Schatz für den König in Besitz genommen haben."

Da schlug der König die Hände zusammen und sprach: „Scheint denn bei euch auch die Sonne? Und läßt der Himmel noch auf euch regnen?" „Alexander antwortete: „Ja." — „So muß es," fuhr er fort, „der unschuldigen Thiere wegen sein, die in eurem Lande leben; denn über solche Menschen sollte keine Sonne scheinen, kein Regen fallen." Herder.

43. Aus „Wilhelm Tell."

Dritter Aufzug. Erste Scene.

Hof vor Tell's Hause.

Er ist mit der Zimmeraxt, Hedwig mit einer häuslichen Arbeit beschäftigt, Walther und Wilhelm in der Tiefe, spielen mit einer kleinen Armbrust.

Walther (singt). Mit dem Pfeil, dem Bogen,
Durch Gebirg und Thal
Kommt der Schütz gezogen
Früh am Morgenstrahl.

Wie im Reich der Lüfte
König ist der Weih,
Durch Gebirg und Klüfte
Herrscht der Schütze frei.

Ihm gehört das Weite;
Was sein Pfeil erreicht,
Das ist seine Beute,
Was da kreucht und fleucht.

(Kommt gesprungen.)

Der Strang ist mir entzwei. Mach' mir ihn, Vater!

Tell. Ich nicht! Ein rechter Schütze hilft sich selbst.

(Knaben entfernen sich.)

Hedwig. Die Knaben fangen zeitig an zu schießen.

Tell. Früh übt sich, was ein Meister werden will.

Hedwig. Ach, wollte Gott, sie lernten's nie!

Tell. Sie sollen Alles lernen. Wer durch's Leben
Sich frisch will schlagen, muß zu Schutz und Trutz
Gerüstet sein.

Hedwig. Ach! es wird Keiner seine Ruh'
Zu Hause finden.

Tell. Mutter! ich kann's auch nicht!
Zum Hirten hat Natur mich nicht gebildet!
Rastlos muß ich ein flüchtig Ziel verfolgen.
Dann erst genieß' ich meines Lebens recht,
Wenn ich mir's jeden Tag auf's Neu' erbeute.

Hedwig. Und an die Angst der Hausfrau denkst Du nicht,
Die sich indessen, Deiner wartend, härmt.
Denn mich erfüllt's mit Grausen, was die Knechte
Von euren Wagefahrten sich erzählen.
Bei jedem Abschied zittert mir das Herz,
Daß Du mir nimmer werdest wiederkehren.
Ich sehe Dich, im wilden Eisgebirg
Verirrt, von einer Klippe zu der andern
Den Fehlsprung thun, seh', wie die Gemse Dich
Rückspringend mit sich in den Abgrund reißt.
Wie eine Windlawine Dich verschüttet,
Wie unter Dir der trügerische Firn
Einbricht und Du herabsinkst, ein lebendig
Begrab'ner in die schauerliche Gruft, —
Ach! den verwegnen Alpenjäger hascht
Der Tod in hundert wechselnden Gestalten!
Das ist ein unglückseliges Gewerb',
Das halsgefährlich führt am Abgrund hin!

Tell. Wer frisch umher späht mit gesunden Sinnen,
Auf Gott vertraut und die gelenke Kraft,
Der ringt sich leicht aus jeder Fahr und Noth.
Den schreckt der Berg nicht, wer darauf geboren.

(Er hat seine Arbeit vollendet, legt das Geräth hinweg.)

Jetzt, mein' ich, hält das Thor auf Jahr und Tag.
Die Axt im Haus erspart den Zimmermann.

(Nimmt den Hut.)

Hedwig. Wo gehst Du hin?
Tell. Nach Altdorf, zu dem Vater.
Hedwig. Sinnst Du auch nichts Gefährliches? Gesteh mir's!
Tell. Wie kommst du darauf, Frau?
Hedwig. Es spinnt sich Etwas
Gegen die Vögte — auf dem Rütli ward
Getagt, ich weiß, und Du bist auch im Bunde.
Tell. Ich war nicht mit dabei — doch werd' ich mich
Dem Lande nicht entziehen, wenn es ruft.
Hedwig. Sie werden Dich hinstellen, wo Gefahr ist;
Das Schwerste wird Dein Antheil sein, wie immer,
Tell. Ein Jeder wird besteuert nach Vermögen.
Hedwig. Den Unterwaldner hast Du auch im Sturme
Ueber den See geschafft. — Ein Wunder war's,
Daß Ihr entkommen. — Dachtest Du denn gar nicht
An Kind und Weib?
Tell. Lieb Weib, ich dacht' an euch;
Drum rettet' ich den Vater seinen Kindern
Hedwig. Zu schiffen in den wüthigen See! das heißt
Nicht Gott vertrauen: das heißt Gott versuchen.
Tell. Wer gar zu viel bedenkt, wird wenig leisten;
Hedwig. Ja, Du bist gut und hülfreich, dienest Allen;
Und, wenn Du selbst, in Noth kommst, hilft Dir Keiner.
Tell. Verhüt' es Gott, daß ich nicht Hülfe brauche!

Schiller.

44. Die seltsamen Menschen.

Ein Mann, der in der Welt sich trefflich umgesehn,
Kam endlich heim von seiner Reise.
Die Freunde liefen schaarenweise
Und grüßten ihren Freund. So pflegt es zu gescheh'n.
Da hieß es alle Mal: „Uns freut' von ganzer Seele,
Dich hier zu sehn; und nun — erzähle!"

Was ward da nicht erzählt! — Hört, sprach er einst, ihr wißt,
Wie weit von uns'rer Stadt zu den Huronen ist.
Eilf hundert Meilen hinter ihnen
Sind Menschen, die mir seltsam schienen.
Sie sitzen oft bis in die Nacht
Beisammen, fest auf einer Stelle
Und denken nicht an Gott und Hölle..
Da wird kein Tisch gedeckt, kein Mund wird naß gemacht;
Es können um sie her die Donnerkeile blitzen,
Zwei Heer' im Kampfe stehn, sollt' auch der Himmel schon
Mit Krachen seinen Einfall droh'n,
Sie blieben ungestöret sitzen;

Denn sie sind taub und stumm. Doch läßt sich dann und wann
Ein halbgebroch'ner Laut aus ihrem Munde hören,
Der nicht zusammenhängt und wenig sagen kann,
Ob sie die Augen schon darüber oft verkehren.
Man sah mich oft erstaunt an ihrer Seite stehen.
Denn wenn dergleichen Ding geschieht,
So pflegt man öfters hinzugehen,
Daß man die Leute sitzen sieht.
Glaubt, Brüder, daß mir nie die gräßlichen Gebehrden
Aus dem Gemüthe kommen werden,
Die ich an ihnen sah! Verzweiflung, Raserei,
Boshafte Freud' und Angst dabei,
Die wechselten auf den Gesichtern.
Sie schienen mir, das schwör' ich euch,
An Wuth den Furien, an Ernst den Höllenrichtern,
An Angst den Missethätern gleich. —

„Allein, was ist ihr Zweck?" so fragten hier die Freunde.
„Vielleicht besorgen sie die Wohlfahrt der Gemeinde?"
Ach nein! — „So suchen sie der Weisen Stein?"— Ihr irrt. —
„So wollen sie des Zirkels Viereck finden?" —
Nein! — „So bereu'n sie alte Sünden?" —
Das ist es Alles nicht. — „So sind sie gar verwirrt,
Wenn sie nicht hören, reden, fühlen,
Noch seh'n; was thun sie denn? — Sie spielen. —

45. Die Nacht auf dem Drachenfels.

Um Mitternacht war schon die Burg erstiegen,
Der Holzstoß flammte auf am Fuß der Mauern
Und wie die Burschen lustig niederkauern,
Erscholl das Lied von Deutschlands heil'gen Siegen.

Wir tranken Deutschlands Wohl aus Rheinweinkrügen,
Wir sahen den Burggeist auf dem Thurme lauern,
Viel dunkle Ritterschaften uns umschauern,
Viel Nebelfrau'n bei uns vorüberfliegen.

Und aus den Trümmern steigt ein tiefes Aechzen,
Es klirrt und rasselt und die Eulen krächzen;
Dazwischen heult des Nordsturms Wuthgebrause.

Sieh nur mein Freund, so eine Nacht durchwacht' ich
Auf hohen Drachenfels, doch leider bracht' ich
Den Schnupfen und den Husten mit nach Hause.

H. Heine.

VOCABULARY.

1.

Das, the; klug, clever; Kind, child; ein, a, one; Bischof, bishop; sagen, to say; einst, once; zu, to; sehr, very; mein, my; ich, I; dir, to thee; Apfel, apple; geben, to give; wenn, if, when; du, thou; mir, to me; wo where; Gott, God; ist, von sein, to be; antworten, to answer; und, and; Ihnen, to you; zwei, two; Sie, you; nicht, not.

2.

Der, the; Platz, place; bei, at, by; Feuer, fire; reisen, to travel; kam...an, ankommen, to arrive; an, to, at; kalt, cold; Abend, evening; Wirth, landlord, host; Haus, house; um, around, in order to; waren, were; besetzen, to occupy; kein, no one; der, of the, pl.; Gast, guest; machen, to make; Miene, look, mien; Miene machen, to look as if; ihm, to him; sein, his; über, over; lassen, to let, leave; überlassen, to abandon; rufen, to call; also, therefore; Stall, stable; Knecht, servant, man; befehlen, to command; derselbe, the same; Pferd, horse; sechs, six; Dutzend, dozen; Auster, oister; zu, to; aber, but; ißt, essen, to eat; doch, however, yet; thun, to do; was, what; erwiedern, to reply; wirst, werden, sign of the fut., shall, will; sehen, to see; ging, gehen, to go; verließen, verlassen, to leave, abandon; jetzt, now; ihr, their; inzwischen, in the mean time; nahm, nehmen, to take; einnehmen, to occupy; bald, soon; nach, after, pref.; nachher, after, afterwards; wieder, again; herein, in; fressen, to eat (of an animal); schon recht, all right; Metze, peck; Hafer, oats.

3.

Esel, ass; Salz, salt; trug, tragen, to carry, bear, wear; indem, whilst; er, he; da, there; mit, with; durch, through; Fluß, river; waten, to wade; glitt, gleiten, to glide, slip; aus, out, out of; auf, on, upon, up; glatt, smooth; Kieselstein, pebble; Stein, stone; fiel, fallen, to fall; sammt, together, with; Sack, bag, sack; ins, contract. of in das; Wasser, water; nachdem, after; stehen, to stand; allmählig, gradually; tropfen, to drip; ab, from, of; spüren, to perceive, trace; daß, that; Last, load, burthen; immer, always, ever; leicht, light, easy; wurde, werden, to become, get; denn, for; geschmolzen, schmelzen, to melt; fließen, to flow; dies, this; merken, to note, notice; künftig, in future; durch, through; mich, me, myself; nieder, down, nether; legen, to lay; dann, then; halb, half; so, so, as; schwer, heavy, difficult; nahe, näher, nächst, near, nearer, nearest; mal, time; Schwamm, sponge; beladen, to load; sollen, shall, to be to; beschlossen, beschließen, to determine; sogen, saugen...ein, to imbite, to suck; unter, under; brach, brechen, to break; beinahe, almost; ertrinken, to drown, to be drowning.

4.

Staar, starling; durstig, thirsty; Flasche, bottle; können, to be able; kurz, short; Schnabel, bill; erreichen, to reach; hacken, to pick; dick, thick; vermochte, vermögen, to be able; zer, pref. to pieces, up; suchen, to seek; versuchen, to try; werfen, to throw; umwerfen, to upset; schwach, weak; endlich, at last; der Einfall, the idea, thought; klein, small; stieg, steigen, to mount; hoch, high; löschen, to quench, put out.

5.

Ward geführt, pass. v., was lead; führen, to lead, guide; Tag, day; wie, as; gewöhnlich, usual; Tränke, watering place; Weg, way, road; Werkstatt, shop

Schneider, tailor; vorbei, by; saß, sitzen, to sit; offen, open; Fenster, window; arbeiten, to work; neben, near, along side of; liegen, to lie; einige, some, a few; strecken, to stretch; Rüssel, trunk; sich, himself, for himself; nach, after to; ander, other; dritte, third; stecken, to stick, to put; stach, stechen, to prick; Nadel, needle; zog, ziehen, to draw; satt, satisfied, sufficient; umrühren, to stir up; Fuß, foot; füllen, to fill; als, when; nun, now; blies, blasen, to blow; arm, poor; Gesicht, face; über, over; ganz, whole; Körper, body.

6.

Sohn, son; singen, to sing; von, of, from; Tag, day; sich neigen, to incline, bow; der Tag neigt sich, the day is almost spent; Eingang, entrance; Fels, rock; Halle, hall; blühen, to bloom; Tochter, daughter; stand, stehen, to stand; schweigen, to be silent; Greis, the old man; da, then, there; fragen, to ask; Sonne, sun; Lauf, course, run; vollenden, to end; roth, red; westlich, western, westerly; Himmel, heaven; Augenblick, moment; Auge, eye; Blick, look, glance; seufzen, to sigh; Vater, father; Jungfrau, maiden; Frau, woman, wife; Morgen, morning; lächeln, to smile; hinzusetzen, to add; auch, also; freundlich, friendly; Antlitz, countenance; hören, to hear; Laut, sound; süß, sweet; Stimme, voice; Klang, sound, ringing; Harfe, harp schweben, to hover; der Geist, spirit, ghost; die Saite, the string (of an instrument); sichtbar, visible; un, pref. not; vernehmen, to hear, to learn; ersterben, to die out; unter, down; ertönen, to resound; leise, soft; säuseln, to rustle, murmur; höher, compar. of hoch, high; Welt, world; schließen, to close; ehe, before; Tod, death; Erde, earth; ruhen, to rest; Nacht, night; Dunkel, darkness; verhüllen, to veil, envelop; nur, only; Stern, star; Glanz, brightness, light; erscheinen, to appear; oben, above; Strahl, beam; berühren, to touch; reichen, to reach; reden, to speak; stürmen, to rush, storm, blow.

7.

Nachtigall, nightingale; Käfig, cage; Landmann, farmer; prächtig, splendid; wohnen, to dwell; reich, rich; vornehm, respectable; hell, clear, bright; Vogel, bird; vergolden, to gild; treten, to step; wehmüthig, melancholy; Herz, heart; lehnen, to lean; hören, to hear, listen; sprechen, to speak; befremden, to astonish; sinnen, to ponder, to brood; ertragen, to bear, suffer; traurig, sad; Klage, complaint, wailing; euer, your; schimmern, to glitter; Thor, fool; versetzen, to reply; dünkt dir, appears to thee; Feld, field; Gebüsch, bushes; mit nichten, by no means; sondern, but; erfüllen, to fill; Ton, the sound; die Weise, the tune, manner; Diener, servant; Spott, scorn; freilich, certainly; unser, our; verkünden, to announce; zwischen, between, amongst; grün, green; Zweig, branch, twig; Lob, praise; verjüngen, to rejuvinate; Schöpfung, creation; blau, blue; Lied, song, hymn; frei, free; Freiheit, freedom; brüten, to brood; Weibchen, mate, female; das Weib, the woman, wife; chen, sign of dimin.; Liebe, love; Wort, word; erhoben, erheben, to raise; laut, loud; Gelächter, shout of laughter; schalten, schelten, to scold, to call; Bauer, peasant; zurückkehren, to return; zurück, back; ländlich, rural; Acker, acre, field, land.

8.

Biene, bee; Blume, flower; gekrochen, kriechen, to creep; pflücken, to pluck; Strauß, bouquet, wreath; heraustreiben, to drive out; herrisch, imperious; zürnen, to be angry; vermuthlich, probably; nie, never; flog, fliegen, to fly; ruhig, quietly; Honig, honey; denken, to think; zu, too; strafen, to punish; Mensch, man, human being; nein, no; es reuet mich, I repent; geschehen, to happen; ach, oh; Stachel, sting; bleiben, to remain; drum, for darum, therefore; starb, sterben, to die; sie, she; erfuhr, erfahren, to learn; spät, late; gern, willingly, with pleasure; wer, he, who; Rache, revenge; üben, to practice; elend, miserable, -bly; machen, to make.

9.

Rabe, raven; schleppen, to drag; tausend, thousand; Ding, thing; Geld, money; Koralle, bead; Perle, pearl; Winkel, corner; schlief, schlafen, to sleep; Hahn, cock; Sache, thing; glücklich, happy; weiß, wissen, to know; damit, so that.

10.

Erst, first; Jahr, year; voll, full, of; Fritz, Fred; Hoffnung, hope; kaum scarcely; die Aeltern, the parents; auskramen, to unpack; gelehrt, learned; Schatz, treasure; Weisheit, wisdom; zeigen, to show; thun, to do (understood); gelt, interj., done! I'll bet! werth, worthy, dear; Herr, Mr.; braten, to roast, to fry; Huhn, chicken, fowl; zwei, two; drei, three; ja, indeed; recht, right; versetzen, to reply; segnen, to bless; Bemühen, exertion.

11.

Der Vogel, the bird; Mädchen, girl; Namens, named; lieb, dear; Thier, animal: früh, early; bis, until; schön, beautiful; gelb, yellow; schwarz, black; Haube, cap, tuft; Samen, seed; kühlen, to cool; Kraut, herb; zuweilen, sometimes; Stück, piece; Zucker, sugar; frisch, fresh; plötzlich, suddenly; trauern, to mourn; weinen, to weep, cry; Mutter, mother; Farbe, colour; jenes, that one; that, thun, to put, to do; allein, but; betrübt, sad; Thräne, tear; verstorben, deceased, dead; Leben, life; hier, here; schlecht, bad; gegen, towards, against; handeln, to act; was, what; pflegen, to nurse, to care for; sein, abbrev. of seiner, of him, of it; sorgfältig, carefully; gebracht, bringen, to bring; erkannte, erkennen; to recognize; heilig, holy; zu Muthe sein, (with the dative) to feel; dankbar, thankful; Grab, grave.

12.

Hund, dog; Fleisch, meat, flesh; das, which; Spitz, the name of a dog; entkommen, to escape; ent, a prefix, indicating escape; verfolgen, to pursue; hinein sehen, to look into; sogleich, immediately; Lust, desire, mind, wish; besiegen, to conquer; Gewalt, power; Neid, envy; schnappen, to snap; weg, away; beides, both; der Geizige, the miser; verlieren, to lose.

13

Gattinn, wife; groß, great; Schule, school; unterwies, unterweisen, to instruct; Volk, people; Wuchs, growth; unterrichten, to inform; Gesetz, law; Söller, flat roof; breiten, to spread; Gewand, garment; Leichnam, corpse; Segen, blessing; gewahr werden, to perceive, to become aware; Becher, cup, goblet; loben, to praise; trinken, to drink; abermals, again; Wein, wine; Mahlzeit, meal; erlauben, allow, permit; vor, ago; wenig, a few; Kleinodie, jewel; Verwahrung, safekeeping; fordern, to demand; Anstand nehmen, to hesitate; Vorwissen, knowledge; wissen, to know; jammern, to lament; wenden, to turn; ergriff, ergreifen, to seize; weigern, to refuse; man, one, people; anvertrauen, to entrust; einstimmen, to join in with, to agree with.

14.

Greis, old man; Schach, shah; Persien, Persia; fand, finden, to find; Jagd, hunt; der, who; pflanzen, to plant; Nuß, nut; Baum, tree; alt, old; anreden, to address; Frucht, fruit; wenn, if; Enkel, grandchild; genoß, genießen, to enjoy; Meister, master; vier, four; Dirhem, a Persian coin; zahlen, to pay; mußte, müssen, must, to be obliged; Anweisung, check; Stelle, spot; erhielt, erhalten, to receive; Belohnung, reward; treffen, to hit, strike; fuhr... fort, fortfahren, to continue; wahr, true; gering, trifling; selten, rare, scarce; folgen, to follow; Huld, favor, kindness; König, king; hervor, forth; kurz, short; locken, to lure; Beutel the bag, purse; blank, bright; schwerlich, hardly; belohnen, to reward.

15.

Kuckuck, cuckoo; fliehen, to flee; entflohen, entfliehen, to escape; fing...an, anfangen, to begin; schreien, to cry; Stadt, town, city; Lerche, lark; Schall, sound; Amsel, black bird, ousel; dort, there; Undank, ingratitude.

16.

Wolf, wolf; Riese, giant; Gebirge, mountain-range; leben, to live; hüten, to guard, to keep; Vieh, cattle; Heerde, herd; Wald, forest; Brei, pap; Napf, bowl; Kuh, cow; weiden, to graze; Wiese, meadow; Wald, forest; inn, fem. term.; Dickicht, thicket; losgehen...auf, to go up to, to attack; packen, to lay hold of; Rock, coat; Röckchen, petty-coat; Innere, interior; nicht mehr, no longer; fehlen, to be missing; Dorf, village; Bote, messenger; sich verirren, to lose one's self; Boden, ground, soil; zufahren auf, to fly, rush at; schlug, schlagen, to strike; stets, always; Holz, wood; Löffel, spoon; Nase, nose; geschwind, quickly; Prügel, a bludgeon; holen, to go for, to fetch; eilen, to hasten; die Kraft, power, strength, might; Heu, hay; Gabel, fork; entgegen kommen, to come to meet; dreschen, to thrash; Flegel, flail, bumpkin; erlegen, to kill; suchen, to seek; empfing, empfangen, to receive; fahren lassen, to let go; fahren, to drive.

17.

Unten, below, down stairs; Stube, room; verzehren, to eat, -up; Abendbrod, supper; außen, out side; Hof, yard, court; oben, up-stairs, above; Zimmer, room; spielen, to play; Mond, moon; etwas, something; Treppe, the stairs; tappen, to walk awkwardly; Thür, door; sprang...auf, aufspringen, to open suddenly; zottig, shaggy; erschrecken, to frighten; krochen, kriechen, to creep; berühren, to touch; Schnautze, snout, nose; streicheln, to stroke; Fußboden, floor; Knabe, boy; sich wälzen, to roll one's self; Versteck spielen, to play hide and go seek; Kopf, head; schwarz, black; Pelz, fur; Trommel, drum; donnern, to thunder; schlug, schlagen, to strike, beat; jeder, each; Gewehr, gun; ordentlich, properly; festhalten, to hold fast; jemand, somebody; aufgehen, to open; Kreide, chalk; weiß, white; nicken, to beckon; vergnügt, pleased; Soldat, soldier; beschützen, to protect.

18.

Maus, mouse; Löwe, lion; Höhle, cave, den; lustig, merry; Schaar, host, band; hervorstehen, to project; herab, down; erwecken, to awake; Tatze, paw; bat, bitten, to pray, request; großmüthig, generous; unbedeutend, insignificant; Geschöpf, creature; beleidigen, to offend; Fehltritt, misstep; nützen, to profit; schenken, to present, give, bestow; lachen, to laugh; möchte, mögen, to like; sich bezeigen, to show, prove one's self; kläglich, lamentable; Gebrüll, roar; brüllen, to roar; Gefahr, danger; umschlungen, umschlingen, to entwine, to envelop; Netz, net; Jäger, hunter; ausspannen, to set, stretch out; Thier, animal; fangen, to catch; Strick, rope; künstlich, artfully; gezogen, ziehen, to draw; weder...noch, neither...nor; Zahn, tooth; gebrauchen, to make use of; zerreißen, to tear; warten, to wait; zernagen, to gnaw; vorder, fore; fesseln, to fetter, chain; Hülfe, help.

19.

Erzählen, to relate, to tell; Sclave, slave; die Waide, meadow, grazing ground; vermissen, to miss; anfallen, to fall upon, to attack; wegen, on account of, for the sake of; ähnlich, resembling, like; Waffe, arm; silbern, silver; Axt, hatchet, ax; Kennzeichen, sign, mark; Gärtner, gardener; arbeiten, to work, labour; Räuber, robber; bloß, merely; in der Absicht, with the intention; scheuchen, to drive off, shy; wirklich, really; Schwung, wielding;

aufhören, to cease; kriegen, to get, to obtain; Leiter, ladder; einfallen, to occur; Bohne, bean; erstaunlich, astonishing; empor, up; wuchsen, wachsen, to grow; sich anranken, to cling to; klettern, to climb; getrost, with a good heart; anlangen, to arrive; mühselig, troublesome; Ort, place; gleichfalls, also; Haufen, heap; Spreu, chaff; Häckerling, chopped straw; Hitze, heat; trocknen, to dry; hinabsteigen, to descend; flocht, flechten, to twine; befestigen, to fasten; Strecke, length of space; hieb...ab, abhauen, to chop off; anknüpfen, to attach, to knot; ziemlich, pretty; weit, far; gelangen, to reach; wiederholen, to repeat; Landgut, estate, farm; Paar, pair; Wolke, cloud; Heftigkeit, violence; solch, such; betäuben, to stun; Loch, hole; Klafter, fathom; sich erholen to recover; Noth, need, necessity; grub, graben, to dig; Nagel, finger-nail; damals, at that time; vierzig, forty; Art, kind; fördern, to further, forward.

20.

Angst, anguish; blicken, to look; Kasten, box; Sünde, sin; Fluth, flood; Berg, mountain; Spitze, top, point; Gefieder, fowls; Rettung, salvation; sich hervordrängen, to press forth; wittern, to smile, to scent; Liebling, favorite; Speise, food; Geschäft, business; vergaß, vergessen, to forget; hing, hangen, to hang, v. n.; Aas, carrion; aus, away; Luft, air; Gift, poison; Dampf, vapour; Dunst, vapour, exhalation; benebeln, to blind, cover with fog; Feder, feather, pen; Gedächtniß, memory; Auge, eye; düster, dark; genießen, to enjoy; häßlich, ugly; zeugen, to produce, engender; Geschlecht, race, sex, gender; entbehren, to do without; Lohn, reward.

21.

Neu, new; Wiederkunft, return; träge, idle; Kundschafter, spy, scout; auswählen, to select; schüchtern, shy; sich anbieten, to offer one's self; senden, to send; Sendung, ambassy; Treue, fidelity; Botschaft, msssage; Flügel, wing; ermatten, to get tired; ergreifen, to seize; Welle, wave; Schlamm, mud; Zunge, tongue; widern, to loathe; rein, clean, pure; müde, tired; genug, enough; der Unvermögende, the incapable one; nirgends, nowhere; schnell, quickly; Wipfel, top; Zuflucht, refuge; verboten, verbieten, to forbid; demüthig, humble, humbly; Fuß, foot; Oelbaum, olive-tree; Oel, oil; brach, brechen, to break; Blatt, leaf; eilen, to hasten; Zweig, branch; Brust, breast; schlummern, to slumber, sleep; erwachen, to awake; riechen, to smell; Geruch, smell, scent; erquicken, to refresh; Friede, peace; erscheinen, to appear; bekräftigen, to corroborate; seitdem, since; Wanderschaft, journey, wandering.

22.

Fuchs, fox; widerstehen, to resist; List, cunning; bekommen, to get; dazu kann Rath werden, that may be done; Rath, advice; morgen früh, to morrow morning; sich einstellen, to appear; zuerst, first; abdanken, to discharge; erst, only; Doppelflinte, double barrelled rifle; Rücken, back, shoulder; Hirschfänger, hunting-knife; Hirsch, stag; Seite, side; sich fortmachen, to get away; erblicken, to perceive; es ist Schade, it is a pity; Kugel, ball; laden, to load; anlegen, to aim; schoß, schießen, to shoot, fire; Schrot, small shot; verziehen, to distort; vorwärts, a'head; Ladung, load; verbeißen, to overcome; Schmerz, pain; zu Leibe rücken, to go up to; links, left; tüchtig, good, thorough; Hieb, cut; bluten, to bleed; heulen, to howl; fertig, ready; vorstellen, to represent; Stock, stick; Schulter, shoulder; kitzeln, to tickle; entsetzlich, terribly; Blitz, lightening; Hagelwetter, hail-storm; Rippe, rib; Leib, body; beinahe, nearly; Prahlhans, boaster.

23.

Güter, goods, chattels; theilen, to divide; Vermögen, fortune; erworben, erwerben, to acquire; Müh, trouble; Diamant, diamond; behalten, to retain;

mittelst, by means of; edel, noble; That, deed; Anspruch, claim; erlangen, to obtain; zerstreuen, to scatter; Mond, month, moon; vergehen, to pass away; sich einstellen, to present one's self; Bruder, brother; fremd, strange; ohne, without; Schein, receipt; getreulich, faithful,-ly; sich gehören, to be proper; sich vernehmen lassen, to let one's self be heard; ehrlich, honest; Pflicht, duty; heißen, to order, command, to be called; unachtsamer Weise, inadvertently; der See, the lake; nachstürzen, to rush after; Zeugniß, witness; schuldig sein, to owe, to be in debt; Schaf, sheep; Feind, enemy; einschlafen, to fall asleep; tief, deep; Abgrund, abyss, precipice; Rand, brink; Muth, courage.

24.

Dorn, thorn; Rose, rose; Märchen, fairy tale; König, king; anstellen, to appoint; Fest, festival, feast; lud...ein, einladen, to invite; bloß, only; Verwandte, relation; Bekannte, acquaintance; gewogen, favorable; dreizehn, thirteen; Reich, realm; zwölf, twelve; Teller, plate; Tugend, virtue; herrlich, glorious, splendid; eilf, eleven; Wunsch, wish; funfzehn, fifteen; Spindel, spindle; übrig, over; aufheben, to annul; mildern, to make milder, mitigate; Befehl, order; einen Befehl ausgehen lassen, te emit an order; abschaffen, to do away with; erfüllen, to fulfil; sittsam, modest; verständig, intelligent; ansehen, to look at; lieb haben, to like; Schloß, castle, lock; allein, alone; besehen, to look at; Kammer, chamber; Thurm, tower; gelangen, to reach, come to; Schlüssel, key; umdrehen, to turn round; emsig, industrious, -ly; Flachs, flax; Kopf, head; herumspringen, to leap round; anrühren, to touch; Verwünschung, malediction; Zauber, enchantment; Hofstaat, household of a prince; Dach, roof; Fliege, fly; Wand, wall; Feuer, fire; Herd, hearth; flackern, to flicker; aufhören, to cease; brötzeln, to hiss; Koch, cook; Küchenjunge, kitchen boy; Küche, kitchen; etwas versehen, to commit something, mistake; Haar, hair; lebendig, living, alive; Athem, breath; Dorn, thorn; Hecke, hedge; umziehen, to surround; Fahne, vane; Sage, tradition; genannt, nennen, to call; dringen in, to penetrate into; möglich, possible; gleichsam, in a manner; es solle, it was said that; abrathen, to dissuade; gerade, exactly; verfließen, to pass; nähern, to approach; lauter, nothing but; sich auseinander thun, to open; unbeschädigt, uninjured; scheckig, pie-bald, pied; Magd, servant-girl; rupfen, to pick; abwenden, to turn away; sich bücken, to stoop; Kuß, kiss; schlug...auf, aufschlagen, to open, to knock open; Auge, eye; sich rütteln, to shake one's self; wedeln, to wag; Ohrfeige, box on the ear; Hochzeit, wedding; feiern, to celebrate; Pracht, splendor.

25.

Was, why, what; Nord, north; fechten, to fence, to fight; Meer, sea; Bord, shore; grau, grey; Haar, hair; Harm, grief; Räuber, robber; Verlies, dungeon; rauben, to rob, to steal; Schande, shame, disgrace; beugen, to bend; Haupt, head, chief; Schlucht, ravine, defile; Hüne, giant; Schwert, sword; Schild, shield; Wächter, guard, watcher; litten, leiden, to suffer; kämpfen, to combat; Reihe, line, row; vergönnen, to allow; Stand halten, to withstand, resist; Mark, marrow; drücken, to press; Klinge, blade; Skalde, bard; verschlingen, to devour; Fluth, flood, waves; horchen, to listen; schäumen, to foam; rauschen, to rustle; Nachen, boat; lauschen, to listen; Toben, turmoil; dumpf, hollow-sounding; Widerhall, echo; bang, anxious; erschaun, to perceive; er, prefix, meaning to obtain; Blut, blood; Heil, hail; Held, hero; rudern, to row, to pull; wonnig, delightful; Ehre, honor; befreien, to free, deliver.

26.

Gleichniß, parable; fromm, pious; ausziehen, to move, draw; abgöttisch, idolatrous; deutsch, German; wehren, to oppose, prevent, resist; Heimath, home, native place; schaffen, to work, effect; wofern, if; begehren, to demand;

Geschichte, history; urtheilen, to judge; etliche, some; Wuth, rage; Grenze, borders; verheeren, to devastate; verwüsten, to desolate; Gegend, district; treffen, to find; Haufen, heap, crowd, lot; nackend, naked; bloß, bare; nagen, to gnaw; Wurzel, root; wühlen, to dig up; jammern, to cause pity, to lament; verbrennen, to burn, — up; Wagen, carriage; bedürfen, to require, want; Kunst, art; sich erbarmen, to take pity upon; verlangen, to long; verwaisen, to become an orphan; gen, inst. of gegen; Götze, idol.

27.

Thal, valley, dale; sacht, slow, -ly; froh, glad, happy; Narr, fool; Scherz, joking, joke; es vergeht mir, it passes away, I lose it; ein Herz fassen, to take heart; ausgelassen, exulting; mäßig, moderate, temperate.

28.

Fürst, prince; preisen, to praise; Rede, speech; Werth, worth, value; Zahl, number; Kaiser, emperor; Sachsen, Saxony; hegen, to contain, to entertain; Schacht, shaft; üppig, luxuriant; Kurfürst, elector; Saat, crop, seed; Kloster, convent, cloister; nachstehen, to be behind, inferior; Bart, beart; Kleinod, jewel; verbergen, to conceal; noch, ever; kühnlich, boldly; Schooß, lap; Edelstein, precious stone.

29.

Schatz, treasure; graben, to dig; krank, sick, ill; Weinbau, cultivation of the vine; Berg, inst. of Weinberg, vineyard; Platz, place; Gruft, grave, vault; Hacke, hoe; Karst, mattock; Spaten, spade; scharren, to scrape; Kloß, clod; Sieb, sieve; Harke, harrow; in die Quer, cross ways; verspüren, to trace; anführen, to deceive, cheat; Weinstock, grape-vine; fach, fold.

30.

Pudel, poodle-dog; Eigenthümer, owner; abrichten, to dress, to train; Kunststück, trick; versichern, to assure; Entfernung, distance; Stunde, hour, half a German mile; in Zweifel ziehen, to doubt; Beutel, purse; zurücklegen, to travel; schnell, quick; Handwerksbursche, journeyman; ermüdet, tired; Strauch, bush; überraschen, to surprise; Seele, soul; Fund, the thing found, catch; dauern, to last; beriechen, to smell; schmeicheln, to flatter; sich gefallen lassen, to put up with; willig, willingly; Thier, animal; Gelegenheit, occasion, opportunity; verkaufen, to sell; fiel ein, einfallen, to occur; redlich, honest; wohlgemuth, in good spirits; übermüthig, arrogant; sich schmecken lassen, to enjoy; schmecken, to taste; Gemach, appartment; anweisen, to show zu ebener Erde, on the lower floor; sich befinden, to be, to find one's self; heiß, hot; kleiden, to dress; Beinkleider, pantaloons; befindlich sein, to be, to live, stay; vergeblich, in vain; Paar, pair; Hosen, pantaloons.

31.

Mährchen, tale, story; Hülle, covering; zudecken, to cover; Lenz, spring; sich schmiegen an, to press close to; Brust, breast; geborgen, safe; einwiegen, to rock a'sleep; träumen, to dream; Thau, dew; berauschen, to intoxicate; Duft, odor; Aue, wet meadow; bunt, variegated; Welle, wave; Bach, brook; kosen mit, to caress, prattle; Schmetterling, butterfly; summen, to hum; zerstieben, to vanish.

32.

Bitten, to pray, to request; ungestüm, stormy, wild; Wetter, weather; bewegen, to move; Regen, rain; bitter, bitter; mit Fleiß, on purpose; plagen, to plague; sauer, difficult, hard, sour; mühsam, with trouble; gebieten, to order; lästern, to abuse; beschirmen, to shelter; Holz, woods; Bogen, bow; die Nässe the wet; schlaff, lax, loose; zielen, to aim; fassen, to aim at, to seize; Pilger, pilgrim; Pfeil, arrow; matt, weak, tired, warm; durchbohren, to pierce; Zorn, anger; erhalten, to sustain, receive.

33.

Kaiser, emperor; Anwalt, lawyer; dienen, to serve; namentlich, particularly; entscheiden, to decide; Schlacht, battle; Rechtshandel, lawsuit; Gericht, court; sich wenden an, to apply to; Beistand, assistance; übertragen, to transfer, to charge with; Beklagte, the accused, defendant; Gefahr, danger; Stellvertreter, substitute; narbig, scarred, full of scars; hindeuten, to point at; rühren, to move; vertheidigen, to defend; Eifer, zeal.

34.

Fluch, curse; hehr, venerable; rings, round; Kranz, wreath; Brunnen, fountain; stolz, proud; Sieg, victory; finster, dark; bleich, pale; sinnen, to ponder; Geißel, scourge; Locke, lock of hair; schmuck, nice, fine; Roß, horse, steed; schreiten, to stride; Genoß, companion; bereit, prepared; anstimmen, to begin to sing, to strike up; zusammennehmen, to gather, collect; es gilt, the object is; Säule, column; Saal, hall; schwoll, schwellen, to swell; Ohr, ear; Chor, quire; selig, blessed; Würde, dignity; heilig, holy; beben, to tremble, to make tremble; Höfling, courtier; Kreis, circle; verlernen, to unlearn, forget; trotzig, bold, haughty; zerfließen, to melt; verführen, to seduce; verlocken, to lead-astray; durchbringen, to penetrate; Strahl, jet, ray; verröcheln, to breathe one's last; Mantel, cloak; schlagen...um, to wrap round; Thor, gate; Marmor, marble; zerschellen, to dash to pieces; schaurig, awfully; gellen, to resound shrilly; Weh, woe; Raum, space; Seufzer, sigh; stöhnen, to moan, groan; scheu, shy; zertreten, to crush, to trample; Schutt, rubbish; Moder, rottenness, decay; entstellen, to disfigure; verdorren, to dry up, to wither; Quell, spring; versiegen, to dry up; veröden, to lay waste; verrucht, atrocious; Sängerthum, minstrelsy; ringen, to strive; Ruhm, fame; tauchen, to steep; ewig, eternal; Röcheln, death rattle, groan; leer empty; verhauchen, to breathe out; Mauer, wall; zerstören, to destroy; verschwinden, to disappear; geborsten, bersten, to crack, burst; stürzen, to fall down, to rush; Haide, heath, heather; Schatten, shade.

35.

Thal, valley; Rast, rest; besonder, particular; Anmerkung, notice; heiter, serene; leise, soft, quiet; Ausdünstung, evaporation; Schnee, snow; kämmen, to comb; Schaumwolle, fleecy wool; Erscheinung, phenomenon; vorkommen, to occur, durchsichtig, transparent; weben, to weave; stocken, to cease, to stand still; Arve, *a river;* abwechseln, to change, vary; Fichte, pine; Gipfel, summit; kahl, hare, bald; spitzig, pointed; Satz, set, range; schließen, to close, enclose; flach, flat, shallow; sachte, soft, light; Stern, star; Milchstraße, milky-way; dicht, dense, close; Standpunkt, position; ändern, to alter; Geheimniß, secret; vergleichen, to compare; Johanniswurm, fire-fly; hervorragen, to project; leuchten, to shine; gehören, to belong; befestigen, to fasten.

36.

Aufmuntern, to encourage; Grille, whim, sorrow; Stirn, brow; Falte, fold, wrinkle; winken, to beckon; scheiden, to part; Scheideweg, cross-way; zerrissen, zerreißen, to tear; Asche, ashes, dust.

37.

Bestrafen, to punish; Anmaßung, presumption; aß, essen, to eat; Tafel, table, dinner; edel, noble; Nachbarschaft, neighborhood; auftreten, to appear; pflegen, to be in the habit of; gegenüber, opposite, auftragen, to serve; reizen, to abstract, charm; der Gaumen, palate; Anspruch, pretension; Pfefferfaß, pepperbox; betroffen, amazed; empört, shocked; Dose, box; schnupfen, to snuff; schütten, to throw.

38.

Abendmahl, sacrament, Lord's supper; zaudern, to hesitate; Erz, arch; Taufe, baptism; Heilige, saint.

39.

Manchmal, often; Schalksstreich, a roguish trick; Jahrmarkt, annual fair Herberge, lodging-house; sich gefallen lassen, to put up with; honett, respectable; Pächter, farmer; ungelegen, inopportune; äußern, to utter, to say; anknüpfen, to commence; Unterhaltung, conversation; eigentlich, properly; Geschäft, business; Scharfrichter, executioner, hangman; Grafschaft, county; viertheilen, to quarter; Spitzbube, rogue; überschnappen, to go crazy; Zeche, reckoning, score; genoß, genießen, to enjoy; Schelm, rogue.

40.

Jagen, to hunt; sich nähern, to feed upon; Ranft, brink; schweifen, to rove, ramble; warten, (with gen.), to tend; das Beet, bed, flower—; laden, to invite; wagen, to dare; Rippe, rib; klettern, to climb; Klippe, cliff; Zinken, pinnacle, top; Grat, top, ridge; jäh, steep, -ly; Pfad, path; flehen, to pray, to implore; losdrücken, to shoot, fire; Spalte, split; schützen, to protect.

41.

Widmen, to dedicate, devote; fordern, to demand; weinen, to weep; Harm, grief; Mannen, men at arms; Kreuz, cross; Helm, helm; genesen, to recover; Segel, sail; blähen, to swell; schiffen, to, travel, steer, sail; Athem, breath; Pforte, gate; anklopfen, to knock; aufthun, to open; Schleier, veil; Braut, bride, affianced; trauen, to marry; Glied, limb; hären, of hair cloth; bauen, to build; Bild, image, picture; einschlafen, to fall a'sleep.

42.

Entlegen, distant; Einwohner, inhabitant; Schale, cup, bowl; die Sitten, manners, morals, customs; Bürger, citizen; Grundstück, property, lots; verbergen, to conceal; gleichwohl, notwithstanding; Gegner, opponent; gewissenhaft, consciencious; Mitbürger, fellow-citizen; wiederholen, to repeat; überlegen, to reflect; verheirathen, to marry; entscheiden, to decide; Ausspruch, decision, sentence; gestehen, confess; Verwahrung, custody; Besitz, possession.

43.

Aufzug, act; Zimmeraxt, carpenter's ax; beschäftigt, busy; Tiefe, background; Armbrust, cross-bow; Schütze, archer; sharp-shooter; Reich, realm; Weih, eagle; Beute, booty; kreucht, kreuchen, inst. of kriechen, to creep; fleucht, inst. of fliegt, fliegen, to fly; Strang, bow-string; entzwei, broken, in two; sich üben, to practice; rüsten, to prepare, to arm; zu Schutz und Trutz, offensively and defensively; Hirte, shepherd; flüchtig, fleeting; Ziel, aim, object; Grausen, horror; Abschied, leave, departure; zittern, to tremble; verirren, to lose one's self; Gemse, chamois; Lawine, avalanche; verschütten, to bury; trügerisch, deceptive; Firn, glazier; lebendig, alive; begraben, to bury; verwegen, bold; haschen, to catch, snatch; wechseln, to change; Gestalt, form; Gewerbe, business, profession; Hals, neck; spähen, to speer, spy; gesund, sound, healthy; Sinn, sense, mind; sich ringen, to wrestle, to save one's self; Fahr for Gefahr;

Geräth, tools; es spinnt sich etwas, something is brewing; tagen, to hold a meeting; Bund, alliance; Antheil, share; besteuern, to tax; Unterwaldner, a man from Underwalden; versuchen, to tempt; gar zu viel, too much altogether; leisten, to effect, execute, do; verhüten, to prevent.

44.

Seltsam, strange; trefflich, thoroughly, well; grüßen, to welcome; Donnerkeil, thunderbolt; blitzen, to lighten, to shine; Heer, host, army; krachen, to crash; drohen, to threaten; stören, to disturb; taub, deaf; stumm, mute; dann und wann, now and then; verkehren, to turn, — up; gräßlich, horrible; Gebehrde, face, grimace; Verzweiflung, despair; Raserei, raving; boshaft, malicious; gleich an, equal in; Missethäter, evil-doer; Zweck, object; besorgen, to care for, to attend to; Wohlfahrt, weal, welfare; Gemeinde, community; Viereck, quadrature, square; bereuen, to repent of; Sünde, sin; verwirrt, crazy, confused.

45.

Der Drachenfels, dragon's rock, a celebrated mountain peack on the Rhine, crowned by the ruins of a castle; Burg, castle; Holzstoß, wood-pile; Bursche, lad, boy, youth; niederkauern, to squat down; Krug, jar, mug; Thurm, tower; lauern, to lurk; umschauern, awfully hush round us; Nebel, vapor, fog; Trümmer, ruins; Aechzen, groaning; klirren, to rattle; rasseln, clatter; krächzen, to croak; brausen, to roar, rush; leider, alas; Schnupfen, cold in the head Husten, cough.

COLLECTION OF WORDS.

(With the following additional words, the sentences contained in the exercises may be increased to any number.)

The world.

Die Welt	the world	die Finsterniß	the darkness	das Thauwetter	the thaw
die Erde	- earth	der Wind	- wind	der Reif	- hoar-frost
die Sonne	- sun	der Sturm	- storm	der Blitz	- flash of lightning
der Mond	- moon	der Orkan	- hurricane	der Donner	- thunder
der Stern	- star	der Osten	- east	der Donnerschlag	- clap of thunder
der Planet	- planet	der Westen	- west	der Regenbogen	- rainbow
das Licht	- light	der Süden	- south	das Erdbeben	- earthquake
das Feuer	- fire	der Norden	- north	die Ebbe	- ebb
das Wasser	- water	das Wetter	- weather	die Fluth	flood.
die Luft	- air	die Wolke	- cloud		
der Himmel	- sky	der Regen	- rain		
der Sonnenstrahl	- sunbeam	der Schnee	- snow		
das Mondlicht	- moonlight	der Hagel	- hail		
		der Thau	- dew		

The earth.

Die Erde	the earth	das Vorgebirge	the promontory	der Fuß des Berges	the foot of the m.
der Berg	- mountain	das Festland	- continent	die Mündung	- mouth of the river
der Hügel	- hill	die Landenge	- isthmus	die Quelle	- well, source
das Gebirge	- chain of mountains	die Küste	- coast	der Bach	- brook
der Fluß	- river	das Ufer	- shore	der Meerbusen	- gulf, bay
der Strom	- stream	die Ebene	- plain	der Canal	- channel canal
das Thal	- valley	der feuerspeiende Berg	- vulcano	der Sund	- sound
das Land	- land	die Wüste	- desert	die Meerenge, die Straße	- strait.
das Wasser	- water	der See	- lake	der Wasserfall	- waterfall
die Stadt	- town, city	die See	- sea		
das Dorf	- village	das Meer	- " , ocean		
die Ansiedelung	- settlement	der Gipfel des Berges	- summit of the mountain		
die Insel	- island				
die Halbinsel	- peninsula				

Time.

die Zeit	the time	das Vierteljahr	the quarter of a year	der Sonnenaufgang	the sunrise
das Jahrhundert	- century	der Morgen	- morning	der Sonnenuntergang	- sunset
das Jahr	- year	der Abend	- evening	der Sonntag	- sunday
der Monat	- month	die Nacht	- night	der Montag	- monday
die Woche	- week	der Tag	day	der Dienstag	- tuesday
der Tag	- day	der Mittag	- mid-day, noon	der (die) Mittwoch	- wednesday
die Stunde	- hour	die Mitternacht	- midnight	der Donnerstag	- thursday
die Minute	- minute	der Vormittag	- forenoon	der Freitag	- friday
die Sekunde	- second	der Nachmittag	- afternoon	der Sonnabend, Samstag	- saturday
eine halbe Stunde	half an hour	der Tagesanbruch	- break of day		
eine viertel Stunde	a quarter of an hour				
Schaltjahr	a leap-year				

Die Jahreszeiten	the seasons	der Pfingsten	whitsuntide	Juni	June
der Frühling	- spring	Neujahrstag	new-years day	Juli	July
der Sommer	- summer	Januar	January	August	August
der Herbst	- autumn	Februar	February	September	September
der Winter	- winter	März	March	October	October
die Weihnacht	christmas	April	April	November	November
Ostern	easter	Mai	Mai	December	December

The human body.

Der Körper	the body	der Schnurrbart	the mustashes	der Fuß	the foot
das Glied	- limb	der Hals	- throat, neck	die Ferse	- heel
der Kopf	- head	der Nacken	- back of the neck	die Zehe	- toe
das Haar	- hair	der Busen	- bosom	der Rest,	- instep
die Stirne	- brow	die Brust	- breast	die Fußsohle	- sole of the foot
der Mund	- mouth	die Schulter	- shoulder	der Knöchel	- ancle
die Lippe	- lip	das Schulterblatt	- shoulder-blade	die Haut	- skin
die Oberlippe	- upper-lip	der Arm	- arm	der Knochen	- bone
die Unterlippe	- under-lip	der linke Arm	- left arm	das Mark	- marrow
die Schleimhaut	- mucous membrane	der rechte Arm	- right arm	das Fleisch	- flesh
der Zahn	- tooth	der Ellenbogen	- elbow	das Fett	- fat
das Zahnfleisch	- gums	die Hand	- hand	das Blut	- blood
die Kehle	- throat	das Handgelenk	- wrist	die Ader	- vein
die Luftröhre	- wind-pipe	der Finger	- finger	die Schlagader	- artery
das Zäpfchen	- uvula	der Daumen	- thumb	der Nerv	- nerve, sinew
das Auge	- eye	der Nagel	- nail	der Muskel	- muscle
die Augenbraune	- eyebrow	die Faust	- fist	der Hirnschädel	- skull
das Augenlied	- eyelid	der Bauch	- belly	die Eingeweide	- entrails
der Augapfel	- pupil	der Leib	- belly, body	der Magen	- stomach
die Augenwimpern	- eyelashes	der Rücken	- back	das Herz	- the heart
das Ohr	- ear	der Rückgrab	- backbone	die Lunge	- lungs
das Ohrläppchen	- ear-lap	die Niere	- kidney	die Leber	- liver
die Ohrtrommel	- tympan	die Rippe	- rib	die Milz	- spleen
die Nase	- nose	das Kreuz	- small of the back	die Galle	- bile
das Nasenloch	- nostril	das Bein	- leg	die Blase	- bladder
die Wange / die Backe	- cheek	der Schenkel	- thigh	das Gesicht	- sight
die Schläfe	- temple	das Knie	- knee	das Gehör	- hearing
das Kinn	- chin	die Wade	- calf of the leg	der Geruch	- smell
der Bart	- beard	das Schienbein	- shin	der Geschmack	- taste
der Backenbart	- whiskers			das Gefühl	- feeling
				der Sinn	- sense

Animals.

Quadrupedes.

Das Thier	the animal	die Hiäne	the hyena	das wilde Schwein	the wild boar
der Löwe	- lion	das Kameel	- camel	der Hase	- hare
der Tiger	- tiger	der Wolf	- wolf	der Hirsch	- stag
der Leopard	- leopard	der Bär	- bear	die Hirschkuh	- hind
der Elephant	- elephant	der Fuchs	- fox		

das Reh the roe, deer
das Kaninchen - rabbit
das Eichhörnchen - squirrel
das Stachelschwein - porcupine
die Ratze - rat
die Maus - mouse
der Affe - ape

der Ochs the ox
die Kuh - cow
das Kalb - calf
das Pferd - horse
der Hengst - stallion
die Stute - mare
das Füllen - colt
der Esel - ass
der Hund - dog

die Katze the cat
der Kater - tom-cat
das Schaf - sheep
das Lamm - lamb
die Ziege - goat
der Ziegenbock - he-goat
das Schwein - pig
das Ferkel - young pig
die Sau - sow

Birds.

Der Vogel the bird
der Adler - eagle
der Strauß - ostrich
die Eule - owl
der Falke - hawk
der Habicht - pigeon-hawk
der Papagei - parrot
der Geier - vulture
die Taube - pigeon
die Ente - duck
die Gans - goose
die Henne - hen
der Hahn - cock
das Huhn - fowl
der welsche Hahn - turkey cock

der Schwan the swan
das Rebhuhn - partridge
der Fasan - pheasant
die Schnepfe - snipe
die Wachtel - quail
die Lerche - lark
die Drossel - thrush
die Nachtigall - nightingale
der Sperling - sparrow
der Kanarienvogel - canary-bird
die Bachstelze - wagtail
der Hänfling - linnet
der Zaunkönig - wren
der Stieglitz - goldfinch
die Buchfinke - bulfinch

die Amsel the black-bird
die Maise - titmouse
der Reiher - heron
der Staar - starling
der Storch - stork
die Fledermaus - bat
die Schwalbe - swallow
der Rohrdommel - bittern
der Rabe - raven
die Krähe - crow
der Kuckuck - cuckoo

Fishes, Insects, &c.

Der Fisch the fish
der Wallfisch - whale
der Haifisch - shark
der Hering - herring
die Sardelle - sardil, sardin
der Stör - sturgeon

der Stockfisch the cod fish
der Hecht - pike
der Delphin - dolphin
der Aal - eel
der Krebs - crab
der Hummer - lobster
der Lachs - salmon

die Neunauge the lamprey
der Weißfisch - whiting
die Auster - oyster
die Alose - shad
die Schildkröte - tortoise
die Krabbe - shrimp

Die Schlange the serpent, snake
die Klapperschlange - rattle-snake
der Scorpion - scorpion
die Eidechse - the lizard
die Schnecke - snail
der Wurm - worm
die Motte - moth

die Spinne the spider
die Ameise - ant
die Fliege - fly
die Wanze - bed-bug
der Floh - flea
der Grashüpfer - grass-hopper
die Heuschrecke - locust
der Frosch - frog

der Maikäfer the may-bug
der Schmetterling - butterfly
der Käfer - beetle
die Biene - bee
die Wespe - wasp
die Raupe - catter-pillar

The town.

die Stadt the town
die Vorstadt - suburb
die Straße, die Gasse - street
der Gang - lane
die Brücke - bridge
das Thor - gate
der Hafen - port, harbor

das Schloß the castle
das Haus - house
das Rathhaus - town-house
das Zeughaus - arsenal
das Gefängniß - jail
das Zuchthaus - house of correction

das Armenhaus the poor house
die Bibliothek - library
die Kirche - church
der Kirchhof - church-yard
der Kirchthurm - steeple
die Börse - exchange

das Theaeer	the theatre	der Tanzboden	the ball-room	der Spazierplatz	the public walk
das Posthaus	- postoffice	der Rennstein	- gutter	die Allee	- walk planted with trees
das Zollhaus	- custom-house	das Pflaster	- pavement	das Museum	- museum
das Speisehaus	- eating-house	die Mühle	- mill	der Thiergarten	- zoological garden
der Laden	- store	die Wasserkunst	- waterwork	der Begräbnißplatz, Gotesacker	- cemetery
der Gerichtshof	- court	das Gasthaus	- hotel		
die Kegelbahn	- ten-pin alley	das Wirthshaus	- inn		
		die Kneipe	- low tavern		

Professions, mechanics, &c.

Der Prediger	the preacher	der Künstler	the artist	der Pflasterer	the paver
der Geistliche	- clergyman	der Schauspieler	- actor	der Schieferdecker	- slater
der Arzt	- physician	die Schauspielerin	- actress	der Tapezier	- paper-hanger
der Apotheker	- apothecary	der Buchhändler	- bookseller	der Küster	- sexton, clerk in a church
der Schriftsteller	- author	der Krämer	- shopkeeper	die Fischfrau	- fish-woman
der Schreiber	- secretary	der Gewürzkrämer	- grocer	der Hutmacher	- hatter
der Wundarzt	- surgeon	der Böttcher, der Küper	- cooper	die Scheuerfrau	- shore-woman
der Zahnarzt	- dentist	der Gerber	- tanner	der Messerschmied	- cutler
der Augenarzt	- oculist	der Barbier	- barber	der Mäkler	- broker
der Commis*	- clerk	der Conditor	- confectionar	der Zinngießer	- tin-man
der Buchhaleer	- book-keeper	der Maurer	- mason	der Briefträger	- letter-carrier, postman
der Uhrmacher	- watch-maker	der Steiuhauer	- stonecutter	das Kammermädchen	- chamber-maid
der Schmied	- smith	der Perückenmacher	- wigmaker	der Kutscher	- coachman
der Schlosser	- lock-smith	der Haarschneider	- hair-cutter	der Schornsteinfeger	- sweep
der Goldschmied	- gold-smith	der Radmacher	- wheel-wright		
der Hufschmied	- farrier				
der Gelehrte	- savant				
der Sattler	- saddler				
der Handwerker	- mechanic				
der Mäher	- mower				

The house.

Das Wohnhaus	the dwelling house	die Planke	the plank	das Zimmer, die Stube	the room
die Hütte	- hut	der Sparren	- rafter	das Schlafzimmer	- bedroom
der Grund	- fondation	der Balken	- beam	das Wohnzimmer	- sitting-room
die Mauer	- wall	das Dach	- roof	das Speisezimmer	- dining-room
die Wand	- wall, partition	das Fenster	- window	das Empfangzimmer	- parlor
der Stein	- stone	der Fensterladen	- shutter	der Keller	- cellar
der Mauerstein	- brick	die Thür	- door	die Kellerküche	- cellar-kitchen
der Ziegel	- tile	das Schloß	- lock	die Küche	- kitchen
die Schindel	- shingle	der Schlüssel	- key	der Boden	- garret
der Kalk	- lime	das Schlüsselloch	- key-hole	die Treppe	- staircase
der Lehm	- clay	der Riegel	- bolt		
der Mörtel	- mortar	das Stockwerk	- story		
das Brett	- board	die Hausflur, die Hausdiele	- hall of a house		

* Auss. kom-me'.

die Stufe	the step	die Decke	the ceiling	der Hof	the yard
das Geländer	- balustrade (banister)	der Brunnen	- well, fountain	der Schornstein	- chimney
der Fußboden	- floor	der Stall	- stable	der Kamin	- fire place

Furniture and Utensils.

Der Spiegel	the looking-glass	das Brett	the board	die Schüssel	the dish
das Gemälde	- picture	die Wiege	- cradle	der Topf	- pot
der Rahmen	- frame	der Korb	- basket	das Gefäß	- vessel
der Teppich	- carpet	die Lampe	- lamp	die Axt	- ax
das Pult	- desk	die Kaffeekanne	- coffee-pot	das Beil	- hatched
der Schemel	- foot-stool	das Handtuch	- towel	der Hammer	- hammer
der Lehnstuhl	- arm-chair	die Serviette	- napkin	die Säge	- saw
der Sopha	- sopha	das Tischtuch	- tablecloth	die Zange	- pincers
der Schrank	- wardrobe	der Ofen	- stove	der Bohrer	- gimlet
die Commode	- chest of drawers *	der Kochofen	- cooking-stove	der Kessel	- kettle
die Schieblade	- drawer	die Feuerzange	- tongs	die Pfanne	- pan
das Bett	- bed	die Feuerschaufel	- fire-shovel	der Sieb	- sieve
die Bettstelle	- bedstead	das Schüreisen	- poker	das Theebrett	- tea-tray
die Matratze	- mattress	der Leuchter	- candle-stick	das Schwefelholz	- match
die Decke	- blanket	die Lichtscheere	- snuffers	die Flasche	- bottle
das Betttuch	- sheet	das Waschbecken	- washhand-basin	der Pfropfen	- cork
das Kopfkissen	- pillow	Waschtisch	- washstand	der Pfropfenzieher	- cork-screw
der Pfühl	- bolster			das Salzfaß	- salt-cellar
das Federbett	- featherbed			die Suppenterrine	- soup-terine
die Gardine / der Vorhang	- curtain				

Clothing, &c.

der Mantel	the cloak	der Schlafrock	the dressing gown	die Haarnadel	- hair-needle
die Hose	- pantaloons	der Schnürleib	- stays, corset	die Schürze	- apron
das Hemd	- shirt, chemise	das Leibchen	- bodice	der Muff	- muff
der Strumpf	- stocking	das Band	- ribbon	die Spitzen, pl.	- lace
der Hosenträger	- suspender	die Trauer	- mourning	der Fächer	- fan
die Unterhose	- drawers	der Anzug	- suit of clothes	der Fingerhut	- thimble
der Pantoffel	- slipper	die Perrücke	- wig	die Brustnadel	- brouch
der Stiefel	- boot	der Ueberrock	- overcoat	die Scheere	- scissors
das Strumpfband	- garter	der Regenschirm	- umbrella	die Wäsche	- linen, clothes
die Mütze	- cap, bonnet	der Sonnenschirm	- parasol	die Juwelen	- jewels
das Halstuch	- neckhandkerchief	die Brille	- spectacles	die Pomade	- pomatum
der Handschuh	- glove,	der Ring	- ring	der Kamm	- comb
das Taschentuch	- pocket-handkerchief	der Ohrring	- earring	die Stecknadel	- pin
der Hut	- hat, bonnet	das Armband	- bracelet	die Nähnadel	- needle
das Kleid	- dress, gown	die Halskette	- chain	die Stricknadel	- knitting-needle
		der Unterrock	petty-coat	die Bürste	- brush
				die Uhr	- watch
				die Dose	- box
				die Börse	- purse

* In Amer. Bureau.

Food.

Das Mittagessen	the dinner	der Schinken	the ham	der Pfirsich	the peach
das Abendessen	- supper	das Gemüse	- vegetables	die Beere	- berry
das Frühstück	- breakfast	der Spargel	- asparagus	die Himbeere	- raspberry
der Rahm	- milk	die Erbse	- pea	die Stachelbeere	- gooseberry
die Milch	- cream	die Bohne	- bean	die Johannisbeere	- currant
das Roggenbrod	- rye bread	die Rübe	- turnip	die Erdbeere	- strawberry
das Weißbrod	wheat bread	die Möhre	- carrot	die Nuß	- nut
die Krume	- crum	die Petersilie	- parsley	die Haselnuß	- hazelnut
die Rinde	- crust	der Essig	- vinegar	die Kastanie	- chestnut
die Sauce	- sauce	der Pfeffer	- pepper	die Apfelsine	- orange
der Fisch	- fish	der Senf	- mustard	die Feige	- fig
der Aal	- eel	die Wurst	- sausage, pudding	die Traube	- grape
der Hecht	- pike	der Meerrettig	- horse-raddish	das Oel	- oil
die Auster	- oister	der Salat	- salad	das Gewürz	- spice
der Lachs	- salmon	der Kohl	- cabbage	der Zimmet	- cinnamon
der Stint	- smelt	der Blumenkohl	- cauliflower	der Piment	- allspice
der Stockfisch	- codfish	das Obst	- fruit	die Gewürznelke	- clove
die Makrele	- mackerel	der Apfel	- apple	der Nachtisch	- dessert
die Forelle	- trout	die Birne	- pear	der Kuchen	- cake
das Schweiuefleisch	- pork	die Pflaume	- plum	die Torte	- tart
		die Kirsche	- cherry	die Pastete	- pie

A FEW ADDITIONAL ADJECTIVES.

niedrig,	low;	freundlich,	friendly;	betrügerisch,	deceitful;
schlank,	slender;	freudig,	joyful;	listig,	cunning;
kurz,	short;	unfreundlich,	unfriendly, disagreeable;	bescheiden,	modest;
breit,	broad;	lasterhaft,	vicious;	unverschämt	impudent;
enge,	narrow, tight	klug,	clever, prudent;	blöde,	bashful;
recht,	right;	weise,	wise;	kühn, dreist,	bold;
link,	left;	thöricht,	foolish;	furchtsam,	afraid;
neu,	new;	wüthend,	enraged;	streitsüchtig,	quarrelsome
mager,	lean;	zornig,	angry;	zänkisch,	"
leer,	empty;	rasend,	raving;	höflich,	courteous;
voll,	full;	toll,	mad;	unhöflich,	impolite;
sanft,	soft, mild;	gerecht,	just;	gemein,	vulgar, rough;
heiß,	hot;	ungerecht,	unjust;	gütig,	kind;
naß,	wet;	tapfer,	brave;	barmherzig,	merciful;
feucht,	damp;	muthig,	courageous;	grausam,	cruel;
schwach,	weak;	feig,	cowardly;	rachsüchtig,	revengeful;
hübsch,	pretty;	heilig,	holy;	gelehrig,	docile;
bucklich,	hunch-backed;	fromm,	pious;	eigensinnig,	stubborn;
stumm,	dumb;	gottlos,	ungodly;	verschwenderisch,	lavish;
nackt,	naked;	stolz,	proud;	sparsam,	saving;
gesund,	healthy, sound;	mitleidig,	compassionate;	geizig,	avaricious;
betrunken,	drunk;	niedrig,	low;	habsüchtig	covetous;
wahr,	true;	demüthig,	humble;	nüchtern,	sober, fasting;
falsch,	false;	aufrichtig,	sincere;	gefräßig,	gluttonous;
lästig,	troublesome;				

faul, träge,	idle, lazy;	feige,	cowardly;	unnütz,	useless;
unbeständig,	fickle;	schmerzhaft,	painful;	nothwendig,	necessary;
verwegen,	rash;	bequem,	convenient;	dunkel,	dark;
muthwillig,	wanton;	unbequem,	inconvenient	biegsam,	pliable;
fähig,	capable;	entschlossen,	determined;	schnell,	quick;
unfähig,	incapable;	verächtlich,	contemptible;	geschwind,	rapid;
bewunderns-würdig,	admirable;			heiser,	hoarse;
		gewöhnlich,	usual;	böse,	wicked; angry;
ruhig,	quiet;	gelb,	yellow;		
untröstlich,	inconsolable;	schwarz,	black;	eifrig,	zealous;
glaublich,	credible;	braun,	brown;	viereckig,	square;
fruchtbar,	fruitful;	frei,	free;	verheirathet,	married;
kahl,	bald;	leer,	empty;	verwundet,	wounded;
fremd,	strange, foreign;	voll,	full;	beschäftigt,	busy;
		möglich,	possible;	eben,	smooth;
günstig,	favorable;	nützlich,	useful;	uneben,	rough;
unschätzbar,	invaluable;				

SOME ADDITIONAL REGULAR VERBS.

(the irregular verbs are all given in the theoretical part.)

Frühstücken,	to breakfast;	tadeln,	to blame;	taumeln,	to stagger;
		entschuldigen,	to excuse;	handeln,	to act;
bewirthen,	to entertain;	siegen,	to be victorious;	sperren,	to bar;
abkürzen,	to abridge;			einsperren,	to lock up;
wachen,	to be awake;	plündern,	to plunder;	benachrichtigen,	to inform;
erwachen,	to awake;	ersticken,	to stifle;		
aufwachen,	to awake;	borgen,	to borrow;	stottern,	to stutter;
bewachen,	to watch;	miethen,	to rent;	rasiren,	to shave;
wecken,	to awake, a.t.	vermiethen,	to let;	stricken,	to knit;
aufwecken,	to awake;	rühren,	to move, stir;	reden,	to speak;
erwecken,	to awake;	berühren,	to touch;	anreden,	to address;
schnarchen,	to snore;	stopfen,	to stuff;	klettern,	to climb;
seufzen,	to sigh;	öffnen,	to open;	rauchen,	to smoke;
ächzen,	to groan;	pflügen,	to plough;	schnupfen,	to snuff;
schluchzen,	to sob;	drücken,	to press;	kauen,	to chew;
niesen,	to sneeze;	bedecken,	to cover;	schauen,	to look;
gähnen,	to yawn;	kämmen,	to comb;	anschauen,	to look at;
bluten,	to bleed;	reinigen,	to clean;	bauen,	to build, cultivate;
kratzen,	to scratch;	malen,	to paint;		
kitzeln,	to tickle;	mahlen,	to grind;	trauen,	to trust;
husten,	to cough;	folgen,	to follow;	hauen,	to hew;
argwöhnen,	to suspect;	fischen,	to fish;	eilen,	to hasten;
beobachten,	to observe;	jagen,	to hunt;	ruhen,	to rest;
		bauen,	to build	erblassen,	to grow pale;
versuchen,	to try, attempt;	auskehren,	to sweep;	messen,	to measure;
übersetzen,	to translate;	scheuern,	to scrub;	einpacken,	to pack up;
antworten,	to answer;	wärmen,	to warm;	legen,	to lay;
warnen,	to warn;	trocknen,	to dry;	verdienen,	to earn, merit
zanken,	to quarrel;	bügeln,	to iron;	absetzen,	to dispose of;
schimpfen,	to abuse;	füllen,	to fill;	einführen,	to import.;
anklagen,	to accuse;	leeren,	to empty;	remittiren,	to remit;
beklagen,	to pity;	horchen,	to listen;	acceptiren,	to accept;
umarmen,	te embrace	athmen,	to breathe;	protestiren,	to protest;
küssen,	to kiss;	saugen,	to suck;	dampfen,	to smoke;
drohen,	to threaten;	säugen,	to suckle;	ausrüsten,	to fit out;
bestrafen,	to punish;	hinken,	to limp;	befrachten,	to charter;

segeln,	to sail;	erstürmen,	to take by storm;	nässen,	to wet;
umlegen,	to tack;			wählen,	to choose;
landen,	to land;	capituliren,	to capitulate;	betteln,	to beg;
trommeln,	to drum;	erwarten,	to expect;	sich sehnen,	to long for
belagern,	to besiege;	erneuern,	to renew;	vernichten,	to annihilate;
verschanzen,	to entrench;	blühen,	to bloom;	zerstören,	to destroy.
stürmen,	to storm;	trocknen,	to dry;		

DIALOGUES.

1. Essen und Trinken. — *Eating and drinking.*

Sind Sie hungrig?	Are you hungry?
Ich habe guten Appetit.	I have a good appetite.
Ich bin sehr hungrig.	I am very hungry.
Essen Sie etwas.	Eat something.
Was wollen Sie essen?	What will you eat?
Was wünschen Sie zu essen?	What do you wish to eat?
Sie essen nicht.	You do not eat.
Ich bitte um Verzeihung. ich esse sehr viel.	I beg your pardon; I eat very heartily.
Ich habe sehr viel gegessen.	I have eaten very heartily.
Ich habe mit gutem Appetit zu Mittag gegessen.	I have dined with a good appetite.
Essen Sie noch ein Stückchen.	Eat another piece.
Ich kann nichts mehr essen.	I can eat no more.
Sind Sie durstig?	Are you thirsty?
Haben Sie keinen Durst?	Are you not thirsty?
Ich bin sehr durstig.	I am very thirsty.
Ich vergehe vor Durst.	I am dying with thirst.
Lassen Sie uns trinken.	Let us drink.
Geben Sie mir zu trinken.	Give me something to drink.
Wollen Sie ein Glas Wein trinken?	Will you drink a glass of wine?
Trinken Sie ein Glas Bier.	Drink a glass of beer.
Trinken Sie noch ein Glas Wein.	Drink another glass of wine.
Mein Herr, ich trinke auf Ihre Gesundheit.	Sir, I drink to your health.
Ich habe die Ehre, auf Ihre Gesundheit zu trinken,	I have the honor, to drink your health.

2. Gehen und Kommen. — *Going and coming.*

Wohin gehen Sie?	Where are you going?
Ich gehe nach Hause.	I am going home.
Ich wollte zu Ihnen.	I was going to your house.
Wo kommen Sie her?	Where do you come from?
Ich komme von meinem Bruder.	I come from my brother's.
Ich komme aus der Kirche.	I am coming from church.
Ich komme so eben aus der Schule.	I just left the school
Wollen Sie mit mir gehen?	Will you go with me?
Wo wollen Sie hingehen?	Whither do you wish to go?
Wir wollen spazieren gehen.	We will go for a walk.
Wir wollen einen Spaziergang machen.	We will take a walk.
Sehr gern, mit Vergnügen.	With all my heart, most willingly.
Welchen Weg wollen wir nehmen?	What road shall we take?

Welchen Weg Sie wollen.	Any way you like.
Lassen Sie uns in den Park gehen.	Let us go into the park.
Lassen Sie uns im Vorbeigehen Ihren Freund abholen.	Let us take your frind in our way.
Wie es Ihnen gefällig ist.	As you please.
Ist Herr B. zu Hause?	Is Mr. B. at home?
Er ist ausgegangen.	He is gone out.
Er ist nicht zu Hause.	He is not at home.
Können Sie uns sagen, wohin er gegangen ist?	Can you tell us, where he is gone?
Ich kann es Ihnen nicht gewiß sagen.	I cannot tell you for certain.
Ich glaube, daß er zu seiner Schwester gegangen ist.	I think he is gone to see his sister.
Wissen Sie wann er zurückkommt?	Do you know, when he will come back?
Nein, er hat nichts davon gesagt als er ausging.	No, he said nothing of it, when he went out.
Dann müssen wir ohne ihn gehen.	Then we must go without nim.

3. Fragen und Antworten. — *Questions and answers.*

Treten Sie näher, ich habe Ihnen etwas zu sagen.	Come nearer; I have something to tell you.
Ich habe Ihnen ein Wörtchen zu sagen.	I have a word to say to you.
Hören Sie mich an.	Listen to me.
Ich möchte mit Ihneu sprechen.	I want to speak to you.
Was steht zu Ihren Diensten?	What is your pleasure?
Ich spreche mit Ihnen.	I am speaking to you.
Ich spreche nicht mit Ihnen.	I am not speaking to you.
Was sagen Sie?	What do you say?
Was haben Sie gesagt?	What did you say?
Ich sage nichts.	I say nothing.
Hören Sie?	Do you hear?
Verstehen Sie, was ich sage?	Do you understand what I say?
Verstehen Sie mich?	Do you understand me?
Wollen Sie so gut sein, zu wiederholen...?	Will you be so kind, as to repeat ....?
Ich verstehe Sie wohl.	I understand you well.
Warum antworten Sie mir nicht?	Why do you not answer me?
Sprechen Sie nicht Französisch?	Do you not speak French?
Sehr wenig, mein Herr.	Very little, Sir,
Ich verstehe es ein wenig, aber ich spreche es nicht.	I understand it a little, but I do not speak it.
Sprechen Sie lauter.	Speak louder.
Sprechen Sie nicht so laut.	Do not speak so loud.
Machen Sie nicht so viel Lärm.	Do not make so much noise.
Schweigen Sie.	Hold your tongue.
Sagten Sie mir nicht daß ....?	Did you not tell me, that ....?
Wer hat Ihnen das gesagt?	Who told you that?
Man hat es mir gesagt.	People have told me so.
Es hat mir's Jemand gesagt.	Somebody has told me so.
Ich habe es gehört.	I have heard it.
Was wollen Sie sagen?	What do you wish to say?
Wozu soll das dienen?	What is that good for?
Wie nennen Sie das?	How do you call that?
Das heißt	That is called.....
Darf ich Sie fragen ....?	May I ask you ....?
Was wünschen Sie?	What do yau wish?
Kennen Sie Herrn G.?	Do you know Mr. G.?
Ich kenne ihn von Ansehen.	I know him by sight.
Ich kenne ihn dem Namen nach.	I know him by name.

4. Das Alter.	*The age.*
Wie alt sind Sie?	How old are you?
Wie alt ist Ihr Herr Bruder?	How old is your brother?
Ich bin zwölf Jahre alt.	I am twelve years old.
Ich bin zehn und ein halbes Jahr alt.	I am ten years and six months old.
Im nächsten Monat werde ich sechzehn Jahre alt.	Next month I shall be sixteen years old
Vergangene Woche bin ich achtzehn Jahre alt geworden.	I was eighteen years old last week.
Sie sehen nicht so alt aus.	You do not look so old.
Sie sehen älter aus.	You look older.
Ich hielt Sie für älter.	I thought you were older.
Ich hielt Sie nicht für so alt.	I did not think you were so old.
Wie alt mag Ihr Oheim sein?	How old may your uncle be?
Er ist ungefähr sechzig Jahre alt.	He is about sixty years old.
Er ist über fünfzig Jahre alt.	He is more than fifty years old.
Er ist ein Mann von fünfzig und einigen Jahren.	He is a man of fifty and upwards.
Er kann etwa sechzig Jahre zählen.	He may be sixty or there about
Er ist über achtzig Jahre.	He is above eighty.
Das ist ein hohes Alter.	That is a great age.
Ist er so alt?	Is he so old?
Er fängt an zu altern.	He begins to grow old.
5. Die Zeit.	*The time.*
Wie viel Uhr ist es?	What o'clock is it?
Ich bitte, sagen Sie mir, welche Zeit es ist	Pray tell me what time it is
Es ist ein Uhr.	It is one o'clock.
Es ist ein Uhr vorbei.	It is past one.
Es hat eins geschlagen.	It has struk one.
Es ist ein Viertel auf zwei (nach eins).	It is a quarter past one.
Es ist halb zwei.	It is half past one.
Es fehlen zehn Minuten an zwei.	It wants ten minutes of two.
Es ist noch nicht zwei Uhr.	It is not yet two o'clock.
Es ist erst zwölf.	It is only twelve o'clock.
Es ist beinahe drei.	It is almost three o'clock.
Es wird gleich drei Uhr schlagen.	It is going to strike three.
Es ist zehn Minuten nach drei.	It is ten minutes past three.
Die Uhr wird sogleich schlagen.	The clock is going to strike.
Da schlägt die Uhr.	There the clock strikes.
Es ist nicht spät.	It is not late.
Es ist später, als ich dachte.	It is later than I thought.
Ich dachte nicht, daß es so spät wäre.	I did not think it was so late.
6. Das Wetter.	*The weather.*
Was ist es für Wetter?	What kind of weather is it?
Es ist schlechtes Weteer.	It is bad weather.
Es ist trübe.	It is very cloudy.
Es ist ein abscheuliches Wetter.	It is dreadful weather.
Es ist schönes Wetter.	It is fine weather.
Wir werden einen schönen Tag haben.	We are going to have a fine day.
Der Thau fällt.	The dew is falling.
Es ist nebelig.	It is foggy.
Es ist regnerisches Wetter.	It is rainy weather.
Es droht zu regnen.	It threatens to rain.

Der Himmel umzieht sich.	The sky bekomes very cloudy.
Der Himmel wird sehr dunkel.	The sky is getting very dark.
Die Sonne fängt an sich zu zeigen.	The sun is coming out.
Das Wetter klärt sich wieder auf.	The weather is clearing up again.
Es ist sehr heiß.	It is very hot.
Es ist eine erstickende Hitze.	The heat is suffocating.
Es ist sehr mild.	It is very mild.
Es ist kalt.	It is cold.
Es ist eine übermäßige Kälte.	It is excessively cold.
Es ist rauhes Wetter.	It is raw weather.
Es regnet.	It rains.
Es hat geregnet.	It has been raining.
Es wird gleich regnen.	It is going to rain.
Ich fühle Regentropfen.	I feel some drops of rain.
Es fallen Regentropfen.	There are some drops of rain falling.
Es hagelt.	It hails.
Es schneit; es fällt Schnee.	It snows; it is snowing.
Es hat geschneit; es ist Schnee gefallen.	It has been snowing.
Es schneit in großen Flocken.	It snows in large flakes.
Es friert.	It freezes.
Es hat gefroren.	It has froozen.
Es fängt an, gelinder zu werden.	It begins to get milder.
Es thauet auf.	It thaws.
Es ist sehr windig.	It is very windy.
Der Wind weht stark.	The wind is very high.
Es weht kein Lüftchen.	There is no air stirring.
Es blitzt.	It lightens.
Es hat die ganze Nacht geblitzt.	It has lightened all night.
Es donnert.	It thunders.
Der Donner rollt.	The thunder roars.
Es hat eingeschlagen.	The lightning has struck.
Es ist stürmisches Wetter.	It is stormy weather.
Wir werden ein Gewitter bekommen.	We shall have a thunder-storm.
Der Himmel fängt an sich aufzuheitern.	The sky begins to clear up.
Das Wetter ist sehr unbeständig.	The weather is very unsettled.
Es ist sehr schmutzig.	It is very muddy.
Es ist sehr staubig.	It is very dusty.
Es ist sehr glatt.	It is very slippery.
Es ist schlechtes Gehen.	It is bad walking.
Es ist Tag.	It is day-light.
Es ist dunkel.	It is dark.
Es ist Nacht.	It is night.

7. Die Eisenbahn. — *The Railroad.*

Im Gasthause. — In the Inn.

Wo ist der Bahnhof der Philadelphia Eisenbahn?	Where is the depot of the Philadelphia railroad?
Er ist auf der andern Seite des Flusses.	It is on the other side of the river.
Wo muß ich hinfahren um mich einzuschiffen?	Where must I drive to, to go on board?
Es geht ein Dampfboot unten von der — Straße ab.	A steamboat leaves the foot of — street.
Wann geht das Boot ab?	When does the boat start?
Es geben täglich sieben Züge ab, wann wünschen Sie zu reisen? [hen.	Seven lines run daily, when do you wish to start.
Ich wünsche mit dem ersten Zuge abzuge-	I wish to start by the first line.

Der nächste Zug geht um zwei Uhr ab.	The next line starts at two o'clock.
Kutscher, fahren Sie nach dem Dampfboote „Susan," hier ist meine Bagage, ein Koffer, einen Mantelsack und eine Hutschachtel.	Driver, to the steamboat Susan, here is my baggage, a trunk, a carpet-bag and a hat-box.
Steigen Sie gefälligst ein mein Herr.	Please to get in, Sir.
Fahren Sie gefälligst schnell, wir haben nur gerade Zeit um vor der Abfahrt da anzukommen.	Please to drive fast, we have but just time to arrive there before the boat leaves.
Sorgen Sie nicht, wir werden vor zwei Uhr am Bord sein.	Do not be afraid, we shall be on board before two o'clock.
Hier sind wir schon.	Here we are.
Wie viel ist das Fuhrlohn?	How much is the fare?
Fünf und siebenzig Cent.	Seventy-five cents.
Hier ist es.	Here it is.
Ich werde Ihre Sachen an den Bagage-Meister abgeben. Hier sind Ihre Marken.	I shall hand your baggage to the baggage-master. Here are your checks.
Man läutet schon.	The bell is already ringing.
Die Räder fangen schon an sich zu bewegen.	The weels are beginning to move.

An Bord.	On Board.
Entschuldigen Sie, mein Herr, ich bin ein Fremder, wie lange dauert wohl die Ueberfahrt nach Jersey City?	Excuse me Sir, I am a stranger, how long does it take us to cross over to Jersey City?
Nur einige Minuten.	Only a few minutes.
Wie lange bleiben wir in Jersey City?	How long do we stay in Jersey City?
Wir fahren ab, sobald die Passagiere eingestiegen sind.	We start as soon as the passengers are all on board.
Hier sind wir schon.	Here we are.
Haben Sie Ihre Karte?	Have you your ticket?
Hier ist sie.	Here it is.
Was wird aus meinem Gepäck?	What becomes of my baggage?
Fürchten Sie nichts, dasselbe ist in dem Gepäckwagen..	Do not trouble yourself, it is in the baggage-wagon.

Auf der Eisenbahn.	On the Railroad.
Steigen wir in diesen Wagen?	Let us go into this car.
Nein, dies ist nicht der rechte, auf unserer Karte steht der Buchstabe A, dieser Wagen ist mit B bezeichnet.	No this is not the right one, on our card is the letter A, this car is marked B.
Hier ist unser Wagen.	Here is our car.
Hier ist der Dampfwagen, der Zug besteht aus zwanzig Wagen.	Here is the locomotive, the train consists of twenty cars.
Wie groß ist die Kraft dieser Maschine?	What is the power of this machine?
Sie hat eine Kraft von hundert Pferden.	It is of a hundred horse-power.
Ist sie stark genug um den Zug zu ziehen?	Is it strong enough to draw the train?
Gewiß.	Certainly.
Jetzt fahren wir ab.	Now we start.
Wie schnell fährt man gewöhnlich auf dieser Bahn?	How fast do they generally go on this road?
Man macht von 20 bis 30 Meilen in der Stunde.	They go from 20 to 30 miles an hour
Hält man lange an?	Do we stop long?
Nur lange genug, um Holz einzunehmen.	Only long enough, to take in wood.
Dies ist ein Schnell-Zug, derselbe hält nur drei oder vier Mal an um Passagiere einzunehmen.	This is a fast line, it only stops three or four times to take up passengers.

Mein Herr, glauben Sie nicht daß es gefährlich ist so schnell zu fahren?	Sir, do you not think, that it is dangerous to go so fast?
Entschuldigen Sie Madame, wir machen jetzt nicht mehr als 25 Meilen die Stunde, ich bin oft 40 Meilen ohne den geringsten Unfall gefahren.	Excuse me Mam., we only go now 25 miles an hour, I have often gone 40 miles, without the slightest accident.
Ach, ich kann es nicht helfen, aber ich fürchte mich, es ist das erste Mal daß ich auf der Eisenbahn fahre.	Oh! I cannot help it, but I am afraid, it is the first time that I travel on a railroad.
Fürchten Sie nichts Madame, seit dem letzten Unfalle, hat man sehr zuverlässige Leute angestellt, und man nimmt alle möglichen Maßregeln, um Unglück zu vermeiden.	Fear nothing Mam., since the last accident, they have appointed very trustworthy people; and they take every precaution, to avoid accidents.
Ich sehe dies ist nur eine einfache Bahn.	I see this is only a single track.
Ja Madame, wir werden gleich halten, um den uns entgenkommenden Zug vorbei zu lassen.	Yes Mam., we shall stop immediately, to let the train, which comes this way, pass.
Hier kommt der Zug, oh wie das sauset.	Here comes the train, oh how is rushes.
Giebt es auf dieser Bahn keinen Tunnel?	Is there no tunnel on this road?
Nein Madame, aber wir kommen über eine Brücke, die fast so dunkel wie ein Tunnel ist.	No Mam., but we shall pass a bridge, which is almost as dark as a tunuel.
Wann werden wir ankommen?	When shall we arrive?
Wir werden um sechs Uhr im Bahnhofe sein.	We shall be at the depot at six o'clock.
Jetzt nähern wir uns der Stadt, dies ist die letzte Station.	We now approach the town, this is the last station.
Wie bekomme ich mein Gepäck?	How do I get my baggage?
Wenn Sie Ihre Marke einem von den Dienern geben, so schickt man Ihnen Ihr Gepäck ins Haus oder nach Ihrem Gasthofe.	If you will give your checks to one of the porters, they will send your baggage to your house or to your hotel.

8. An Bord eines Dampfbootes zwischen New York und Fall River. — *On board of a steamboat between New York and Fall River.*

Wann geht das Dampfboot ab?	When does the steamboat leave?
Es geht um fünf Uhr ab, meine Herren, Sie haben keine Zeit zu verlieren.	She leaves at five o'clock, Gentlemen, you have no time to lose.
Geben Sie uns unsere Karten, wir wollen gleich an Bord, unser Gepäck ist schon hier.	Give us our tickets, we shall go on board immediately, our baggage is already here.
Dies ist ein sehr schönes Boot.	This is a very handsome boat.
Es ist stark gebaut und ist sehr elegant möblirt.	It is strongly built and is very elegantly furnished.
Ißt man zu Abend am Bord?	Do they serve supper on board?
Ja mein Herr, man ißt um sieben Uhr zu Abend.	Yes Sir, supper is served at seven o'clock.
Und wann kommen wir in Fall River an?	And when do we arrive in Fall River?
Morgen früh um fünf Uhr.	To morrow morning at five o'clock.
Wissen Sie wie bald ein Zug von da nach Boston geht?	Do you know how soon a train goes from there to Boston?
Der erste Zug geht um 6 Uhr, der andere um 8 Uhr.	The first train starts at 6 o'clock, the next at 8 o'clock.
Da läutet man schon zum letzten Mal.	There the bell is ringing for the last time.

Jetzt zieht man die Laufplanke ein und schließt das Steuerungsventil. Wir fahren ab.	Now they are pulling in the gang-boards and closing the safety-valve. We are off.
Wollen wir nicht hinuntergehen und unsere Betten in Beschlag nehmen?	Shall we not go below and look at our berths?
Mit Vergnügen, welche Nummer haben Sie?	With pleasure, what number have you?
Ich habe Nummer 97	I have number 97.
Und ich Nummer 95.	And I number 95.
Da sind wir über einander.	Then we are one over the other.
Ich finde daß das Boot bedeutend schlingert.	I find that the boat rolls considerably.
Das ist nicht so unangenehm als wenn es stampft.	That is not as disagreeable as when it pitches.
Ich fange schon an mich unwohl zu befinden.	I commence already to feel indisposed.
Kommen Sie schnell auf das Verdeck, in der freien Luft werden Sie sich besser fühlen.	Come on deck, in the fresh air you will feel more comfortable.
Ich will es versuchen, aber ich fürchte, daß ich an der Seekrankheit leiden werde.	I will try it, but I fear, I shall suffer from sea-sickness.
Ich bin niemals seekrank, aber es muß sehr unangenehm sein.	I am never sea-sick, but it must be very disagreeable.
Giebt es kein Mittel gegen dieses Übel?	Is there no remedy for this sickness.
O ja, sehr viele aber sie helfen nur nichts.	Oh, yes, a great many but they do not cure it.
Das ist schlimm, da werde ich nie eine lange Seereise machen können.	That is bad, then I shall never be able to make a long sea-voyage.
O, doch! bei den meisten Leuten ist die Seekrankheit nur ein vorübergehendes Uebel.	Oh, you may!, with most persons sea-sickness is only a temporary evil.
Warum sind Kinder der Seekrankheit weniger und auf kürzere Zeit ausgesetzt als Erwachsene?	Why are children exposed to sea-sickness less and for a shorter time, than grown persons?
Weil Kinder ungeachtet des Uebels, doch Nahrung zu sich nehmen, wenn Erwachsene diesem Beispiel folgen wollten, sobald Sie fühlen daß der Magen leer ist, so würden Sie sich bald besser befinden.	Because children, nothwithstanding the sickness, will take food; if grown persons would follow this example, as soon as they feel their stomach empty, they would soon be better.
Ich werde mir dieses merken.	I shall remember this.
Es ist wahr, es gehört etwas Muth dazu.	It is true, it requires a little courage.
Ich glaube wir werden eine stürmische Nacht haben, der Wind nimmt zu.	I think we shall have a stormy night, the wind is increasing.
Haben Sie schon das Leuchten des Meeres gesehen?	Have you ever seen the phospherescent light at sea?
Ich habe oft davon gehört, aber ich habe es nie gesehen.	I have often heard of it, but I have never seen it.
Lassen Sie uns nach dem Hintertheile des Schiffes gehen. Sehen Sie, das Kielwasser leuchtet wie fließendes Gold.	Let us go to the stern of the vessel. Look, the wake shines like molden gold.
Das ist ein herrlicher Anblick.	That is a splendid sight.
Es wird jetzt aber sehr kühl, und wir werden wohl thun uns zu Bette zu legen.	But it is growing very cool now, and we shall do well to go to bed.
Schlafen Sie wohl mein Herr und werden Sie nicht seekrank.	A pleasant night to you, Sir, and do not get sea-sick.
Ich danke Ihnen recht sehr, es würde mir leid thun, Sie zu beunruhigen.	I thank you very much, I should be sorry to disturb you.

CONTENTS.

PART I.

PART II.

THE GERMAN READER.

www.ingramcontent.com/pod-product-compliance
Lightning Source LLC
Chambersburg PA
CBHW031113020726
47495CB00007B/2185
9783337387389